THE ADVENTURES
OF KATHLYN

HAROLD MACGRATH

1st WORLD
LIBRARY
Literary Society

The Adventures of Kathlyn

Harold MacGrath

© 1st World Library, 2007
PO Box 2211
Fairfield, IA 52556
www.1stworldlibrary.com
First Edition

LCCN: 2007927845

Softcover ISBN: 978-1-4218-4546-3
Hardcover ISBN: 978-1-4218-4462-6
eBook ISBN: 978-1-4218-4630-9

Purchase *"The Adventures of Kathlyn"*
as a traditional bound book at:
www.1stWorldLibrary.com/purchase.asp?ISBN=978-1-4218-4546-3

1st World Library is a literary, educational organization
dedicated to:

- Creating a free internet library of downloadable ebooks

- Hosting writing competitions and offering book
publishing scholarships.

Interested in more 1st World Library books?
contact: literacy@1stworldlibrary.com
Check us out at: www.1stworldlibrary.com

1ˢᵗ World Library Literary Society

Giving Back to the World

"If you want to work on the core problem, it's early school literacy."

- James Barksdale, former CEO of Netscape

"No skill is more crucial to the future of a child, or to a democratic and prosperous society, than literacy."

- Los Angeles Times

"Literacy... means far more than learning how to read and write... The aim is to transmit... knowledge and promote social participation."

- UNESCO

"Literacy is not a luxury, it is a right and a responsibility. If our world is to meet the challenges of the twenty-first century we must harness the energy and creativity of all our citizens."

- President Bill Clinton

"Parents should be encouraged to read to their children, and teachers should be equipped with all available techniques for teaching literacy, so the varying needs and capacities of individual kids can be taken into account."

- Hugh Mackay

TO W. N. SELIG

CONTENTS

CHAPTER I

THE GOLDEN GIRL

Under a canopied platform stood a young girl, modeling in clay. The glare of the California sunshine, filtering through the canvas, became mellowed, warm and golden. Above the girl's head—yellow like the stalk of wheat—there hovered a kind of aureola, as if there had risen above it a haze of impalpable gold dust.

A poet I know might have cried out that here ended his quest of the Golden Girl. Straight she stood at this moment, lovely of face, rounded of form, with an indescribable suggestion of latent physical power or magnetism. On her temples there were little daubs of clay, caused doubtless by impatient fingers sweeping back occasional wind blown locks of hair. There was even a daub on the side of her handsome sensitive nose.

Her hand, still filled with clay, dropped to her side, and a tableau endured for a minute or two, suggesting a remote period, a Persian idyl, mayhap. With a smile on her lips she stared at the living model. The chatoyant eyes of the leopard stared back, a flicker of restlessness in their brilliant yellow deeps. The tip of the tail twitched.

"You beautiful thing!" she said.

She began kneading the clay again, and with deft fingers added bits here and there to the creature which had grown up under her strong supple fingers.

"Kathlyn! Oh, Kit!"

The sculptress paused, the pucker left her brow, and she turned, her face beaming, for her sister Winnie was the apple of her eye, and she brooded over her as the mother would have done had the mother lived. For Winnie, dark as Kathlyn was light, was as careless and aimless as thistledown in the wind.

A collie leaped upon the platform and began pawing Kathlyn, and shortly after the younger sister followed. Neither of the girls noted the stiffening mustaches of the leopard. The animal rose, and his nostrils palpitated. He hated the dog with a hatred not unmixed with fear. Treachery is in the marrow of all cats. To breed them in captivity does not matter. Sooner or later they will strike. Never before had the leopard been so close to his enemy, free of the leash.

"Kit, it is just wonderful. However can you do it? Some day we'll make dad take us to Paris, where you can exhibit them."

A snarl from the leopard, answered by a growl from the collie, brought Kathlyn's head about. The cat leaped, but toward Winnie, not the collie. With a cry of terror Winnie turned and ran in the direction of the bungalow. Kathlyn, seizing the leash, followed like the wind, hampered though she was by the apron. The cat loped after the fleeing girl, gaining at each bound. The yelping of the collie brought forth from various points low rumbling sounds, which presently developed into roars.

Winnie turned sharply around the corner of the bungalow toward the empty animal cages, to attract her father and at the same time rouse some of the keepers. Seeing the door of an empty cage open, and that it was approached by a broad runway, she flew to it, entered and slammed the door and held it. The cat, now hot with the lust to kill, threw himself against the bars, snarling and spitting.

Kathlyn called out to him sharply, and fearlessly approached him. She began talking in a monotone. His ears went flat against his head, but he submitted to her touch because invariably it soothed him, and because he sensed some undefinable power whenever his gaze met hers. She snapped the leash on his collar just as her father came running up, pale and disturbed. He ran to the door and opened it.

"Winnie, you poor little kitten," he said, taking her in his arms, "how many times have I told you never to take that dog about when Kit's leopard is off the leash?"

"I didn't think," she sobbed.

"No. Kit here and I must always do your thinking for you. Ahmed!"

"Yes, Sahib," answered the head keeper.

"See if you can stop that racket over there. Sadie may lose her litter if it keeps up."

The lean brown Mohammedan trotted away in obedience to his orders. He knew how to stop captive lions from roaring. He knew how to send terror to their hearts. As he ran he began to hiss softly.

Colonel Hare, with his arm about Winnie, walked toward

the bungalow.

"Lock your pet up, Kit," he called over his shoulder, "and come in to tea."

Kathlyn spoke soothingly to the leopard, scratched his head behind the ears, and shortly a low satisfied rumble stirred his throat, and his tail no longer slashed about. She led him to his own cage, never ceasing to talk, locked the door, then turned and walked thoughtfully toward the bungalow.

She was wondering what this gift was that put awe into the eyes of the native keepers on her father's wild animal farm and temporary peace in the hearts of the savage beasts. She realized that she possessed it, but it was beyond analysis. Often some wild-eyed keeper would burst in upon her. Some newly captive lion or tiger was killing itself from mere passion, and wouldn't the Mem-sahib come at once and talk to it? There was a kind of pity in her heart for these poor wild things, and perhaps they perceived this pity, which was fearless.

"She gets a little from me, I suppose," Colonel Hare had once answered to a query, "for I've always had a way with four footed things. But I think Ahmed is right. Kathlyn is heaven born. I've seen the night when Brocken would be tame beside the pandemonium round-about. Yet half an hour after Kit starts the rounds everything quiets down. The gods are in it."

The living-room of the bungalow was large and comfortable. The walls were adorned with the heads of wild beasts and their great furry hides shared honors with the Persian rugs on the floor. Hare was a man who would pack up at a moment's notice and go to the far ends of the world to find a perfect black panther, a cheetah with a litter, or a great horned rhinoceros. He was tall and broad, and amazingly active, for all that his hair and mustache were almost white. For thirty years or more he had gone about the hazardous enterprise of supplying zoological gardens and circuses with wild beasts. He was known from Hamburg to Singapore, from Mombassa to Rio Janeiro. The Numidian lion, the Rajput tiger, and the Malayan panther had cause to fear Hare Sahib. He was even now preparing to return to Ceylon for an elephant hunt.

The two daughters went over to the tea tabouret, where a matronly maid was busying with the service. The fragrant odor of tea permeated the room. Hare paused at his desk. Lines suddenly appeared on his bronzed face. He gazed for a space at the calendar. The day was the fifteenth of July. Should he go back there, or should he give up the expedition? He might never return. India and the border countries! What a land, full of beauty and romance and terror and squalor, at once barbaric and civilized! He loved it and hated it, and sometimes feared it, he who had faced on foot many a wounded tiger.

He shrugged, reached into the desk for a box of Jaipur brass enamel and took from it a medal attached to a ribbon. The golden disk was encrusted with uncut rubies and emeralds.

"Girls," he called. "Come here a moment. Martha, that will be all," with a nod toward the door. "I never showed you this before."

"Goodness gracious!" cried Winnie, reaching out her hand.

"Why, it looks like a decoration, father," said Kathlyn. "What lovely stones! It would make a beautiful pendant."

"Vanity, vanity, all is vanity," said the colonel, smiling down into their charming faces. "Do you love your old dad?"

"Love you!" they exclaimed in unison, indignantly, too, since the question was an imputation of the fact.

"Would you be lonesome if I took the Big Trek?" whimsically.

"Father!"

"Dad!"

They pressed about him, as vines about an oak.

"Hang it, I swear that this shall be the last hunt. I'm rich. We'll get rid of all these brutes and spend the rest of the years seeing the show places. I'm a bit tired myself of jungle fodder. We'll go to Paris, and Berlin, and Rome, and Vienna. And you, Kit, shall go and tell Rodin that you've inherited the spirit of Gerome. And you, Winnie, shall make a stab at grand opera."

Winnie gurgled her delight, but her sister searched her father's eyes. She did not quite like the way he said those words. His voice lacked its usual heartiness and spontaneity.

"Where did you get this medal, father?" she asked.

"That's what I started out to tell you."

"Were you afraid we might wish to wear it or have it made over?" laughed Winnie, who never went below the surface of things.

"No. The truth is, I had almost forgotten it. But the preparations for India recalled it to mind. It represents a royal title conferred on me by the king of Allaha. You have never been to India, Kit. Allaha is the name we hunters give that border kingdom. Some day England will gobble it up; only waiting for a good excuse."

"What big thing did you do?" demanded Kathlyn, her eyes still filled with scrutiny.

"What makes you think it was big?" jestingly.

"Because," she answered seriously, "you never do anything but big things. As the lion is among beasts, you are among men."

"Good lord!" The colonel reached embarrassedly for his pipe, lighted it, puffed a few minutes, then laid it down. "India is full of strange tongues and strange kingdoms and principalities. Most of them are dominated by the British Raj, some are only protected, while others do about as they please. This state"—touching the order—"does about as it did since the days of the first white rover who touched the shores of Hind. It is small, but that signifies nothing; for you can brew a mighty poison in a small pot. Well, I happened to save the old king's life."

"I knew it would be something like that," said Kathlyn. "Go on. Tell it all."

The colonel had recourse to his pipe again. He smoked on till the coal was dead. The girls waited patiently. They knew that his silence meant that he was only marshaling the events in their chronological order.

"The king was a kindly old chap, simple, yet shrewd, and with that slumbrous oriental way of accomplishing his ends, despite all obstacles. Underneath this apparent simplicity I discovered a grim sardonic humor. Trust the Oriental for always having that packed away under his bewildering diplomacy. He was all alone in the world. He was one of those rare eastern potentates who wasn't hampered by parasitical relatives. By George, the old boy could have given his kingdom, lock, stock and barrel, to the British government, and no one could say him nay. There was a good deal of rumor the last time I was there that when he died England would step in actually. The old boy gave me leave to come and go as I pleased, to hunt where and how I would. I had a mighty fine collection. There are tigers and leopards and bears and fat old pythons, forty feet long. Of course, it isn't the tiger country that Central India is, but the brutes you find are bigger. I have about sixty beasts there now, and that's mainly why I'm going back. Want to clean it up and ship 'em to Hamburg, where I've a large standing order. I'm going first to Ceylon, for some elephants."

The colonel knocked the ash from his pipe. "The old boy used to do some trapping himself, and whenever he'd catch a fine specimen he'd turn it over to me. He had a hunting lodge not far from my quarters. One day Ahmed came to me with a message saying that the king commanded my presence at the lodge, where his slaves had trapped a fine leopard. Yes, my dears, slaves. There is even a slave mart at the capital this day. A barbaric fairy-land, with its good genii and its bad djinns."

"*The Arabian Nights*," murmured Winnie, snuggling close to Kathlyn.

"The Oriental loves pomp," went on the colonel. "He can't give you a chupatty—"

"What's that?" asked Winnie.

"Something like hardtack. Well, he can't give you that without ceremonial. When I arrived at the lodge with Ahmed the old boy—he had the complexion of a prima donna—the old boy sat on his portable throne, glittering with orders. Standing beside him was a chap we called Umballa. He had been a street rat. A bit of impudence had caught the king's fancy, and he brought up the boy, clothed, fed him, and sent him away down to Umballa to school. When the boy returned he talked Umballa morning, noon and night, till the soldiers began to call him that, and from them it passed on to the natives, all of whom disliked the upstart. Hanged if I can recall his real name. He was ugly and handsome at the same time; suave, patient, courteous; yet somehow or other I sensed the real man below—the Tartar blood. I took a dislike to him, first off. It's the animal sense. You've got it, Kit. Behind the king sat the Council of Three—three wise old ducks I wouldn't trust with an old umbrella."

Winnie laughed.

"While we were salaaming and genuflecting and using grandiloquent phrases the bally leopard got loose, somehow. Maybe some one let him loose; I don't know. Anyhow, he made for the king, who was too thunder-struck to dodge. The rest of 'em took to their heels, you may lay odds on that. Now, I had an honest liking for the king. Seeing the brute make for him, I dashed forward. You see, at ceremonials you're not permitted to carry arms. It had to be with my hands. The leopard knocked the old boy flat and began to maul him. I kicked the brute in the face, swept the king's turban off his head and flung it about the head of the leopard. Somehow or other I got him down. Some of the frightened natives came up, and with the help of Ahmed we got the brute tied up securely. When the king came around he silently shook hands with me and smiled peculiarly at Umballa, who now came running up."

"And that's how you got those poor hands!" exclaimed Kathlyn, kissing the scars which stood out white against the tan.

"That's how," raising the hands and putting them on Kathlyn's head in a kind of benediction.

"Is that all?" asked Winnie breathlessly.

"Isn't that enough?" he retorted. "Well, what is it, Martha? Dinner? Well, if I haven't cheated you girls out of your tea!"

"Tea!" sniffed Winnie disdainfully. "Do you know, dad, you're awfully mean to Kit and me. If you'd take the trouble you could be more interesting than any book I ever read."

"He doesn't believe his stories would interest vain young ladies," said Kathlyn gravely.

Her father eyed her sharply. Of what was she thinking? In those calm unwavering eyes of hers he saw a question, and he feared in his soul she might voice it. He could evade the questions of the volatile Winnie, but there was no getting by Kathlyn with evasions. Frowning, he replaced the order in the box, which he put away in a drawer. It was all arrant nonsense, anyhow; nothing could possibly happen; if there did, he would feel certain that he no longer dwelt in a real workaday world. The idle whim of a sardonic old man; nothing more than that.

"Father, is the king dead?"

"Dead! What makes you ask that, Kit?"

"The past tense; you said he was, not is."

"Yes, he's dead, and the news came this morning. Hence, the yarn."

"Will there be any danger in returning?"

"My girl, whenever I pack my luggage there is danger. A cartridge may stick; a man may stumble; a man you rely on may fail you. As for that, there's always danger. It's the penalty of being alive."

On the way to the dining-room Kathlyn thought deeply. Why had her father asked them if they loved him? Why did he speak of the Big Trek? There was something more than this glittering medal, something more than this simple tale of bravery. What? Well, if he declined to take her into his confidence he must have good reason.

After dinner that night the colonel went the rounds, as was his habit nightly. By and by he returned to the bungalow, but did not enter. He filled his cutty and walked to and fro in the moonlight, with his head bent and his hands clasped behind his back. There was a restlessness in his stride not unlike that of the captive beasts in the cages near by. Occasionally he paused at the clink clink of the elephant irons or at the "whuff" as the uneasy pachyderm poured dust on his head.

Bah! It was madness. A parchment in Hindustani, given jestingly or ironically by a humorous old chap in orders and white linen and rhinoceros sandals. . . . A throne! Pshaw! It was bally nonsense. As if a white man could rule over a brown one by the choice of the latter! And yet, that man Umballa's face, when he had shown the king the portraits of his two lovely daughters! He would send Ahmed. Ahmed knew the business as well as he did. He would send his abdication to the council, giving them the right to choose his successor. He himself would remain home with the girls. Then he gazed up at the moon and smiled grimly.

"Hukum hai!" he murmured in Hindustani. "It is the orders. I've simply got to go. When I recall those rubies and emeralds and pearls. . . . Well, it's not cupidity for myself. It's for the girls. Besides; there's the call, the adventure. I've simply got to go. I can't escape it. I must be always on the go . . . since she died."

A few days later he stood again before the desk in the living-room. He was dressed for travel. He sat down and penned a note. From the box which contained the order he extracted a large envelope heavily sealed. This he balanced in his hand for a moment, frowned, laughed, and swore softly. He would abdicate, but at a snug profit. Why not? . . . He was an old fool. Into a still larger envelope he put the sealed envelope and his own note, then wrote upon it. He was blotting it as his daughters entered.

"Come here, my pretty cubs." He held out the envelope. "I want you, Kit, to open this on December thirty-first, at midnight. Girls like mysteries, and if you opened it any time but midnight it wouldn't be mysterious. Indeed, I shall probably have you both on the arms of my chair when you open it."

"Is it about the medal?" demanded Winnie.

"By George, Kit, the child is beginning to reason out things," he jested.

Winnie laughed, and so did Kathlyn, but she did so because occultly she felt that her father expected her to laugh. She was positively uncanny sometimes in her perspicacity.

"On December thirty-first, at midnight," she repeated. "All right, father. You must write to us at least once every fortnight."

"I'll cable from Singapore, from Ceylon, and write a long letter from Allaha. Come on. We must be off. Ahmed is waiting."

Some hours later the two girls saw the Pacific Mail steamer move with cold and insolent majesty out toward the Golden Gate. Kathlyn proved rather uncommunicative on the way home. December thirty-first kept running through her mind. It held a portent of evil. She knew something of the Orient, though she had never visited India. Had her father made an implacable enemy? Was he going into some unknown, unseen danger? December thirty-first, at midnight. Could she hold her curiosity in check that long?

Many of the days that followed dragged, many flew—the first for Kathlyn, the last for Winnie, who now had a beau, a young newspaper man from San Francisco. He came out regularly every Saturday and returned at night. Winnie became, if anything, more flighty than ever. Her father never had young men about. The men he generally gathered round his board were old hunters or sailors. Kathlyn watched this budding romance amusedly. The young man was very nice. But her thoughts were always and eternally with her father.

During the last week in December there arrived at the Palace Hotel in San Francisco an East Indian, tall, well formed, rather handsome. Except for his brown turban he would have passed unnoticed. For Hindus and Japanese and Chinamen and what-nots from the southern seas were every-day affairs. The brown turban, however, and an enormous emerald on one of his fingers, produced an effect quite gratifying to him. Vanity in the Oriental is never conspicuous for its absence. The reporters gave him scant attention, though, for this was at a time when the Gaikwar of Baroda was unknown.

The stranger, after two or three days of idling, casually asked the way to the wild animal farm of his old friend, Colonel Hare. It was easy enough to find. At the village inn he was treated with tolerant contempt. These brown fellows were forever coming and going, to and fro, from the colonel's.

At five o'clock in the afternoon of the thirty-first day of December, this East Indian peered cautiously into the French window of the Hare bungalow. The picture he saw there sent a thrill into his heart. She was as fair and beautiful as an houri of Sa'adi. She sat at a desk, holding a long white envelope in her hand. By and by she put it away, and he was particular to note the drawer in which she placed it. That the dark-haired girl at the tea tabouret was equally charming did not stir the watcher. Dark-haired women were plentiful in his native land. Yonder was the girl of the photograph, the likeness of which had fired his heart for many a day. With the patience of the Oriental he stood in the shadow and waited. Sooner or later they would leave the room, and sooner or later, with the deftness of his breed, he would enter. The leopard he had heard about was nowhere to be seen.

"Winnie," said Kathlyn, "I dread it."

Winnie set down the teacup; her eyes were brimming.

"What can it all mean? Not a line from father since

Colombo, five months gone."

"Do you think—"

"No, no!" replied Kathlyn hastily. "Father sometimes forgets. He may be hunting miles from telegraph wires and railroads; it is only that he should forget us so long. Who knows? He may have dropped down into Borneo. He wanted some pythons, so I heard him say."

The elder sister did not care to instil into the heart of her charge the fear which was in her own.

"Who knows but there may be good news in the envelope? Dad's always doing something like that. New Year's!"

The collie, released from the kitchen, came bounding in. In his exuberance he knocked over a cloisonne vase. Both girls were glad to welcome this diversion. They rose simultaneously and gave chase. The dog headed for the outdoor studio, where they caught him and made believe they were punishing him.

Quietly the watcher entered through the window, alert and tense. He flew to the desk, found the envelope, steamed it open at the kettle, extracted the sealed envelope and Colonel Hare's note. He smiled as he read the letter and changed his plans completely. He would not play messenger; he would use a lure instead. With his ear strained for sounds, he wrote and substituted a note. This houri of Sa'adi would not pause to note the difference in writing; the vitalness of the subject would enchain her thoughts. It was all accomplished in the space of a few minutes. Smiling, he passed out into the fast settling twilight.

They were shipping a lion to San Francisco, and the roaring and confusion were all very satisfactory to the trespasser.

Midnight. From afar came the mellow notes of the bells in the ancient Spanish mission. The old year was dead, the new year was born, carrying with it the unchanging sound of happiness and misery, of promises made and promises broken, of good and evil.

"The packet!" cried Winnie.

Kathlyn recognized in that call that Winnie was only a child. All the responsibility lay upon her shoulders. She ripped the cover from the packet and read the note.

"Kathlyn: If not heard from I'm held captive in Allaha. Sealed document can save me. Bring it yourself to Allaha by first steamer.

"Father."

"I knew it," said Kathlyn calmly. The fear in her heart had, as the brown man had anticipated, blinded her to the fact that this was not her father's characteristic blunt scrawl.

"Oh, Kit, Kit!"

"Hush, Winnie! I must go, and go alone. Where's the evening paper? Ah, there it is. Let me see what boat leaves San Francisco to-morrow. The *Empress of India*, six a. m. I must make that. Now, you're your father's daughter, too, Winnie. You must stay behind and be brave and wait. I shall come back. I shall find father, if I have to rouse all India. Now, to pack."

When they arrived at the station the passenger train had just drawn out. For a while Kathlyn felt beaten. She would be compelled to wait another week. It was disheartening.

"Why not try the freight, then?" cried Winnie.

"You little angel! I never thought of that!"

But the crew would not hear of it. It was absolutely against the company's rules. Kathlyn could have cried.

"It isn't money, miss, it's the rules," said the conductor kindly. "I can't do it."

Kathlyn turned in despair toward the station. It was then she saw the boxed lion on the platform. She returned to the conductor of the freight.

"Why isn't that lion shipped?"

"We can't carry a lion without an attendant, miss. You ought to know that."

"Very well," replied Kathlyn. She smiled at the conductor confidently. "I'll travel as the lion's attendant. You certainly can not object to that."

"I guess you've got me," admitted the conductor. "But where the dickens will we put the cat? Every car is closed and locked, and there is not an empty."

"You can easily get the lion in the caboose. I'll see that he doesn't bother any one."

"Lions in the caboose is a new one on me. Well, you know your dad's business better than I do. Look alive, boys, and get that angora aboard. This is Miss Hare herself, and she'll take charge."

"Kit, Kit!"

"Winnie!"

"Oh, I'll be brave. I've just got to be. But I've never been left alone before."

The two girls embraced, and Winnie went sobbing back to the maid who waited on the platform.

What happened in that particular caboose has long since been newspaper history. The crew will go on telling it till it becomes as fabulous as one of Sindbad's yarns. How the lion escaped, how the fearless young woman captured it alone, unaided, may be found in the files of all metropolitan newspapers. Of the brown man who was found hiding in the coat closet of the caboose nothing was said. But the sight of him dismayed Kathlyn as no lion could have done. Any-dark skinned person was now a subtle menace. And when, later, she saw peering into the port-hole of her stateroom, dismay became terror.

Who was this man?

CHAPTER II

THE UNWELCOME THRONE

Kathlyn sensed great loneliness when, about a month later, she arrived at the basin in Calcutta. A thousand or more natives were bathing ceremoniously in the ghat—men, women and children. It was early morn, and they were making solemn genuflections toward the bright sun. The water-front swarmed with brown bodies, and great wheeled carts drawn by sad-eyed bullocks threaded slowly through the maze. The many white turbans, stirring hither and thither, reminded her of a field of white poppies in a breeze. India! There it lay, ready for her eager feet. Always had she dreamed about it, and romanced over it, and sought it on the wings of her spirit. Yonder it lay, ancient as China, enchanting as storied Persia.

If only she were on pleasure bent! If only she knew some one in this great teeming city! She knew no one; she carried no letters of introduction, no letters of credit, nothing but the gold and notes the paymaster at the farm had hastily turned over to her. Only by constant application to maps and guide books had she managed to arrange the short cut to the far kingdom. She had been warned that it was a wild and turbulent place, out of the beaten path, beyond the reach of iron rails. Three long sea voyages: across the Pacific (which wasn't), down the bitter Yellow Sea, up the blue Bay of Bengal, with many a sea change and many a strange picture. What though her heart ached, it was impossible that her young eyes should not absorb all she saw and marvel over it. India!

The strange elusive Hindu had disappeared after Hongkong. That was a weight off her soul. She was now assured that her imagination had beguiled her. How should he know anything about her? What was more natural than that he should wish to hurry back to his native state? She was not the only one in a hurry. And there were Hindus of all castes on all three ships. By now she had almost forgot him.

There was one bright recollection to break the unending loneliness. Coming down from Hongkong to Singapore she had met at the captain's table a young man by the name of Bruce. He was a quiet, rather untalkative man, lean and sinewy, sun and wind bitten. Kathlyn had as yet had no sentimental affairs. Absorbed in her work, her father and the care of Winnie, such young men as she had met had scarcely interested her. She had only tolerated contempt for idlers, and these young men had belonged to that category. Bruce caught her interest in the very fact that he had but little to say and said that crisply and well. There was something authoritative in the shape of his mouth and the steadiness of his eye, though before her he never exercised this power. A dozen times she had been on the point of taking him into her confidence, but the irony of fate had always firmly closed her lips.

And now, waiting for the ship to warp into its pier, she realized what a fatal mistake her reticence had been. A friend of her father!

Bruce had left the Lloyder before dinner (at Singapore),

and as Kathlyn's British-India coaster did not leave till morning she had elected to remain over night on the German boat.

As Bruce disappeared among the disembarking passengers and climbed into a rickshaw she turned to the captain, who stood beside her.

"Do you know Mr. Bruce?"

"Very well," said the German. "Didn't he tell you who he is? No? *Ach*! Why, Mr. Bruce is a great hunter. He has shot everything, written books, climbed the Himalayas. Only last year he brought me the sack of a musk deer, and that is the most dangerous of all sports. He collects animals."

Then Kathlyn knew. The name had been vaguely familiar, but the young man's reticence had given her no opportunity to dig into her recollection. Bruce! How many times her father had spoken of him! What a fool she had been! Bruce knew the country she was going to, perhaps as well as her father; and he could have simplified her journey to the last word. Well, what was done could not be recalled and done over.

"My father is a great hunter, too," she said simply, eying wistfully the road taken by Bruce into town.

"What? *Herr Gott*! Are you Colonel Hare's daughter?" exclaimed the captain.

"Yes."

He seized her by the shoulders. "Why did you not tell me? Why, Colonel Hare and I have smoked many a Burma cheroot together on these waters. *Herr Gott*! And you never said anything! What a woman for a man to marry!" he laughed. "You have sat at my table for five days, and only now I find that you are Hare's daughter! And you have a sister. *Ach*, yes! He was always taking out some photographs in the smoke-room and showing them to us old chaps."

Tears filled Kathlyn's eyes. In an Indian prison, out of the jurisdiction of the British Raj, and with her two small hands and woman's mind she must free him! Always the mysterious packet lay close to her heart, never for a moment was it beyond the reach of her hand. Her father's freedom!

The rusty metal sides of the ship scraped against the pier and the gangplank was lowered; and presently the tourists flocked down with variant emotions, to be besieged by fruit sellers, water carriers, cabmen, blind beggars, and maimed, naked little children with curious, insolent black eyes, women with infants straddling their hips, stolid Chinamen; a riot of color and a bewildering babel of tongues.

Kathlyn found a presentable carriage, and with her luggage pressing about her feet directed the driver to the Great Eastern Hotel.

Her white sola-topee (sun helmet) had scarcely disappeared in the crowd when the Hindu of the freight caboose emerged from the steerage, no longer in bedraggled linen trousers and ragged turban, but dressed like a native fop. He was in no hurry. Leisurely he followed Kathlyn to the hotel, then proceeded to the railway station. He had need no longer to watch and worry. There was nothing left now but to greet her upon her arrival, this golden houri from the verses of Sa'adi. The two weeks of durance vile among the low castes in the steerage should be amply repaid. In six days he would be beyond the hand of the meddling British Raj, in his own country. Sport! What was more beautiful to watch than cat play? He was the cat, the tiger cat. And what would the Colonel Sahib say when he felt the claws? Beautiful, beautiful, like a pattern woven in an Agra rug.

Kathlyn began her journey at once. Now that she was on land, moving toward her father, all her vigor returned. She felt strangely alive, exhilarated. She knew that she was not going to be afraid of anything hereafter. To enter the strange country without having her purpose known would be the main difficulty. Where was Ahmed all this time? Doubtless in a cell like his master.

Three days later she stood at the frontier, and her servant set about arguing and bargaining with the mahouts to engage elephants for the three days' march through jungles and mountainous divides to the capital. Three elephants were necessary. There were two howdah elephants and one pack elephant, who was always lagging behind. Through long aisles of magnificent trees they passed, across hot blistering deserts, dotted here and there by shrubs and stunted trees, in and out of gloomy defiles of flinty rock, over sluggish and swiftly flowing streams. The days were hot, but the nights were bitter cold. Sometimes a blue miasmic haze settled down, and the dry raspy hides of the elephants grew damp and they fretted at their chains.

Rao, the khidmutgar Kathlyn had hired in Calcutta, proved invaluable. Without him she would never have succeeded in entering the strange country; for these wild-eyed Mohammedan mahouts (and it is pertinent to note that only Mohammedans are ever made mahouts, it being against the tenets of Hinduism to kill or ride anything that kills) scowled at her evilly. They would have made way with her for an anna-piece. Rao was a Mohammedan himself, so they listened and obeyed.

All this the first day and night out. On the following morning a leopard crossed the trail. Kathlyn seized her rifle and broke its spine. The jabbering of the mahouts would have amused her at any other time.

"Good, Mem-sahib," whispered Rao. "You have put fear into their devils' hearts. Good! Chup!" he called. "Stop your noise."

After that they gave Kathlyn's dog tent plenty of room.

One day, in the heart of a natural clearing, she saw a tree. Its blossoms and leaves were as scarlet as the seeds of a pomegranate.

"Oh, how beautiful! What is it, Rao?"

"The flame of the jungle, Mem-sahib. It is good luck to see it on a journey."

About the tree darted gay parrakeets and fat green parrots. The green plumage of the birds against the brilliant scarlet of the tree was indescribably beautiful. Everywhere was life, everywhere was color. Once, as the natives seated themselves of the evening round their dung fire while Kathlyn busied with the tea over a wood fire, a tiger roared near by. The elephants trumpeted and the mahouts rose in terror. Kathlyn ran for her rifle, but the trumpeting of the elephants was sufficient to send the striped cat to other hunting-grounds. Wild ape and pig abounded, and occasionally a caha wriggled out of the sun into the brittle grasses. Very few beasts or reptiles are aggressive; it is only when they feel cornered that they turn. Even the black panther, the most savage of all cats, will rarely offer battle except when attacked.

Meantime the man who had followed Kathlyn arrived at the city.

Five hours later Kathlyn stepped out of her howdah, gave Rao the money for the mahouts and looked about. This was the gate to the capital. How many times had her father passed through it? Her jaw set and her eyes flashed. Whatever dangers beset her she was determined to meet them with courage and patience.

"Rao, you had better return to Calcutta. What I have to do must be done alone."

"Very good. But I shall remain here till the Mem-sahib returns." Rao salaamed.

"And if I should not return?" affected by this strange loyalty.

"Then I shall seek Bruce Sahib, who has a camp twenty miles east."

"Bruce? But he is in Singapore!"—a quickening of her pulses.

"Who can say where Bruce Sahib is? He is like a shadow, there to-day, here to-morrow. I have been his servant, Mem-sahib, and that is how I am to-day yours. I received a telegram to call at your hotel and apply to you for service. Very good. I shall wait. The mahout here will take you directly to Hare Sahib's bungalow. You will find your father's servants there, and all will be well. A week, then. If you do not send for me I seek Bruce Sahib, and we shall return with many. Some will speak English at the bungalow."

"Thank you, Rao. I shall not forget."

"Neither will Bruce Sahib," mysteriously. Rao salaamed.

Kathlyn got into the howdah and passed through the gates. Bruce Sahib, the quiet man whose hand had reached out over seas thus strangely to reassure her! A hardness came into her throat and she swallowed desperately. She was only twenty-four. Except for herself there might not be a white person in all this sprawling, rugged principality. From time to time the new mahout turned and smiled at her curiously, but she was too absorbed to note his attentions.

Durga Ram, called lightly Umballa, went directly to the palace, where he knew the Council of Three solemnly awaited his arrival. He dashed up the imposing flight of marble steps, exultant. He had fulfilled his promise; the golden daughter of Hare Sahib was but a few miles away. The soldiers, guarding the entrance, presented their arms respectfully; but instantly after Umballa disappeared the expression on their faces was not pleasing.

Umballa hurried along through the deep corridor, supported by exquisitely carved marble columns. Beauty in stone was in evidence everywhere and magnificent brass lamps hung from the ceiling. There was a shrine topped by an idol in black marble, incrusted with sapphires and turquoises. Durga Ram, who shall be called Umballa, nodded slightly as he passed it. Force of habit, since in his heart there was only one religion—self.

He stopped at a door guarded by a single soldier, who saluted but spat as soon as Umballa had passed into the throne room. The throne itself was vacant. The Council of Three rose at the approach of Umballa.

"She is here," he said haughtily.

The council salaamed.

Umballa stroked his chin as he gazed at the huge candles flickering at each side of the throne. He sniffed the Tibetan incense, and shrugged. It was written. "Go," he said, "to Hare Sahib's bungalow and await me. I shall be there presently. There is plenty of time. And remember our four heads depend upon the next few hours. The soldiers are on the verge of mutiny, and only success can pacify them."

He turned without ceremony and left them. With oriental philosophy they accepted the situation. They had sought to overturn him, and he held them in the hollow of his hand. During the weeks of his absence in America his spies had hung about them like bees about honey. They were the fowlers snared.

Umballa proceeded along the corridor to a flight of stairs leading beneath the palace floor. Here the soldiers were agreeable enough; they had reason to be. Umballa gave them new minted rupees for their work, many rupees. For they knew secrets. Before the door of a dungeon Umballa paused and listened. There was no sound. He returned upstairs and sought a chamber near the harem. This he entered, and stood with folded arms near the door.

"Ah, Colonel Sahib!"

"Umballa?" Colonel Hare, bearded, unkempt, tried to stand erect and face his enemy. "You black scoundrel!"

"Durga Ram, Sahib. Words, words; the patter of rain on stone roofs. Our king lives no more, alas!"

"You lie!"

"He is dead. Dying, he left you this throne—you, a white man, knowing it was a legacy of terror and confusion. You knew. Why did you return? Ah, pearls and sapphires and emeralds! What? I offer you this throne upon conditions."

"And those conditions I have refused."

"You have, yes, but now—" Umballa smiled. Then he suddenly blazed forth: "Think you a white man shall sit upon this throne while I live? It is mine. I was his heir."

"Then why didn't you save him from the leopard? I'll tell you why. You expected to inherit on the spot, and I spoiled the game. Is that not true?"

"And what if I admit it?" truculently.

"Umballa, or Durga Ram, if you wish, listen. Take the throne. What's to hinder you? You want it. Take it and let me begone."

"Yes, I want it; and by all the gods of Hind I'll have it— but safely. Ah! It would be fine to proclaim myself when mutiny and rebellion stalk about. Am I a pig to play a game like that? Tch! Tch!" He clicked his tongue against the roof of his mouth in derision. "No; I need a buckler till all this roily water subsides and clears."

"And then, some fine night, Hare Sahib's throat? I am not afraid of death, Umballa. I have faced it too many times. Make an end of me at once or leave me to rot here, my answer will always be the same. I will not become a dishonorable tool. You have offered me freedom and jewels. No; I repeat, I will free all slaves, abolish the harems, the buying and selling of flesh; I will make a man of every poor devil of a coolie who carries stones from your quarries."

Umballa laughed. "Then remain here like a dog while I put your golden daughter on the throne and become what the British Raj calls prince consort. She'll rebel, I know; but I have a way." He stepped outside and closed the door.

"Umballa?"

"Well?"

"Kit, my daughter? Good God, what is she doing here when I warned her?" Hare tugged furiously at his chains. "Durga Ram, you have beaten me. State your terms and I will accept them to the letter. . . . Kit, my beautiful Kit, in this hellhole!"

"Ah, but I don't want you to accept now. I was merely amusing myself." The door shut and the bolt shot home.

Hare fell upon his knees. "My head, my head! Dear God, save me my reason!"

* * * * * *

The moment Kathlyn arrived at the animal cages of her father she called for Ahmed.

"My father?"

"Ah, Mem-sahib, they say he is dead. I know not. One night—the second after we arrived—he was summoned to the palace. He never came back."

"They have killed him!"

"Perhaps. They watch me, too; but I act simple. We wait and see."

Kathlyn rushed across the ground intervening between the animal cages and the bungalow. There was no one in sight. She ran up the steps . . . to be greeted inside by the suave Umballa.

"You?" her hand flying to her bosom.

"I, Miss Hare." He salaamed, with a sweeping gesture of his hands.

Sadly the wretch told her the tale; the will of the king, his death and the subsequent death of her father in his, Durga Ram's, arms. Yonder urn contained his ashes. For the first time in her young life Kathlyn fainted. She had been living on her nerves for weeks, and at the sight of that urn something snapped. Daintily Umballa plucked forth the packet and waited. At length she opened her eyes.

"You are a queen, Miss Hare."

"You are mad!"

"Nay; it was the madness of the king. But mad kings often make laws which must be obeyed. You will accuse me of perfidy when I tell you all. The note which brought you here was written by me and substituted for this."

Duly Kathlyn read:

"Kathlyn—if not heard from, I'm held captive in Allaha. The royal title given to me by the king made me and my descendants direct heirs to the throne. Do not come to

Allaha yourself. Destroy sealed document herewith.

"Father."

The Council of Three entered noiselessly from the adjoining room. At the four dark, inscrutable faces the bewildered girl stared, her limbs numb with terror. Gravely the council told her she must come with them to the palace.

"It is impossible!" she murmured. "You are all mad. I am a white woman. I can not rule over an alien race whose tongue I can not speak, whose habits I know nothing of. It is impossible. Since my father is dead, I must return to my home."

"No," said Umballa.

"I refuse to stir!" She was all afire of a sudden: the base trickery which had brought her here! She was very lovely to the picturesque savage who stood at her elbow.

As he looked down at her, in his troubled soul Umballa knew that it was not the throne so much as it was this beautiful bird of paradise which he wished to cage.

"Be brave," he said, "like your father. I do not wish to use force, but you must go. It is useless to struggle. Come."

She hung back for a moment; then, realizing her utter helplessness, she signified that she was ready to go. She needed time to collect her stunned and disordered thoughts.

Before going to the palace they conducted her to the royal crypt. The urn containing her father's ashes was deposited in a niche. Many other niches contained urns, and

Umballa explained to her that these held the ashes of many rulers. Tears welled into Kathlyn's eyes, but they were of a hysterical character.

"A good sign," mused Umballa, who thought he knew something of women, like all men beset with vanity. Oddly enough, he had forgot all about the incident of the lion in the freight caboose. All women are felines to a certain extent. This golden-haired woman had claws, and the day was coming when he would feel them drag over his heart.

From the crypt they proceeded to the palace zenana (harem), which surrounded a court of exceeding beauty. Three ladies of the harem were sitting in the portico, attended by slaves. All were curiously interested at the sight of a woman with white skin, tinted like the lotus. Umballa came to a halt before a latticed door.

"Here your majesty must remain till the day of your coronation."

"How did my father die?"

"He was assassinated on the palace steps by a Mohammedan fanatic. As I told you, he died in my arms."

"His note signified that he feared imprisonment. How came he on the palace steps?"

"He was not a prisoner. He came and went as he pleased in the city." He bowed and left her.

Alone in her chamber, the dullness of her mind diminished and finally cleared away like a fog in a wind. Her dear, kind, blue-eyed father was dead, and she was virtually a prisoner, and Winnie was all alone. A queen!

They were mad, or she was in the midst of some hideous nightmare. Mad, mad, mad! She began to laugh, and it was not a pleasant sound. A queen, she, Kathlyn Hare! Her father was dead, she was a queen, and Winnie was all alone. A gale of laughter brought to the marble lattice many wondering eyes. The white cockatoo shrilled his displeasure. Those outside the lattice saw this marvelous white-skinned woman, with hair like the gold threads in Chinese brocades, suddenly throw herself upon a pile of cushions, and they saw her shoulders rock and heave, but heard no sound of wailing.

After a while she fell asleep, a kind of dreamless stupor. When she awoke it was twilight in the court. The doves were cooing and fluttering in the cornices and the cockatoo was preening his lemon colored topknot. At first Kathlyn had not the least idea where she was, but the light beyond the lattice, the flitting shadows, and the tinkle of a stringed instrument assured her that she was awake, terribly awake.

She sat perfectly still, slowly gathering her strength, mental and physical. She was not her father's daughter for nothing. She was to fight in some strange warfare, instinctively she felt this; but from what direction, in what shape, only God knew. Yet she must prepare for it; that was the vital thing; she must marshal her forces, feminine and only defensive, and watch.

Rao! Her hands clutched the pillows. In five days' time he would be off to seek John Bruce; and there would be white men there, and they would come to her though a thousand legions of these brown men stood between. She would play for time; she must pretend docility and meet quiet guile with guile. She could get no word to her faithful khidmutgar; none here, even if open to bribery, could be made to understand. Only Umballa and the council spoke English or understood it. She had ten days' grace; within that time she hoped to find some loophole.

Slave girls entered noiselessly. The hanging lamps were lighted. A tabouret was set before her. There were quail and roast kid, fruits and fragrant tea. She was not hungry, but she ate.

Within a dozen yards of her sat her father, stolidly munching his chupatties, because he knew that now he must live.

* * * * * *

One of the chief characteristics of the East Indian is extravagance. To outvie one another in celebrations of births, weddings, deaths and coronations they beggar themselves. In this the Oriental and the Occidental have one thing in common. This principality was small, but there was a deal of wealth in it because of its emerald mines and turquoise pits. The durbar brought out princes and princelings from east, south and west, and even three or four wild-eyed ameers from the north. The British government at Calcutta heard vaguely about this fete, but gave it scant attention for the simple fact that it had not been invited to attend. Still, it watched the performance covertly. Usually durbars took months of preparation; this one had been called into existence within ten days.

Elephants and camels and bullocks; palanquins, gharries, tongas; cloth of gold and cloth of jewels; color, confusion, maddening noises, and more color. There was very little semblance of order; a rajah preceded a princeling, and so on down. The wailing of reeds and the muttering of kettle drums; music, languorous, haunting, elusive, low minor chords seemingly struck at random, intermingling a droning chant; a thousand streams of incense, crossing and recrossing; and fireworks at night, fireworks which had come all the way across China by caravan—these things Kathlyn saw and heard from her lattice.

The populace viewed all these manifestations quietly. They were perfectly willing to wait. If this white queen proved kind they would go about their affairs, leaving her in peace; but they were determined that she should be no puppet in the hands or Umballa, whom they hated for his cruelty and money leeching ways. Oh, everything was ripe in the state for murder and loot—and the reaching, holding hand of the British Raj.

As Kathlyn advanced to the canopied dais upon which she was to be crowned, a hand filled with flowers reached out. She turned to see Ahmed.

"Bruce Sahib," she whispered.

Ahmed salaamed deeply as she passed on. The impression that she was dreaming again seized her. This could not possibly be real. Her feet did not seem to touch the carpets; she did not seem to breathe; she floated. It was only when the crown was placed upon her head that she realized the reality and the finality of the proceedings.

"Be wise," whispered Umballa coldly. "If you take off that crown now, neither your gods nor mine could save you from that mob down yonder. Be advised. Rise!"

She obeyed. She wanted to cry out to that sea of bronze faces: "People I do not want to be your queen. Let me go!" They would not understand. Where was Rao? Where was Bruce? What of the hope that now flickered and died in her heart, like a guttering candle light? There was a small dagger hidden in the folds of her white robe; she could always use that. She heard Umballa speaking in the native tongue. A great shouting followed. The populace surged.

"What have you said to them?" she demanded.

"That her majesty had chosen Durga Ram to be her consort and to him now forthwith she will be wed." He salaamed.

So the mask was off! "Marry you? Oh, no! Mate with you, a black?"

"Black?" he cried, as if a whiplash had struck him across the face.

"Yes, black of skin and black of heart. I have submitted to the farce of this durbar, but that is as far as my patience will go. God will guard me."

"God?" mockingly.

"Yes, my God and the God of my fathers!"

To the mutable faces below she looked the Queen at that instant. They saw the attitude, but could not interpret it.

"So be it. There are other things besides marriage."

"Yes," she replied proudly; "there is death."

CHAPTER III

THE TWO ORDEALS

Umballa was not a coward; he was only ruthless and predatory after the manner of his kind. A thrill of admiration tingled his spine. The women of his race were chattels, lazy and inert, without fire, merely drudges or playthings. Here was one worth conquering, a white flame to be controlled. To bend her without breaking her, that must be his method of procedure. The skin under her chin was as white as the heart of a mangosteen, and the longing to sweep her into his arms was almost irresistible.

A high priest spoke to Kathlyn.

"What does he say?" she asked.

"That you must marry me."

"Tell him that I refuse!"

Umballa shrugged and repeated her words. Here the Council of Three interposed, warning Kathlyn that she must submit to the law as it read. There was no appeal from it.

"Then I shall appeal to the British Raj."

"How?" asked Umballa urbanely.

Swiftly she stepped to the front of the platform and extended her arms. It was an appeal. She pointed to Umballa and shook her head. Her arms went out again. A low murmur rippled over the pressing crowd; it grew in volume; and a frown of doubt flitted over Umballa's brow. The soldiers were swaying restlessly. Kathlyn saw this sign and was quick to seize upon its possibilities. She renewed her gesture toward them. It seemed that she must burst forth in their maddening tongue: "I appeal to the chivalry of Allaha! . . . Soldiers, you now wear my uniform! Liberate me!" But her tongue was mute; yet her eyes, her face, her arms spoke eloquently enough to the turbulent soldiers. Besides, they welcomed the opportunity to show the populace how strong they were and how little they feared Umballa. At a nod from their leader they came romping up the steps to this dais and surrounded Kathlyn. A roar came from the populace; an elephant trumpeted; the pariah dogs barked.

Umballa stepped back, his hand on his jeweled sword. He was quite unprepared for any such flagrant mutiny— mutiny from his angle of vision, though in law the troopers had only responded to the desire of their queen. He turned questioningly to the council and the priests. He himself could move no further. His confreres appreciated the danger in which their power stood. They announced that it was decreed to give the queen a respite of seven days in which to yield. It would at least hold the bold troopers on the leash till they could be brought to see the affair in its true light by the way of largess in rupees. Umballa consented because he was at the bottom of the sack. A priest read from a scroll the law, explaining that no woman might rule unmarried. Because the young queen was not conversant with the laws of the state she would be given seven days. Thus the durbar ended.

With a diplomacy which would have graced a better man Umballa directed the troopers to escort Kathlyn to her chamber in the zenana. He had in mind seven days. Many things could be accomplished in that space of time.

"For the present," he said, smiling at Kathlyn, "the God of your fathers has proven strongest. But to-morrow! . . . Ah, to-morrow! There will be seven days. Think, then, deeply and wisely. Your khidmutgar Rao is a prisoner. It will be weeks ere your presence is known here. You are helpless as a bird in the net. Struggle if you will; you will only bruise your wings. The British Raj? The British Raj does not want a great border war, and I can bring down ten thousand wild hillmen outlaws between whom and the British Raj there is a blood feud; ten thousand from a land where there is never peace, only truce. In seven days. Salaam, heaven born!"

She returned his ironical gaze calmly over the shoulder of a trooper.

"Wait," she said. "I wish you to understand the enormity of your crime."

"Crime?" with elevated eyebrows.

"Yes. You have abducted me."

"No. You came of your own free will."

"The white men of my race will not pause to argue over any such subtlety. Marry you? I do not like your color."

A dull red settled under Umballa's skin.

"I merely wish to warn you," she went on, "that my blood will be upon your head. And woe to you if it is. There are white men who will not await the coming of the British Raj."

"Ah, yes; some brave hardy American; Bruce Sahib, for instance. Alas, he is in the Straits Settlements! Seven days."

"I am not afraid to die."

"But there are many kinds of death," and with this sinister reflection he stepped aside.

The multitude, seeing Kathlyn coming down from the dais, still surrounded by her cordon of troopers, began reluctantly to disperse. "Bread and the circus!"—the mobs will cry it down the ages; they will always pause to witness bloodshed, from a safe distance, you may be sure. There was a deal of rioting in the bazaars that night, and many a measure of bhang and toddy kept the fires burning. Oriental politics is like the winds of the equinox: it blows from all directions.

The natives were taxed upon every conceivable subject, not dissimilar to the old days in Urdu, where a man paid so much for the privilege of squeezing the man under him. Mutiny was afoot, rebellion, but it had not yet found a head. The natives wanted a change, something to gossip about during the hot lazy afternoons, over their hookas and coffee. To them reform meant change only, not the alleviation of some of their heavy burdens. The talk of freeing slaves was but talk; slaves were lucrative investments; a man would be a fool to free them. An old man, with a skin white like this new queen's and hair like spun wool, dressed in a long black cloak and a broad brimmed hat, had started the agitation of liberating the slaves. More than that, he carried no idol of his God, never bathed in the ghats, or took flowers to the temples, and seemed always silently communing with the simple iron cross suspended from his neck. But he had died during the last visitation of the plague.

They had wearied of their tolerant king, who had died mysteriously; they were now wearied of the council and Umballa; in other words, they knew not what they wanted, being People.

Who was this fair-skinned woman who stood so straight before Umballa's eye? Whence had she come? To be ruled by a woman who appeared to be tongue-tied! Well, there were worse things than a woman who could not talk. Thus they gabbled in the bazaars, round braziers and dung fires. And some talked of the murder. The proud Ramabai had been haled to prison; his banker's gold had not saved him. Oh, this street rat Umballa generally got what he wanted. Ramabai's wife was one of the beauties of Hind.

Through the narrow, evil smelling streets of the bazaars a man hurried that night, glancing behind frequently to see if by any mischance some one followed. He stopped at the house of Lal Singh, the shoemaker, whom he found drowsing over his water pipe.

"Is it well?" said the newcomer, intoning.

"It is well," answered Lal Singh, dropping the mouthpiece of his pipe. He had spoken mechanically. When he saw who his visitor was his eyes brightened. "Ahmed?"

"Hush!" with a gesture toward the ceiling.

"She is out merrymaking, like the rest of her kind. The old saying: if a man waits, the woman comes to him. I am alone. There is news?"

"There is a journey. Across Hind to Simla."

"The hour has arrived?"

"At least the excuse. Give these to one in authority with the British Raj, whose bread we eat." Ahmed slid across the table a very small scroll. "The Mem-sahib is my master's daughter. She must be spirited away to safety."

"Ah!" Lal Singh rubbed his fat hands. "So the time nears when we shall wring the vulture's neck? Ai, it is good! Umballa, the toad, who swells and swells as the days go by. Siva has guarded him well. The king picks him out of the gutter for a pretty bit of impudence, sends him afar to Umballa, where he learns to speak English, where he learns to wear shoes that button and stiff linen bands round the neck. He has gone on, gone on! The higher up, the harder the fall."

"The cellar?"

"There are pistols and guns and ammunition and strange little wires by which I make magic fires."

"Batteries?"

"One never knows what may be needed. You have the key?"

"Yes."

"Hare Sahib's daughter. And Hare Sahib?" with twinkling eyes.

"In some dungeon, mayhap. There all avenues seemed closed up."

"Umballa needs money," said Lal Singh, thoughtfully. "But he will not find it," in afterthought.

"To-morrow?"

"At dawn."

These two men were spiders in that great web of secret service that the British Raj weaves up and down and across Hind, to Persia and Afghanistan, to the borders of the Bear.

Even as Lal Singh picked up his mouthpiece again and Ahmed sallied forth into the bazaars Umballa had brought to him in the armory that company of soldiers who had shown such open mutiny, not against the state but against him.

Gravely he questioned the captain.

"Pay our wages, then, heaven born," said the captain, with veiled insolence. "Pay us, for we have seen not so much as betel money since the last big rains."

"Money," mused Umballa, marking down this gallant captain for death when the time came.

"Ai, money; bright rupees, or, better still, yellow British gold. Pay us!"

"Let us be frank with each other," said Umballa, smiling to cover the fire in his eyes.

"That is what we desire," replied the captain with a knowing look at his silent troopers.

"I must buy you."

The captain salaamed.

"But after I have bought you?" ironically.

"Heaven born; our blood is yours to spill where and when you will."

From under the teak table Umballa drew forth two heavy bags of silver coin. These he emptied upon the table dramatically; white shining metal, sparkling as the candle flames wavered. Umballa arranged the coin in stacks, one of them triple in size.

"Yours, Captain," said Umballa, indicating the large stack.

The captain pocketed it, and one by one his troopers passed and helped themselves and fell back along the wall in military alignment, bright-eyed and watchful.

"Thanks, heaven born!"

The captain and his troopers filed out. Umballa fingered the empty bags, his brow wrinkled. Cut off a cobra's head and it could only wriggle until sunset. Umballa gave the vanishing captain two weeks. Then he should vanish indeed.

The next morning while the council and Umballa were in session relative as to what should be done with Kathlyn in the event of her refusal to bend, two soldiers entered, bringing with them a beautiful native young woman, one Pundita, wife of Ramabai, found in murder.

Umballa wiped his betel stained lips and salaamed mockingly. Not so long ago he had been attentive to this young woman—after her marriage. She had sent him about his business with burning ears and a hot cheek, made so by the contact of her strong young hand. Revenge, great or small, was always sweet to Umballa.

To the slave girl who attended Pundita he said: "Go summon the queen. It is for her to decide what shall be done with this woman."

Through the veil Pundita's black eyes sparkled with hatred.

When Kathlyn came in it was at once explained to her that the woman's husband had been taken for murder; by law his wife became the queen's property, to dispose of as she willed. The veil was plucked from Pundita's face. She was ordered to salaam in submission to her queen. Pundita salaamed, but stoutly refused to kneel. They proceeded to force her roughly, when Kathlyn intervened.

"Tell her she is free," said Kathlyn.

"Free?" came from the amazed Pundita's lips.

"You speak English?" cried Kathlyn excitedly.

"Yea, Majesty."

Kathlyn could have embraced her for the very joy of the knowledge. A woman who could talk English, who could understand, who perhaps could help! Yes, yes; the God of her fathers was good.

Umballa smiled. All this was exactly what he had reason to expect. Seven days of authority; it would amuse him to watch her.

"Tell me your story," urged Kathlyn kindly. "Be not

afraid of these men. I shall make you my lady in waiting . . . so long as I am queen," with a searching glance at Umballa's face. She learned nothing from the half smile there.

Pundita's narrative was rather long but not uninteresting. She had learned English from the old white priest who had died during the last plague. She was of high caste; and far back in the days of the Great Mogul in Delhi her forebears had ruled here; but strife and rebellion had driven them forth. In order that her immediate forebear might return to their native state and dwell in peace they had waived all possible rights of accession. They had found her husband standing over a dead man in the bazaars. He was innocent.

Umballa smoothed his chin. Pundita had not told her queen how he, Umballa, had made the accusation, after having been refused money by Ramabai. He secretly admired the diplomacy of the young woman. He did not at this moment care to push his enmity too far. As a matter of fact, he no longer cared about her; at least, not since his arrival at the Hare wild animal farm in California.

"Where is this man Ramabai confined?" demanded Kathlyn.

"In the murderers' pit in the elephant arena."

"Send and bring him here. I am certain that he is innocent."

So they brought in Ramabai in chains. Behind him came a Nautch girl, at whom Umballa gazed puzzledly. What part had she in this affair? He soon found out.

"Who are you?" he asked.

"I am Lalla Ghori, and I live over the shoemaker, Lal Singh, in the Kashmir Gate bazaar. I dance."

"And why are you here?"

"I saw the murder. Ramabai is innocent. He came upon the scene only after the murderer had fled. They were fighting about me," naively. "I was afraid to tell till now."

"Knock off those chains," said Kathlyn. Of Pundita she asked: "Does he, too, speak English?"

"Yes, heaven born."

"Then for the present he shall become my bodyguard. You shall both remain here in the palace."

"Ah, Your Majesty!" interposed Umballa. Pundita he did not mind, but he objected to Ramabai, secretly knowing him to be a revolutionist, extremely popular with the people and the near-by ryots (farmers), to whom he loaned money upon reasonable terms.

"If I am queen, I will it," said Kathlyn firmly. "If I am only a prisoner, end the farce at once."

"Your majesty's word is law," and Umballa bowed, hiding as best he could his irritation.

The next afternoon he began to enact the subtle plans he had formed regarding Kathlyn. He brought her certain documents and petitions to sign and went over them carefully with her. Once, as she returned a document, he caught her hand and kissed it. She withdrew it roughly, flaming with anger. He spread his hands apologetically.

He was on fire for her, but he possessed admirable control. He had the right to come and go; as regent he could enter the zenana without being accompanied by the council. But, thereafter, when he arrived with the day's business she contrived to have Pundita near and Ramabai within call. On the sixth day he cast all discretion to the winds and seized her violently in his arms. And, though she defended her lips, her cheeks and neck were defiled. She stepped back; the hidden dagger flashed.

"A step nearer," she cried, low voiced, "and I will strike."

Umballa recoiled. This was no longer Sa'adi's houri but the young woman who had mastered the lion in the railway train. Rage supplanted the passion in his heart. Since she would not bend, she should break. As her arm sank he sprang forward like a cat and seized her wrist. He was not gentle. The dagger tinkled as it struck the marble floor. He stooped for it.

"Since you will not bend, break!" he said, and left the chamber, cold with fury.

Kathlyn sank weakly upon her pillows as Pundita ran to her side.

"What shall I do, Pundita?"

"God knows, Mem-sahib!"

"Are you a Christian?"

"Yes."

And so they comforted each other.

There was a garden in the palace grounds, lovely indeed.

A fountain tinkled and fat carp swam about in the fluted marble basin. There were trellises of flowers, too. Persian roses, despite the fact that it was still winter. It was called the garden of brides.

Kathlyn, attended by Pundita, awaited there the coming of Umballa and the council. Her heart ached with bitterness and she could not think clearly. The impression that all this was some dreadful nightmare recurred to her vividly. What terrors awaited her she knew not nor could conceive. Marry that smiling demon?—for something occult told her that he was a demon. No; she was ready to die . . . And but a little while ago she had been working happily in the outdoor studio; the pet leopard sprawled at her feet; from the bungalow she heard the nightingale voice of Winnie, soaring in some aria of Verdi's; her father was dozing on the veranda. Out of that, into this! It was incredible. From time to time she brushed her forehead, bewildered.

In this mood, bordering on the hysterical (which is sometimes but a step to supreme courage), Durga Ram, so-called Umballa, and the council found her. The face of the former was cold, his eyes steady and expressionless.

"Has your majesty decided?" asked the eldest of the council.

"Yes," quietly.

"And your decision is?"

"No, absolutely and finally. There is no reason why I should obey any of your laws; but there is a good reason why all of you shall some day be punished for this outrage."

"Outrage! To be made queen of Allaha?" The spokesman for the council stamped his foot in wrath.

"Think!" said Umballa.

"I have thought. Let us have no more of this cat-and-mouse play. I refuse to marry you. I'd much prefer any beggar in the street. There is nothing more to be said."

"There are worse things than marriage."

"What manner of indignities have you arranged for me?" Her voice was firm, but the veins in her throat beat so hardily that they stifled her.

Said the spokesman of the council: "We have found a precedent. We find that one hundred and ninety years ago a like case confused the council of that day. They finally agreed that she must submit to two ordeals with wild beasts of the jungle. If she survived she was to be permitted to rule without hindrance. It would be a matter for the gods to decide."

"Are you really human beings?" asked Kathlyn, her lips dry. "Can you possibly commit such a dreadful crime against one who has never harmed you, who asks for nothing but the freedom to leave this country?"

Pundita secretly caught Kathlyn's hand and pressed it.

"Once more!" said Umballa, his compassion touched for the first time. But he had gone too far; for the safety of his own head he must go on.

"I am ready!"

The four men salaamed gravely. They turned, the flowing

Harold MacGrath

yellow robes of the council fluttering in the wind, the sun lighting with green and red fires the hilt of Umballa's sword. Not one of them but would have emptied his private coffers to undo what he had done. It was too late. Already a priest had announced the ordeals to the swarming populace. You feed a tiger to pacify him; you give a populace a spectacle.

That night Umballa did not rest particularly well. But he became determined upon one thing: no actual harm should befall Kathlyn. He would have a marksman hidden near by in both ordeals. What a woman! She was a queen, and he knew that he would go through all the hells of Hind to call her his. Long ere this he would have looted the treasure chests and swept her up on his racing elephant had he dared. Sa'adi's houri!

A thousand times he heard it through the night:

"I am ready!"

CHAPTER IV

HOW TIME MOVES

Meantime Lal Singh was hurrying on a racing camel toward the railway, toward Simla, more than a thousand miles away. He was happy. Here was the long delayed opportunity for the hand of the British Raj: a captive white woman. What better excuse was needed? There would be armed Sikhs and Gurhas and Tommies near Rawal Pindi. Ai! how time moved, how fate twisted! How the finest built castle in schemes came clattering down! At the very moment when he had secretly worked upon the king to throw himself into the protecting arms of the British Raj—assassinated! The council? Umballa? Some outsider, made mad by oppression? The egg of Brahma was strangely hatched—this curious old world!

Ahmed remained hidden in the bazaars, to await the ordeals. Nothing should harm his mistress; he was ready now and at all times to lay down his life for her; in this the British Raj came second. He had sent a courier to Bruce Sahib's bungalow, but the man had returned to report that it was still unoccupied.

And while he bit his nails in futile wrath and smoked till his tongue grew bitter, some miles away there was much confusion in the jungle by the water. Tents were being set up, native bearers and coolies were running to and fro, building fires, carrying water, hobbling the pack elephants. Wandering in and out of this animated scene was a young man, clean shaven, deeply tanned, with blue eyes which were direct, small pupiled, yet kindly. Presently he called to one of the head men.

"Ali, you might send three or four men on to the bungalow to clean up things. We shall make it tomorrow. It's but two hours' ride, but there's no hurry; and besides there's a herd of elephants behind us somewhere. They've come up far for this time of year."

"Any news worth while?"

"Yes, Sahib."

Ali made a gesture; it signified a great many things.

"Bruce Sahib will not believe."

"Believe what?" said Bruce, emptying his pipe against his heel.

"There is a white queen in the city."

"What? What bally nonsense is this?"

"It is only what I've been told, Sahib. Hare Sahib is dead."

Bruce let his pipe slip through his fingers. "Hare? Good lord!"

"Yes, Sahib. But that is not all. It seems the king went mad after we went to Africa. You remember how Hare Sahib saved him from the leopard? Well, he made Hare Sahib his heir. He had that right; the law of the childless

king has always read so in Allaha. The white queen is
Hare Sahib's daughter."

Bruce leaned against a tent pole. "Am I dreaming or are
you?" he gasped.

"It is what they tell me, Sahib. I know it not as a fact."

"The king dead, Hare dead, and his daughter on the
throne! How did she get here? And what the devil is a
chap to do?" Bruce stooped and recovered his pipe and
swore softly. "Ali, if this is true, then it's some devil
work; and I'll wager my shooting eye that that sleek
scoundrel Umballa, as they call him, is at the bottom of it.
A white woman, good old Hare's daughter. I'll look into
this. It's the nineteenth century, Ali, and white women are
not made rulers over the brown, not of their own free will.
Find out all you can and report to me," and Bruce
dismissed his servant and fell to pacing before his tent.

The native who had spread this astounding news in
Bruce's camp was already hastening back to the city,
some fourteen miles away. He had been a bheestee (water
carrier) to the house of Ramabai up to the young banker's
incarceration. To him, then, he carried the news that a
white hunter had arrived outside the city—"Bruce Sahib
has returned!"

Ramabai lost no time in taking this news to Kathlyn.

"Ramabai, I have saved your life; save mine. Go at once
to him and tell him that I am a prisoner but am called a
queen; tell him I am Colonel Hare's daughter, she who
traveled with him on the same ship from Hongkong to
Singapore. Go! Tell him all, the death of my father and
Umballa's treachery. Hasten!"

Bruce was eating his simple evening meal when Ramabai arrived.

"Bruce Sahib?"

"Yes. Your face is familiar."

"You have been twice to my bank. I am Ramabai."

"I remember. But what are you doing here?"

"I have come for aid, Sahib, aid for a young woman, white like yourself."

"Then it is true? Go ahead and let me have all the facts. She is Hare Sahib's daughter; Ali told me that. Precious rigmarole of some sort. The facts!"

"She is also the young lady who traveled in the same boat from Hongkong to Singapore." Ramabai paused to see the effect of this information.

Bruce lowered his fork slowly. The din about him dwindled away into nothing. He was again leaning over the rail, watching the phosphorescence trail away, a shoulder barely touching his: one of the few women who had ever stirred him after the first glance. In God's name, why hadn't she said something? Why hadn't she told him she was Colonel Hare's daughter? How was he to know? (For Hare, queerly enough, had never shown his young friend the photographs of his daughters.) Perhaps he had been at fault; he, too, had scarcely stirred from his shell. And where was that scoundrel Rao?

"I shall enter the city as soon as I can settle my bungalow. This rather knocks me out."

"No, Sahib; don't wait: come back with me!" Quickly he outlined the desperate straits in which Kathlyn stood. "To-morrow may be too late."

"Ali!" called Bruce, rising.

"Yes, Sahib."

"The Pasha. No questions. Give him water. Use the hunting howdah. Both guns and plenty of cartridges. That's all." The young man ran into his sleeping tent and presently came forth with a pair of ugly looking Colts; for this was before the days of the convenient automatics. "All aboard, Ramabai!" Bruce laughed; the sound was as hard and metallic as the click of the cartridge belt as he slung it round his waist; but it was music to Ramabai's ears. "Trust me. There shan't be any ordeals; not so you would notice it. . . . Great God! A white woman, one of my kind! . . . All right, Ali; quick work. Thanks!"

"There will be many pitfalls, Sahib," said Ramabai.

"Indeed!"

"I have some influence with the populace, but Umballa has the army, paid for. The priests and the council are back of him. And, after all, the priests are most to be feared. They can always sway the people through fear."

Bruce laughed again. "Either Kathlyn Hare will be free to-morrow or Umballa and the council meat for the jackals . . . or I shall be," he added, in afterthought. "Now, do not speak till I speak. I wish to think, for I've got to act quickly; I can't make any mistakes when I get there."

Far away a brown figure in clout and drab turban watched the young man. When he saw the elephant with the hunting howdah he knew that he had the information for which his master had detailed him to follow, night and day, the young banker Ramabai. The white hunter was coming hot-foot to the city. He turned and ran. Running was his business; he was as tireless as a camel and could run twenty and thirty miles at a stretch. The soles of his feet were as tough as elephant's hide. Thus he reached the city an hour before Bruce and Ramabai.

When Bruce and the native banker arrived at the gate coolies stood about with torches. Suddenly beyond the gate half a regiment drew up. The officer in charge raised his hand warningly.

"The white hunter is Bruce Sahib?"

"Yes." Bruce spoke the dialects with passable fluency.

"Good. The Sahib will be pleased to dismount."

"I am on my way to the palace."

"That is impossible, Sahib." At a sign from the officer the troopers extended their guns at half aim. It was a necessary precaution. These white sahibs were generally a mad people and were quick to shoot. "Please dismount, Sahib. It is the orders."

Bruce's mahout, who was a Rajput Mohammedan, turned his head to learn what his master had to say. Bruce, pale under his tan, nodded. The mahout reached down with his silver tipped goad and touched the elephant on the knee. The big brute slowly and ponderously kneeled. Bruce stepped out of the howdah, followed by Ramabai, who saw that in some unaccountable manner they had been betrayed. He was sick at heart.

Two troopers stepped forward and took possession of the rifles which were slung on each side of the howdah. Bruce accepted the situation philosophically; argument or protest was futile. Next they took away his cartridge belt. He trembled for a moment with apprehension, but the troopers did not search him further; and he thanked God for the wisdom which had made him strap his revolvers under his armpits.

"What now?" he demanded.

"The Sahib will be given his guns and ammunition the hour he starts back to camp."

"And in the meantime?"

"The Sahib is free to come and go about the city so long as he does not approach the palace. If he is found in the vicinity of the zenana he will be arrested and imprisoned."

"This is all very high-handed."

"Sahib, there is no British Raj here. The orders of the regent and the council are final. Submit."

"Very well."

"Ramabai!"

Ramabai stepped forward. By a kind of clairvoyance he saw what was coming.

"Ramabai, the orders are that you shall retire to your house and remain there till further orders."

"I am the queen's body-guard."

"Ai! Well said! But I do not take my orders from the queen—yet. Obey. The Sahib may accompany you if he wishes; there are no orders against that. The Sahib's elephant will be lodged in the royal stables; the mahout will see that he is fed and watered."

"We have been betrayed," said Ramabai. "I know not how."

"You were followed. A moment," said Bruce, turning to the officer. "I have a servant by the name of Rao. I believe he acted as bearer to the young lady at the palace. What has become of him?"

The officer smiled and shook his head.

"Rao is a prisoner, then," thought the young man. "That black scoundrel Umballa is at least thorough." Aloud he said: "We shall go at once to your house, Ramabai."

And all through the night they planned and planned, but not knowing where the first ordeal was to take place, nor the hour, they found themselves going round in a circle, getting nowhere. To a man of action like Bruce it was maddening. He walked out of the house into the garden and back again at least a dozen times, always to find Ramabai with his head held despairingly in his hands. Another time Bruce opened the door to the street; two troopers squatted on each side of the threshold. Umballa was in earnest. The rear gate was also guarded. How to get Ramabai out, that was the problem.

He slept a little before dawn, and was aroused by voices below. He listened.

"I am Jawahir Lal, the water carrier. Each day at dawn I water the garden of Ramabai to pay a debt."

Bruce looked toward Ramabai, who slept the sleep of the profoundly wearied. A bheestee, perhaps a messenger.

"Go around to the rear gate, which can be opened," said the trooper.

Bruce went to the window overlooking the garden. He saw the water carrier enter through the bamboo gate, heard the water slosh about jerkily as the bheestee emptied his goatskin. He watched the man curiously; saw him drop the skin and tiptoe toward the house, glance to right and left alertly. Then he disappeared. Presently at the head of the stairs Bruce heard a whisper—"Ramabai!"

"Who is it?" Bruce whispered in the dialect.

"Ahmed."

Ahmed. Who was Ahmed?

Bruce shook Ramabai. "Ahmed is here. Who is he?" he asked softly.

"Ahmed?" drowsily. Then, wide awake enough: "Ahmed? He was Hare Sahib's head animal man. Where is he?"

"Hush! Not so loud. Come up, Ahmed; I am Bruce. Let us speak in English."

"Good!" Ahmed came into the chamber. "To see Bruce Sahib is good. To-morrow my master's daughter is to be carried into the jungle. The Mem-sahib is to be tied inside a tiger trap, bait for the cat. That is the first ordeal."

"Shaitan!" murmured Ramabai.

"Go on, Ahmed."

"The cage will be set near the old peepul tree, not far from the south gate. Now, you, Sahib, and you, Ramabai, must hide somewhere near. It is the law that if she escapes the ordeal from unexpected sources she is free, at least till the second ordeal. I know not what that is at present or when it is to take place. The troops will be there, and the populace, the council, the priest and Umballa. I shall have two swift camels near the clump of bamboo. I may not be there, but some one will. She must be hurried off before the confusion dies away. Must, Sahib. There must be no second ordeal."

"But how am I to get out of here?" asked Ramabai. "Guards all about, and doubtless bidden to shoot if I stir!"

"Tch! Tch!" clicked Ahmed. He unwound his dirty turban and slipped out of the ragged shirtlike frock. "These and the water skin below. A bheestee entered, a bheestee goes out. What is simpler than that? It is not light enough for the soldiers to notice. There is food and water here. Trust me to elude those bhang-guzzlers outside. Am I a ryot, a farmer, to twist naught but bullocks' tails?"

"Ahmed," said Bruce, holding out his hand, "you're a man."

"Thanks, Sahib," dryly. "But hasten! At dawn to-morrow, or late to-night, Ramabai returns with a full water skin. The Mem-sahib must at least stand the ordeal of terror, for she is guarded too well. Yet, if they were not going to bind her, I should not worry. She has animal magic in her eye, in her voice. I have seen wild beasts grow still when she spoke. Who knows? Now, I sleep."

Bruce and Ramabai had no difficulty in passing the guards. The white hunter was free to come and go, and the sleepy soldiers saw the water skin which Ramabai threw carelessly over his head. They sat down against the wall again and replenished the dung fire. Bruce and Ramabai wisely made a wide detour to the peepul tree, which they climbed, disturbing the apes and the parrakeets.

Somewhere near eight o'clock they heard the creaking of wheels and a murmur of voices. Shortly into their range of vision drew a pair of bullocks, pulling a tiger trap toward the clearing. This cage was of stout wood with iron bars. The rear of the cage was solid; the front had a falling door. The whole structure rested upon low wheels, and there was a drop platform which rested upon the ground. An iron ring was attached to the rear wall, and to this was generally tied a kid, the bleating of which lured the tiger for which the trap was laid. The moment the brute touched the bait the falling door slid down, imprisoning the prowler.

When Bruce saw this damnable thing he understood, and he shook with horror and voiceless rage. He caught Ramabai by the arm so savagely that a low cry came from the brown man's lips.

"Patience, Sahib!" he warned. "Without you what will the Mem-sahib do? They will tie her in that and liberate a tiger. The rest lies with you, Sahib."

"Ramabai, as God hears me, some one shall pay for this! . . . The nineteenth century, and I am wide awake! I may not be able to kill the brute with these revolvers, but I'll stop him, even if I have to use my bare hands. . . . Kathlyn Hare!"

"Hush!" again warned Ramabai, hugging his perch.

Later by half an hour Bruce witnessed a spectacle such as

few white men, happily for their reason, are permitted to see. Kathlyn, in her royal robes (for ordeals of this character were ceremonials), a necklace of wonderful emeralds about her throat, stepped from her palanquin and stood waiting. From other vehicles and conveyances stepped Umballa, the council and the yellow robed priests. Troops also appeared, and behind them the eager expectant populace. They were to be amused. There were many of them, however, who hoped that a miracle would happen.

"Ramabai," whispered Bruce, "she is as beautiful as a dream. If I had only known! Well, there's going to be a miracle. See how straight she stands; not a sign of fear in her face. There's a woman . . . a woman for me!" he added under his breath.

He saw the bejeweled turban of Umballa bend toward the girl, and it was hard to resist taking a pot at the man. Kathlyn shook her head. Thereupon she was led to the trap, her hands bound and the rope round her waist attached securely to the ring.

Ah, they talked about it that night in the surging bazaars, in the palace, wherever two persons came together: how the white hunter had appeared from nowhere, rushed toward the trap as the tiger approached, entered and dropped the door, blazed away at the beast, who turned tail and limped off into the jungle. Ai! It was a sight for eyes. They could laugh behind Umballa's back, the gutter born, the iron heeled upstart; they could riddle (confidentially) the council with rude jests. The law was the law; and none, not even the priests in their shaven polls and yellow robes, might slip beyond the law as it read. The first ordeal was over. Nor, as the law read, could they lay hands upon this brave young man. Ai! it was good. Umballa must look elsewhere for his chief wife; the Mem-sahib would not adorn his zenana. It was more than good, for now there would be a second ordeal; more amusement, perhaps another miracle. True, they had taken away the pistols of the white Sahib, but he had his hands.

"Thank you," Kathlyn had said. "Somehow I knew you would come." And what she had seen in his eyes had made her tremble visibly for the first time that day.

She was conducted back to the palace. The populace howled and cheered about her palanquin to the very gates. Not in many a big rain had they had such excitement.

The fury in Umballa's heart might have disquieted Bruce had he known of its existence.

Kathlyn, arriving in her chamber, flung herself down upon her cushions and lay there like one dead, nor would she be comforted by the worshiping Pundita. Bruce had saved her this time, but it was not possible that he could repeat the feat.

Having convinced Umballa and the council that she would not marry her persecutor, the council announced to the populace that on the next fete day the queen would confront the lions in the elephant arena. What could one man do against such odds? Lions brought from the far Nubian deserts, fierce, untamable.

That night there was a conference between Bruce, Ahmed and Ramabai.

"They have taken my guns away, and God knows I can't do the impossible. Where the devil were your camels, Ahmed?"

"Umballa has his spies, Ramabai," said Ahmed, smiling, as he got into his bheestee rags, which Ramabai had surrendered willingly enough: "Ramabai, thou conspirator, what about the powder mines you and your friends hid when the late king signified that he was inclined toward British protectorate? Eh? What about the republic thou hadst dreams of? Poor fool! It is in our blood to be ruled by kings, oppressed; we should not know what to do with absolute freedom. There! Fear not. Why should I betray thee? The mines. The arena is of wood."

"But there will be many of my friends there," said the bewildered Ramabai. Who was this strange man who seemed to know everything?

"Put the mines in the center of the arena. What we want is merely terror and confusion. Pouf! Bang! There's your miracle. And a little one under the royal pavilion. And Umballa and the council sleep in Shaitan's arms. Welcome, my lambs!" And Ahmed laughed noiselessly.

"By the lord!" gasped Bruce. "But the fuses? No, no, Ahmed; it can not be done."

"In the house of my friend Lal Singh there is a cellar full of strange magic—magic with copper wires that spit blue fires. Eh, Sahib? You and I know; we have traveled."

"Batteries, here, in this wilderness?"

"Even so. To you, Ramabai, the powder; to me, the spitting wires; to you, Bruce Sahib, patience. Umballa shall yet wear raw the soles of his feet in the treadmill. He shall grind the poor man's corn. I know what I know. Now I must be off. I shall return to-morrow night and you, Ramabai, shall gather together your fellow conspirators (who would blow up the palace!) and bring the mines to the arena."

And while Kathlyn gazed through the marble lattice at the bright stars another gazed at the sunny heavens in a far country, a sprite of a girl with dark tearful eyes. Father gone, sister gone; silence.

But a few yards away from Kathlyn a man plucked at his chains, praying to God that he might not lose his reason. With the finished cruelty of the East, Umballa had not visited Colonel Hare again. There is nothing like suspense to squeeze hope and courage from the heart of man.

*　*　*　*　*　*

On the night before the ordeal men moved cautiously about the elephant arena. It was only after much persuasion and argument could Bruce hold the men. At the testing of Lal Singh's wires and batteries they had started to fly. This was devil's fire.

At the end of the arena, in a box which Bruce was to occupy, by order of the council (where they proposed to keep an eye upon Umballa and to wring his heart), the key to the wires was laid. This box was directly over a wooden canopy where the mahouts loafed between fights. Back of this canopy was a door which led outside. Through this Bruce proposed to lead Kathlyn during the confusion created by the explosion. They had carried off the keeper (who was also guardian of the arena), and the key to this door reposed in Bruce's pocket.

On the day of the ordeal only the bedridden remained at home. The temples, the palaces, the bazaars, all were deserted as thoroughly as if the black wings of the plague had swept through the city. Even the crows and the kites were there, the one chattering; the other soaring high above.

Ramabai was forced to sit with the council, much to his terror. After much pleading the council was prevailed upon to permit him to sit with Bruce. A cordon of soldiers was accordingly detailed to surround Bruce's box at the rear.

When Kathlyn arrived she was placed under the canopy: another bit of kindly attention on the part of Umballa to twist the white man's heart. But nothing could have happened more to the satisfaction of Bruce.

"Kathlyn Hare," he called out softly in Spanish, "do you hear and understand me?"

"Yes," she replied in the same tongue. "Do nothing desperate. Don't throw away your life. I have a sister in America. Will you tell her?"

"Listen. Under no circumstances leave the canopy. The lions come from the other side. We are not only going to rescue but save you. Attend me carefully. Behind you is a door. There will be an explosion in the center of the arena. There was to be another under our friend Umballa, but the battery was old. Press over toward that door. I have the key."

"Ah, Mr. Bruce!"

"Kathlyn, my name is John."

"The lions, the lions!" howled the populace.

It seemed to Bruce that he had been suddenly flung back into antiquity and that Nero sat yonder, squinting through his polished emerald. The great, tawny African brutes blinked and turned their shaggy heads this way and that, uneasily. Kathlyn stood very still. How, how could they save her? At length the lions espied her, attracted by the white of her robe. One bounded forward, growling. The others immediately started in pursuit.

Suddenly the center of the arena opened and a tremendous roar followed. A low wail of terror ran round the arena. Surely this Mem-sahib had all the gods with her. A great crevice had opened up between Kathlyn and the lions, one of which lay dead. Then came the rush toward the exits, a mad frantic rush. Not even Umballa, who knew that not the gods, but man had contrived this havoc, not even Umballa waited, but fled, beating down all those who blocked his path.

Bruce and Ramabai dropped over the railing to Kathlyn's side. But the key upon which their escape depended would not unlock the door.

Harold MacGrath

CHAPTER V

THE COURT OF THE LION

When Bruce dropped down into the arena to Kathlyn's side he had never given a thought to the possibility of the key not being the right one. Trapped!—and Ahmed but a few yards away with a zenana gharry, ready to convey them to the camp, freedom! It took the heart out of him for a moment. The confusion all about, the pall of dust, the roaring of the frightened lions which had escaped destruction, the shrill cries of the panic-stricken populace, who now looked upon the white Mem-sahib as the daughter of Shaitan, these dulled his inventive faculties for the nonce. Here was the confusion, properly planned, and he could not make use of it. Possibly, when no further explosion shook the air, the mob and the soldiers would return out of curiosity. And then, good-by!

But the sight of a lion emerging from the murk, the wrong side of the crevice, roused him thoroughly.

"Save yourself!" said Kathlyn in despair: "there is no possible way of saving me. I have never in all my life injured any one, and yet God makes me go through all this. . . . I am mad, you are, the whole world is! . . . Run!"

Bruce laughed; it was that kind of laughter with which

men enter battle. He drew Lal Singh's revolvers and thrust one into her hand.

"Shoot at the keyhole. Leave the lion to me. With the pandemonium no one will note the shots, or if they do, will think that more explosions are on the way. I'll get you out of this nightmare; that's what I was born for."

"Nightmare!"

"There, now!"—as Kathlyn leaned dizzily against one of the supports.

"I've gone through a good deal," she said. Without more ado she pressed the muzzle of the revolver into the keyhole and fired. She heard a shot behind her, another and another; but she kept on firing into and about the keyhole till the revolver was empty.

A firm hand drew her aside.

"The lion?"

"Gone to sleep. Let me have a whack at that door."

"Where's Ramabai?"

"Went back over the wall. Probably to warn Ahmed; maybe gone directly off toward camp. Anyhow, he has faith in me."

"And, oh! so have I, so have I!"

Bruce bore his weight savagely against the door, once, twice, thrice; and pitched forward on his knees, outside. He was up instantly. He caught Kathlyn by the hand and hurried her along; and all she could think of was Winnie romping toward the canopied studio, her father half asleep on the veranda and the leopard cat sprawled on the divan!

"Sahib! Huzoor!" a voice called. "This way!"

"Ahmed! Ahmed!" cried Kathlyn.

"Yes, heaven born; but hurry, hurry! Umballa will return to search as soon as he can get the better of his legs. Siva take that battery that was worn out! Heaven born, you are now a queen in fact. . . ."

"I want to go home, Ahmed, home!"

"Here's the gharry. Here, Sahib!" He held out a handful of cartridges toward Bruce. "These fit Lal Singh's pistols. Hurry, hurry!"

Bruce helped Kathlyn into the vehicle and jumped in beside her, and Ahmed struck the horse. The gharry was a rickety old contrivance, every hinge creaking like some lost soul; but Ahmed had reasoned that the more dilapidated the vehicle, the less conspicuous it would be. He urged the horse. He wanted the flying mob to think that he was flying, too, which, indeed, he was. The gharry rolled and careened like a dory in a squall. A dozen times Bruce and Kathlyn were flung together, and quite unconsciously she caught hold of his lean, strong brown hand. It would not be true to say that he was unconscious of the act.

Presently they entered the paved streets of the bazaars, and the going improved. Kathlyn leaned back.

"I am Kathlyn Hare, and this is the year . . ."

"Come now, Miss Kathlyn, no thinking; leave the whole

business to me, the worry and the planning. If we can reach my elephants, all right; we'll be in Delhi within seven days. The rest of the going will be as simple as falling off a log."

That Yankee phrase did more to rehabilitate her than all his assurances.

From time to time Bruce stole a glance through the curtained window. Stragglers were hastening along close to the walls, and there were soldiers who had forgot to bring their guns from the elephant arena. Once he heard the clatter of hoofs. A horseman ran alongside the gharry, slowed up, peered down and shrugged. Kathlyn shrank toward Bruce. The rider proceeded on his way. Ahmed recognized him as the ambassador from the neighboring principality, ruled by a Kumor, who was in turn ruled by the British Raj. Kathlyn could not shut out the leer on his face.

By midafternoon the gharry reached Bruce's camp. Ramabai and Pundita greeted Kathlyn with delight. All their troubles were over. They had but to mount the elephants and ride away.

"Ahmed," urged Kathlyn, "leave the gharry and come with us."

"No, Mem-sahib,"—Ahmed gazed at her strangely—"I have work to do, much work. Allah guard you!" He struck the horse with his bamboo stick and careened away.

"Let us be off!" cried Bruce. "We have sixty miles to put between us and freedom in fact. We can not make the railway. Ali, pack! Go to the bungalow and remain there. You will be questioned. Tell the truth. There is not an elephant in the royal stables that can beat Rajah. All aboard! No stops!"—smiling as he helped Kathlyn into the howdah. "We shall be forced to ride all night."

The elephants started forward, that ridden by Bruce and Kathlyn in the lead, Ramabai and Pundita following a few yards in the rear.

"Mr. Bruce, I am sure Ahmed has some information regarding father. I don't know what. Who knows? They may have lied to me. He may be alive, alive!"

"I'll return and find out, once I've got you safe. I don't blame you for thinking all this a nightmare. God knows it is nightmarish. Do you know, I've been thinking it over. It appears to me that the king latterly took a dislike to his protege, Umballa, and turned this little trick to make him unhappy. I dare say he thought your father wise enough to remain away. Umballa hangs between wind and water; he can go neither forward nor backward. But poor Ramabai back there will lose his gold for this."

"Ramabai has always been very kindly to the poor, and the poor man generally defends his benefactor when the night-time comes. To Umballa I was only a means to the end. If he declared himself king, that would open up the volcano upon which he stands; but as my prince consort, that would leave him fairly secure."

"Only a means," mused Bruce inwardly, stealing a glance at her sad yet lovely profile. Umballa was a man, for all his color; he was human; and to see this girl it was only human to want her. "Your father was one of the best friends I had. But, oddly enough, I never saw a photograph of you. He might have been afraid we young chaps . . ." He paused embarrassedly. "If only you had taken me into your confidence on board the *Yorck*!"

"Ah, but did you offer me the chance?" she returned.

"I never realized till now that a chap might be too close lipped sometimes. Well, here we are, in flight together!"

That night for the first time in many hours Kathlyn closed her eyes with a sense of security. True, it was not the most comfortable place to sleep in, the howdah; there were ceaseless rollings from side to side, intermingled with spine racking bumps forward, as the elephant occasionally hastened his stride. Kathlyn succeeded in stealing from the god of sleep only cat naps. Often the cold would awaken her, and she would find that Bruce had been bracing her by extending his arm across the howdah and gripping the rail.

"You mustn't do that," she protested feebly. "You will be dead in the morning."

"You might fall out."

"Then I shan't go to sleep again till the journey ends. You have been so good and kind to me!"

"Nonsense!"

They came out into the scrub jungle, and the moonlight lay magically over all things. Sometimes a shadow crossed the whitened sands; scurried, rather; and quietly Bruce would tell her what the animals were—jackals, with an occasional prowling red wolf. They were not disturbed by any of the cat family. But there was one interval of suspense. Bruce spied in the distance a small herd of wild elephants. So did Rajah, who raised his trunk and trumpeted into the night. The mahout, fully awake to the danger, beat the old rascal mightily with his goad. Yet that would have failed to hold Rajah. Bruce averted the danger by shooting his revolvers into the air. The wild elephants stampeded, and Rajah, disgruntled, was brought to the compass.

"Strange thing about a gunshot," said Bruce. "They may never have heard one before; but instinct tells them quickly of the menace. Years ago at home, when I used to fish for bass, during the closed season I'd see thousands of duck and geese and deer. Yet a single gunshot when the season opened and you never could get within a mile of them."

"That is true. I have fished and hunted with father."

"Surely! I keep forgetting that it's ten to one you know more about game than I do."

Silence fell upon them again. On, on, without pausing. Bruce was getting sleepy himself, so he began munching biscuits. Lighter and lighter grew the east; the moon dimmed, and by and by everything grew gray and the chill in the air seemed sharpest yet.

They were both awake.

Sunup they stopped by a stream. Bruce dismounted without having the elephant kneel and went to the water to fill his canteen. The hunter in him became interested in the tracks along the banks. A tiger, a leopard, some apes, and a herd of antelopes had been down to drink during the night. Even as he looked a huge gray ape came bounding out, head-on toward Rajah, who despised these foolish beasts. Perhaps the old elephant missed Ali, perhaps he was still somewhat upset by his failure to join his wild brothers the night before; at any rate, without warning, he set off with that shuffling gait which sometimes carried him as swiftly as a horse. An elephant never trots nor really runs according to our conception of the terms; he shuffles, scarcely lifting his feet off the ground.

The mahout yelled and belabored the elephant on the skull. Rajah did not mind this beating at all. Whatever his idea was, he evidently proposed to see it fulfilled.

Cunningly he dashed under some branches, sweeping the mahout off his neck. The branches, with a crash as of musketry, struck the howdah, but it held, thanks to the stoutness of the belly bands and the care with which they had been adjusted round the huge barrel.

Bruce stood up, appalled. For a time he was incapable of movement. Short as the time was, it was enough to give Rajah such headway as he needed. He disappeared from sight. Bruce saw the futility of shooting at the beast. The only thing he could do was to mount up beside Ramabai and Pundita and give chase; and this he did in short order, dragging up the bruised and shaken mahout with him. The pursuing elephant, with this extra handicap, never brought Rajah into sight. But the trail was clear, and they followed.

Surely that poor girl was marked for misfortune. In all the six years Bruce had possessed Rajah he had never exhibited anything but docility. The elephant was not running amuck, though he might eventually work himself into that blind ungovernable rage. Off like that, without the slightest warning! If Kathlyn could only keep him clear of the trees, for the old rogue would do his best to scrape off the irksome howdah.

Kathlyn heard the shouts from behind, but she could not understand whether these were warnings or advice. Could they overtake her before she was flung off? She tried to recall the "elephant talk" Ahmed had taught her in the old days at the farm, but just now she was too dazed. At the end of an hour all sounds from the rear ceased; no more pistol shots to encourage her with the knowledge that friends were near. Rajah must have outstripped them two or three miles.

At length she came into a small clearing amid the tall jungle grass, a dead and brittle last year's growth. She saw two natives in the act of kicking out a dung fire. Rajah headed directly toward them, the fire evidently being in the line of path he had chosen. This rare and unexpected freedom, this opportunity to go whither he listed, was as the giant fern he used to eat in the days when he was free and wild in Ceylon.

Kathlyn called out to the men, but they turned and fled in terror. To them Rajah was amuck. The elephant passed the fire so closely that the wind of his passing stirred the fire into life again; and this time it crept toward the highly inflammable grass. A few hundred yards beyond Kathlyn turned to see the flames leaping along the grass. Rajah, getting a whiff of the acrid smoke, quickened his stride. The fire followed with amazing rapidity and stopped only when it reached the bed of a trickling stream, no doubt a torrent during the big rains. A great pall of smoke blotted out everything in the rear; blotted out hope, for Bruce could never pick up the trail now.

Kathlyn's eyes were feverishly dry and bright. It was only a matter of time when the howdah would slip down the brute's side. She prayed that she might die instantly. Strange fancies flitted through her mind, disordered by all these days of suspense and terror. . . .

And suddenly the jungle came to an end, and a long plowed field opened into view. Beyond this field rose a ruined wall, broken by a crumbling gate, and lounging in the gateway were soldiers. Near by were two elephants employed in piling logs.

Rajah, perforce, slackened his gait. The soldiers became animated. Immediately the two mahouts charged their brutes toward Rajah, who stopped. He had had his sport. He swayed to and fro. One of the mahouts reached forward and clouted Rajah on the knee. He slowly kneeled. The soldiers ran forward to help Kathlyn out of the howdah. At the sight of her skin their astonishment was great.

She was very weak and faint, and the increasing babel of tongues was like little triphammers beating upon her aching head. One of the soldiers gave her a drink of water. He held his canteen high, so that the water trickled into her mouth; no lips but his own must touch the nozzle, otherwise, being a Brahmin, he would be denied. Natives instantly flocked about, jabbering in wonder. Some of the bolder touched her bare arms. The soldiers drove them back angrily. Through the press a horseman pushed forward. The rider stared at the strange captive, started and uttered an astonished cry.

"The white queen of Allaha, whom mine own eyes saw crowned at the durbar there!" he murmured. "By the shroud of the prophet what can this mean? Stop!" he called to the soldiers. Kathlyn looked up dully. "Convey her to his highness the Kumor!" The prince should decide what should be done with her.

The Kumor was big and lazy and sensual. He gazed upon Kathlyn with eyes which sparkled evilly, like a cat's.

"Who is this woman?" he demanded.

"Highness, she is the white queen of Allaha, but who may

say that she is here?" with a smile as evil as his master's.

"But how came she here?"

The horseman briefly recounted the events as he had seen them in the capital of Allaha.

"Who are you, maiden?" the Kumor asked in English, for, like all potentates, little or great, in India, he spoke English. It presented the delectable pastime of conspiring in two languages; for, from Bombay to Calcutta, from Peshawar to Madras, India seethes, conspires and takes an occasional pot shot at some poor devil of a commissioner whose only desire is to have them combine religion and sanitation.

"I am an American. Please take me to the English commissioner." Somehow instinct told her that she might not expect succor from this man with the pearls about his gross neck.

"I regret that his excellency the commissioner has gone to Bombay. Besides, I do not know that you tell the truth. Still, I can offer you what pearls and emeralds you may find to your liking."

"Your Highness, there are those whose coming shortly will cause you much annoyance if you refuse to give me proper aid. There is no possible way for you to cover up my appearance here. Send me to the commissioner's bungalow, where I may await the coming of my friends."

"Indeed!" The Kumor saw here a conflict not altogether to his liking. He was lazy, and there was the damnable, unrelenting hand of the British Raj looming in the distance. He shrugged. "Achmet, call the captain of the guard and have him convey this runaway queen to Allaha.

Surely, I may not meddle with the affairs of a friendly state." With a wave of his fat bejeweled hand he appeared to dismiss the matter from his mind.

Kathlyn was led away. The human mind can stand only so many shocks.

Outside the palace courtyard stood Rajah, the howdah securely attached once more, Kathlyn was bidden to mount. A water bottle and some cakes were placed in the howdah beside her. Then a drunken mahout mounted behind Rajah's ears. The elephant did not like the feel of the man's legs, and he began to sway ominously. Nevertheless, he permitted the mahout to direct him to one of the city gates, the soldiers trooping alongside.

It appeared that there was a much shorter route to Allaha. Time being essential, Bruce had had to make for the frontier blindly, as it were. The regular highway was a moderately decent road which led along the banks of one of those streams which eventually join the sacred Jumna. This, of course, was also sacred. Many Hindus were bathing in the ghats. They passed by these and presently came upon a funeral pyre.

Sometimes one sleeps with one's eyes open, and thus it was with Kathlyn. Out of that funeral pyre her feverish thoughts builded a frightful dream.

* * * * * *

The drunken mahout slid off Rajah; the soldiers turned aside. Hired female mourners were kneeling about, wailing and beating their breasts, while behind them stood the high caste widow, her face as tragic as Dido's at the pyre of Aeneas. Suddenly she threw her arms high over her head.

"I am suttee!"

Suttee! It was against the law of the British Raj. The soldiers began arguing with the widow, but only half heartedly. It was a pious rite, worthy of the high caste Hindu's wife. Better death on the pyre than a future like that of a pariah dog. For a wife who preferred to live after her husband was gone was a social outcast, permitted not to wed again, to exist only as a drudge, a menial, the scum and contempt of all who had known her in her days of prosperity.

The widow, having drunk from a cup which contained opium, climbed to the top of the pyre where her husband lay, swathed in white. She gazed about wildly, and her courage and resolve took wings. She stumbled down. A low hissing ran about.

"Make the white woman suttee in her place!" cried the drunken mahout.

The cry was taken up by the spectators. Kathlyn felt herself dragged from the elephant, bound and finally laid beside the swathed figure. There could be no horror in the wide world like it. Smoke began to curl up from the underbrush. It choked and stifled her. Sparks rose and dropped upon her arms and face. And through the smoke and flame came Rajah. He lifted her with his powerful trunk and carried her off, for hours and hours, back into the trackless jungle. . . .

Kathlyn found herself, all at once, sitting against the roots of an aged banyan tree. A few yards away an ape sat on his haunches and eyed her curiously. A little farther off Rajah browsed in a clump of weeds, the howdah at a rakish angle, like the cocked hat of a bully. Kathlyn stared at her hands. There were no burns there; she passed a hand over her face; there was no smart or sting. A dream; she had dreamed it; a fantasy due to her light-headed state of mind. A dream! She cried and laughed, and the ape jibbered at her uneasily.

In reality, Rajah, freed of his unwelcome mahout, had legged it down the road without so much as trumpeting his farewell, and the soldiers had not been able to stop him.

How she had managed to get down would always remain a mystery to her. Food and water, food and water; in her present state she must have both or die. Let them send her back to Allaha; she was beaten; she was without the will to resist further. All she wanted was food and water and sleep, sleep. After that they might do what they pleased with her.

For the first time since the extraordinary flight from Allaha Kathlyn recollected the "elephant talk" which Ahmed had taught her. She rose wearily and walked toward Rajah, who cocked his ears at the sound of her approach. She talked to him for a space in monotone. She held out her hands; the dry raspy trunk curled out toward them. Rajah was evidently willing to meet her half-way. She ordered him to kneel. Without even pausing to think it over Rajah bent his calloused knees, and gratefully Kathlyn crawled back into the howdah. Food and water: these appeared at hand as if by magic. So she ate and drank. If she could hold Rajah to a walk the howdah would last at least till she came to some village.

Later, in the moonshine, she espied the ruined portico of a temple.

CHAPTER VI

THE TEMPLE

In the blue of night the temple looked as though it had been sculptured out of mist. Here and there the heavy dews, touched by the moon lances, flung back flames of sapphire, cold and sharp. To Kathlyn the temple was of marvelous beauty. She urged Rajah toward the crumbling portico.

It was a temple in ruins, like many in Hind. Broken pillars, exquisitely carved, lay about, and some of the tall windows of marble lace were punctured, as if the fist of some angry god had beaten through. Under the decayed portico stood an iron brazier. Near this reposed a cracked stone sarcophagus: an unusual sight in this part of the world. It was without its lid. But one god now brooded hereabouts—Silence. Not a sound anywhere, not even from the near-by trees. She saw a noiseless lizard slide jerkily across a patch of moonshine and dissolve into the purple shadow beyond.

What was this temple? What gods had been worshiped here? And why was it deserted? She had heard her father tell of the ruined city of Chitor. Plague? . . . Kathlyn shuddered. Sometimes villages, to the last soul in them, were brushed from existence and known no more to man.

And this might be one of them. Yet indications of a village were nowhere to be seen. It was merely a temple, perhaps miles from the nearest village, deserted save by prowling wild beasts, the winds, the sunshine and the moonshine. She looked far and wide for any signs of human habitation.

She commanded Rajah to kneel. So held by the enchanting picture was Kathlyn that the elephant's renewed restlessness (and he had reason, as will be seen) passed unobserved by her. He came to his knees, however, and she got out of the howdah. Her legs trembled for a space, for her nerves were in a pitiable condition. Suddenly Rajah's ears went forward, he rose, and his trunk curled angrily. With a whuff he wheeled and shuffled off toward the jungle out of which he had so recently emerged.

"Halt!" cried Kathlyn. What had he heard? What had he seen? "Halt!" But even as she called the tall grass closed in behind the elephant. What water and food she had disappeared with him.

She paused by the brazier, catching hold of it for support. She laughed hysterically: it was so funny; it was all so out of joint with real things, with every-day life as she had known it. Weird laughter returned to mock her astonished ears, a sinister echo. And then she laughed at the echo, being in the grip of a species of madness. In the purple caverns of the temple she suddenly became conscious of another presence. A flash as of moonlight striking two chrysoberyls took the madness out of her mind. This forsaken temple was the haunt of a leopard or a tiger.

She was lost. That magnetism which ordinarily was hers was at its nadir. She hesitated for a second, then climbed into the empty sarcophagus, crouching low. Strangely enough, as she did so a calm fell upon her; all the terrors

Harold MacGrath

of her position dropped away from her as mists from the mountain peaks. She had, however, got into the hiding-place none too soon.

She heard the familiar pad-pad, the whiff-whiff of a big cat. Immediately into the moonlight came an African lion, as out of place here as Kathlyn herself; his tail slashed, there was a long black streak from his mane to his tail where the hair had risen. Kathlyn crouched even lower. The lion trotted round the sarcophagus, sniffing. Presently he lifted his head and roared. The echoes played battledore and shuttlecock with the sound. The lion roared again, this time at the insulting echoes. For a few minutes the noise was deafening. A rumble as of distant thunder, and the storm died away.

By and by she peered out cautiously. She saw the lion crossing the open space between the temple and the jungle. She saw him pause, bend his head, then lope away in the direction taken by Rajah.

To Kathlyn it seemed that she had no longer anything to do with the body of Kathlyn Hare. The soul of another had stepped into this wearied flesh of hers and now directed its physical manifestations, while her own spirit stood gratefully and passively aloof. Nothing could happen now; the world had grown still and calm. The spirit drew the sleeves of the robe snugly about her arms and laid Kathlyn's head upon them and drew her down into a profound slumber.

Half a mile to the north of the ruined temple there lay, all unsuspected by Kathlyn, a village—a village belonging solely to the poor, mostly ryots or tillers of the soil. The poor in Asia know but two periods of time—for rarely do they possess such a thing as a watch or a clock—sunset and sunrise. Perhaps the man of the family may sit a while at dusk on his mud door-sill, with his bubbling water pipe (if he has one), and watch the stars slowly swing across the arch. A pinch of very bad tobacco is slowly consumed; then he enters the hunt [Transcriber's note: hut?], flings himself upon his matting (perhaps a cotton rug, more likely a bundle of woven water reeds) and sleeps. No one wakes him; habit rouses him at dawn. He scrubs his teeth with a fibrous stick. It is a part of his religious belief to keep his teeth clean. The East Indian (Hindu or Mohammedan) has the whitest, soundest teeth in the world if the betel-nut is but temperately used.

Beyond this village lay a ruined city, now inhabited by cobras and slinking jackals.

Dawn. A few dung fires smoldered. From the doorway of one of the mud huts came a lean man, his naked torso streaked with wet ashes, his matted hair hanging in knots and tangles on his emaciated shoulders. His aspect was exceedingly filthy; he was a holy man, which in this mad country signifies physical debasement, patience and fortitude such as would have adorned any other use. A human lamprey, sticking himself always at the thin and meager board of the poor, a vile parasite, but holy!

The holy man directed his steps to the narrow beaten pathway which led to the temple, where, every morning, he performed certain rites which the poor benighted ryots believed would some day restore the ruined city and the prosperity which attends fat harvests. The holy man had solemnly declared that it would take no less than ten years to bring about this miracle. And the villagers fell down with their foreheads in the dust. He was a Brahmin; the caste string hung about his neck; he was indeed holy, he who could have dwelt on the fat of the land, in maharajahs' courts. The least that can be said is that he performed his duties scrupulously.

So, then, the red rim of the March sun shouldered up above the rolling jungle as he came into the beaten clay court which fronted the temple. The lion stalked only at night, rarely appearing in the daytime. Once a month he was given a bullock, for he kept tiger and leopard away, and the villagers dwelt in peace. The lion had escaped from Allaha, where the species were kept as an additional sport. Since he had taken up his abode in the temple there had been fewer thefts from the cattle sheds.

The holy man was about to assume his squatting posture in the center of the court, as usual, when from out of the sarcophagus rose languidly a form, shrouded in white. The form stretched its lovely arms, white as alabaster, and presently the hands rubbed a pair of sleepy eyes. Then the form sat down within the sarcophagus, laid its arms on the rim, and wearily hid its face in them.

The watcher was the most dumfounded holy man in all India. For the first time in his hypocritical life he found faith in himself, in his puerile rites. He had conjured up yonder spirit, unaided, alone. He rose, turned, and never a holy man ran faster. When he arrived, panting and voiceless, at the village well, where natives were coming and going with water in goatskins and jars and copper vessels, he fell upon his face, rose to his knees, and poured hands full of dust upon his head.

"Ai, ai!" he called. "It is almost done, my children. The first sign has come from the gods. I have brought you in human form the ancient priestess!" And he really believed he had. "O my children, my little ones, my kids! I have brought her who will now attend to the sacred fires; for these alone will restore the city as of old, the fat corn, the plentitude of fruit. Since the coming of the lion two rains ago the leopard and the striped one have forsaken their lairs. One bullock a month is better than fire, together with the kids and the children. Ai!" More dust.

Naturally the villagers set down their water skins and jars and copper vessels and flocked about this exceptional holy man. They wanted to believe him, but for years nothing had happened but the advent of the lion, whence no one exactly knew, though the holy man had not been backward in claiming it was due to his nearness to the god Vishnu.

They followed him eagerly to the temple. What they beheld transfixed them. A woman with skin like the petals of the lotus and hair like corn sat in the sacred sarcophagus and braided her hair, gazing the while toward the bright sun.

The intake of many breaths produced a sound. Kathlyn turned instantly toward this sound, for a moment expecting the return of the lion. Immediately holy man and villagers threw themselves upon the ground, striking their foreheads against the damp clay. The alien spirit still ruled the substance; Kathlyn eyed them in mild astonishment, not at all alarmed.

"Ai!" shrilled the holy man, springing to his feet. "Ai! She is our ancient priestess, rising from her tomb of centuries! Ai, ai! O thou unholy children, to doubt my word! Behold! Henceforth she shall share the temple with the lion, and later she will give us prosperity, and my name shall ever be in your households."

Having secured a priestess, he was now determined that he should not lose her. The future was roseate indeed, and when he took his next pilgrimage to holy Benares they would bestrew his pathway with lotus flowers.

"Wood to start the sacred fires!" he commanded.

Harold MacGrath

The villagers flew to obey his orders. He was indeed a holy man. Not in the memory of the oldest had a miracle such as this happened. Upon their return with wood and embers the holy man built the fire, handing a lighted torch to Kathlyn and signifying for her to touch the tinder. The spirit in Kathlyn told her that these people meant her no immediate harm, so she stepped out of the sarcophagus and applied the torch. The moment the flames began to crackle the villagers prostrated themselves again and the holy man besmeared his bony chest with more ashes.

A second holy man appeared upon the scene, wanting in breath. His jaw dropped and his eyes started to leave their sockets. Knowing his ilk so thoroughly well, he flung himself down before the brazier and beat his forehead upon the ground; not in any chastened spirit, but because he had overslept that morning. This glory might have been his! Ai, ai!

Later the two conferred. During the day they should guard the priestess, because, having taken human form, she might some day tire of this particular temple. At night she would be well guarded by the lion.

Several awestricken women came forward with bowls of cooked rice and fruits and a new copper drinking vessel. These they reverently placed at Kathlyn's feet.

Gradually the spirit which had comforted Kathlyn withdrew, and at length Kathlyn became keenly alive. It entered her mind clearly that these poor foolish people really believed her a celestial being, and so long as they laid no hand upon her she was not alarmed. She had recently passed through too many terrors to be disturbed by a bit of kindness, even if stirred into being by a religious fanaticism.

Kathlyn ate.

By pairs the villagers departed, and soon none remained save her self-appointed guardians, the two holy men. Kathlyn felt a desire to explore this wonderful temple. She discovered what must have been the inner shrine. The chamber was filled with idols; here and there a bit of gold leaf, centuries old, glistened upon the bronze, the clay, the wood. The caste mark on the largest idol's head was a polished ruby, overlooked doubtless during the loot. She swept the dust from the jewel with the tip of her finger, and the dull fire sent a shiver of delight over her. She was still a woman.

As she wandered farther in her foot touched something and she looked down. It was a bone; in fact, the floor was strewn with bones. She quickly discerned, much to her relief, that none of these bones was human. This was, or had been, the den of the lion. There was an acrid unpleasant odor, so she hurried back to the brazier. Vaguely she comprehended that she must keep the fire replenished from time to time in order to pacify the two holy men. At night it would fend off any approach of the lion.

Where was Bruce? Would he ever find her? That philosophy which she had inherited from her father, that quiet acceptance of the inevitable, was the one thing which carried her through her trials sanely. An ordinary woman would have died from mere exhaustion.

Bruce, indeed! At that very moment he was rushing out of the Kumor's presence, wild to be off toward the road to Allaha, since Kathlyn had not been seen upon it. He found where Rajah had veered off into the jungle again, and followed the trail tirelessly. But it was to be his misfortune always to arrive too late.

To Kathlyn the day passed with nothing more than the curiosity of the natives to disturb her. They brought her cotton blankets which she arranged in the sarcophagus. There were worse beds in the world than this; at least it shielded her from the bitter night wind.

She ate again at sundown and builded high the sacred fire and tried to plan some manner of escape; for she did not propose to be a demi-goddess any longer than was necessary. From Pundita she had learned many words and a few phrases in Hindustani, and she ventured to speak them to the holy men, who seemed quite delighted. They could understand her, but she on her part could make little or nothing of their jabbering. Nevertheless, she pretended.

Finally the holy men departed, after having indicated the sacred fire and the wood beside it. This fire pleased Kathlyn mightily. While it burned brightly the lion would not prowl in her immediate vicinity. She wondered where this huge cat had come from, since she knew her natural history well enough to know that African lions did not inhabit this part of the globe. Doubtless it had escaped from some private menagerie.

The fire, then, giving her confidence, she did not get into the sarcophagus, but wandered about, building in her fancy the temple as it had stood in its prime. The ceilings had been magnificently carved, no two subjects alike; and the walls were of marble and jasper and porphyry. A magic continent this Asia in its heyday. When her forefathers had been rude barbarians, sailing the north seas or sacrificing in Druidical rites, there had been art and culture here such as has never been surpassed. India, of splendid pageants, of brave warriors and gallant kings! Alas, how the mighty had fallen! About her, penury, meanness, hypocrisy, uncleanliness, thievery and unbridled passions. . . . What was that? Her heart missed a beat.

That pad-pad; that sniffling noise!

She whirled about, knocking over an idol. It came down with a crash and, being of clay, lay in shards at her feet. (Unfortunately it was the holy of holies in this temple.) How she gained the shelter of the sarcophagus she never knew, but gain it she did, and cowered down within. She could hear the beast trotting round and round, sniffling and rumbling in his throat. Then the roaring of the preceding night was repeated. The old fellow evidently could not find those other lions who roared back at him so valiantly. Evidently fire had no terrors for him. For an hour or more he patrolled the portico, and all this time Kathlyn did not stir, hardly daring to breathe for fear he might undertake to peer into the sarcophagus.

Silence. A low roar from the inner shrine told her that for the present she was safe. To-morrow she must fly, whither did not matter. Toward four o'clock she fell into a doze and was finally awakened by the sound of voices raised in anger.

Poor sheep! They had discovered the shattered idol. It did not matter at all that the return of their ancient goddess was to bring back prosperity. She had broken their favorite idol. Damnation would come in a devil's wind that night.

The holy man who had missed the chance of claiming the miraculous appearance of Kathlyn as a work of his own now saw an opportunity to rehabilitate himself in the eyes of those who had made his holiness a comfortable existence. With a piece of the idol in his hand, he roused Kathlyn and shook the clay before her face, jabbering violently. Kathlyn understood readily enough. She had unwittingly committed a sacrilege.

The natives gathered about and menaced her. Kathlyn rose, standing in the sarcophagus, and extended her hands for silence. She was frightened, but it would never do to let them see it. What Hindustani she knew would in this case be of no manner of use. But we human beings can, by facial expression and gesture, make known our messages with understandable clearness. From her gestures, then, the holy men gathered that she could recreate the god. She pointed toward the sun and counted on her fingers.

The premier holy man, satisfied that he understood Kathlyn's gestures, turned to the justly angered villagers and explained that with his aid their priestess would, in five suns, recreate Vishnu in all his beauty. Instantly the villagers prostrated themselves.

"Poor things!" murmured Kathlyn.

The holy men sent the natives away, for it was not meet that they should witness magic in the making. They then squatted in the clay court and curiously waited for her to begin. There was a well in the inner shrine. To this she went with caution. The lion was evidently foraging in the jungle. Kathlyn filled the copper vessel with water and returned. Next, she gathered up what pieces of the idol she could find and pieced them together. Here was her model. She then approached one of the fakirs and signified that she had need of his knife. He demurred at first, but at length consented to part with it. She dug up a square piece of clay. In fine, she felt more like the Kathlyn of old than she had since completing the leopard in her outdoor studio. It occupied her thoughts, at least part of them, for she realized that mayhap her life depended upon her skill in reproducing the hideous idol.

As the two old hypocrites saw the clay take form and

shape and the mocking face gradually appear, they were assured that Kathlyn was indeed the ancient priestess; and deep down in their souls they experienced something of the awe they had often inspired in the poor trusting ryot.

Kathlyn had talent bordering on genius. The idol was an exact replica of the original one; more, there was a subtle beauty now where before there had been a frank repulsiveness. It satisfied the holy men, and the unveiling was greeted by the villagers with such joy that Kathlyn forgave them and could have wept over them. She had made a god for them, and they fell down and worshiped it.

Five more days passed. On the afternoon of the fifth day Kathlyn was feeding the fire. The holy men sat in the court at their devotions, which consisted in merely remaining motionless. Kathlyn returned from the fire to see them rise and flee in terror. She in turn fled, for the lion stood between her and the sarcophagus! The lion paused, lashing his tail. The many recent commotions within and without the temple had finally roused his ire. He hesitated between the holy men and Kathlyn, and finally concluded that she in the fluttering robes would be the most desirable.

There was no particular hurry; besides, he was not hungry. The cat in him wanted to play. He loped after Kathlyn easily. At any time he chose a few swift bounds would bring him to her side.

Beyond the temple lay the same stream by which, miles away, Kathlyn had seen the funeral pyre and about which she had so weird a fantasy. If this stream was deep there was a chance for life.

Harold MacGrath

CHAPTER VII

QUICKSANDS

When Kathlyn came to the river she swerved toward the broadest part of it. Twice she stumbled over boulders, but rose pluckily and, bruised and breathless, plunged into the water. It was swift running and shoulder deep, and she was forced to swim strongly to gain the opposite shore. She dragged herself up to the bank and, once there, looked back. What she saw rather astonished her. She could not solve the riddle at first. The lion seemed to be struggling with some invisible opponent. He stood knee deep in the sands, tugging and pulling. He began to roar. Even as Kathlyn gazed she saw his chest touch the sand and his swelling flanks sink lower. Fascinated, she could not withdraw her gaze. How his mighty shoulders heaved and pulled! But down, down, lower and lower, till nothing but the great maned head remained in view. Then that was drawn down; the sand filled the animal's mouth and stopped his roaring; lower, lower . . .

Quicksands! The spot where he had disappeared stirred and glistened and shuddered, and then the eternal blankness of sand.

She was not, then, to die? Should she return to the temple? Would they not demand of her the restoration of the lion? She must go on, whither she knew not. She regretted the peace of the temple in the daytime. She could see the dome from where she stood. Like Ishmael, she must go on, forever and forever on. Was God watching over her? Was it His hand which stayed the onslaught of the beast and defeated the baser schemes of men? Was there to be a haven at the end? She smiled wanly. What more was to beset her path she knew not, nor cared just then, since there was to be a haven at the end.

Perhaps prescience brought to her mind's eye a picture; she saw her father, and Bruce, and Winnie, and her sweetheart, and they seemed to be toasting her from the end of a long table, under the blue California sky. This vision renewed her strength. She proceeded onward.

She must have followed the river at least a mile when she espied a raft moored to a clump of trees. Here she saw a way of saving her weary limbs many a rugged mile. She forded the stream, freed the raft, and poled out into the middle of the stream.

It happened that the Mohammedan hunters who owned the raft were at this moment swinging along toward the temple. On the shoulders of two rested a pole from which dangled the lifeless body of a newly killed leopard. They were bringing it in as a gift to the head man of the village, who was a thoroughgoing Mohammedan, and who held in contempt Hinduism and all its amazing ramifications.

The white priestess was indeed a puzzle; for, while the handful of Mohammedans in the village were fanatical in their belief in the true prophet and his Koran, and put little faith in miracles and still less in holy men who performed them, the advent of the white priestess deeply mystified them. There was no getting around this: she was there;

with their own eyes they saw her. There might be something in Hinduism after all.

When the hunters arrived at the portico of the temple they found two greatly terrified holy men, shrilling their "Ai! Ai!" in lamentation and beating their foreheads against the earth.

"Holy men, what is wrong?" asked one of the hunters, respectfully.

"The lion has killed our priestess; the sacred fires must die again! Ai! Ai!"

"Where is the lion?"

"They fled toward the river, and there he has doubtless destroyed her, for in evil, Siva, represented by the lion, is more powerful than Vishnu, reincarnated in our priestess. Ai! Ai! She is dead and we are undone!"

"Come!" said the chief huntsman. "Let us run to the river and see what these queer gods are doing. We'll present the skin of Siva to our master!" He laughed.

The leopard carriers deposited their burden and all started off at a dog-trot. They had always been eager regarding this lion. In the temple he was inviolable; but at large, that was a different matter.

Arriving at the river brink, they saw the foot-prints of the lion on the wet sand which ran down to the water. To leap from this spot to the water was not possible for any beast of the jungle. Yet the lion had vanished completely, as though he had been given wings. They stood about in awe till one of the older hunters knelt, reached out, and dug his hand into the innocent looking sand. Instantly he leaped to his feet and jumped back.

"The sucking sand!" he cried. "To the raft!"

They skirted the dangerous quicksands and dashed along the banks to discover that their raft was gone. Vishnu, then, as reincarnated, required solid transportation, after the manner of human beings? They became angry. A raft was a raft, substantial, necessary; and there was no reason why a god who had ten thousand temples for his own should stoop to rob a poor man of his wherewithal to travel in safety.

"The mugger!" exclaimed one, "let the high priestess beware of the mugger, for he is strong enough to tip over the raft!"

Nearly every village which lies close to a stream has its family crocodile. He is very sacred and thrives comfortably upon suicides and the dead, which are often cast into the river to be purified. The Hindus are a suicidal race; the reverse of the occidental conception, suicide is a quick and glorious route to Heaven.

The current of the stream carried Kathlyn along at a fair pace; all she had to do was to pole away from the numerous sand-bars and such boulders as lifted their rugged heads above the water.

Round a bend the river widened and grew correspondingly sluggish. She sounded with her pole. Something hideous beyond words arose—a fat, aged, crafty crocodile. His corrugated snout was thrust quickly over the edge of the raft. She struck at him wildly with the pole, and in a fury he rushed the raft, upsetting Kathlyn.

The crocodile sank and for a moment lost sight of

Kathlyn, who waded frantically to the bank, up which she scrambled. She turned in time to see the crocodile's tearful [Transcriber's note: fearful?] eyes staring up at her from the water's edge. He presently slid back into his slimy bed; a few yellow bubbles, and he was gone.

Kathlyn's heart became suddenly and unaccountably swollen with rage; she became primordial; she wanted to hurt, maim, kill. Childishly she stooped and picked up heavy stones which she hurled into the water. The instinct to live flamed so strongly in her that the crust of civilization fell away like mist before the sun, and for a long time the pure savage (which lies dormant in us all) ruled her. She would live, live, live; she would live to forget this oriental inferno through which she was passing.

She ran toward the jungle, all unconscious of the stone she still held in her hand. She lost all sense of time and compass; and so ran in a half circle, coming out at the river again.

The Indian twilight was rising in the east when she found herself again looking out upon the water, the stone still clutched tightly. She gazed at the river, then at the stone, and again at the river. The stone dropped with a thud at her feet. The savage in her had not abated in the least; only her body was terribly worn and wearied and the robe, muddied and torn, enveloped her like a veil of ice. Above her the lonely yellow sky; below her the sickly river; all about her silence which held a thousand menaces. Which way should she go? Where could she possibly find shelter for the night?

The chill roused her finally and she swung her arms to renew the circulation. Near by she saw a tree, in the crotch of which reposed a platform, and upon this platform sat a shrine. A few withered flowers hung about the gross neck of the idol, and withered flowers lay scattered at the base of the tree. There was also a bundle of dry rushes which some devotee had forgotten. At least, yonder platform would afford safety through the night. So, with the last bit of strength at her command, she gathered up the rushes and climbed to the platform, arranging her bed behind the idol. She covered her shoulders with the rushes and drew her knees up to her chin. She had forgotten her father, Bruce, the happy days in a far country; she had but a single thought, to sleep. What the want of sleep could not perform exhaustion could; and presently she lay still.

Thus, she neither saw nor heard the pious pilgrims who were on their way to Allaha to pray in that temple known to offer protection against wild beasts. Fortunately, they did not observe her.

The pilgrim is always a pilgrim in India; it becomes, one might say, a fascinating kind of sport. To most of them, short pilgrimages are as tame as rabbits would be to the hunter of lions. They will walk from Bombay to Benares, from Madras to Llassa, begging and bragging all the way. Eventually they become semi-holy, distinguished citizens in a clutter of mud huts.

They deposited some corn and fruit at the foot of the tree and departed, leaving Kathlyn in peace. But later, when the moon poured its white, cold radiance over her face it awakened her, and it took her some time to realize where she was.

Below, belly deep in the river, stood several water buffaloes, their sweeping horns glistening like old ivory in the moonshine. Presently a leopard stole down to the brink and lapped the water greedily, from time to time throwing a hasty, apprehensive glance over his sleek shoulders. The buffaloes never stirred; where they were it was safe. Across the river a bulky shadow moved into the light, and a fat, brown bear took his tithe of the water. The leopard snarled and slunk off. The bear washed his face, possibly sticky with purloined wild honey, and betook himself back to his lair.

Kathlyn suddenly became aware of the fact that she was a spectator to a scene such as few human beings are permitted to see: truce water, where the wild beasts do not kill one another. She grew so interested that she forgot her own plight. The tree stood only a few feet from the water, so she saw everything distinctly.

Later, when his majesty the tiger made his appearance dramatically, the buffaloes simply moved closer together, presenting a formidable frontage of horns.

Never had Kathlyn seen such an enormous beast. From his great padded paws to his sloping shoulders he stood easily four feet in height, and his stripes were almost as broad as her hand. He drank, doubtless eying the buffaloes speculatively; some other time. Then he, too, sat on his haunches and washed his face, but with infinite gracefulness. It occurred to the watcher that, familiar as she was with the habits of wild beasts, never had she witnessed a tiger or a lion enact this domestic scene. Either they were always pacing their cages, gazing far over the heads of those who watched them, or they slept. Even when they finished a meal of raw meat they merely licked their chops; there was no toilet.

Here, however, was an elaborate toilet. The great cat licked his paws, drew them across his face; then licked his beautiful sides, purring; for the night was so still and the beast was so near that she could see him quite plainly. He stretched himself, took another drink, and trotted off to the jungle.

Then came a herd of elephants, for each species seemed to have an appointed time. The buffaloes emerged and filed away into the dark. The elephants plunged into the water, squealing, making sport, squirting water over their backs, and rolling, head under; and they buffeted one another amiably, and there was a baby who seemed to get in everybody's way and the grown-ups treated him shabbily. By and by they, too, trooped off. Then came wild pigs and furtive antelopes and foolish, chattering apes.

At last the truce water became deserted and Kathlyn lay down again, only to be surprised by a huge ape who stuck his head up over the edge of the platform. The surprise was mutual. Kathlyn pushed the idol toward him. The splash of it in the water scared off the unwelcome guest, and then Kathlyn lay down and slept.

A day or so later Bruce arrived at the temple. Day after day he had hung to the trail, picking it up here and losing it there. He found Rajah, the elephant, the howdah gone, and only the ornamental headpiece discovered to Bruce that he had found his rogue. Rajah was docile enough; he had been domesticated so long that his freedom rather irked him.

Bruce elicited from the mourning holy men the amazing adventure in all its details. Kathlyn had disappeared in the jungle and not even the tried hunters could find her. She was lost. Bruce, though in his heart of hearts he believed her dead, took up the trail again. But many weary weeks were to pass ere he learned that she lived.

He shook his fist toward Allaha. "Oh, Durga Ram, one of

these fine days you and I shall square accounts!"

* * * * * *

Kathlyn had just completed herself a dress of grass. Three years before she had learned the trick from the natives in Hawaii. The many days of hardship had made her thinner, but never had she been so hardy, so clear eyed, so quick and lithe in her actions. She had lived precariously, stealing her food at dusk from the tents of the ryots; raw vegetables, plantains, mangoes. Sometimes she recited verses in order that she might break the oppressive silence which always surrounded her.

She kept carefully out of the way of all human beings, so she had lost all hope of succor from the brown people, who had become so hateful to her as the scavengers of the jungle. There was something to admire in the tiger, the leopard, the wild elephant; but she placed all natives (perhaps wrongly) in a class with the unclean jackals and hyenas.

Tanned deeply by wind and sun, Kathlyn was darker than many a native woman. Often she thought of Bruce, but hope of his finding her had long since died within her. Every night when she climbed to her platform she vowed she would start south the next morning; south, toward the land where there were white people; but each morning found her hesitant.

Behind her tree there was a clearing, then a jumble of thickly growing trees; beyond those was another clearing, upon which stood a deserted elephant stockade. The grass had grown rank in it for want of use. She was in the act of putting on grass sandals when she saw, to her dismay, the approach of men and elephants. Two elephants were ridden by mahouts. Two other elephants were being jostled toward the stockade, evidently new captives. They proceeded passively, however, for elephants submit to captivity with less real trouble than any other wild beast. Kathlyn crouched low in the grass and waited till the men and elephants entered the stockade; then she ran quickly toward her haven, the platform in the tree. She never went very far from this, save in search of food. She had also recovered the idol and set it back in its place. It was not, fortunately, a much frequented spot. It was for the benefit of the occasional pilgrim, the ryots having shrines more conveniently situated.

She nestled down among her rushes and waited. She could not see the stockade from where she now was, but she could hear shouts from the mahouts.

Recently she had discovered a leopard's lair near the stockade and was very careful to avoid it, much as she wanted to seize the pretty cubs and run away with them. By this time she knew the habits, fears, and hatreds of these people of the jungle, and she scrupulously attended her affairs as they attended theirs. Sometimes the great striped tiger prowled about the base of the tree, sharpened his claws on the bark, but he never attempted to ascend to the platform. Perhaps he realized the uselessness of investigation, since the platform made it impossible for him to see what was up there. But always now, to and from the truce water, he paused, looked up, circled the tree, and went away mystified.

Only the grass eating beasts came down to water that night, and Kathlyn understood by this that the men and the elephants were still in the stockade.

The following morning she went down to the stream to bathe; at the same time the parent leopards came for drink. They had not cared to seek their lair during the night on account of the fires; and, worrying over their cubs, they were not in the most agreeable mood.

Kathlyn saw their approach in time to reach her platform. They snarled about the tree, and the male climbed up as far as the platform. Kathlyn reached over with a stout club and clouted the brute on his tender nose.

A shot broke the silence and a bullet spat angrily against the tree trunk. Two cats fled. Immediately there came a squealing and trumpeting from the stockade.

This is what had happened: The chief mahout had discovered the cubs and had taken them into the stockade just as another hunter had espied the parent leopards. The rifle shot had frightened one of the wild elephants. With a mighty plunge he had broken the chain which held him prisoner to the decoy elephant and pushed through the rotten stockade, heading straight for the river.

Kathlyn saw his bulk as it crashed straight through the brush. He shuffled directly toward her tree. The ground about was of clay, merging into sand as it sloped toward the river. The frantic runaway slipped, crushed against the tree trunk, recovered himself, and went splashing into the water.

Kathlyn was flung headlong and only the water saved her from severe bodily harm. When she recovered her senses she was surrounded by a group of very much astonished Mohammedans.

They jabbered and gesticulated to one another and she was conducted to the stockade. She understood but two words—"Allaha" and "slave."

CHAPTER VIII

THE SLAVE MART

Having decided upon the fate of Kathlyn, the natives set about recapturing the wild elephant. It took the best part of the morning. When this was accomplished the journey to Allaha was begun. But for the days of peace and quiet of the wilderness and the consequent hardness of her flesh, Kathlyn would have suffered greatly. Half the time she was compelled to walk. There was no howdah, and it was a difficult feat to sit back of the mahout. The rough skin of the elephant had the same effect upon the calves of her legs that sandpaper would have had. Sometimes she stumbled and fell, and was rudely jerked to her feet. Only the day before they arrived was she relieved in any way: she was given a litter, and in this manner she entered the hateful city.

In giving her the litter the chief mahout had been inspired by no expressions of pity; simply they desired her to appear fresh and attractive when they carried her into the slave mart.

In fitful dreams all that had happened came back to her—the story her father had told about saving the old king's life, and the grim, ironical gratitude in making Colonel Hare his heir—as if such things could be! And then her own journey to Allaha; the nightmarish durbar, during which she had been crowned; the escape from the ordeals with John Bruce; the terrors of the temple of the sun; the flight from there . . . John Bruce! She could still see the fire in his eyes; she could still feel the touch of his gentle yet tireless hand. Would she ever see him again?

On the way to the mart they passed under the shadow of the grim prison walls of the palace. The elephants veered off here into a side street, toward the huge square where horses and cattle and elephants were bought and sold. The litter, in charge of the chief mahout, proceeded to the slave mart. Kathlyn glanced at the wall, wondering. Was her father alive? Was he in some bleak cell behind that crumbling masonry? Did he know that she was here? Or was he really dead? Ah, perhaps it were better that death should have taken him—better that than having his living heart wrung by the tale of his daughter's unspeakable miseries.

Even as she sent a last lingering look at the prison the prisoner within, his head buried in his thin wasted hands, beheld her in a vision—but in a happy, joyous vision, busying about the living room of the bungalow.

And far away a younger man beheld a vision as very tenderly he gazed at Kathlyn's discarded robe and resumed his determined quest. Often, standing beside his evening fires, he would ask the silence, "Kathlyn, where are you?" Even then he was riding fast toward Allaha.

A slave mart is a rare thing these days, but at the time these scenes were being enacted there existed many of them here and there across the face of the globe. Men buy and sell men and women these times—enlightened, so they say—but they do it by legal contract or from vile hiding places.

Allaha had been a famous mart in its prime. It had drawn the agents of princes from all over India. Persia, Beloochistan, Afghanistan, and even southern Russia had been rifled of their beauties to adorn the zenanas of the slothful Hindu princes.

The slave mart in the capital town of Allaha stood in the center of the bazaars, a great square platform with a roof, but open on all four sides. Here the slaves were exhibited, the poor things intended for dalliance and those who were to struggle and sweat and die under the overseer's lash.

Every fortnight a day was set aside for the business of the mart. Owners and prospective buyers met, chewed betel-nut, smoked their hookas, sipped coffee and tea, and exchanged the tattle of the hour. It was as much an amusement as a business; indeed, it was the oriental idea of a club, and much the same things were discussed. Thus, Appaji bought a beautiful girl at the last barter and Roya found a male who was a good juggler, and only night before last they had traded. The bazaars were not what they used to be. Dewan Ali had sold his wife to a Punjab opium merchant. Aunut Singh's daughter had run away with the son of a bheestee. All white people ate pig. And no one read the slokas, or moral, stanzas, any more. Yes, the English would come some day, when there would be enough money to warrant it.

All about there were barkers, and fruit sellers, and bangle wallas (for slave girls should have rings of rupee silver about their ankles and wrists), and solemn Brahmins, and men who painted red and ocher caste marks on one's forehead, and ash covered fakirs with withered hands, Nautch girls, girls from the bazaars, peripatetic jewelers, kites, and red-headed vultures—this being a proper place for them.

The chief mahout purchased for Kathlyn a beautiful saree, or veil, which partially concealed her face and hair.

"Chalu!" he said, touching Kathlyn's shoulder, whenever she lagged, for they had dispensed with the litter, "Go on!"

She understood. Outwardly she appeared passive enough, but her soul was on fire and her eyes as brilliant as those of the circling, whooping kites, watching that moment which was to offer some loophole. On through the noisy bazaars, the object of many a curious remark, sometimes insulted by the painted women at the windows, sometimes jested at by the idlers around the merchants' booths. Vaguely she wondered if some one of her ancestors had not been terribly wicked and that she was paying the penalty.

It seemed to her, however, that a film of steel had grown over her nerves; nothing startled her; she sensed only the watchfulness she had often noted in the captives at the farm.

At length they came out into the busy mart. The old mahout congratulated himself upon the docility of his find. It would stiffen the bidding to announce that she was gentle. He even went so far as to pat her on the shoulder. The steel film did not cover all her nerves, so it would seem; the patted shoulder was vulnerable. She winced, for she read clearly enough what was in the mind back of that touch.

She had made her plans. To the man who purchased her she would assume a meekness of spirit in order to lull his watchfulness. To the man who purchased her . . . Kathlyn Hare! She laughed. The old man behind her nodded approvingly, hearing the sound but not sensing its import.

Ah, when the moment came, when the fool who bought her started to lead her home, she would beguile him and at the first sign of carelessness she would trust to her heels. She knew that she was going to run as never a woman ran before; back to the beasts of the jungle, who at least made no effort to molest her so long as she kept out of their way.

Wild and beautiful she was as the old mahout turned her over to a professional seller.

"Circassian!"

"From the north!"

"A bride from the desert!"

"A yellow-hair!"

"A daughter of the north seas!"

The old mahout squatted close by and rubbed his hands. He would be a rich man that night; bags of rupees; a well thatched house to cover his gray hairs till that day they placed him on the pyre at the burning ghat. The gods were good.

Durga Ram, known familiarly as Umballa, at this hour came forth into the sunshine, brooding. He was not in a happy frame of mind. Many things lay heavy upon his soul; but among these things there was not one named remorse. To have brought about all these failures this thought irked him most. Here was a crown almost within reach of his greedy fingers, the water to Tantalus. To have underestimated this yellow haired young woman, he who knew women so well—there lay the bitter sting. He had been too impetuous; he should have waited till all her fears had been allayed. That spawn of Siva, the military, was insolent again, and rupees to cross their palms were scarce. Whither had she blown? Was she dead? Was she alive?

The white hunter had not returned to his camp yet, but the sly Ahmed was there. The perpetual gloom on the face of the latter was reassuring to Umballa. Ahmed's master had not found her. To wring the white man's heart was something. He dared not put him out of the way; too many knew.

And the council was beginning to grow uneasy. How long could he hold them in leash?

What a woman! As magnificent as the daughter of Firoz, shah of Delhi. Fear she knew not. At one moment he loved her with his whole soul, at another he hated her, longed to get her into his hands again, to wreak his vengeance upon her for the humiliation she had by wit and courage heaped upon him. "I am ready!" He could hear it yet. When they had led her away to the ordeals—"I am ready!" A woman, and not afraid to die!

Money! How to get it! He could not plunge his hand into the treasury; there were too many about, too many tongues. But Colonel Hare knew where the silver basket lay hidden, heaped with gold and precious stones; and torture could not wring the hiding-place from him. May he be damned to the nethermost hell! Let him, Durga Ram, but bury his lean hands in that treasure, and Daraka swallow Allaha and all its kings! Rubies and pearls and emeralds, and a far country to idle in, to be feted in, to be fawned upon for his riches!

And Ramabai and his wife, Pundita, let them beware; let them remain wisely in their house and meddle not with affairs of state.

"A thousand rupees!"

Umballa looked up with a start. Unconsciously he had wandered into the slave mart. He shrugged and would have passed on but for the strange, unusual figure standing on the platform. A golden haired woman with neck and arms like Chinese bronze and dressed in a skirt of grass! He paused.

"Two thousand rupees!"

"What!" jeered the professional seller. "For an houri from paradise? O ye of weak hearts, what is this I hear? Two thousand rupees?—for an houri fit to dwell in the zenana of heaven!"

A keen-eyed Mohammedan edged closer to the platform. He stared and sucked in his breath. He found himself pulled two ways. He had no money, but he had knowledge.

"Who sells this maiden?" he asked.

"Mohammed Ghori."

"Which is he?"

"He squats there."

The Mohammedan stopped and touched the old mahout on the shoulder.

"Call off this sale, and my master will make you rich."

The old sinner gingerly felt of the speaker's cotton garb.

"Ah! 'My master' must be rich to dress thee in cotton. Where is your gold? Bid," satirically.

"Two thousand rupees!" shouted the professional seller.

"I have no gold, but my master will give 10,000 rupees for yonder maid. Quick! Old fool, be quick!"

"Begone, thou beggar!"

And the old man spat.

"Mem-sahib," the Mohammedan called out in English, "do not look toward me, or all will be lost. I am Ali, Bruce Sahib's chief mahout; and we have believed you dead! Take care! I go to inform Ahmed. Bruce Sahib has not returned."

Kathlyn, when she heard that voice, shut her eyes.

Umballa had drawn closer. There was something about this half veiled slave that stirred his recollection. Where had he seen that graceful poise? The clearness of the skin, though dark; the roundness of the throat and arms. . . .

"Three thousand rupees!"

The old mahout purred and smoothed his palms together. Three thousand rupees, a rajah's ransom! He would own his elephant; his wife should ride in a gilded palanquin, and his children should wear shoes. Three thousand rupees! He folded his arms and walked gently to and fro.

"Five thousand rupees!" said Umballa, impelled by he knew not what to make this bid.

A ripple of surprise ran over the crowd. The regent, the

powerful Durga Ram, was bidding in person for his zenana.

Kathlyn's nerves tingled with life again, and the sudden bounding of her heart stifled her. Umballa! She was surely lost. Sooner or later he would recognize her.

The mahout stood up, delighted. He was indeed fortunate. He salaamed.

"Huzoor, she is gentle," he said.

The high-caste who had bid 3,000 rupees salaamed also.

"Highness, she is yours," he said. "I can not bid against my regent."

It was the custom to mark a purchased slave with the caste of her purchaser. Umballa, still not recognizing her, waved her aside toward the Brahmin caste markers, one of whom daubed her forehead with a yellow triangle. Her blue eyes pierced the curious brown ones.

"The sahib at the river," she whispered in broken Hindustani. "Many rupees. Bring him to the house of Durga Ram." This in case Ali failed.

The Brahmin's eyes twinkled. Her Hindustani was execrable, but "sahib" and "river" were plain to his understanding. There was but one sahib by the river, and he was the white hunter who had rescued the vanished queen from the ordeals. He nodded almost imperceptibly. Inwardly he smiled. He was not above giving the haughty upstart a Thuggee's twist. He spoke to his neighbor quietly, assigned to him his bowls and brushes, rose, and made off.

"Follow me," said Umballa to the happy mahout. Presently he would have his bags of silver, bright and twinkling.

Fate overtook Ali, who in his mad race to Hare's camp fell and badly sprained his ankle. Moaning, less from the pain than from the attendant helplessness, he was carried into the hut of a kindly ryot and there ministered to.

The Brahmin, however, filled with greed and a sly humor, reached his destination in safety. Naturally cunning, double tongued, sly, ingratiating, after the manner of all Brahmins, who will sink to any base level in order to attain their equivocal ends his actions were unhampered by any sense of treachery toward Umballa. A Thuggee's twist to the schemes of the street rat Umballa, who wore the Brahmin string, to which he had no right! The Brahmin chuckled as he paused at the edge of Bruce's camp. A fat purse lay yonder. He approached, his outward demeanor a mixture of pride and humility.

Bruce had returned but half an hour before, mind weary, bone tired. He sat with his head in his hands, his elbows propped upon his knees. His young heart was heavy. He had searched the bewildering jungle as one might search a plot of grass before one's door, blade by blade. A hundred times he had found traces of her; a hundred times he had called out her name, only to be mocked and gibbered at by apes. She had vanished like a perfume, like a cloud shadow in the wind.

His soul was bitter; for he had built many dreams, and always this fair haired girl had ridden upon them. So straight she stood, so calm in the eyes, mannered with that gentleness, known of the brave. . . . Gone, and skilled as he was in jungle lore, he could not find her.

"Sahib, a Brahmin desires audience."

"Ask him what he wants."

"It is for the sahib's ear alone."

"Ah! Bring him to me quickly."

The Brahmin approached, salaamed.

"What do you wish?" Bruce asked curtly.

"A thousand rupees, Huzoor!" blandly.

"And what have you that is worth that many rupees?" irritably.

The Brahmin salaamed again. "Huzoor, a slave this day was purchased by Durga Ram, Umballa, so-called. She has skin the color of old tusks, and eyes like turquoise, and lips like the flame of the jungle, and hair like the sands of Ganges, mother of rivers."

Bruce was upon his feet, alive, eager. He caught the Brahmin by the arm.

"Is this woman white?" harshly.

"Huzoor, the women of Allaha are always dark of hair."

"And was sold as a slave?"

"To Durga Ram, the king without a crown, Huzoor. It is worth a thousand rupees," smiling.

"Tell me," said Bruce, stilling the tremor in his voice, "tell me, did she follow him without a struggle?"

"Yes. But would a struggle have done any good?"

Bruce took out his wallet and counted out a thousand rupees in Bank of India notes. "Now, listen. Umballa must not know that I know. On your head, remember."

"Huzzor, the word of a Brahmin."

"Ah, yes; but I have lived long here. Where is Ali?" cried Bruce, turning to one of his men.

"He went into the city this morning, Sahib, and has not returned."

"Come," said Bruce to the waiting Brahmin, "We'll return together." He now felt no excitement at all; it was as if he had been immersed in ice water. It was Kathlyn, not the least doubt of it, bought and sold in the slave mart. Misery, degradation . . . then he smiled. He knew Kathlyn Hare. If he did not come to her aid quickly she would be dead.

Now, when Umballa took her into his house, Kathlyn was determined to reveal her identity. She had passed through the ordeals; she was, in law, a queen, with life and death in her hands.

"Do not touch me!" she cried slowly in English.

Umballa stepped back.

"I am Kathlyn Hare, and if all the world is not made up of lies and wickedness, I am the queen you yourself made. I can speak a few words, enough to make myself known to the populace. I will make a bargain with you. I will give you five times five thousand rupees if you will deliver me safely in Peshawer. On my part, I promise to say nothing, nothing."

Umballa raised both his hands in astonishment. He knew now why that form had stirred his recollection.

"You!" He laughed and clapped his hands to summon his servants. Kathlyn, realizing that it was useless to attempt to move this man, turned and started to run, but he intercepted her. "My queen, my bride that was to be, the golden houri! Five times five thousand rupees would not purchase a hair of your head."

"I am your queen!" But she said it without heart.

"What! Do you believe that? Having passed the ordeals you nullified the effect by running away. You will be whatever I choose! Oh, it will be legally done. You shall go with me to the council, and the four of us shall decide. Ah, you would not be my wife!"

"You shall die, Durga Ram," she replied, "and it will be the death of a pariah dog."

"Ah! Still that spirit which I loved. Why, did I not buy you without knowing who you were? Are you not mine? At this very moment I could place you in my zenana and who would ever know? And soon you would not want any one to know."

"Are you without mercy?"

"Mercy? I know not the word. But I have an ambition which surpasses all other things. My wife you shall be, or worse. But legally, always legally!" He laughed again and swiftly caught her in his arms. She struggled like a tigress, but without avail. He covered her face and neck with kisses, then thrust her aside. "Poor little fool! If you had whined and whimpered I should have let you go long since. But there burns within you a spirit I must conquer, and conquer I will!"

Kathlyn stood panting against a pillar. Had she held a weapon in her hand she would have killed him without compunction, as one crushes a poisonous viper.

"Legally! Why, all the crimes in Hind are done under that word. It is the shibboleth of the British Raj. Legally! Come!"

"I will not stir!"

"Then be carried," he replied, beckoning his servants.

"No, no!"

"Ah! Well, then, we'll ride together in the palanquin."

To struggle would reward her with nothing but shame and humiliation; so she bent her head to the inevitable. A passionate longing to be revenged upon this man began to consume her. She wanted the feel of his brown throat in her fingers; wanted to beat him down to his knees, to twist and crush him. But she was a woman and she had not the strength of a man.

"Behold!" cried Umballa later, as he entered the presence of the council, "behold a slave of mine!" He pushed Kathlyn forward. "This day I bought her for five thousand rupees."

The council stirred nervously.

"Do you not recognize her?" exultantly.

The council whispered to one another.

"Legally she is mine, though she has been a queen. But by running away she has forfeited her rights to the law of the ordeals. Am I not right?"

The council nodded gravely. They had not yet wholly recovered from their bewilderment.

"On the other hand, her identity must remain a secret till I have developed my plans," continued Umballa.

"You are all courting a terrible reprisal," said Kathlyn. "I beg of you to kill me at once; do not prolong my torture, my misery. I have harmed none of you, but you have grievously harmed me. One even now seeks aid of the British Raj; and there are many soldiers."

The threat was ill timed.

The head of the council said to Umballa: "It would be wise to lock her up for the present. We all face a great complication."

"A very wise counsel," agreed Umballa, knowing that he had but to say the word to destroy them all. "And she shall have company. I would not have her lonely. Come, majesty; deign to follow your humble servant." Umballa salaamed.

Kathlyn was led to a cell in the palace prison, whose walls she had but a little while ago viewed in passing, and thrust inside. A single window admitted a faint light. Umballa remained by the door, chuckling softly. Presently, her eyes becoming accustomed to the dark, Kathlyn discovered a man chained to a pillar. The man suddenly leaned forward.

"Kit, my Kit!"

"Father!"

She caught him to her breast in her strong young arms, crooned to him, and kissed his matted head. And they stood that way for a long time.

At this very moment there appeared before the council a wild eyed, disheveled young man. How he had passed the palace guard none of them knew.

"A white woman was brought into this room forcibly a few minutes ago. I demand her! And by the God of my father I will cut out the heart of every one of you if you deny me! She is white; she is of my race!"

"There is no white woman here, Bruce Sahib."

"You lie!" thundered the young man.

Two guards came in quickly.

"I say you lie! She was seen to enter here!"

"This man is mad! Besides, it is sacrilege for him to enter our presence in this manner," cried one of the council. "Seize him!"

A fierce struggle between the guards and Bruce followed; but his race to the city and the attendant excitement had weakened him. He was carried away, still fighting manfully.

In the meantime Umballa concluded that the reunion had lasted long enough. He caught Kathlyn roughly by the shoulder and pulled her away.

"Behold, Colonel Sahib! Mine! I bought her this day in the slave mart. Legally mine! Now will you tell me where that silver basket lies hidden, with its gold and game?"

"Father, do not tell him!" warned Kathlyn. "So long as we do not tell him he does not put us out of the way!"

"Kit!"

"Dad, poor dad!"

"Little fool!" said Umballa.

Kathlyn struggled to reach her father again, but could not. Umballa folded his arms tightly about her and attempted to kiss her. This time her strength was superhuman. She freed her hands and beat him in the face, tore his garments, dragged off his turban. The struggle brought them within the radius of the colonel's reach. The prisoner caught his enemy by the throat, laughing insanely.

"Now, you black dog, die!"

CHAPTER IX

THE COLONEL IN CHAINS

The colonel and Umballa swayed back and forth. Umballa sank to his knees and then fought madly to rise but the hands at his throat were the hands of a madman, steel, resistless. The colonel's chains clinked sharply. Lower and lower went Umballa's head; he saw death peering into the cell. His cry rattled in his throat.

Not a sound from Kathlyn. She watched the battle, unfeeling as marble. Let the wretch die; let him feel the fear of death; let him suffer as he had made others suffer. What new complications might follow Umballa's death did not alarm her. How could she be any worse off than she was? He had polluted her cheeks with his kisses. He had tortured and shamed her as few white women have been. Mercy? He had said that day that he knew not the word.

"Ah, you dog! Haven't I prayed God for days for this chance? You black caha! Die!"

But Umballa was not to die at that moment or in that fashion.

That nervous energy which had infused the colonel with

the strength of a lion went out like a spark, and as quickly. Umballa rolled from his paralyzed fingers and lay on the floor, gasping and sobbing. Hare fell back against the pillar, groaning. The cessation of dynamic nerve force filled him with racking pains and a pitiable weakness. But for the pillar he would have hung by his chains.

Kathlyn, with continued apathy, stared down at her enemy. He was not dead. He would kill them both now. Why, she asked with sudden passion, why this misery? What had she done in her young life to merit it? Under-fed, dressed in grass, harassed by men and wild beasts—why?

Umballa edged out of danger and sat up, feeling tenderly of his throat. Next he picked up his turban and crawled to the open door. He pulled himself up and stood there, weakly. But there was venom enough in his eyes. The tableau lasted a minute or two; then slowly he closed the door, bolted it, and departed.

This ominous silence awoke the old terror in Kathlyn's heart far more than oral threats would have done. There would be reprisal, something finished in cruelty.

"My dear, my dear!" She ran over to her father and flung her arms about him, supporting him and mothering him. An hour passed.

"All in, Kit, all in; haven't the strength of a cat. Ah, great God; if that strength had but lasted a moment longer. Well, he's still alive. But, O, my Kit, my golden Kit, to see you here is to be tortured like the damned. And it is all my fault, all mine!" The man who had once been so strong sobbed hysterically.

"Hush, hush!"

Harold MacGrath

"There were rare and wonderful jewels of which I alone knew the hiding place. But God knows that it was not greed; I wanted them for you and Winnie . . . I knew you were here. Trust that black devil to announce the fact to me . . . God! what I haven't suffered in the way of suspense! Kit, Kit, what has he done to you?"

Briefly she recounted her adventures, and when she had done he bowed his head upon her bare shoulder and wept as only strong men, made weak, weep.

To Kathlyn it was terrible. "Father, don't, don't! You hurt me! I can't stand it!"

After a while he said: "What shall we do, Kit; what shall we do?"

"I will marry him, father," she answered quietly. "We can take our revenge afterward."

"What!"

"If it will save you."

"Child, let me rot here. What! Would you trust him, knowing his false heart as you do? The moment you married him would be my death warrant. No, no! If you weaken now I shall curse you, curse you, my Kit! There has been horror enough. I can die."

"Well, and so can I, father."

Silence. After a cockatoo shrilled; a laugh came faintly through the window, and later the tinkle of music. Up above the world was going on the same as usual. Trains were hurrying to and fro; the great ships were going down the sapphire seas; children were at play, and the world wide marts were busying with the daily affairs of men.

"Jewels!" she murmured, gazing at the sky beyond the grilled window. Was there ever a precious stone that lay not in the shadow of blood and misery? Poor, poor, foolish father! As if jewels were in beauty a tithe of the misery they begot!

"Ay, Kit, jewels; sapphires and rubies and emeralds, diamonds and pearls and moonstones. And I wanted them for my pretty cubs! Umballa knew that I would return for them and laid his plans. But were they not mine?"

"Yes, if you intended to rule these people; no, if you thought to take them away. Do you not know that to Winnie and me a hair of your head is more precious than the Koh-i-noor? We must put our heads together and plan some way to get out."

She dropped her arms from his shoulders and walked about the cell, searching every stone. Their only hope lay in the window, and that appeared impossible since she had no means of filing through her father's chains and the bars of the window. She returned and sat down beside her father and rested her aching head on her knees, thinking, thinking.

Bruce, struggling with the soldiers (and long since their fat flesh had been stung into such activity!) saw Umballa appear in the corridor.

"Durga Ram," he cried, with a furious effort to free his arms. "Durga Ram, you damnable scoundrel, it would be wise for you to kill me, here and now, for if I ever get free. God help you! O, I shan't kill you; that would be too merciful. But I'll break your bones, one by one, and never more shall you stand and walk. Do you hear me? Where is

Kathlyn Hare? She is mine!"

Umballa showed his teeth in what was an attempt to smile. He still saw flashes of fire before his eyes, and it was yet difficult to breathe naturally. Still, he could twist this white man's heart, play with him.

"Take him away. Put him outside the city gates and let him go."

Bruce was greatly astonished at this sign of clemency.

"But," added Umballa, crossing his lips with his tongue, "place him against a wall and shoot him if he is caught within the city. He is mad, and therefore I am lenient. There is no white woman in the palace or in the royal zenana. Off with him!"

"You lie, Durga Ram! You found her in the slave mart to-day."

Umballa shrugged and waved his hand. He could have had Bruce shot at once, but it pleased him to dangle death before the eyes of his rival. He was no fool; he saw the trend of affairs. This young white man loved Kathlyn Hare. All the better, in view of what was to come.

Bruce was conducted to the gate and rudely pushed outside. He turned savagely, but a dozen black officers convinced him that this time he would meet death. Ah, where was Ali, and Ahmed, and the man Lal Singh, who was to notify the English? He found Ali at camp, the chief mahout having been conducted there in an improvised litter. He recounted his experiences.

"I was helpless, Sahib."

"No more than I am, Ali. But be of good cheer; Umballa and I shall meet soon, man to man."

"Allah is Allah; there is no God but God."

"And sometimes," said Bruce, moodily, "he watches over the innocent."

"Ahmed is at Hare Sahib's camp."

"Thanks, Ali; that's the best news I have heard yet. Ahmed will find a way. Take care of yourself. I'm off!"

When Umballa appeared before the council their astonishment knew no bounds. The clay tinted skin, the shaking hands, the disheveled garments—what had happened to this schemer whom ill luck had made their master?

He explained. "I went too near our prisoner. A flash of strength was enough. They shall be flogged."

"But the woman!"

"Woman? She is a tiger-cat, and tiger-cats must sometimes be flogged. It is my will. Now I have news for you. There is another sister, younger and weaker. Our queen," and he salaamed ironically, "our queen did not know that her father lived, and there I made my first mistake."

"But she will now submit to save him!"

"Ah, would indeed that were the case. But tiger-cats are always tiger-cats, and nothing will bend this maid; she must be broken, broken. It is my will," with a flash of fire in his eyes.

The council salaamed. Umballa's will must of necessity

be theirs, hate him darkly as they might.

The bungalow of Colonel Hare was something on the order of an armed camp. Native animal keepers, armed with rifles, patrolled the menagerie. No one was to pass the cordon without explaining frank his business, whence he came, and whither he was bound.

By the knees of one of the sentries a little native child was playing. From time to time the happy father would stoop and pat her head.

Presently there was a stir about camp. An elephant shuffled into the clearing. He was halted, made to kneel, and Ahmed stepped out of the howdah.

The little girl ran up to Ahmed joyfully and begged to be put into the howdah. Smiling, Ahmed set her in the howdah, and the mahout bade the elephant to rise, but, interested in some orders by Ahmed, left the beast to his own devices. The child called and the elephant walked off quietly. So long as he remained within range of vision no one paid any attention to him. Finally he passed under a tree near the cages and reached up for some leaves. The child caught hold of a limb and gleefully crawled out upon it some distance beyond the elephant's reach. Once there, she became frightened, not daring to crawl back.

She prattled "elephant talk," but the old fellow could not reach her. The baboon in the near-by cage set up a chattering. The child ordered the elephant to rise on his hind legs. He placed his fore legs on the roof of the baboon's cage, which caved in, rather disturbing the elephant's calm. He sank to the ground.

The baboon leaped through the opening and made off to test this unexpected liberty. He was friendly and tame, but freedom was just then paramount.

The elephant remained under the trees, as if pondering, while the child began to cry loudly. One of the natives saw her predicament and hastened away for assistance.

Achmed was greatly alarmed over the loss of the baboon. It was a camp pet of Colonel Hare's and ran free in camp whenever the colonel was there. He had captured it when a mere baby in British East Africa. The troglodyte, with a strange reasoning yet untranslatable, loved the colonel devotedly and followed him about like a dog and with a scent far keener. So Ahmed and some of the keepers set off in search of the colonel's pet.

He went about the search with only half a heart. Only a little while before he had received the news of what had happened in the slave mart that afternoon. It seemed incredible. To have her fall into Umballa's hands thus easily, when he and Bruce Sahib had searched the jungle far and wide! Well, she was alive; praise Allah for that; and where there was life there was hope.

Later Kathlyn was standing under the cell window gazing at the yellow sunset. Two hours had gone, and no sign of Umballa yet. She shuddered. Had she been alone she would have hunted for something sharp and deadly. But her father; not before him. She must wait. One thing was positive and absolute: Umballa should never embrace her; she was too strong and desperate.

"Kit!"

"Yes, father."

"I have a sharp piece of metal in my pocket. Could you . . . My God, by my hand! . . . when he comes?"

"Yes, father; I am not afraid to die, and death seems all that remains. I should bless you. He will be a tiger now."

"My child, God was good to give me a daughter like you."

She turned to him this time and pressed him to her heart.

"It grows dark suddenly," he said.

Kathlyn glanced toward the window.

"Why, it's a baboon!" she exclaimed.

"Jock, Jock!" cried her father excitedly.

The baboon chattered.

"Kit, it's Jock I used to tell you about. He is tame and follows me about like a dog. Jock, poor Jock!"

"Father, have you a pencil?"

"A pencil?" blankly.

"Yes, yes! I can write a note and attach it to Jock. It's a chance."

"Good lord! and you're cool enough to think like that." The colonel went through his pockets feverishly. "Thank God, here's an old stub! But paper?"

Kathlyn tore off a broad blade of grass from her dress and wrote carefully upon it. If it fell into the hands of the natives they would not understand, If the baboon returned to camp . . . It made her weak to realize how slender the chance was. She took the tabouret and placed it beneath the window and stood upon it.

"Jock, here, Jock!"

The baboon gave her his paws. Deftly she tied the blade of grass round his neck. Then she struck her hands together violently. The baboon vanished, frightened at this unexpected treatment.

"He is gone."

The colonel did not reply, but began to examine his chains minutely.

"Kit, there's no getting me out of here without files. If there is any rescue you go and return. Promise."

"I promise."

Then they sat down to wait.

And Ahmed in his search came to the river. Some natives were swimming and sporting in the water. Ahmed put a question. Oh, yes, they had seen the strange-looking ape (for baboons did not habitate this part of the world); he had gone up one of the trees near by. Colonel Hare had always used a peculiar whistle to bring Jock, and Ahmed resorted to this device. Half an hour's perseverance rewarded him; and then he found the blade of grass.

"Dungeon window by tree. Kathlyn."

That was sufficient for Ahmed. He turned the baboon over to the care of one of his subordinates and hurried away to Bruce's camp, only to find that he had gone to the colonel's. Away went Ahmed again, tireless. He found Bruce pacing the bungalow frontage.

"Ahmed."

"Yes, Sahib. Listen." He told his tale quickly.

"The guards at all the gates have orders to shoot me if they catch me within the walls of the city. I must disguise myself in some way."

"I'll find you an Arab burnoose, hooded, Sahib, and that will hide you. It will be dark by the time we reach the city, and we'll enter by one of the other gates. That will allay suspicion. First we must seek the house of Ramabai. I need money for bribery."

Bruce searched his wallet. It was empty. He had given all he had to the Brahmin.

"You lead, Ahmed. I'm dazed."

In the city few knew anything about Ahmed, not even the keenest of Umballa's spies. Umballa had his suspicions, but as yet he could prove nothing. To the populace he was a harmless animal trainer who was only too glad not in any way to be implicated with his master. So they let him alone. Day by day he waited for the report from Lal Singh, but so far he had heard nothing except that the British Raj was very busy killing the followers of the Mahdi in the Soudan. It was a subtle inference that for the present all aliens in Allaha must look out for themselves.

"Sahib," he whispered, "I have learned something. Day after day I have been waiting, hoping. Colonel Sahib lives, but where I know not."

"Lives!"

"Ai! In yonder prison where later we go. He lives. That is enough for his servant. He is my father and my mother, and I would die for him and his. Ah! Here is the north gate. Bend your head, Sahib, when we pass."

They entered the city without mishap. No one questioned them. Indeed, they were but two in a dozen who passed in at the same time. They threaded the narrow streets quickly, skirting the glow of many dung fires for fear that Bruce's leggings might be revealed under his burnoose.

When at length they came to the house of Ramabai they did not seek to enter the front, but chose the gate in the rear of the garden. The moon was up and the garden was almost as light as day.

"Ramabai!" called Bruce in a whisper.

The dreaming man seated at a table came out of his dream with a start. A servant ran to the gate.

"Who calls?" demanded Ramabai, suspicious, as all conspirators ever are.

"It is I, Bruce," was the reply in English, flinging aside his burnoose.

"Bruce Sahib? Open!" cried Ramabai. "What do you here? Have you found her?"

Ramabai's wife, Pundita, came from the house. She recognized Bruce immediately.

"The Mem-sahib! Have you found her?"

"Just a moment. Kathlyn Mem-sahib is in one of the palace dungeons. She must be liberated to-night. We need money to bribe what sentries are about." Bruce went on to relate the incident of the baboon. "This proves that the note was written not more than three hours ago. She will probably be held there till morning. This time we'll place her far beyond the reach of Umballa."

"Either my money or my life. In a month from now . . ."

"What?" asked Ahmed.

"Ah, I must not tell." Pundita stole close to Ramabai.

Ahmed smiled.

"We have elephants but a little way outside the city. We have pulling chains. Let us be off at once. It is not necessary to enter the city, for this window, Ahmed says, is on the outside. We can easily approach the wall in a roundabout way without being seen. Have you money?"

From his belt Ramabai produced some gold.

"That will be sufficient. To you, then, the bribing. The men, should there be any, will hark to you. Come!" concluded Bruce, impatient to be off.

"And I?" timidly asked Pundita.

"You will seek Hare Sahib's camp," said Ramabai. "This is a good opportunity to get you away also."

Ahmed nodded approvingly.

Pundita kissed her husband; for these two loved each other, a circumstance almost unknown in this dark mysterious land of many gods.

"Pundita, you will remain at the camp in readiness to receive us. At dawn we shall leave for the frontier. And when we return it will be with might and reprisal.

Umballa shall die the death of a dog." Ramabai clenched his hands.

"But first," cooed Ahmed, "he shall wear out the soles of his pig's feet in the treadmill. It is written. I am a Mohammedan. Yet sometimes these vile fakirs have the gift of seeing into the future. And me has seen . . ." He paused.

"Seen what?" demanded Bruce.

"I must not put false hopes in your hearts. But this I may say: Trials will come, bitter and heart burning: a storm, a whirlwind, a fire; but peace is after that. But Allah uses us as his tools. Let us haste!"

"And I?" said Ramabai, sending a piercing glance at Ahmed.

But Ahmed smiled and shook his head. "Wait and see, Ramabai. Some day they will call you the Fortunate. Let us hurry. My Mem-sahib waits."

"What did this fakir see?" whispered Bruce as he donned his burnoose again.

"Many wonderful things; but perhaps the fakir lied. They all lie. Yet . . . hurry!"

The quartet passed out of the city unmolested. Ramabai's house was supposed to be under strict surveillance; but the soldiers, due to largess, were junketing in the bazaars. Shortly they came up to two elephants with howdahs. They were the best mannered of the half dozen owned or rented by Colonel Hare. Mahouts sat astride. Rifles reposed in the side sheaths. This was to be no light adventure. There might be a small warfare.

Pundita flung her arms around Ramabai, and he consoled her. She was then led away to the colonel's camp.

"Remember," Ramabai said at parting, "she saved both our lives. We owe a debt."

"Go, my Lord; and may all the gods—no, the Christian God—watch over you!"

"Forward!" growled Ahmed. First, though, he saw to it that the pulling chains were well wrapped in cotton blankets. There must be no sound to warn others of their approach.

"Ahmed," began Bruce.

"Leave all things to me, Sahib," interrupted Ahmed, who assumed a strange authority at times that confused and puzzled Bruce. "It is my Mem-sahib, and I am one of the fingers of the long arm of the British Raj. And there are books in Calcutta in which my name is written high. No more!"

Through the moon-frosted jungle the two elephants moved silently. A drove of wild pigs scampered across the path, and the wild peacock hissed from the underbrush sleepily. All silence again. Several times Ahmed halted, straining his ears. It seemed incredible to Bruce that the enormous beasts could move so soundlessly. It was a part of their business; they were hunters of their kind.

At length they came out into the open at the rear of the prison walls. Here Ramabai got down, and went In search of any sentries. He returned almost at once with the good news that there was none.

The marble walls shimmered like clusters of dull opals.

What misery had been known behind their crumbling beauty!

Ahmed marked the tree and raised his hand as a sign.

"Bruce Sahib!" he called.

"Yes, Ahmed. I'll risk it first."

Bruce moved the elephant to the barred window. His heart beat wildly. He leaned down from his howdah and strove to peer within.

"Kathlyn Hare?" he whispered.

"Who is it?"

"Bruce."

"Father, father!" Bruce heard her cry; "they have found us!"

Ahmed heard the call; and he sighed as one who had Allah to thank. God was great and Mahomet was His prophet.

"Listen," said Bruce. "We shall hook chains to the bars and pull them out, without noise if possible. The moment they give . . . have you anything to stand on?"

"Yes, a tabouret."

"That will serve. You stand on it, and I'll pull you up and through. Then your father."

"Father is in chains."

"Ahmed, he is in chains. What in God's name shall we do?"

"Return for me later," said Hare. "Don't bother about me. Get Kit away, and quickly. Umballa may return at any moment. To work, to work, Bruce, and God bless you!"

They flew to the task. Round the hooks Ahmed had wrapped cloths to ward against the clink of metal against metal. The hooks were deftly engaged. The chains grew taut. So far there was but little noise. The elephants leaned against the chains; the bars bent and sprang suddenly from their ancient sockets.

Kathlyn was free.

CHAPTER X

WAITING

Kathlyn flung herself into her father's arms.

"Dad, dad! To leave you alone!"

"Kit, you are wasting time. Be off. Trust me; I wasn't meant to die in this dog's kennel, curse or no curse. Kiss me and go!"

"Curse? What do you mean, father?"

"Ahmed will tell you. In God's name go, child!"

"Come, Miss Kathlyn," Bruce called anxiously.

Kathlyn then climbed up to the window, and Bruce lifted her into his howdah, bidding her to lie low. How strong he was, she thought. Ah, something had whispered to her day by day that he would come when she needed him. Suddenly she felt her cheeks grow hot with shame. She snuggled her bare legs under her grass dress. Till this moment she had never given her appearance a single thought. There had been things so much more vital. But youth, and there is ever the way of a man with a maid.

Now, Kathlyn did not love this quiet, resourceful young man, at least if she did she was not yet aware of it; but the touch of his hand and the sound of his voice sent a shiver over her that was not due to the chill of the night. She heard him give his orders, low voiced.

"Do not lift your head above the howdah rim, Miss Kathlyn, till we are in the jungle. And don't worry about your father. He's alive, and that's enough for Ahmed and me. What a strange world it is, and how fate shuffles us about! Forward!"

The curse: what did her father mean by that? It seemed to Kathlyn that hours passed before Bruce spoke again.

"Now you may sit up. What in the world have you got on? Good heavens, grass! You poor girl!" He took off his coat and threw it across her shoulders, and was startled by the contact of her warm flesh.

"I can not thank you in words," she said faintly.

"Don't. Pshaw, it was nothing. I would have gone—" He stopped embarrassedly.

"Well?" Perhaps it was coquetry which impelled the query; perhaps it was something deeper.

He laughed. "I was going to say that I would have gone into the depths of hell to serve you. We'll be at your father's bungalow in a minute or so, and then the final stroke. Umballa is not dependable. He may or may not pay a visit to the cell to-night. I can only pray that he will come down the moment I arrive."

But he was not to meet Umballa that night. Umballa had won his point in regard to having his prisoners flogged;

but, Oriental that he was, he went about the matter leisurely. He ate his supper, changed his clothes and dallied in the zenana for an hour. The rascal had made a thorough study of the word "suspense"; he knew the exquisite torture of making one's victim wait. For the time being his passion for Kathlyn had subsided. He desired above all things just than revenge for the humiliating experience in the ceil; he wanted to put pain and terror into her heart. Ah, she would be on her knees, begging, begging, and her father would struggle in vain at his shackles. Spurned; so be it. She should have a taste of his hate, the black man's hate. Two should hold her by the arms while the professional flogger seared the white soft back of her. She would soon come to him begging. He had been too kind. The lash of the zenana, it should bite into her soft flesh. He would break her spirit and her body together and fling her into his own zenana to let her gnaw her heart out in suspense. She should be the least of his women, the drudge.

First, however, the lash should bite the father till he dropped in his chains; thus she would be able to anticipate the pain and degradation.

And always there would remain the little dark-haired sister. She would marry him; she would do it to save her father and sister. Then the filigree basket heaped with rubies and pearls and emeralds and sapphires! As for the other, what cared he if he rotted? It gave him the whip hand over the doddering council. Master he would be; he would blot out all things which stood in his path. A king, till he had gathered what fortune he needed. Then let the jackals howl.

Accompanied by torch bearers, servants and the professional flogger, he led the way to the cell and flung open the door triumphantly. For a moment he could not

Harold MacGrath

believe his eyes. She was gone, and through yonder window! Hell of all hells of Hind! She was gone, and he was robbed!

"Out of your reach this time, you black devil!" cried the colonel. "Go on. Do what you please to me, I'm ready."

Umballa ran to the tabouret and jumped upon it. He saw the trampled grass. Elephants. And these doubtless had come from the colonel's camp. He jumped off the tabouret and dashed to the door.

"Follow me!" he cried. "Later, Colonel Hare, later!" he threatened.

The colonel remained silent.

Up above, in the palace, Umballa summoned a dozen troopers and gave them explicit orders. He was quite confident that Kathlyn would be carried at once to her father's bungalow, if only for a change of clothes. It was a shrewd guess.

As the iron door changed upon the sill Colonel Hare leaned against the pillar and closed his eyes, praying silently.

At the bungalow Pundita fell at Kathlyn's feet and kissed them.

"Mem-sahib!" she cried brokenly.

"Pundita!" Kathlyn stooped and gathered her up in her arms.

After that Ramabai would have died for her under any torture.

"Now, Ahmed, what did my father mean when he said 'curse or no curse'?"

"It's a long story, Mem-sahib," said Ahmed evasively.

"Tell it."

"It was in a temple in the south. The Colonel Sahib took a sapphire from an idol's eye. The guru, a very wise and ancient priest, demanded the return of it. The Colonel Sahib, being a young man, refused. The guru cursed him. That is all."

"No, Ahmed; there must be more. Did not the guru curse my father's children and their children's children?"

"Ah, Mem-sahib, what does the curse of a Hindu amount to?"

"Perhaps it is stronger than we know," glancing down at her dress.

Further discussion was interrupted by one of the armed keepers, who came rushing up with the news that armed soldiers were approaching. Bruce swore frankly. This Umballa was supernaturally keen. What to do now?

"Quick!" cried Ahmed. "Get the howdahs off the elephants." It was done. "Hobble them." It was immediately accomplished. "Into the bungalow, all of you. Mem-sahib, follow me!"

"What are you going to do?" asked Bruce.

"Hide her where none will dare to look," answered Ahmed.

He seized Kathlyn by the hand and urged her to run. She had implicit faith in this old friend, who had once dandled her on his knees. They disappeared behind the bungalow and ran toward the animal cages. He stopped abruptly before one of the cages.

"A leopard, but harmless. You'll know how to soothe him if he becomes nervous. Enter."

Kathlyn obeyed.

This cage was not a movable one, and had a cavity underneath. The heavy teak flooring was not nailed.

The soldiers arrived at the bungalow, boisterously threatening the arrest of the entire camp if Durga Ram's slave was not produced forthwith.

"You are mistaken," said Bruce. "There is no slave here. Search."

"You stand in extreme danger, Sahib. You have meddled with what does not concern you," replied the captain, who had thrown his fortunes with Umballa, sensing that here was a man who was bound to win and would be liberal to those who stood by him during the struggle.

"Search," repeated Bruce.

The captain and his men ran about, but not without a certain system of thoroughness. They examined the elephants, but were baffled there, owing to Ahmed's foresight. They entered the native quarters, looked under the canvases into the empty cages, from cellar to roof in the bungalow, when suddenly the captain missed Ahmed.

"Where is the Colonel Sahib's man?" he asked bruskly.

"Possibly he is going the rounds of the animal cages," said Bruce, outwardly calm and shaking within.

"And thou, Ramabai, beware!"

"Of what, Captain?" coolly.

"Thou, too, hast meddled; and meddlers burn their fingers."

"I am innocent of any crime," said Ramabai. "I am watched, I know; but there is still some justice in Allaha."

"Bully for you!" said Bruce in English.

The captain eyed him malevolently.

"Search the animal cages," he ordered.

Bruce, Ramabai and Pundita followed the captain. He peered into the cages, one by one, and at length came to the leopard's cage. And there was the crafty Ahmed, calmly stroking the leopard, which snarled suddenly. Ahmed stood up with a fine imitation of surprise. The captain, greatly mystified, turned about; he was partially convinced that he had had his work for nothing. Still, he had his tongue.

"Thou, Ramabai, hast broken thy parole. Thou wert not to leave thy house. It shall be reported." Then he took a shot at Bruce: "And thou wilt enter the city on the pain of death."

With this he ordered the soldiers right about and proceeded the way he had come.

"Ahmed, where is she?" cried Bruce, who was as

mystified as the captain.

Smiling, Ahmed raised one of the broad teak boards, and the golden head of Kathlyn appeared.

"Ahmed," said Bruce, delighted, "hereafter you shall be chief of this expedition. Now, what next?"

"Secure files and return for my master."

"Wait," interposed Kathlyn, emerging. "I have a plan. It will be useless to return to-night. He will be too well guarded. Are you brave, Pundita?"

"I would die for the Mem-sahib."

"And I, too," added Ramabai.

Ahmed and Bruce gazed at each other.

"What is your plan, Mem-sahib?" asked Ahmed, replacing the board and helping Kathlyn out of the cage, the door of which he closed quickly, as the leopard was evincing a temper at all this nocturnal disturbance.

"It is a trap for Umballa."

"He is as wise as the cobra and as suspicious as the jackal," said Ahmed doubtfully.

"Reason forbids that we return to-night. Umballa will wait, knowing me. Listen. Pundita, you shall return to the city. Two men will accompany you to the gate. You will enter alone in the early morning."

Pundita drew close to her husband.

"You will seek Umballa and play traitor. You will pretend to betray me."

"No, no, Mem-sahib!"

"Listen. You will demand to see him alone. You will say that you are jealous of me. You will tell him that you are ready to lead him to my hiding-place."

"No, Miss Kathlyn; that will not do at all," declared Bruce emphatically.

To this Ahmed agreed with a slow shake of the head.

"Let me finish," said Kathlyn. "You will tell him, Pundita, that he must come alone. He will promise, but by some sign or other he will signify to his men to follow. Well, the guard may follow. Once Umballa steps inside the bungalow we will seize and bind him. His life will depend upon his writing a note to the council to liberate my father. If he refuses, the leopard."

"The leopard?"

"Yes; why not? A leopard was the basic cause of all this misery and treachery. Let us give Umballa a taste of it. Am I cruel? Well, yes; all that was gentle and tender in me seems either to have vanished or hardened. He has put terror into my heart; let me put it into his."

"It is all impractical," demurred Bruce.

"He will never follow Pundita," said Ahmed.

"Then shall we all sit down and wait?" Kathlyn asked bitterly. "At least let me try. He will not harm Pundita, since it is I he wants."

"She is right," averred Pundita. "A woman can do more at this moment than a hundred men. I will go, Mem-sahib; and, more, I will bring him back."

"But if he should hold you as a hostage?" suggested the harried Ahmed. "What then?"

"What will be will be," answered Pundita with oriental philosophy.

"You shall go, Pundita," said Ramabai; "and Durga Ram shall choke between these two hands if he harms a hair of your head."

"And now to bed," said Ahmed.

Well for Kathlyn that she had not the gift of clairvoyance. At the precise moment she put her head upon the pillow her father was writhing under the lash; but never a sound came from his lips. Kit was free. Kit was free!

"To-morrow and to-morrow's to-morrow you shall feel the lash," cried Umballa when he saw that his victim could stand no more. "Once more, where is the filigree basket?"

Feebly the colonel shook his head.

"To-morrow, then! Up till now you have known only neglect. Now you shall feel the active hatred of the man you robbed and cheated. Ah, rubies and pearls and emeralds; you will never see them."

"Nor shall you!"

"Wait and see. There's another way of twisting the secret from you. Wait; have patience." Umballa laughed.

And this laughter rang in the colonel's ears long after the door had closed. What new deviltry had he in mind?

The next morning Kathlyn came into the living-room dressed, for the first time in weeks. She felt strangely uncomfortable. For so long a time her body had been free that the old familiar garments of civilization (are they civilized?) almost suffocated her.

"You are not afraid, Pundita?"

"No, Mem-sahib. Ahmed will have me carried to within a few yards of the gate, and after that it will be easy to find Durga Ram. Ah, Mem-sahib, if you but knew how I hate him!"

After Pundita had departed Ahmed brought in the leopard. Kathlyn petted it and crooned, and the magic timbre of her tones won over the spotted cat. He purred.

And now they must wait. An hour flew past. Kathlyn showed signs of restlessness, and this restlessness conveyed itself to the leopard, who began to switch his tail about.

"Mem-sahib, you are losing your influence over the cat," warned Ahmed. "Go walk; go talk elephant; and you, Bruce Sahib, go with her. I'll take care of the cat."

So Bruce and Kathlyn went the rounds of the cages. She was a veritable enigma to Bruce. Tigers lost their tense-ness and looked straight into her eyes. A cheetah with cubs permitted her to touch the wabbly infants, whereas the keeper of this cage dared not go within a foot of it. By the time she reached the elephants a dozen keepers were following her, their eyes wide with awe. They had heard often of the Mem-sahib who calmed the wild ones, but they had not believed. With the elephants she did about as she pleased.

"Miss Kathlyn, I am growing a bit afraid of you," said Bruce.

"And why?"

"I've never seen animals act like that before. What is it you do to them?"

"Let them know that I am not afraid of them and that I am fond of them."

"I am not afraid of them and am also fond of them. Yet they spit at me whenever I approach."

"Perhaps it is black art." The shadow of a smile crossed her lips. Then the smile stiffened and she breathed deeply. For the moment she had forgot her father, who stood chained to a pillar in a vile cell. She put her hand over her eyes and swayed.

"What is it?" he cried in alarm.

"Nothing. I had almost forgot where I am."

"I, too. I am beginning to let Ahmed think for me. Let us get back to the bungalow."

He loved her. And he feared her, too. She was so unlike any young woman he had ever met that she confused his established ideas of the sex. The cool blood of her disturbed him as much as anything. Not a sign of that natural hysteria of woman, though she had been through enough to drive insane a dozen ordinary women. He loved the fearless eye of her, the flat back, the deep chest, the spring with which she measured her strides. Here at last was the true normal woman. She was of the breed which produced heroes.

He loved her, and yet was afraid of her. A wall seemed to surround her, and nowhere could he discover any breach. Vaguely he wondered how the Viking made love to the Viking's daughter. By storm, or by guile? Yes, he was afraid of her; afraid of her because she could walk alone. He locked up his thoughts in his heart; for instinct advised him to say nothing now; this was no time for the declaration of love.

"It is best," said Ahmed, "that we all remain inside the bungalow. Ramabai, have you any plan in case Pundita does not return?"

Ramabai's breast swelled. "Yes, Ahmed. I have a thousand friends in yonder city, ready at my call. Only, this is not the time. Still, I can call to them, and by to-morrow there will not be a stone of the palace upon another. Be not alarmed. Pundita will return, but mayhap alone."

So they waited.

Now, Pundita, being a woman, was wise in the matter of lure. She entered the city unquestioned. She came to the palace steps just as Umballa was issuing forth. She shivered a little—she could not help it; the man looked so gloomy and foreboding. The scowl warned her to walk with extreme care.

He stopped when he saw her and was surprised into according her the salute one gave to a woman of quality.

"Ah!"

"Durga Ram," she began, "I am seeking you." Her voice trembled ever so little.

"Indeed! And why do you seek me, who am your enemy, and who always will be?"

"A woman loves where she must, not where she wills."

Umballa seemed to ponder over this truth.

"And why have you sought me?"

"A woman's reasons. My husband and the Mem-sahib—"

"You know, then, where she is?" quickly.

"Aye, Durga Ram; I alone know where she is hiding."

He sent a shrewd glance into her eyes. Had she wavered, ill would have befallen her.

"Tell me."

"Follow."

He laughed. Near by stood two of the palace guards. "All women are liars. Why should I trust you?"

"That is true. Why indeed should you trust me?" She turned and with bowed head started to walk away.

"Wait!" he called to her, at the same time motioning to the guards to follow at a distance.

"If I lead you to the Mem-sahib, it must be alone."

"You say that you alone know where she is?"

"I meant that I alone will lead you to her. And you must decide quickly, Durga Ram, for even now they are preparing for night, and this time they will go far."

"Lead on."

"Send the guards back to the palace."

Umballa made a sign with his hand, but another with his eyes. The guards fell back to the palace steps, understanding perfectly that they and others were to follow unseen. Umballa knew instinctively that this was a trap. He would apparently walk into it unsuspectingly; but those who sprung the trap would find no rat, but a tiger. And after the manner of hungry tigers, he licked his chops. A trap; a child could have discerned it. But having faith in his star he followed Pundita. Only once during the journey did he speak.

"Pundita, remember, if you have lied you will be punished."

"Durga Ram, I have not lied. I have promised to lead you to her, and lead you to her I shall."

"Durga Ram," he mused. She did not give him his title of prince; indeed, she never had. She was really the rightful heir to this crown; but her forbears had legally foresworn. Ah! the Colonel Sahib's camp. Good! He knew now that in Kathlyn's escape he had the man Ahmed to reckon with. Presently.

"She is there, Durga Ram."

"And what more?" ironically.

His coolness caused her some uneasiness. Had he, by

means unknown to her, signed to the guards to follow?

Umballa entered the living-room of the bungalow. It was apparently deserted. He cast a quick glance about. The curtains trembled suspiciously, and even as he noted it, Bruce, Ramabai and Ahmed sprang forth, carrying ropes. Umballa made a dash for the door, but they were too quick for him. Struggling, he was seized and bound; but all the while he was laughing inwardly. Did they dream of trapping him in this childish fashion? By now twenty or thirty of his paid men were drawing a cordon about the camp. All of them should pay the full penalty for this act. What mattered a few ropes? He was rather puzzled as to the reason of their leaving his right arm free.

Next, the curtains were thrown back, and Kathlyn stood revealed. Near her a leopard strained impatiently on the leash. Umballa eyed her wonderingly. She was like the woman who had arrived weeks ago. And yet to him she seemed less beautiful than when he paid five thousand rupees for her in the slave mart. He waited.

"Umballa, write an order for my father's release."

"And if I refuse?" Umballa wanted to gain time.

"You shall be liberated at the same time as this leopard. You have had experience with leopards. Do you not recall the one my father killed, saving the life of your benefactor?"

"I will free him in exchange for yourself."

"Write."

She offered the pen to him.

He shrugged and made no effort to take it.

"Very well," said Kathlyn. "Leave us." Once alone she said: "Can you run as fast as this cat?" She approached and began at the knots of the ropes.

He saw by the thin determined line of her lips that she meant to do exactly as she threatened. He concluded then to sign the paper. His men would arrive before a messenger could reach the city.

"I will sign," he said. "For the present you have the best of me. But what of the afterwards?"

"We are going to hold you as hostage, Umballa. When my father arrives we intend to escort you to the frontier and there leave you."

"Give me the pen." His men were drawing nearer and nearer. He signed the order of release. He knew that even if it reached the council it would not serve, lacking an essential.

Kathlyn joyfully caught up the order and called to her friends. Ramabai smiled and shook his head. It was not enough, he said. He took the jeweled triangle from Umballa's turban.

"Go, Ramabai," said Kathlyn, strangely tender all at once; "go bring my father back to me. Rest assured that if aught happens to you, Umballa shall pay."

"With his head," supplemented Bruce. "Look not so eagerly toward the west, Umballa. Your troopers will remain at the edge of the clearing. They have been informed that a single misstep on their part and their master dies."

Umballa sat up stiffly in the chair. They had beaten him by a point. The heat of his rage swept over him like fire, and he closed his eyes.

Ramabai passed the guards, giving them additional warning to remain exactly where they were. The captain shrugged; it was all in a day's work, women were always leading or driving men into hell.

When Ramabai appeared before the council he did so proudly. He salaamed as etiquette required, however, and extended the written order for Colonel Hare's release. At first they refused to regard it as authentic. Ramabai produced the jeweled triangle.

"The prince has made this order imperative," he said. "Colonel Hare will proceed in my custody."

"Where is Durga Ram?"

"At the bungalow of Colonel Hare, where he found the daughter."

Ah, that cleared up everything. Umballa had some definite plan in releasing Colonel Hare. It would confuse the public, who had been given to understand that the hunter was dead; but they would claim that it was an affair of state, in nowise concerning the populace. So Colonel Hare was brought up. Ramabai instantly signaled him to smother his joy. But it was not necessary for the colonel to pretend dejection. He was so pitiably weak that he could scarcely stand and only vaguely understood that he was to follow this man Ramabai, whom he did not recognize.

Ramabai, comprehending his plight, gave him the support of his arm, and together they left the palace. So far all had gone smoothly.

The council had no suspicions. Twenty men had followed Durga Ram and without doubt they were at this moment with him.

"Free!" breathed the colonel, as Ramabai beckoned to a public litter.

"Hush! You are supposed to be my prisoner. Make no sign of jubilation." Ramabai helped the broken man into the litter and bade the coolies to hurry. "Elephants will be ready to start the moment we reach your camp. This time I believe we can get away in safety."

"And Umballa?"

"Shall go with us as hostage."

But Umballa did not go with them as hostage. On the contrary, the moment they left him alone he quickly undid his bonds. He tiptoed past the leopard which flew at him savagely, ripping the post from its socket and wrecking the banisters. Umballa, unprepared for this stroke, leaped through the window, followed by the hampered leopard. It would have gone ill with Umballa even then had not some keepers rushed for the leopard. In the ensuing confusion Umballa escaped.

"He is gone!" cried Bruce. "Ahmed, send a runner to warn Ramabai to head for my camp! Quick! Get the elephants ready! Come, Kathlyn; come, Pundita!" He hastened them toward the elephants. "Umballa made his escape east; it will take him some minutes to veer round to his men. Come!"

They waited at Bruce's camp an hour. A litter was seen

swaying to and fro, with coolies on the run. Ahmed ran forward and hailed it. A moment later Kathlyn and her father were reunited.

"In God's name, Bruce, let us get out of this damnable country; I am dying for want of light, air, food!"

They lifted the colonel into a howdah and started south, urging the elephants at top speed. No sooner had they left the river than some native boats landed at the broken camp, gleefully picking up things which had been left behind in the rush.

"Our troubles are over, father."

"Perhaps! So long as I remain in India, there is that curse. Ah, I once laughed at it; but not now."

Umballa at length found his captain.

"Follow me'" he cried in a fury.

He led them back to the colonel's camp, but those he sought had flown. He reasoned quickly. The trail led toward the camp of Bruce Sahib, and along this he led his men, arriving in time to find the native boatmen leaving for their boats.

A hurried question or two elicited the direction taken by the fugitives. Umballa commandeered the boats. There was some protest, but Umballa threatened death to those who opposed him, and the frightened natives surrendered. The soldiers piled into the boats and began poling down-stream rapidly. A mile or two below there was a ford and to go south the pursued must cross it.

Later, pursuer and pursued met, and a real warfare began,

with a death toll on both sides. Bruce and Ahmed kept the elephants going, but in the middle of the ford a bullet struck Kathlyn, and she tumbled headlong into the water.

The curse had not yet lifted its evil hand.

CHAPTER XI

THE WHITE ELEPHANT

It was the shock of the bullet rather than the seriousness of the wound that had toppled Kathlyn into the river. In the confusion, the rattle of musketry, the yelling of the panic-stricken pack coolies who had fled helter-skelter for the jungle, the squealing of the elephants, she had forgot to crouch low in the howdah. There had come a staggering blow, after which sky and earth careened for a moment and became black; then the chill of water and strangulation, and she found herself struggling in the deepest part of the ford, a strange deadness in one arm. She had no distinct recollection of what took place; her one thought was to keep her head above water.

Instantly the firing ceased; on one side because there were no more cartridges, on the other for fear of hitting the one person who had made this pursuit necessary.

Kathlyn struggled between the elephant which carried Ramabai and Pundita and the boat or barge which held the eager Umballa and his soldiers. The mahout, terrorized, had slid off and taken to his heels ingloriously. Thus, Ramabai could do nothing to aid Kathlyn. Nor could the elephant ridden by the colonel and Bruce be managed.

Umballa was quick to see his advantage, and, laughing, he urged his men toward the helpless girl. The colonel raised his rifle and aimed at Umballa, but there was no report, only a click which to the frantic man's ears sounded like the gates of hell closing in behind him.

"Forward!" shouted Umballa.

She was his again; he would have the pleasure of taking her from under the very eyes of her father and lover. His star never faltered.

Bruce stood up in the howdah, ready to dive; but the colonel restrained him.

"Don't waste your life! My God, we can't help her! Not a bullet in either gun. God's curse on all these worthless stones men call guns! . . . There, he's got her! Not a shell left! Kit! Kit! Kit!" The colonel broke down and cried like a child. As for Bruce, hot irons could not have wrung a tear from his eyes; but Kit, in the hands of that black devil again!

"Colonel," said Bruce, "I'd going to get some cartridges."

He realized then that Kathlyn's future depended upon him alone. The colonel was a broken man. So he struck the elephant, who lumbered ashore. The moment Kathlyn was safe in the barge Umballa would probably give orders to resume firing. He could do so now with impunity.

The soldiers drew Kathlyn into the barge. Umballa saw that she was wounded in the fleshy part of the arm. Quickly he snatched off the turban of one of the soldiers, unwound it and began to bandage Kathlyn's arm.

The man, for all his oriental craftiness, was still guileless enough to expect some sign of gratitude from her; but; as he touched her she shrank in loathing. His anger flamed and he flung her roughly into a seat.

"Suffer, then, little fool!"

Meantime the colonel and Bruce dismounted and tried to stem the tide of fleeing coolies; but it was no more effective than blowing against the wind. They found, however, an abandoned pack containing cartridge cases, and they filled their pockets, calling to Ramabai and Pundita to follow them along the river in pursuit of Umballa's barge, which was now being rapidly poled up-stream. They might be able to pick off enough soldiers, sharpshooting, to make it impossible to man the barge. They were both dead shots, and the least they could do would be to put the fight on a basis of equality so far as numbers were concerned.

The colonel forgot all about how weak he was. The rage and despair in his heart had once more given him a fictitious strength.

"The curse, the curse, always the curse!"

"Don't you believe that, Colonel. It is only misfortune. Now I'm going to pot Umballa. That will simplify everything. Without a head the soldiers will be without a cause, and they'll desert Kathlyn as quickly as our coolies deserted us."

"Where is Ahmed?"

"Ahmed? I had forgot all about him! But we can't wait now. He'll have to look out for himself. Hark!"

Squealing and trumpeting and thunderous crashing in

the distance.

"Wild elephants!" cried the colonel, the old impulse wheeling him round. But the younger man caught hold of his arm significantly.

The soldiers poled diligently, but against the stream, together with the clumsiness of the barge, they could not make headway with any degree of speed. It was not long before Bruce could see them. He raised his rifle and let go; and in the boat Umballa felt his turban stir mysteriously. The report which instantly followed was enough to convince him that he in particular was being made a target. He crouched behind Kathlyn, while two or three of the soldiers returned the shot, aiming at the clump of scrub from which a film of pale blue smoke issued. They waited for another shot, but none came.

The reason was this: the herd of wild elephants which Bruce and the colonel had heard came charging almost directly toward them, smashing young trees and trampling the tough underbrush. Some of them made for the water directly in line with the passing boats. Kathlyn, keenly alive to the fact that here was a chance, jumped overboard before Umballa could reach out a staying hand.

To Kathlyn there was only death in the path of the elephants; to remain on the barge was to face eventually that which was worse than death. Her arm throbbed painfully, but in the desperate energy with which she determined to take the chance she used it. Quite contrary to her expectations, her leap was the best thing she could have done. Most of the barges were upset and the great beasts were blundering across the river between her and the barges.

Bruce witnessed Kathlyn's brave attempt and dashed into

the water after her. It took him but a moment to bring her to land, where her father clasped her in his arms and broke down again.

"Dad, dad!" she whispered. "Don't you see our God is powerfulest? I believed I was going to be trampled to death, and here I am, with you once more."

They hurried back as fast as Kathlyn's weakness would permit to where they had left their own elephants, doubting that they should find them, considering that it was quite probable that they had joined their wild brethren. But no; they were standing shoulder to shoulder, flapping their ears and curling their trunks. So many years had they been trained to hunt elephants that they did not seem to know what to do without some one to guide them.

Bruce ordered one of them to kneel, doubtfully; but the big fellow obeyed the command docilely, and the colonel and Bruce helped the exhausted girl into the howdah. The colonel followed, while Bruce took upon his own shoulders the duties of mahout. Pundita got into the other howdah and Ramabai imitated Bruce. The elephants shuffled off, away from the river. For the time being neither Bruce nor Ramabai gave mind to the compass. To make pursuit impossible was the main business just then.

Later Umballa, dulled and stupefied from his immersion, stood on the shore, with but nine of the twenty soldiers he had brought with him. Evidently, his star had faltered. Very well; he would send for the other sister. She was the Colonel Sahib's daughter, and young; she would be as wax in his hands. A passion remained in Umballa's heart, but it was now the passion of revenge.

When he had recovered sufficiently he gave orders to one of the soldiers to return to the city, to bring back at once servants, elephants and all that would be required for a long pursuit. The messenger was also to make known these preparations to the council, who would undertake to forward the cable submitted to them. All these things off his mind, Umballa sat down and shivered outwardly, while he boiled within. He was implacable; he would blot out his enemy, kith and kin. Colonel Hare should never dip his fingers into the filigree basket—never while he, Durga Ram, lived.

Quite unknown, quite unsuspected by him, for all the activity of his spies, a volcano was beginning to grumble under his feet. All tyrants, the petty and the great, have heard it: the muttering of the oppressed.

Perhaps the fugitives had gone thirty miles when suddenly the jungle ended abruptly and a desert opened up before them. Beyond stood a purple line of rugged hills. Ramabai raised his hand, and the elephants came to a halt.

"I believe I know where I am," said Ramabai. "Somewhere between us and yonder hills is a walled city, belonging to Bala Khan, a Pathan who sometimes styles himself as a rajah. He has a body of fierce fighting men; and he lives unmolested for two reasons: looting would not be worth while and his position is isolated and almost impregnable. Now, if I am right, we shall find shelter there, for he was an old friend of my father's and I might call him a friend of mine, since I sell sheep for him occasionally."

"Bala Khan?" mused Bruce, reminiscently. "Isn't he the chap who has a sacred white elephant?"

"It is the same," answered Ramabai. "We can reach there before sundown. It would be wise to hasten, however, as this desert and those hills are infested with lawless nomadic bands of masterless men—brigands, you call them. They would cut the throat of a man for the sake of his clothes."

"Let us go on," said the colonel. "I don't care where. I am dead for want of food and sleep."

"And I, too," confessed Kathlyn; "My arm pains me badly."

"My poor Kit!" murmured her father gloomily. "And all this because I told you half a truth, because in play I tried to make a mystery out of a few plain facts. I should have told you everything, warned you against following in case I failed to turn up."

"I should have followed you just the same."

"Shall I rebind the arm?" asked Bruce, turning.

"No, thanks." She smiled down at him. "This bandage will serve till we reach Bala Khan's."

"By the way, Colonel, is there a pair of binoculars in the howdah?"

"Yes. Do you want them?"

"No. Just to be sure they were there. We may have occasion to use them later, in case this place Ramabai is taking us to should turn out hostile. I like to know what is going on ahead of me."

"Poor Kit!" reiterated the colonel.

"Never mind, dad; you meant it all for the best; and you must not let our present misfortunes convince you that

that yogi or guru cast a spell of evil over you. That is all nonsense."

"My child, this is the Orient, Asia. Things happen here that are outside the pale of logic. Bruce, am I not right?"

"I have seen many unbelievable things here in India," replied Bruce reluctantly. "Think of yesterday and to-day, Miss Kathlyn."

"Yes; but the curse of a priest who believes in different gods, who kotows before a painted idol! I just simply can't believe anything so foolish. Dad, put the thought out of your mind for my sake. So long as we have the will to try we'll see California again before many weeks."

"Do you feel like that?" curiously.

"In my soul, dad, in my soul." She stared dreamily toward the empurpling hills. "I can't explain, but that's the way I feel. Some day we shall be free again, reenter the life we have known and all this will resolve itself into an idle dream. Ahmed has said it."

"No, he is alive somewhere back there."

Bruce turned to look at her again, but Kathlyn was still gazing at the hills without seeing them.

"A white elephant," mused the colonel. "Do you know it for a fact that this Bala Khan has a white elephant?" he called across to Ramabai.

"I have never seen it Sahib. It is what they say."

"A pair of mottled ears is the nearest I ever came to seeing a white elephant, and I've hunted them for thirty years, here, in Ceylon, in Burma, in Africa. There was once a tiger near Madras that hadn't any stripes. The natives would not permit him to be killed because they held that, being unique, he was sacred. A sacred white elephant! Poor simple-minded fools!" The colonel felt in his pockets, then dropped his hands dispiritedly. How long since he had tasted tobacco? "Bruce, have you got a cheroot in your pocket? I think a smoke would brace me up."

Bruce laughed and passed up a broken cigar, which the colonel lighted carefully. The weariness seemed to go out of his face magically.

"This Bala Khan should be Mohammedan," said Bruce. "The Pathan despises the Hindu."

"There are Hindus in yonder city; quite as many," said Ramabai, "as there are Mohammedans. Even the Pathan expects that which he can not understand."

"Isn't that the wall behind that sand-hill? Let me have the glasses a moment. Colonel. . . . H'm! The walled city, all right. Some people moving about outside. Dancers, I should say."

"Professional," explained Ramabai.

"Nothing religious, then? By George!"

"What is it?" asked the colonel.

"Take a look. There's an elephant being led into the city gates."

The colonel peered eagerly through the glasses.

"The sun is shining on him. . . . No! he is . . . white! A white elephant! I'd give ten thousand this minute to own it. There, it's entered the gate. Well, well, well! And I've lived to see it! Poor old Barnum, to have carried around a tinted pachyderm! He's white as any elephant flesh could be. Those dancing chaps are going in, too. What caste would those dancers be, Ramabai?"

"Pariahs, quite possibly; probably brigands."

The rim of the sun was sinking rapidly as Bruce drew his elephant to a halt before the gate of the white walled city. The guard ran out, barring the way.

"I am Ramabai, a friend of Bala Khan. I am come to pay him a visit. Direct me to his house or his palace."

The authority in Ramabai's voice was sufficient for the guard, who gave the necessary directions. The party continued on into town. It was an odd place for a walled city. There wasn't a tree about, not a sign of boscage, except some miles away where the hills began to slope upward. Bruce wondered what the inhabitants fed upon. It was more like an Egyptian village than anything he had ever seen in India. Bruce asked for his rifle, which he laid carelessly in the crook of his arm. One never could tell.

Presently they came upon a group in the center of which were the dancers at their vocations. They ceased their mad whirlings at the sight of the two elephants. There were nine of these men, fierce of eye and built muscularly. No effeminate Hindus here, mused Bruce, who did not like the looks of them at all. The surrounding natives stared with variant emotions. Many of them had never seen a white man before. Their gaze centered upon the colonel. Kathlyn was almost as dark as Pundita, and as for Bruce, only his European dress distinguished him from Ramabai, for there was scarcely a shade difference in color. But the colonel, having been weeks in prison, was as pale as alabaster and his hair shone like threads of silver.

On through the narrow streets, sometimes the sides of the elephants scraping against the mud and plaster of the buildings, and one could easily look into the second stories. No one seemed hostile; only a natural curiosity was evinced by those standing in doorways or leaning out of windows.

The house of Bala Khan was not exactly a palace, but it was of respectable size. A high wall surrounded the compound. There was a gateway, open at this moment. A servant ran out and loudly demanded what was wanted.

"Say to your master, Bala Khan, that Ramabai, son of Maaho Singh, his old friend, awaits with friendly greetings."

"Kit," whispered Kathlyn's father, "this chap Ramabai wouldn't make a bad king. And look!" excitedly. "There's the sacred elephant, and if he isn't white, I'll eat my hat!"

Kathlyn sighed gratefully. That her father could be interested in anything was a good sign for the future. A few days' rest and wholesome food would put him half-way on his legs. Her own vitality was an inheritance from her father. The male line of the family was well known for its recuperative powers.

The servant ran back into the compound and spoke to a dignified man, who proved to be a high caste Brahmin, having in his charge the care of the white elephant. He disappeared and returned soon with the Khan. The pleasant face, though proudly molded, together with the simplicity of his appearance, conveyed to Kathlyn the fact that here was a man to be trusted, at least for the present. He greeted Ramabai cordially, struck his hands and ordered out the servants to take charge of what luggage there was and to lead away the elephants to be fed and watered.

Courteously he asked Kathlyn how she had become injured and Ramabai acted as interpreter. He then ushered them into his house, spread rugs and cushions for them to sit upon and mildly inquired what had brought the son of his old friend so far.

Colonel Hare spoke several dialects fluently and briefly told (between sips of tea and bites of cakes which had been set out for the guests) his experiences in Allaha.

"The rulers of Allaha," observed Bala Khan, "have always been half mad."

Ramabai nodded in agreement.

"You should never have gone back," went on Bala Khan, lighting a cigarette and eying Kathlyn with wonder and interest. "Ah, that Durga Ram whom they call Umballa! I have heard of him, but fortunately for him our paths have not crossed in any way." He blew a cloud of smoke above his head. "Well, he has shown wisdom in avoiding me. In front of me, a desert; behind me, verdant hills and many sheep and cattle, well guarded. I am too far away for them to bother. Sometimes the desert thieves cause a flurry, but that is nothing. It keeps the tulwar from growing rusty," patting the great knife at his side.

Bala Khan was muscular; his lean hands denoted work; his clear eyes, the sun and the wind. He was in height and building something after the pattern of the colonel.

"And to force a crown on me!" said the colonel.

"You could have given it to this Umballa."

"That I would not do."

"In each case you showed forethought. The Durga Ram, when he had you where he wanted you—" Bala Khan drew a finger suggestively across his throat. "Ramabai, son of my friend, I will have many sheep for you this autumn. What is it to me whether you Hindus eat beef or not?" He laughed.

"I am not a Hindu in that sense," returned Ramabai. "I have but one God."

"And Mahomet is His prophet," said the host piously.

"Perhaps. I am a Christian."

Bruce stirred uneasily, but his alarm was without foundation.

"A Christian," mused Bala Khan. "Ah, well; have no fear of me. There is no Mahdi in these hills. There is but one road to Paradise and argument does not help us on the way."

Lowly and quickly Pundita translated for Kathlyn so that she might miss none of the conversation.

"The Colonel Sahib looks worn."

"I am."

"Now, in my travels I have been to Bombay, and there I dressed like you white people. I have the complete.

Perhaps the Colonel Sahib would be pleased to see if he can wear it? And also the use of my barber?"

"Bala Khan," cried the colonel, "you are a prince indeed! It will tonic me like medicine. Thanks, thanks!"

"It is well."

"You have a wonderful elephant out there in the compound," said Bruce, who had remained a silent listener to all that had gone before.

"Ah! That is a curiosity. He is worshiped by Hindus and reverenced by my own people. I am his official custodian. There is a saying among the people that ill will befall me should I lose, sell, or permit him to be stolen."

"And many have offered to buy?" inquired the colonel.

"Many."

When the colonel appeared at supper, simple but substantial, he was a new man. He stood up straight, though his back still smarted from the lash. Kathlyn was delighted at the change.

After the meal was over and coffee was drunk, the Khan conducted his guests to his armory, of which he was very proud. Guns of all descriptions lined the walls. Some of them Bruce would have liked to own, to decorate the walls of his own armory, thousands of miles away.

The colonel whispered a forgotten prayer as, later, he laid down his weary aching limbs upon the rope bed. Almost immediately he sank into slumber as deep and silent as the sea.

Kathlyn and Bruce, however, went up to the hanging gardens and remained there till nine, marveling over the beauty of the night. The Pathan city lay under their gaze with a likeness to one of those magic cities one reads about in the chronicles of Sindbad the Sailor. But they spoke no word of love. When alone with this remarkable young woman, Bruce found himself invariably tongue-tied.

At the same hour, less than fifty miles away, Umballa stood before the opening of his elaborate tent, erected at sundown by the river's brink, and scowled at the moon. He saw no beauty in the translucent sky, in the silvery paleness of the world below. He wanted revenge, and the word hissed in his brain as a viper hisses in the dark of its cave.

Dung fires twinkled and soldiers lounged about them, smoking and gossiping. They had been given an earnest against their long delinquent wages; and they were in a happy frame of mind. Their dead comrades were dead and mourning was for widows; but for them would be the pleasures of swift reprisals. The fugitives had gone toward the desert, and in that bleak stretch of treeless land it would not be difficult to find them, once they started in pursuit.

Midnight.

In the compound the moonlight lay upon everything; upon the fat sides and back of the sacred white elephant, upon the three low caste keepers, now free of the vigilant eye of their Brahmin chief. The gates were barred and closed; all inside the house of Bala Khan were asleep. Far away a sentry dozed on his rifle, on the wall. The three keepers whispered and chuckled among themselves.

"Who will know?" said one.

"The moon will not speak," said another.

"Then, let us go and smoke."

The three approached the elephant. A bit of gymnastics and one of them was boosted to the back of the elephant to whom this episode was more or less familiar. Another followed; the third was pulled up, and from the elephant's back they made the top of the wall and disappeared down into the street. Here they paused cautiously, for two guards always patrolled the front of the compound during the night. Presently the three truants stole away toward the bazaars which in this desert town occupied but a single street. Down they went into a cellar way and the guru's curse stalked beside them. For opium is the handmaiden of all curses.

Perhaps twenty minutes later slight sounds came from the front of the compound wall. A rifle barrel clattered upon the cobbles. Then, over the wall, near the elephant, a head appeared, then a body. This was repeated four times, and four light-footed nomads of the desert lowered themselves into the compound. They ran quickly to the gate and noiselessly unbarred it. Outside were five more desert nomads, gathered about the insensible bodies of the sentries.

These nine men were the dancers who had entered the town in advance of Kathlyn. For weeks they had lain in wait for this moment. They had spied upon the three low caste keepers and upon learning of their nocturnal junkets into the opium den had cast the die this night.

With the utmost caution they approached the sacred elephant, took off his chains and led him from the compound. Immediately six of the marauders trotted far ahead toward the gate they knew to be the least guarded. The sacred elephant, passing through the streets, attended by three men, aroused no suspicions in any straggler who saw. So remote was the walled city, so seemingly impregnable, and so little interfered with that it was only human that its guardians should eventually grow careless.

When the keepers, straggling under the fumes of the drug, returned near daybreak, first to find the gate open, second to find their sacred charge gone, they fled in terror; for it would be death, lingering and painful, for them to stay and explain how and why they had left their post.

The wild and lawless brigands knew exactly what they were about. There were several agents of European and American circuses after this white elephant, and as it could not be purchased there was no reason why it could not be stolen.

When the Brahmin arrived at sunrise to find his vocation gone he set up a wailing which awakened the household. The Khan was furious and ordered a general search. He vowed death to the foul hands which had done this sacrilege!

Kathlyn and the others were genuinely sorry when they heard the news. They were in the armory when the Khan announced what had taken place.

Said he: "Come, you are all skilled hunters. Find me my elephant and these guns and newer and surer ones shall protect you from Durga Ram, should he take it into his head to come this way."

The colonel, Bruce and Ramabai set off at once. After they had gone a camel rider entered the compound and sought audience with Bala Khan. Kathlyn and Pundita were in the compound at the time and the former was greatly interested in the saddlebags, attached to one of which was a binocular case. Kathlyn could not resist the inclination to open this case. It contained an exceptionally fine pair of glasses, such as were used in that day in the British army. No doubt they were a part of some loot.

Suddenly an idea came to her. She asked permission (through Pundita) to ride the camel outside the town. After some argument the servant in charge consented.

Upon a knoll outside the city—a hillock of sand three or four hundred feet in height—Kathlyn tried the glasses. From this promontory she had a range of something like fifteen to twenty miles. Back and forth her gaze roved and suddenly paused.

CHAPTER XII

THE PLAN OF RAMABAI

When Kathlyn returned to the compound it was with the news that she had discovered a group of men, some twelve or fifteen miles to the west. They had paused at what appeared to be a well, and with them was the sacred white elephant. Bala Khan was for giving orders at once to set out with his racing camels to catch and crucify every mother's son of them on the city walls. But Ramabai interposed.

"As I came toward the compound I was given a message. The man who gave it to me was gone before I could get a good look at his face. These men who stole the sacred white elephant are brave and desperate. At the first sign of pursuit they promise to kill the elephant."

"And by the beard of the prophet," cried Bala Khan, his face purpling with passion, "these men of the desert keep their promises. And so do I. I promise later to nail each one of them to the walls to die hanging to nails!"

"But just now," said Ramabai quietly, "the main thing is to rescue the elephant, and I have a plan."

"Let me hear it."

"From what you told me last night," went on Ramabai, "those nomads or brigands are opium fiends."

Bala Khan nodded.

"Bruce Sahib, here, and I will undertake to carry them doctored opium. I know something about the drug. I believe that we saw the thieves last evening as we came through the streets. My plan is this: we will take five racing camels, go north and turn, making the well from the west. That will not look like pursuit."

"But five camels?" Bala Khan was curious.

"Yes. In order to allay the suspicions of the brigands, Kathlyn Mem-sahib and my wife must accompany us."

The colonel objected, but Kathlyn overruled his objections.

"But, Kit, they will recognize us. They will not have forgot me. They will know that we have come from the town, despite the fact that to all appearances we come from the West."

Bruce also shook his head. "It doesn't look good, Ramabai. Why not we three men?"

"They would be suspicious at once. They would reason, if they saw Kathlyn Mem-sahib and my wife with us that we were harmless. Will you trust me?"

"Anywhere," said the colonel. "But they will simply make us prisoners along with the elephant."

"Ah, but the Colonel Sahib forgets the opium." Ramabai laid his hand upon the colonel's arm. "Let them make prisoners of us. The very first thing they will do will be to search the saddle-bags. They will find the opium. In a quarter of an hour they will be as dead and we can return."

"It is a good plan," said Bala Khan, when the conversation was fully translated to him. "And once the elephant is back in the compound I'll send a dozen men back for the rogues. Ah! they will play with me; they will steal into my town, overcome my guards, take the apple of my eye! Ramabai, thou art a friend indeed. Haste and Allah fend for thee! Umballa may arrive with an army, but he shall not enter my gates."

Guided by a servant, Bruce and Ramabai set off for the opium den. The proprietor understood exactly what they desired. There were times when men entered his place who were in need of a long sleep, having money tucked away in their fantastic cummerbunds.

So, mounted upon five swift camels, the party started off on a wide circle. Whether they caught the brigands at the well or on the way to their mountain homes was of no great importance. Ramabai was quite certain that the result would be the same. The colonel grumbled a good deal. Supposing the rascals did not smoke; what then?

"They will smoke," declared Ramabai confidently. "The old rascal of whom we bought the opium has entertained them more than once. They are too poor to own pipes. Have patience, Colonel Sahib. A good deal depends upon the success of our adventure this morning. If I know anything about Umballa, he will shortly be on the march. Bala Khan has given his word."

Had it not been for liberal use of opium the night before, the brigands would not have tarried so long at the well;

but they were terribly thirsty, a bit nerve shattered and craved for the drug. The chief alone had fully recovered. He cursed and raved at his men, kicked and beat them. What! After all these weeks of waiting, to let sleep stand between them and thousands of rupees! Dogs! Pigs! Did they not recollect that Bala Khan had a way of nailing thieves outside the walls of his city? Well, he for one would not wait. He would mount the sacred white elephant and head toward the caves in the hills. Let them who would decorate the walls of Bala Khan. The threat of Bala Khan put life into the eight followers, and they were getting ready to move on, when one of them discovered a small caravan approaching from the west.

Camels? Ha! Here was a chance of leaving Bala Khan's city far in the rear. And there would be loot besides. Those helmets were never worn by any save white men. The chief scowled under his shading palm. Women! Oh, this was going to be something worth while.

When the caravan came within hailing distance the chief of the brigands stepped forward menacingly. The new arrivals were informed that they were prisoners, and were bidden to dismount at once.

"But we are on the way to the city of Bala Khan," remonstrated Ramabai.

"Which you left this morning!" jeered the chief.

"Dismount!"

"But I am selling opium there!"

"Opium!"

"Where is it? Give it to us!" cried one of the brigands.

The chief thought quickly. If his men would smoke they should suffer the penalty of being left at the well to await the arrival of the tender Bala Khan. The white elephant was worth ten thousand rupees. He might not be obliged to share these bags of silver. His men could not complain. They had discharged him. Let them have the pipes. He himself would only pretend to smoke.

But the first whiff of the fumes was too much for his will power. He sucked in the smoke, down to the bottom of his very soul, and suddenly found peace. The superdrug with which the poppy had been mixed was unknown to Ramabai, but he had often witnessed tests of its potency. It worked with the rapidity of viper venom. Within ten minutes after the first inhalation the nine brigands sank back upon the sand, as nearly dead as any man might care to be.

At once the elephant was liberated, and the party made off toward the town. Colonel Hare, suspicious of everything these days, marveled over the simplicity of the trick and the smoothness with which it had been turned. He began to have hope for the future. Perhaps this time they were really going to escape from this land accursed.

There was great powwowing and salaaming at the gate as the sacred white elephant loomed into sight. The old Brahmin who had charge of him wept for joy. He was still a personage, respected, salaamed to, despite the preponderance of Mohammedans. His sacred elephant!

Bala Khan was joyous. Here was the sacred elephant once more in the compound, and not a piece out of his treasure chest. He was in luck. In the midst of his self-congratulations came the alarming news that a large body of men were seen approaching across the desert from the direction of Allaha. Bala Khan, his chiefs and his guests climbed to the top of the wall and beheld the spectacle in truth. It required but a single look through the binoculars to discover to whom this host belonged.

"Umballa!" said Ramabai,

"Ah! Durga Ram, to pay his respects." Bala Khan rubbed his hands together. It had been many moons since he had met a tulwar.

The colonel examined his revolver coldly. The moment that Umballa came within range the colonel intended to shoot. This matter was going to be settled definitely, here and now. So long as Umballa lived, a dread menace hung above Kathlyn's head. So, then, Umballa must die.

Bala Khan was for beginning the warfare at once, but Bruce argued him out of this idea. Let them first learn what Umballa intended to do. There was no need of shedding blood needlessly.

"You white people must always talk," grumbled the Khan, who was a fighting man, born of a race of fighters yet to bow the head to the yoke. "It is better to kill and talk afterward. I have given my word to protect you, and the word of Bala Khan is as sound as British gold."

"For that," said Bruce, "thanks."

"Keep your men from the walls," cried Kathlyn, "and bring me the white elephant. I would deal with this man Umballa."

Her request was granted. So when Durga Ram and has soldiers arrived before the closed gates they beheld Kathlyn mounted on the white elephant alone.

"What wish you here, Durga Ram?" she called down to the man on the richly caparisoned war elephant.

"You! Your father and those who have helped you to escape."

"Indeed! Well, then, come and take us."

"I would speak with Bala Khan," imperiously.

"You will deal with me alone," declared Kathlyn.

Umballa reached for his rifle, but a loud murmur from the men stayed his impulse.

"It is the sacred white elephant, Highness. None dare fire at that," his captain warned him. "Those with him or upon him are in sanctity."

"Tell Bala Khan," said Umballa, controlling his rage as best he could, "tell Bala Khan that I would be his friend, not his enemy."

"Bala Khan," boomed a voice from the other side of the wall, "cares not for your friendship. Whatever the Mem-sahib says is my word. What! Does Allaha want war for the sake of gratifying Durga Ram's spite? Begone, and thank your evil gods that I am not already at your lying treacherous throat. Take yourself off, Durga Ram. The people of Bala Khan do not make war on women and old men. The Mem-sahib and her friends are under my protection."

"I will buy them!" shouted Umballa, recollecting the greed of Bala Khan.

"My word is not for sale!" came back.

Kathlyn understood by the expression on Umballa's countenance what was taking place. She smiled down at her enemy.

"So be it, Bala Khan," snarled Umballa, his rage no longer on the rein. "In one month's time I shall return, and of your city there will not be one stone upon another when I leave it!"

"One month!" Ramabai laughed.

"Why are you always smiling, Ramabai?" asked Bruce.

"I have had a dream, Sahib," answered Ramabai, still smiling. "Umballa will not return here."

"You could tell me more than that."

"I could, but will not," the smile giving way to sternness.

"If only I knew what had become of Ahmed," said the colonel, when the last of Umballa's soldiers disappeared whence they had come, "I should feel content."

"We shall find him, or he will find us, if he is alive," said Kathlyn. "Now let us make ready for the last journey. One hundred miles to the west is the Arabian gulf. It is a caravan port, and there will be sailing vessels and steamships." She shook him by the shoulders joyously. "Dad, we are going home, home!"

"Kit, I want to see Winnie!"

The word sent a twinge of pain through Bruce's heart. Home! Would he ever have a real one? Was she to go out of his life at last? Kathlyn Hare.

"But you, Ramabai?" said Kathlyn.

"I shall return to Allaha, I and Pundita," replied Ramabai.

"It will be death!" objected Bruce and Kathlyn together.

"I think not," and Ramabai permitted one of his mysterious smiles to stir his lips.

"Ramabai!" whispered Pundita fearfully.

"Yes. After all, why should we wait?"

"I?"

"Even so!"

"What is all this about?" inquired Kathlyn.

"Allaha is weary of Umballa's iron heel, weary of a vacillating council. And the time has arrived when the two must be abolished. A thousand men await the turn of my hand. And who has a better right to the throne of Allaha than Pundita, my wife?"

"Good!" cried Kathlyn, her eyes sparkling. "Good! And if we can help you—"

"Kit," interposed the colonel, "we can give Ramabai and Pundita only our good wishes. Our way lies to the west, to the seaport and home."

Ramabai bowed.

And the party returned to the compound rather subdued. This quiet young native banker would go far.

"And if I am ever queen, will my beautiful Mem-sahib come back some day and visit me?"

"That I promise, Pundita, though I have no love for Allaha."

"We will go with you to the coast," said Ramabai, "and on our return to Allaha will see what has become of the faithful Ahmed."

"For that my thanks," responded the colonel. "Ahmed has been with me for many years, and has shared with me many hardships. If he lives, he will be a marked man, so far as Umballa is concerned. Aid him to come to me. The loss of my camp and bungalow is nothing. The fact that we are all alive to-day is enough for me. But you, Bruce; will it hit you hard?"

Bruce laughed easily. "I am young. Besides, it was a pastime for me, though I went at it in a business way."

"I am glad of that. There is nothing to regret in leaving this part of the world." Yet the colonel sighed.

And Kathlyn heard that sigh, and intuitively understood. The filigree basket of gems. Of such were the minds of men.

But the colonel was taken ill that night, and it was a week before he left his bed, and another before he was considered strong enough to attempt the journey. Bala Khan proved to be a fine host, for he loved men of deeds, and this white-haired old man was one of the right kidney. He must be strong ere he took the long journey over the hot sands to the sea.

A spy of Umballa's watched and waited to carry the news

to his master, the day his master's enemies departed from the haven of Bala Khan's walled city.

When the day came the Khan insisted that his guests should use his own camels and servants, and upon Ramabai's return the elephants would be turned over to him for his journey back to Allaha. Thus, one bright morning, the caravan set forth for what was believed to be the last journey.

And Umballa's spy hastened away.

All day long they wound in and out, over and down the rolling mounds of sand, pausing only once, somewhere near four o'clock, when they dismounted for a space to enjoy a bite to eat and a cup of tea. Then on again, through the night, making about sixty miles in all. At dawn they came upon a well, and here they decided to rest till sunset. Beyond the well, some twenty-five miles, lay the low mountain range over which they must pass to the sea. At the foot of these hills stood a small village, which they reached about ten o'clock that night.

They found the village wide awake. The pariah dogs were howling. And on making inquiries it was learned that a tiger had been prowling about for three or four nights, and that they had set a trap cage for the brute. The colonel and Bruce at once assumed charge. The old zest returned with all its vigor and allurement. Even Kathlyn and Pundita decided to join the expedition, though Pundita knew nothing of arms.

Now, this village was the home of the nine brigands, and whenever they were about they dominated the villagers. They were returning from a foraging expedition into the hills, and discovered the trap cage with the tiger inside. Very good. The tiger was no use to any but themselves, since they knew where to sell it. They were in the act of pulling the brush away from the cage when they heard sounds of others approaching. With the suspicion which was a part of their business they immediately ran to cover to see who it was.

Instantly the chief of the brigands discovered that these new arrivals were none other than the white people who had given him and his men a superdrug and thereby mulcted them out of the sacred white elephant which was to have brought them a fortune.

Unfortunately, the men of Kathlyn's party laid aside their weapons on approaching the cage to tear away the brush. Eight brigands, at a sign from their chief, surrounded the investigators, who found themselves nicely caught.

The natives fled incontinently. So did Bala Khan's camel men.

"Death if you move!" snarled the chief. "Ah, you gave us bad opium, and we dropped like logs! Swine!" He raised his rifle threateningly.

"Wait a minute," said Bruce coolly. "What you want is money."

"Ay, money! Ten thousand rupees!"

"It shall be given you if you let us go. You will conduct us over the hills to the sea, and there the money will be given you."

The chief laughed long and loudly. "What! Am I a goat to put my head inside the tiger's jaws? Nay, I shall hold you here for ransom. Let them bring gold. Now, take hold," indicating the trap cage. "We shall take this fine man eater along with us. I am speaking to you, white men, and you, pig of a Hindu! Chalu! I will kill any one who falters. Opium! Ah, yes! You shall pay for my headache and the sickness of my comrades. Chalu! And your white woman; she shall give a ransom of her own!"

The village jutted out into the desert after the fashion of a peninsula. On the west of it lay another stretch of sand. They followed the verdure till they reached the base of the rocky hills, which were barren of any vegetation; huge jumbles of granite the color of porphyry. During the night they made about ten miles, and at dawn were smothered by one of those raging sand-storms, prevalent in this latitude. They had to abandon the trap cage and seek shelter in a near-by cave. Here they remained huddled together till the storm died away.

"It has blown itself out," commented the chief. Then he spoke to Ramabai. "Who is this man?" with a nod toward the colonel.

"He is an American."

"He came for Allaha?"

"Yes," said Ramabai unsuspiciously.

"Ha! Then that great prince did not lie."

"What prince?" cried Ramabai, now alarmed.

"The Prince Durga Ram. Three fat bags of silver, he said, would he pay me for the white hunter with the white hair. It is the will of Allah!"

The colonel's head sank upon his knees. Kathlyn patted his shoulder.

"Father, I tell you mind not the mouthings of a vile guru. We shall soon be free."

"Kit, this time, if I return to Allaha, I shall die. I feel it in my bones."

"And I say no!"

The chief turned to Ramabai. "You and the woman with you shall this day seek two camels of the five you borrowed from Bala Khan. You will journey at once to Allaha. But do not waste your time in stopping to acquaint Bala Khan. At the first sign of armed men each of those left shall die in yonder tiger cage."

"We refuse!"

"Then be the first to taste the tiger's fangs!"

The chief called to his men to seize Ramabai and Pundita, when Kathlyn interfered.

"Go, Ramabai; it is useless to fight against these men who mean all they say, and who are as cruel as the tiger himself."

"It shall be as the Mem-sahib says," replied Ramabai resignedly.

* * * * * *

One morning Umballa entered the judgment hall of the palace, disturbed in mind. Anonymous notes, bidding him not to persecute Ramabai and his wife further, on pain of death. He had found these notes at the door of his zenana, in his stables, on his pillows. In his heart he had sworn the death of Ramabai; but here was a phase upon which he had set no calculation. Had there not been unrest abroad he would have scorned to pay any attention to these warnings; but this Ramabai—may he burn in hell!—was a power with the populace, with low and high castes alike, and for the first time, now that he gave the matter careful thought, his own future did not look particularly clear. More than ever he must plan with circumspection. He must trap Ramabai, openly, lawfully, in the matter of sedition.

Imagine his astonishment when, a few minutes after his arrival, Ramabai and Pundita demanded audience, the one straight of back and proud of look, the other serene and tranquil! Umballa felt a wave of bland [Transcriber's note: blind?] hatred surge over him, but he gave no sign. Ramabai stated his case briefly. Colonel Hare and his daughter were being held prisoners for ransom. Three bags of silver—something like five thousand rupees— were demanded by the captors.

The council looked toward Umballa, who nodded, having in mind the part of the good Samaritan, with reservations, to be sure. Having trod the paths of the white man, he had acquired a certain adroitness in holding his people. They had at best only the stability of chickens. What at one moment was a terror was at another a feast. For the present, then, he would pretend that he had forgot all about Ramabai's part in the various unsuccessful episodes.

To the council and the gurus (or priests) he declared that he himself would undertake to assume the part of envoy; he himself would bring the legal king of Allaha back to his throne. True, the daughter had been crowned, but she had forfeited her rights. Thus he would return with Colonel Hare as soon as he could make the journey and return.

"He is contemplating some treachery," said Ramabai to his wife. "I must try to learn what it is."

In his shop in the bazaars Lal Singh had resumed his awl. He had, as a companion, a bent and shaky old man, whose voice, however, possessed a resonance which belied the wrinkles and palsied hands.

"The rains," said Lal Singh, "are very late this year. Leather will be poor."

"Aye."

All of which signified to Ahmed that the British Raj had too many affairs just then to give proper attention to the muddle in Allaha.

"But there is this man Ramabai. He runs deep."

"So!"

"He has been conspiring for months."

"Then why does he not strike?"

"He is wary. He is wary; a good sign." Lal Singh reached for his pipe and set the water bubbling. "In a few weeks I believe all will be ready, even the British Raj."

"Why will men be sheep?"

Lal Singh shrugged. "Only Allah knows. But what about this guru's curse you say follows the Colonel Sahib?"

"It is true. I was there," said Ahmed. "And here am I, with a price on my head!"

"In the business we are in there will always be a price on our heads. And Umballa will bring back the Colonel Sahib. What then?"

"We know what we know, Lal Singh," and the face under the hood broke into a smile.

Five days passed. The chief of the brigands was growing restless. He finally declared that unless the ransom was delivered that night he would rid himself of them all. The tiger was starving. In order to prove that he was not chattering idly he had the prisoners tied to the wheels of the cage. It would at least amuse him to watch their growing terror.

"Look! Some one is coming!" cried Kathlyn.

The chief saw the caravan at the same time, and he set up a shout of pleasure. Three fat bags of silver rupees!

Umballa, the good Samaritan, bargained with the chief. He did not want all the prisoners, only one. Three bags of silver would be forthcoming upon the promise that the young woman and the young man should be disposed of.

"By the tiger?"

Umballa shrugged. To him it mattered not how. The chief, weary of his vigil, agreed readily enough, and Umballa turned over the silver.

"The guru, my Kit! You see? This is the end. Well, I am tired. A filigree basket of gems!"

"So!" said Umballa, smiling at Kathlyn. "You and your lover shall indeed be wed—by the striped one! A sad tale I shall take back with me. You were both dead when

I arrived."

Presently Bruce and Kathlyn were alone. They could hear the brute in the cage, snarling and clawing at the wooden door.

CHAPTER XIII

LOVE

The golden sands, the purple cliffs, the translucent blue of the heavens, and the group of picturesque rascals jabbering and gesticulating and pressing about their chief, made a picture Kathlyn was never to forget.

"Patience, my little ones!" said the chief, showing his white strong teeth in what was more of a snarl than a smile. "There is plenty of time."

Bruce leaned toward Kathlyn.

"Stand perfectly still, just as you are. I believe I can reach the knot back of your hands. This squabbling is the very thing needed. They will not pay any attention to us for a few minutes, and if I can read signs they'll all be at one another's throats shortly."

"But even if we get free what can we do?"

Kathlyn was beginning to lose both faith and heart. The sight of her father being led back to Allaha by Durga Ram, after all the misery to which he had been subjected, shook the courage which had held her up these long happy weeks. For she realized that her father was still weak, and that any additional suffering would kill him.

"You mustn't talk like that," said Bruce. "You've been in tighter places than this. If we can get free, leave the rest to me. So long as one can see and hear and move, there's hope."

"I'm becoming a coward. Do what you can. I promise to obey you in all things."

Bruce bent as far as he could, and went desperately to work at the knot with his teeth. Success or failure did not really matter; simply, he did not propose to die without making a mighty struggle to avoid death. The first knot became loose, then another. Kathlyn stirred her hands cautiously.

"Now!" he whispered.

She twisted her hands two or three times and found them free.

"Mine, now!" said Bruce. "Hurry!"

It was a simple matter for her to release Bruce.

"God bless those rupees!" he murmured. "There'll be a fine row in a minute. Keep perfectly still, and when the moment comes follow me into the cave. They have left their guns in there."

"You are a brave and ready man, Mr. Bruce."

"You called me John once."

"Well, then, John," a ghost of a smile flitting across her lips. Men were not generally sentimental in the face of death.

"There are nine of us!" screamed one of the brigands.

"And I claim one bag because without my help and brains you would have had nothing," roared the chief. "Who warned you against the opium? Ha, pig!"

The first blow was struck. Instantly the chief drew his knife and lunged at the two nearest him.

"Treachery!"

"Ha! Pigs! Dogs! Come, I'll show you who is master!"

"Thief!"

The remaining brigands closed in upon their leader and bore him upon his back.

"To the tiger with him!"

"Now!" cried Bruce.

He flung the rope from his hands, caught Kathlyn by the arm, and running and stumbling, they gained the cave, either ignored or unobserved by the victorious brigands.

They dragged the stunned leader to his feet and haled him to the cage, lashing him to a wheel. Next, they seized the rope which operated the door and retired to the mouth of the cave.

"Rob us, would he!"

"Take the lion's share when we did all the work!"

"Swine!"

"I will give it all to you!" whined the whilom chief, mad with terror.

"And knife us in the back when we sleep! No, no! You have kicked and cuffed us for the last time!"

Bruce picked up one of the rifles and drew Kathlyn farther into the cave.

"Get behind me and crouch low. They'll come around to us presently."

The rascals gave the rope a savage pull, and from where he stood Bruce could see the lean striped body of the furious tiger leap to freedom.

"Keep your eyes shut. It will not be a pleasant thing to look at," he warned the girl.

But Kathlyn could not have closed her eyes if she had tried. She saw the brute pause, turn and strike at the helpless man at the wheel, then lope off, doubtless having in mind to test his freedom before he fed. The remaining brigands rushed out and gathered up the bags of rupees.

This was the opportunity for which Bruce had waited.

"Come. There may be some outlet to this cave. Here is another rifle. Let us cut for it! When thieves fall out; you know the old saying."

They ran back several yards and discovered a kind of chasm leading diagonally upward.

"Thank God! We can get out of this after all. Are you

Harold MacGrath

strong enough for a stiff climb?"

"I've got to be—John!"

"Trust me, Kathlyn," he replied simply. He had but one life, but he determined then and there to make it equal or outlast the six lives which stood between him and liberty.

The brigands, having succeeded in their mutiny, bethought themselves of their prisoners, only to find that they had vanished. Familiar with the cave and its outlet, they started eagerly in pursuit. They reasoned that if an old man was worth three bags of rupees, two young people might naturally be worth twice as much. And besides, being tigers, they had tasted blood.

A shout caused Bruce to turn. Instantly he raised his rifle, and pulled the trigger. The result was merely a snap. The gun had not been loaded. He snatched Kathlyn's rifle, but this, too, was useless. The brigands yelled exultantly and began to swarm up the ragged cliff. Bruce flung aside the gun and turned his attention to a boulder. Halfway up the chasm had a width which was little broader than the shoulders of an ordinary man. He waited till he saw the wretches within a yard or so of this spot, then pushed this boulder. It roared and crashed and bounded, and before it reached the narrow pathway Bruce had started a mate to it. Then a third followed. This caused a terrific slide of rocks and boulders, and the brigands turned for their lives.

"That will be about all for the present," said Bruce, wiping his forehead. "Now if we can make that village we shall be all right. Bala Khan's men will not leave with the camels till they learn whether we are dead or alive. It will be a hard trek, Miss Kathlyn. Ten miles over sand is worse than fifty over turf. I don't think we'll see any more of those ruffians."

"Kathlyn," she said.

"Well—Kathlyn!"

"Or, better still, at home they call me Kit."

They smiled into each other's eyes, and no words were needed. Thus quickly youth discards its burdens!

That he did not take her into his arms at once proved the caliber of the man. And Kathlyn respected him none the less for his control. She knew now; and she was certain that her eyes had told him as frankly as any words would have done; and she fell into his stride, strangely embarrassed and not a little frightened. The firm grasp of his hand as here and there he steadied her sent a thrill of exquisite pleasure through her.

Love! She laughed softly; and he stopped and eyed her in astonishment.

"What is it?"

"Nothing," she answered.

But she went on with the thought which had provoked her laughter. Love! Danger all about, unseen, hidden; misery in the foreground, and perhaps death beyond; her father back in chains, to face she knew not what horrors, and yet she could pause by the wayside and think of love!

"There was something," he insisted. "That wasn't happy laughter. What caused it?"

"Some day I will tell you—if we live."

"Live?" Then he laughed.

And she was not slow to recognize the Homeric quality of his laughter.

"Kit, I am going to get you and your father out of all this, if but for one thing."

"And what is that?" curious in her turn.

"I'll tell you later." And there the matter stood.

The journey to the village proved frightfully exhausting. The two were in a sorry plight when they reached the well.

The camel men were overjoyed at the sight of them. For hours they had waited in dread, contemplating flight which would take them anywhere but to Bala Khan, who rewarded cowardice in one fashion only. For, but for their cowardly inactivity, their charges might by now be safe in the seaport toward which they had been journeying. So they brought food for the two and begged that they would not be accused of cowardice to Bala Khan.

"Poor devils!" said Bruce. "Had they shown the least resistance those brigand chaps would have killed them off like rats." He beckoned to the head man. "Take us back to Bala Khan in the morning, and we promise that no harm shall befall you. Now, find us a place to sleep."

Nevertheless, it was hard work to keep that promise. Bala Khan stormed and swore that death was too good for the watery hearts of his camel men. They should be crucified on the wall. Kathlyn's diplomacy alone averted the tragedy. Finally, with a good deal of reluctance, Bala Khan gave his word.

So Bruce and Kathlyn planned to return to Allaha, and it

was the Khan himself who devised the method. The two young people should stain their skins and don native dress. He would give them two camels outright, only they would be obliged to make the journey without servants.

"But if harm comes to you, and I hear of it, by the beard of the prophet, I'll throw into Allaha such a swarm of stinging bees that all Hind shall hear of it. Now go, and may Allah watch over you, infidels though you be!"

* * * * * *

Umballa sent a messenger on before, for he loved the theatrical, which is innate in all Orientals. He desired to enter the city to the shrilling of reeds and the booming of tom-toms; to impress upon this unruly populace that he, Durga Ram, was a man of his word, that when he set out to accomplish a thing it was as good as done. His arrival was greeted with cheers, but there was an undertone of groans that was not pleasant to his keen ears. Deep in his heart he cursed, for by these sounds he knew that only the froth was his, the froth and scum of the town. The iron heel; so they would have it in preference to his friendship. Oh, for some way to trap Ramabai, to hold him up in ridicule, to smash him down from his pedestal, known but as yet unseen!

He wondered if he would find any more of those anonymous notes relating to the inviolable person of Ramabai. Woe to him who laid them about, could he but put his hand upon him! He, Durga Ram, held Allaha in the hollow of his hand, and this day he would prove it.

So he put a rope about the waist of Colonel Hare, and led him through the streets, as the ancient Romans he had read about did to the vanquished. He himself recognized the absurdity of all these things, but his safety lay in the fact that the populace at large were incapable of reasoning for themselves; they saw only that which was visible to the eye.

On the palace steps he harangued the people, praising his deeds. He alone had gone into the wilderness and faced death to ransom their lawful king. Why these bonds? The king had shirked his duty; he had betrayed his trust; but in order that the people should be no longer without a head, this man should become their prisoner king; he should be forced to sign laws for their betterment. Without the royal signature the treasury could not be touched, and now the soldiers should be paid in full.

From the soldiers about came wild huzzahs.

Ahmed and Lal Singh, packed away in the heart of the crowd, exchanged gloomy looks. Once the army was Umballa's, they readily understood what would follow: Umballa would acclaim himself, and the troops would back him.

"We have a thousand guns and ten thousand rounds of ammunition," murmured Lal Singh.

"Perhaps we had best prevail upon Ramabai to strike at once. But wait. The Colonel Sahib understands. He knows that if he signs anything it will directly proved his death-warrant. There is still an obstacle at Umballa's feet. Listen!"

Sadly Umballa recounted his adventure in full. The daughter of the king and his friend, the American hunter, were dead. He, Umballa, had arrived too late.

The colonel, mad with rage, was about to give Umballa the lie publicly, when he saw a warning hand uplifted, and below that hand the face of Ahmed. Ahmed shook his head. The colonel's shoulders drooped. In that sign he read danger.

"They live," said Ahmed. "That is enough for the present. Let us begone to the house of Ramabai."

"The Colonel Sahib is safe for the time being."

"And will be so long as he refuses to open the treasury door to Umballa. There is a great deal to smile about, Lal Singh. Here is a treasury, guarded by seven leopards, savage as savage can be. Only two keepers ever dare approach them, and these keepers refuse to cage the leopards without a formal order from the king or queen. Superstition forbids Umballa to make way with the brutes. The people, your people and mine, Lal Singh, believe that these leopards are sacred, and any who kills them commits sacrilege, and you know what that amounts to here. So there he dodders; too cowardly to fly in the face of superstition. He must torture and humiliate the Colonel Sahib and his daughter. Ah, these white people! They have heads and hearts of steel. I know."

"And Umballa has the heart of a flea-bitten pariah dog. When the time comes he will grovel and squirm and whine."

"He will," agreed Ahmed. "His feet are even now itching for the treadmill."

The colonel was taken to one of the palace chambers, given a tub and fresh clothing. Outside in the corridors guards patrolled, and there were four who watched the window. He was a king, but well guarded. Well, they had crowned him, but never should Umballa, through any signature of his, put his hand into the royal treasury.

Besides, this time he had seen pity and sympathy in the faces of many who had looked upon his entrance to the city. The one ray of comfort lay in the knowledge that faithful Ahmed lived.

He dared not think of Kathlyn. He forced his mind to dwell upon his surroundings, his own state of misery. Bruce was there, and Bruce was a man of action and resource. He would give a good account of himself before those bronze devils in the desert made away with him. He feared not for Kathlyn's death, only her future. For they doubtless had lied to Umballa. They would not kill Kathlyn so long as they believed she was worth a single rupee.

Umballa came in, followed by four troopers, who stationed themselves on each side of the door.

"Your Majesty—"

"Wait!" thundered the colonel. Suddenly he turned to the troopers. "Am I your king?"

"Yes, Majesty!"

The four men salaamed.

"Then I order you to arrest this man Durga Ram for treason against the person of your king!"

The troopers stared, dumfounded, first at the colonel, then at Umballa.

"I command it!"

Umballa laughed. The troopers did not stir.

"Ah," said the colonel. "That is all I desire to know. I am not a king. I am merely a prisoner. Therefore those papers which you bring me can not lawfully be signed by me." The colonel turned his back to Umballa, sought the latticed window and peered forth.

"There are ways," blazed forth Umballa.

"Bah! You black fool!" replied the colonel, wheeling. "Have I not yet convinced you that all you can do is to kill me? Don't waste your time in torturing me. It will neither open my lips nor compel me to take a character brush in my hand. If my daughter is dead, so be it. At any rate, she is at present beyond your clutches. You overreached yourself. Had you brought her back it is quite possible I might have surrendered. But I am alone now."

"You refuse to tell where the filigree basket is hidden?"

"I do."

"You refuse to exercise your prerogative to open the doors of the treasury?"

"I do."

Umballa opened the door, motioning to the troopers to pass out. He framed the threshold and curiously eyed this unbendable man. Presently he would bend. Umballa smiled.

"Colonel Sahib, I am not yet at the end of my resources," and with this he went out, closing the door.

That smile troubled the colonel. What deviltry was the scoundrel up to now? What could he possibly do?

Later, as he paced wearily to and fro, he saw something white slip under the door. He stooped and picked up a note, folded European fashion. His heart thrilled as he read the stilted script:

"Ahmed and I shall watch over you. Be patient. This time I am pretending to be your enemy, and you must act accordingly. A messenger has arrived from Bala Khan. Your daughter and Bruce Sahib are alive, and, more, on the way to Allaha in native guise. Be of good cheer, Ramabai.'"

And Umballa, as he lifted his fruit dish at supper, espied another of those sinister warnings. "Beware!" This time he summoned his entire household and threatened death to each and all of them if they did not immediately disclose to him the person who had placed this note under the fruit dish. They cringed and wept and wailed, but nothing could be got out of them. He had several flogged on general principles.

Kathlyn and Bruce returned to Allaha without mishap. Neither animal nor vagabond molested them. When they arrived they immediately found means to acquaint Ramabai, who with Pundita set out to meet them.

In their picturesque disguises Kathlyn and Bruce made a handsome pair of high caste natives. The blue eyes alone might have caused remarks, but this was a negligible danger, since color and costume detracted. Kathlyn's hair, however, was securely hidden, and must be kept so. A bit of carelessness on her part, a sportive wind, and she would be lost. She had been for dyeing her hair, but Bruce would not hear of this desecration.

So they entered the lion's den, or, rather, the jackal's.

At Ramabai's house Ahmed fell on his knees in thankfulness; not that his Mem-sahib was in Allaha, but that she was alive.

During the evening meal Ramabai outlined his plot to circumvent Umballa. He had heard from one of his faithful followers that Umballa intended to force the colonel into a native marriage; later, to dispose of the colonel and marry the queen himself. Suttee had fallen in disuse in Allaha. He, Ramabai, would now apparently side with Umballa as against Colonel Hare, who would understand perfectly. As the colonel would refuse to marry, he, Ramabai, would suggest that the colonel be married by proxy. However suspicious Umballa might be, he would not be able to find fault with this plan. The betrothal would take place in about a fortnight. The Mem-sahib would be chosen as consort out of all the assembled high caste ladies of the state.

Ahmed threw up his hands in horror, but Lal Singh bade him be patient. What did the Mem-sahib say to this? The Mem-sahib answered that she placed herself unreservedly in Ramabai's hands; that Umballa was a madman and must be treated as one.

"Ramabai, why not strike now?" suggested Ahmed.

"The promise Umballa has made to the soldiers has reunited them temporarily. Have patience, Ahmed." Lal Singh selected a leaf with betel-nut and began to chew with satisfaction.

"Patience?" said Ahmed? "Have I none?"

So the call went forth for a bride throughout the principality, and was answered from the four points of the compass.

Between the announcement and the fulfilment of these remarkable proceedings there arrived in the blazing city of Calcutta a young maid. Her face was very stern for one so youthful, and it was as fearless as it was stern. Umballa's last card, had she but known the treachery which had lured her to this mystic shore. The young maid was Winnie, come, as she supposed, at the urgent call of her father and sister, and particularly warned to confide in no one and to hide with the utmost secrecy her destination.

CHAPTER XIV

THE VEILED CANDIDATES

From the four ends of the principality they came, the veiled candidates; from the north, the east, the south and west. They came in marvelous palanquins, in curtained howdahs, on camels, in splendid bullock carts. Many a rupee resolved itself into new-bought finery, upon the vague chance of getting it back with compound interest.

What was most unusual, they came without pedigree or dowry, this being Ramabai's idea; though, in truth, Umballa objected at first to the lack of dowry. He had expected to inherit this dowry. He gave way to Ramabai because he did not care to have Ramabai suspect what his inner thoughts were. Let the fool Ramabai pick out his chestnuts for him. Umballa laughed in his voluminous sleeve.

Some one of these matrimonially inclined houris the colonel would have to select; if he refused, then should Ramabai do the selecting. More, he would marry the fortunate woman by proxy. There was no possible loophole for the colonel.

The populace was charmed, enchanted, as it always is over a new excitement. Much as they individually

Harold MacGrath

despised Umballa, collectively they admired his ingenuity in devising fresh amusements. Extra feast days came one after another. The Oriental dislikes work; and any one who could invent means of avoiding it was worthy of gratitude. So, then, the populace fell in with Umballa's scheme agreeably. The bhang and betel and toddy sellers did a fine business during the festival of Rama.

There was merrymaking in the streets, day and night. The temples and mosques were filled to overflowing. Musicians with reeds and tom-toms paraded the bazaars. In nearly every square the Nautch girl danced, or the juggler plied his trade, or there was a mongoose-cobra fight (the cobra, of course, bereft of its fangs), and fakirs grew mango trees out of nothing. There was a flurry in the slave mart, too.

The troops swaggered about, overbearing. They were soon to get their pay. The gold and silver were rotting in the treasury. Why leave it there, since gold and silver were minted to be spent?

There were elephant fights in the reconstructed arena; tigers attacked wild boars, who fought with enormous razor-like tusks, as swift and deadly as any Malay kris. The half forgotten ceremony of feeding the wild pig before sundown each day was given life again. And drove after drove came in from the jungles for the grain, which was distributed from a platform. And wild peacocks followed the pigs. A wonderful sight it was to see several thousand pigs come trotting in, each drove headed by its fighting boar. When the old fellows met there was carnage; squealing and grunting, they fought. The peacocks shrilled and hopped from back to back for such grain as fell upon the bristly backs of the pigs. Here and there a white peacock would be snared, or a boar whose tusks promised a battle royal with some leopard or tiger.

And through all this turmoil and clamor Ahmed and Lal Singh moved, sounding the true sentiments of the people. They did not want white kings or white queens; they desired to be ruled by their kind, who would not start innovations but would let affairs drift on as they had done for centuries.

Nor was Bruce inactive. Many a time Umballa had stood within an arm's length of death; but always Bruce had resisted the impulse. It would be rank folly to upset Ramabai's plans, which were to culminate in Umballa's overthrow.

But upon a certain hour Ramabai came to Bruce, much alarmed. During his absence with Pundita at some palace affair his home had been entered, ransacked, and ten thousand rupees had been stolen. His real fortune, however, was hidden securely. The real trouble was that these ten thousand rupees would practically undo much of what had been accomplished. He was certain that Umballa had instigated this theft, and that the money would be doled out to the soldiers. For upon their dissatisfaction rested his future.

"Take Bala Khan at his word," suggested Bruce, "and ask him for his five thousand hillmen."

Ramabai smiled. "And have Bala Khan constitute himself the king of Allaha! No, Sahib; he is a good friend, but he is also a dangerous one. We must have patience."

"Patience!" exploded Bruce.

"I have waited several years. Do you not see that when I strike I must succeed?"

"But these warnings to Umballa?"

"He is not molesting me, is he?" returned Ramabai calmly.

"Well, it is more than I could stand."

"Ah, you white people waste so much life and money by acting upon your impulses! Trust me; my way is best; and that is, for the present we must wait."

"God knows," sighed Bruce, "but I am beginning to believe in the colonel's guru."

"Who can say? There are some in this land who possess mighty wills, who can make man sleep by looking into his eyes, who can override and destroy weaker minds. I know; I have seen. You have heard of suspended animation? Well, I have seen examples of it; and so have my people. Can you wonder at their easiness in being swayed this way and that? But these men I refer to do not sit about in the bazaars with wooden bowls for coppers. It is said, however, that all curses die with their makers. It depends upon how old the Colonel Sahib's guru is. I know priests who are more than a hundred years old, and wrinkled like the bride of Hathi, the god of elephants."

"But a child could see through all this rigmarole."

"Can Bruce Sahib?" Again Ramabai smiled. "My people are sometimes children in that they need constant amusement. Have patience, my friend; for I understand. Do I not love Pundita even as you love the Mem-sahib?"

"What do you mean?" demanded Bruce roughly,

"I have eyes."

"Well, yes; it is true. Behind you are your people; behind

us, nothing. That is why I am frantic. Umballa, whenever he finds himself checkmated, digs up what he purports to be an unused law. There is none to contest it. I tell you, Ramabai, we must escape soon, or we never will. You suggested this impossible marriage. It is horrible."

"But it lulls Umballa; and lulled, he becomes careless. Beyond the north gate there are ever ready men and elephants. And when the moment arrives, thither we shall fly, all of us. But," mysteriously, "we may not have to fly. When Umballa learns that the Colonel Sahib will refuse to sign the necessary treasury release the soldiers will understand that once again they have been trifled with."

"We must wait. But it's mighty hard."

The garden of brides has already been described. But on this day when the ten veiled candidates sat in waiting there was spring in the air; and there were roses climbing trellises, climbing over the marble walls, and the pomegranate blossoms set fire to it all. At the gate stood Ramabai, dressed according to his station, and representing by proxy the king. Presently a splendid palanquin arrived, and within it a tardy candidate. She was laden with jewels, armlets, anklets and head ornaments; pearls and uncut sapphires and rubies. Upon lifting her veil she revealed a beautiful high caste face. Ramabai bade her pass on. No sooner had she taken her place than still another palanquin was announced, and this last was drawn by fat sleek bullocks, all of a color.

Ramabai held up his hand. The bullock drivers stopped their charges, and from the palanquin emerged a veiled woman. This was Kathlyn.

The selected candidates were now all present. As master of ceremonies, Ramabai conducted them into the palace, thence into the throne room gaily decorated for the occasion. In a balcony directly above the canopy of the throne were musicians, playing the mournful harmonies so dear to the oriental heart.

Upon the throne sat Colonel Hare, gorgeously attired, but cold and stern of visage, prepared to play his part in this unutterable buffoonery. Near by stood Durga Ram, so-called Umballa, smiling. It was going to be very simple; once yonder stubborn white fool was wedded, he should be made to disappear; and there should be another wedding in which he, Durga Ram, should take the part of the bridegroom. Then for the treasury, flight, and, later, ease abroad. Let the filigree basket of gems stay where it was; there were millions in the treasury, the accumulated hoardings of many decades.

The council and high priests also wore their state robes, and behind them were officers and other dignitaries.

There was a stir as Ramabai entered with the veiled candidates. The colonel in vain tried to hide his interest and anxiety. Kathlyn was there, somewhere among these kotowing women; but there was nothing by which he could recognize her. As the women spread about the throne, Ramabai signified to the musicians to cease.

Silence.

Then Ramabai brought candidate after candidate close to the colonel, so that he alone might see the face behind the veil. At each uplifting of the veil the colonel shook his head. A dark frown began to settle over Umballa's face. If the colonel refused the last candidate for nuptial honors, he should die. But as Ramabai lifted the veil of this last woman the colonel nodded sharply; and Kathlyn, for a brief space, gazed into her father's eyes. The same thought occurred to both; what a horrible mockery it all was, and where would it lead finally?

"Take care!" whispered Kathlyn as she saw her father's fingers move nervously with suppressed longing to reach out and touch her.

The spectators of this little drama which was hidden from them evinced their approval by a murmuring which had something like applause in it. A queen was chosen! A real queen at last had been chosen. Ramabai had accomplished by diplomacy what yonder Durga Ram had failed to do by force. But Umballa secretly smiled as he sensed this undercurrent. Presently they should see.

The colonel extended his hand and drew Kathlyn up beside him; and now for a moment the whole affair trembled in the balance: Kathlyn felt herself possessed with a wild desire to laugh.

The chain of gold, representing the betrothal, was now ordered brought from the treasury.

The populace, outside the palace, having been acquainted with what was taking place, burst out into cheers.

The treasure room, guarded by leopards in charge of incorruptible keepers, was now approached by Umballa and his captain of the guard. Umballa presented his order on the treasury. The leopards were driven into their cages, and the magic door swung open. The two gasped for breath; for Umballa had never before looked within. Everywhere gold and gems; fabulous riches, enough to make a man ten times a king.

"Highness," whispered the captain, "there is enough riches here to purchase the whole of Hind!"

As he stared Umballa surrendered to a passing dream. Presently he shook himself, sought the chain for which he had come, and reluctantly stepped out into the corridor again. He would return soon to this door. But for that fool of a white man who had saved the king from the leopard, he would have opened this door long since. As he walked to the outer door he thought briefly of the beauty of Kathlyn. She was dead, and dead likewise was his passion for her.

Beyond the gate to the garden of brides Ahmed and Lal Singh waited with elephants. From here they would make the north gate, transfer to new elephants, and leave Allaha and its evil schemes behind. They created no suspicion. There were many elephants about the palace this day. In one of the howdahs sat Bruce, armed; in the other, Pundita, trembling with dread. So many arms had Siva, that evil spawn, that Pundita would not believe all was well till they had crossed the frontier.

"They will be coming soon, Sahib," said Ahmed. Bruce wiped the sweat from his palms and nodded.

Now, when Umballa and his captain of the guard departed with the betrothal chain they did not firmly close the outer door, which shut off the leopards from the main palace. The leopards were immediately freed and began their prowling through the corridors, snarling and growling as they scented the air through which the two men had just passed. One paused by the door, impatiently thrusting out a paw.

The door gave.

In the throne room the mockery of the betrothal was gone through, and then the calm Ramabai secretly signified that the hour for escape was at hand; for everywhere, now that the ceremony was done, vigilance would be lax.

Immediately the high priest announced that the successful candidate would be conducted to the palace zenana and confined there till the final ceremonies were over.

Umballa dreamed of what he had seen.

To Ramabai was given the exalted honor of conducting the king and his betrothed to their respective quarters. Once in the private passageway to the harem, or zenana, Ramabai threw caution to the winds.

"We must go a roundabout way to the garden of brides, which will be deserted. Outside the gate Bruce Sahib and Ahmed and Lal Singh await with elephants. Once we can join them we are safe. And in a month's time I shall return."

Meantime one of the leopard keepers rushed frantically into the throne room, exclaiming that the seven guardian leopards were at large. Even as he spoke one of the leopards appeared in the musicians' balcony. The panic which followed was not to be described. A wild scramble ensued toward all exits.

The fugitives entered the royal zenana. Kathlyn proceeded at once to the exit which led to the garden of brides. There she waited for her father and Ramabai, who had paused by the door of one of the zenana chambers. Between them and Kathlyn lay the plunge.

Ramabai addressed the lady of the zenana, telling her that if guards should come to state that Kathlyn was concealed in her own chamber. To this the young woman readily agreed.

Suddenly a leopard appeared behind the colonel and Ramabai. Kathlyn, being first to discover the presence of the animal, cried out a warning.

"Fly, Kit! Save yourself! I am accursed!" called the colonel.

Ramabai and the young woman at the chamber door hurriedly drew the colonel into the chamber and shut the door. The colonel struggled, but Ramabai held him tightly.

"We are unarmed, Sahib," he said; "and the Mem-sahib never loses her head."

"Ramabai, I tell you I shall die here. It is useless to attempt to aid me. I am accursed, accursed! Kit, Kit!"

The leopard stood undecided before the door which had closed in his face. Then he discovered Kathlyn, fumbling at the wicker door at the far side of the swimming pool. There was something upon which to wreak his temper; for all this unusual commotion and freedom had disturbed him greatly. Kathlyn opened the wicker door, closing it behind her. Clear headed, as Ramabai had said, she recollected the palanquin which had been last to enter the garden of brides. She ran into the garden, flew to the palanquin just as she heard the leopard crash through the flimsy wicker door. She reached and entered the palanquin not a moment too soon. She huddled down close to the door. The leopard trotted round and round, snarling and sniffing. Presently he was joined by another. From afar she could hear shouting. She readily understood. Through some carelessness the leopards of the treasury were at liberty, and that of her own and her father was in jeopardy. Just without the garden of brides was Bruce and help, and she dared not move!

Bruce, from his howdah, heard the noise in the palace; female shrieks, commands, a shot from a musket. What in heaven's name had happened? Where was Kathlyn? Why did she not appear? He fingered his revolvers. But Ahmed signaled to him not to stir. The knowledge of whatever had happened must be brought to them; on their lives they dared not go in search of it.

"This comes from your damnable oriental way of doing things. If I had had my way, Umballa would be dead and buried."

"All in good time, Sahib."

The elephants stirred restlessly, for they scented the cat whom they hated.

Within the palanquin Kathlyn dared scarcely to breathe; for outside seven leopards prowled and sniffed and snarled!

CHAPTER XV

THE SEVEN LEOPARDS

Crouched in the palanquin Kathlyn waited for the onslaught of the leopards. Once she heard a tremendous scratching at the rear of her hiding-place; the palanquin tottered. But the animal was not trying to get inside; he was merely sharpening his claws after the manner of his kind, claws which were sharp enough, heaven knew, since, regularly, once a month the keepers filed them to needle-points.

An elephant trumpeted near by, and Kathlyn could have wept in despair. Outside the wall were friends, doubtless by this time joined by her father and Ramabai, and all wondering where she was. She dared not call out for fear of attracting the leopards, whose movements she could hear constantly: the jar of their padded feet as they trotted under and about the palanquin, the sniff-sniff of their wet noses, an occasional yawning.

By and by her curiosity could not be withstood, even though she might be courting death. Cautiously and soundlessly she moved the curtain which faced the wall. A mass of heavy vines ran from the ground to the top of this wall. If only she could reach it; if only she dared try! Presently the keepers, armed with goads and ropes, would be forthcoming, and all hope of flight banished. Umballa, upon close inspection, would recognize her despite her darkened skin and Indian dress.

From the other window she peered. There, in the path, were two leopards, boxing and frolicking in play. As she watched, always interested in the gambols of such animals, she noticed that two other leopards left off prowling, approached, sat upon their haunches, and critically followed the friendly set-to. Then the other three, seeking diversity, sauntered into view. Kathlyn quickened with life and hope. The seven leopards were at least half a dozen yards away. It was but a step to the vines sprawling over the wall.

To think that all depended upon the handle of the palanquin door! If it opened without noise there was a chance. If it creaked she was lost; for she would fall into the hands of the keepers if not under the merciless paws of the cats.

But the longer she hesitated the less time she would have. Bravely, then, she tried her hand upon the door handle and slowly but firmly turned it. There was no sound that she could hear. She pressed it outward with a slow steady movement. Fortunately the dress of the Hindu was short, somewhat above the ankles, and within her strong young body was free of those modern contrivances known as corsets and stays.

She sprang out, dashed for the vines and drew herself up rapidly. In unison the seven leopards whirled and flew at her. But the half a dozen yards which they had first to cover to reach the wall saved her. Up, up, desperately, wildly, with a nervous energy which did far more for her than her natural strength. The cats leaped and snarled at her heels. She went on. Beneath her the leopards tore at

Harold MacGrath

the vines and tried to follow, one succeeding in tearing her skirt with a desperate slash of his paw. He lost his hold and tumbled back among his mates.

But every minute the vines, sturdy as they were, threatened to come tumbling to the ground.

Her long and lonely experiences in the jungle had taught her the need of climbing quickly yet lightly. She flung herself across the top of the wall, exhausted. For the time being, at least, she was safe. She hung there for a few minutes till she had fully recovered her breath. Below the leopards were still leaping and striking futilely! and even in her terror she could not but admire their grace and beauty. And, oddly, she recalled the pet at home. Doubtless by this time he had fallen back into his savage state.

When she dared risk it she gained a securer position on the wall and sat up, flinging her legs over the side of it. She saw things in a bit of blur at first, her heart had been called upon so strenuously; but after a little objects resumed their real shapes, and she espied the two elephants. She called, waving her hands.

"It is Kathlyn!" cried Bruce.

"Kit!" shouted the colonel, who shared the howdah with Bruce. "Kit, hang on for a moment longer! Ahmed, to the wall!"

The colonel and Ramabai had left the zenana by one of the windows overlooking the passage which ran past the garden of brides. They had had no trouble whatever in reaching the elephants. But the subsequent waiting for Kathlyn had keyed them all up to the breaking point. The pity of it was, they dared not stir, dared not start in search of her. Had it been leopards only, Bruce would have made short work of it; but it would have been rank folly to have gone in search of the girl. If she had been made captive, she needed their freedom to gain her own. Besides, the council of both Ahmed and Lal Singh was for patience.

Ahmed had the greatest faith in the world in Kathlyn's ability to take care of herself. Think of what she had already gone through unscathed! Kathlyn Mem-sahib bore a charmed life, and all the wild beasts of the jungles of Hind could not harm her. It was written.

And then Bruce discovered her upon the wall. It took but a moment to bring the elephant alongside; and Kathlyn dropped down into the howdah.

"A narrow squeak, dad," was all she said.

"Let us get on our way," said the colonel hoarsely. "And remember, shoot to kill any man who attempts to stop us. My Kit!" embracing Kathlyn. "Perhaps the escape of the leopards is the luckiest thing that could have happened. It will keep them all busy for an hour or more. Since Umballa believes you to be dead, he will be concerned about my disappearance only. And it will be some time ere they learn of my escape. Forward, Ahmed! This time . . ."

"Don't, father!" interrupted Kathlyn. "Perhaps we shall escape, but none of us is sure. Let us merely hope. I'm so tired!"

Bruce reached over and pressed her hand reassuringly; and the colonel eyed him as from a new angle.

"Good!" he murmured under his breath; "nothing better could happen. He is a man, and a tried one, I know. Good!

Harold MacGrath

If once we get clear of this hell, I shall not stand in their way. But Winnie, Winnie; what in God's name will that kitten be doing all these terrible weeks? Will she try to find us? The first telegraph office we reach I must cable her under no circumstances to stir from home. Ahmed," he said aloud, "how far are we from the nearest telegraph station?"

"Three days, Sahib."

"Shall we be obliged to stop at the gate to change our mounts?"

"No, Sahib; only to take supplies enough to last us."

"Lose as little time as you can. Now drop the curtains, Bruce."

So through the streets they hurried, unmolested. Those who saw the curtained howdah took it for granted that some unsuccessful candidate was returning to her home.

It was well for Kathlyn that she had made up her mind to leap for the vines at the moment she did. For the elephants had not left the first turn in the street when keepers and soldiers came running pell-mell into the street with ropes and ladders, prepared for the recapture of the treasury leopards, which, of course, were looked upon as sacred.

At the ancient gate the fugitives paused for the supplies awaiting them. Ahmed was not known to the guards there; that was good fortune. In the dialect he jested with them, winked and nodded toward the curtained howdah. The guards laughed; they understood. Some disappointed houri was returning whence she had come. Ahmed took his time; he had no reason to hurry. Nothing must pass which would arouse the suspicions of the guards; and haste always alarmed the Oriental.

To the colonel, however, things appeared to lag unnecessarily. He finally lost patience and swept back the curtain despite Bruce's restraining hand. A native mahout, who had been loitering in town that day, recognized at once the royal turban which the colonel still wore. The colonel's face meant nothing; the turban, everything. The mahout stood stock-still for a moment, not quite believing his eyes. By this time, however, Ahmed was comfortably straddled back of his elephant's ears and was jogging along the road.

"The king!" shouted the surprised mahout to the guards, who had not seen the man or the turban.

"What king, fool?" returned the guards.

"The white king who was betrothed this day! Ai, ai! I have seen the royal turban. It is he!"

The guards derided him. So, finding no hope in them, he ran to his elephant, mounted and rode back into town. Durga Ram would pay well for this news.

"Father," said Kathlyn reproachfully, "that mahout recognized you. I warned you not to move the curtain."

Bruce shrugged.

"But, Kit," returned her father, "Ahmed was so infernally slow! He could spend time in chattering to the guards."

Ahmed heard, but said nothing.

"Never mind," interposed Bruce pacifically. "At any rate we shall have the advantage of a couple of hours, and

Umballa will not catch us with the elephants he has at hand. By the time he starts his expedition we shall be thirty miles away. Let us be cheerful!"

"Kit," said her father, "I couldn't help it. I can't think quickly any more. I am like a man in a nightmare. I've been down to hell, and I can't just yet realize that I am out of it. I'm sorry!"

"Poor dad!" Kathlyn pressed him in her arms, while Bruce nodded enviously but approvingly.

By and by they drew aside the curtains. Kathlyn saw here and there objects which recalled her first journey along this highway. If only she had known!

"One thing is forecast," said Bruce. "When Ramabai returns it will be to fight. He will not be able to avoid it now. I shouldn't mind going back with him. Ahmed, what is this strange hold Umballa has over the actions of the Council of Three? They always appear to be afraid of him."

"Ah, Sahib," said Ahmed, resting his ankus or goad on the skull of his mount, "there is said to be another prisoner in the palace prison. Lal Singh knows, I believe."

"What's your idea?"

"Sahib, when I put you all safe over the frontier I am coming back to Allaha to find out." And that was all Ahmed would say regarding the subject.

"I'll wager he knows," whispered Bruce.

"But who can it be? Another poor devil of a white man? Yet how could a white man influence the actions of the council?" The colonel spoke irritably.

"Look!"—from Kathlyn; "there is one of those wonderful trees they call the flame of the jungle." She called their attention to the tree merely to cause a diversion. She wanted to keep her father's thoughts away from Allaha.

So they journeyed on into the sunset, into twilight, into the bright starry night.

Back in the city the panic was already being forgot as a thing of the past. The leopards were back at their patrolling; the high officials and dignitaries, together with the unsuccessful candidates, had gone their several ways. Umballa alone paced the halls, well satisfied with the events of the day, barring the disturbance caused by the escape of the leopards.

His captain entered and saluted.

"Highness, a mahout has news."

"News? Of what?"

"He claims that he saw the king's turban in a howdah which passed the ancient gate about an hour gone."

"That is not possible," replied Umballa.

"I told him that the king was in his chamber."

"So he is. Wait! I will go myself and see," all at once vaguely perturbed. He was back in a very short time, furious.

"It is true! Woe to those who permitted him to escape!"

"Highness, the escape of the leopards and the confusion which followed . . ."

"By all the gods of Hind, and 'twas you who left the door open! You opened it for me to pass out first. Summon the council. Off with you, and give this handful of silver to the only man who has sense enough to believe his eyes. Hare Sahib is mine, and I will follow him into the very house of the British Raj! Guards and elephants! And the bride to be, what of her? Look and see. Nay, I will go with you."

Umballa found an empty chamber; the future queen was gone. More, he found one of the women of the zenana—his favorite—bound and gagged with handkerchiefs. Quickly he freed her.

"Highness, the bride's face was dark like my own, but her arms were as light as clotted cream! And she spake the tongue of the white people."

Kathlyn Hare! She lived; she had escaped the brigands; she had fooled him! And Ramabai had played with him as a cat plays with a wounded mouse. Oh, they should see this time!

Suddenly he laughed. It echoed down the corridor, and one of the treasury leopards roared back at the sinister sound.

"Highness!" timidly.

"Enough! I hold you blameless." He rushed from the palace.

Poor fools! Let them believe that they had escaped. There was still the little sister; in a short time now she would be inside the city walls. The Colonel Sahib would return; indeed, yes. There would be no further difficulty regarding the filigree basket of gold and gems. Still, he would pursue them, if only for the mere sport of it. If he failed to catch them all he had to do was to sit down and wait for them to return of their own volition.

Ramabai, however, was a menace; and Umballa wondered how he was going to lay hold of him. While waiting for his elephants to be harnessed he summoned the council. Ramabai's property must be confiscated and Ramabai put to death. Here for the first time the council flatly refused to fall in with Umballa's plans. And they gave very good reasons. Yes, Ramabai was a menace, but till the soldiery was fully paid, to touch Ramabai would mean the bursting forth of the hidden fire and they would all be consumed.

"Open the treasury door for me, then!"

"We dare not. The keepers understand. They would loose the leopards, which we dare not shoot. The law . . ."

"What is the law to us?" demanded Umballa frankly. "Let us make laws to suit our needs. The white man does. And we need money; we need one another," pointing a finger suggestively toward the floor.

"Only when we have the troops," replied the council firmly. "We have bent our heads to your will so far in everything, but we refuse to sacrifice these heads because of a personal spite against Ramabai, whom we frankly and wisely fear. We dare not break into the treasury. The keepers are unbribable; the priests are with them, and the people are with the priests. Bring back the white man and his daughter. If that is impossible, marry this second daughter and we will crown her; and then you may work your will upon Ramabai. You have failed in all directions so far. Succeed but once and we are ready to follow you."

Umballa choked back the hot imperious words that crowded to his lips. These were plain unvarnished facts, and he must bow to the inevitable, however distasteful it might be. For the present then, Ramabai should be permitted to go unharmed. But Ramabai might die suddenly and accidentally in the recapture of the Colonel Sahib. An accidental death would certainly extinguish any volcanic fires that smoldered under Allaha. So, with this secret determination in mind, Umballa set forth.

Ahmed, his mind busy with a thousand things, forgot the thousand and first, at that stage most important of all; and this was the short cut, a mere pathway through the jungle, but which lessened the journey by some thirty miles. And this pathway Umballa chose. The three hours' headway was thus pared down to minutes, and at the proper time Umballa would appear, not behind the pursued, but in the road in front of them.

There was, to be sure, a bare possibility of the colonel and his party getting beyond the meeting of the path and the road, that is, if he kept going forward all through the night, which, by the way, was exactly what the astute Ahmed did. But Kathlyn's curiosity the next morning neutralized the advantage gained.

A group of masked dancers, peripatetic, was the cause. Confident that they had outstripped pursuit, she saw no reason why she should not witness the dancing.

How Umballa came upon them suddenly, like a thunderbolt, confiscating the elephants; how they fled to a nearby temple, bribed the dancers for masks and garments, fled still farther into the wooded hills, and hid there with small arms ready, needs but little telling. Umballa returned to the city satisfied. He had at least deprived them of their means of travel. Sooner or later they would founder in the jungle, hear of the arrival of the younger daughter and return.

Ahmed was grave. Lal Singh had gone. Now that the expedition had practically failed, his place was back in the shoe shop in the bazaars. Yes, Ahmed was grave. He was also a trifle disheartened. The fakir had said that there would be many disappointments, but that in the end . . . He might be a liar like all the other Hindus. Yet one part of his foretelling was correct: many disappointments.

"Kit," said her father, "Ahmed warned you not to stop."

"I am sorry."

It was on the tip of her tongue to retort that his own carelessness was the basic cause of the pursuit; but she remembered in time what her father had been through.

"There is a village not far," reminded Ahmed. "They are a friendly people. It is quite possible, with the money we have, to buy some horses, small but sturdy. But there is one thing I do not understand, Sahib."

"And what is that?" asked the colonel.

"The readiness with which Umballa gave up the pursuit. It's a long walk; let us be getting forward."

Late that afternoon they were all mounted once more, on strong tractable ponies, with water and provisions. And the spirits of all rose accordingly. Even Ahmed became cheerful.

"We'll make it, please God!" said the colonel. "Give me a telegraph office. That's all I need just now."

"Two days, Sahib," said Ahmed, "we will reach the sea."

They rode all through the night, stopping only at dawn for breakfast and a cat nap after. Then forward again till they came upon a hunter's rest house, deserted. Here they agreed to spend the night. Beyond the rest house were half a dozen scattered mud huts, occupied by natives who pretended friendliness, lulling even the keen Ahmed into a sense of security. But at dawn, when they awoke cheerfully to pick up the trail, they found their horses and provisions gone.

The colonel, Bruce and Ahmed, still armed, never having permitted the rifles out of their keeping, set out grimly in pursuit of the thieves, while Kathlyn proceeded to forage on her own initiative.

She came presently upon a magnificent ravine, half a mile in depth. There was a broad ledge some fifteen feet below. It was evidently used as a goat path, for near at hand stood a shepherd's hut. Stirred by the spirit of investigation, she made preparations for descent by attaching the rope she had brought along to a stout boulder.

Panthers!

They were coming up the pathway behind her. It would be simple enough to descend; but how to get back to the rest house? There was no time to plan; she must act at once. She must drop down to the ledge and trust to her star.

She called out loudly as she swung downward. The

shepherd came running out of his hut, dumfounded at what he saw.

Harold MacGrath

CHAPTER XVI

THE RED WOLF

With the assistance of the shepherd Kathlyn went down the rope agilely and safely. Once firmly on her feet, she turned to thank the wild-eyed hillman. But her best Hindustani (and she was able to speak and understand quite a little by now) fell on ears which heard but did not sense what she said. The man, mild and harmless enough, for all his wild eyes, shrank back, for no woman of his kind had ever looked like this. Kathlyn, with a deal of foreboding, repeated the phrase, and asked the way back to the hunter's rest house. He shook his head; he understood nothing.

But there is one language which is universal the world over, and this is sign language. Kathlyn quickly stooped and drew in the dust the shape of the rest house. Then she pointed in the direction from whence she had come. He smiled and nodded excitedly. He understood now. Next, being unarmed, she felt the need of some sort of weapon. So she drew the shape of a rifle in the dust, then produced four rupees, all she had. The shepherd gurgled delightedly, ran into the hut, and returned with a rifle of modern make and a belt of cartridges. With a gesture he signified that it was useless to him because he did not know how to use it.

He took the rupees and Kathlyn took the rifle, vaguely wondering how it came into the possession of this poverty-stricken hillman. Of one thing she was certain; it had become his either through violence of his own or of others. She examined the breech and found a dead shell, which she cast out. The rifle carried six cartridges, and she loaded skillfully, much to the astonishment of the hillman. Then she swung the butt to her shoulder and fired up at the ledge where the panthers had last been seen.

The hillman cried out in alarm and scuttled away to his hut. When he peered forth again Kathlyn made a friendly gesture, and he approached timidly. Once more she pointed to the dust, at the picture of the rest house; and then, by many stabs of his finger in the air, he succeeded in making the way back sufficiently clear to Kathlyn, who smiled, shouldered the rifle and strode confidently down the winding path; but also she was alert and watchful.

There was not a bit of rust on the rifle, and the fact that one bullet had sped smoothly convinced her that the weapon was serviceable. Some careful hunter had once possessed it, for it was abundantly oiled. To whom had it belonged? It was of German make; but that signified nothing. It might have belonged to an Englishman, a Frenchman, or a Russian; more likely the latter, since this was one of the localities where they crossed and recrossed with their note-books to be utilized against that day when the Bear dropped down from the north and tackled the Lion.

Kathlyn had to go down to the very bottom of the ravine. She must follow the goat path, no matter where it wound, for this ultimately would lead her to the rest house. As she started up the final incline, through the cedars and pines, she heard the bark of the wolf, the red wolf who hunted in packs of twenty or thirty, in reality far more menacing than a tiger or a panther, since no hunter could kill a whole pack.

To this wolf, when hunting his kill, the tiger gave wide berth; the bear took to his cave, and all fleet-footed things of the jungles fled in panic.

Kathlyn climbed as rapidly as she could. She dared not mount a tree, for the red wolf would outwit her. She must go on. The bark, or yelp, had been a signal; but now there came to her ears the long howl. She had heard it often in the great forests at home. It was the call of the pack that there was to be a kill. She might shoot half a dozen of them, and the living rend the dead, but the main pack would follow on and overtake her.

She swung on upward, catching a sapling here, a limb there, pulling herself over hard bits of going. Once she turned and fired a chance shot in the direction of the howling. Far away came the roar of one of the mountain lions; and the pack of red wolves became suddenly and magically silent. Kathlyn made good use of this interval. But presently the pack raised its howl again, and she knew that the grim struggle was about to begin.

She reached the door of the rest house just as the pack, a large one, came into view, heads down, tails streaming. Pundita, who was at the fire preparing the noon meal, seized Kathlyn by the arm and hurried her into the house, barricading the door. The wolves, arriving, flung themselves against it savagely. But the door was stout, and only a battering-ram in human hands could have made it yield.

Unfortunately, there was no knowing when the men-folk would return from their chase of the horses, nor how long the wolves would lay siege. The two women tried shooting, though Pundita was the veriest tyro, being more frightened at the weapon in her hands than at the howling animals outside. They did little or no damage to the wolves, for the available cracks were not at sufficiently good angles. An hour went by, Kathlyn could hear the wolves as they crowded against the door, sniffing the sill.

The colonel, Bruce, Ramabai and Ahmed had found the horses half a dozen miles away; and they had thrashed the thieving natives soundly and instilled the right kind of fear in their breasts. At rifle point they had forced the natives back to the rest house. The crack of their rifles soon announced to Kathlyn that the dread of wolves was a thing of the past. She wisely refrained from recounting her experiences. The men had worry enough.

After a hasty meal the journey toward the sea-port began in earnest. Umballa's attack had thrown them far out of the regular track. They were now compelled to make a wide detour. Where the journey might have been made in three days, they would be lucky now if they reached the sea under five. The men took turns in standing watch whenever they made camp, and Kathlyn nor Pundita had time for idleness. They had learned their lessons; no more carelessness, nothing but the sharpest vigilance from now on.

One day, as the pony caravan made a turn round a ragged promontory, they suddenly paused. Perhaps twenty miles to the west lay the emerald tinted Persian Gulf. The colonel slipped off his horse, dragged Kathlyn from hers, and began to execute a hornpipe. He was like a boy.

"The sea, Kit, the sea! Home and Winnie; out of this devil's cauldron! You will come along with us, Bruce?"

"I haven't anything else to do," Bruce smiled back.

Then he gazed at Kathlyn, who found herself suddenly filled with strange embarrassment. In times of danger sham and subterfuge have no place. Heretofore she had met Bruce as a man, to whom a glance from her eyes had told her secret. Now that the door to civilization lay but a few miles away, the old conventions dropped their obscuring mantles over her, and she felt ashamed. And there was not a little doubt. Perhaps she had mistaken the look in his eyes, back there in the desert, back in the first day when they had fled together from the ordeals. And yet . . . !

On his part, Bruce did not particularly welcome the sea. There might be another man somewhere. No woman so beautiful as Kathlyn could possibly be without suitors. And when the journey down to the sea was resumed he became taciturn and moody, and Kathlyn's heart correspondingly heavy.

The colonel was quite oblivious to this change. He swung his legs free of the primitive stirrups and whistled the airs which had been popular in America at the time of his departure.

There was no lightness in the expressions of Ramabai and Pundita. They were about to lose these white people forever, and they had grown to love, nay, worship them. More, they must return to face they knew not what.

As for Ahmed, he displayed his orientalism by appearing unconcerned. He had made up his mind not to return to America with his master. There was much to do in Allaha, and the spirit of intrigue had laid firm hold of him. He wanted to be near at hand when Ramabai struck his blow. He would break the news to the Colonel Sahib before they sailed.

It was four o'clock when the caravan entered the little seaport town. A few tramp steamers lay anchored in the offing. A British flag drooped from the stem of one of them. This meant Bombay; and Bombay, in turn, meant Suez, the Mediterranean and the broad Atlantic.

The air was still and hot, for the Indian summer was now beginning to lay its burning hand upon this great peninsula. The pale dust, the white stucco of the buildings, blinded the eyes.

They proceeded at once to the single hotel, where they found plenty of accommodation. Then the colonel hurried off to the cable office and wired Winnie. Next he ascertained that the British ship Simla would weigh anchor the following evening for Bombay; that there they could pick up the *Delhi*, bound for England. There was nothing further to do but wait for the answer to the colonel's cable to Winnie, which would arrive somewhere about noon of the next day.

And that answer struck the hearts of all of them with the coldness of death. Umballa had beaten them. Winnie had sailed weeks ago for Allaha, in search of father and sister!

Ahmed spat out his betel-nut and squared his shoulders. Somehow he had rather expected something like this. The reason for Umballa's half-hearted pursuit stood forth clearly.

"Sahib, it is fate," he said. "We must return at once to Allaha. Truly, the curse of that old guru sticks like the blood leeches of the Bengal swamps. But as you have faith in your guru, I have faith in mine. Not a hair of our heads shall be harmed."

"I am a very miserable man, Ahmed! God has forsaken me!" The colonel spoke with stoic calm; he was more like the man Ahmed had formerly known.

"No, Allah has not forsaken; he has forgot us for a time." And Ahmed strode out to make the arrangements for the return.

"Bruce," said the colonel, "it is time for you to leave us. You are a man. You have stood by us through thick and thin. I can not ask you to share any of the dangers which now confront us, perhaps more sinister than any we have yet known."

"Don't you want me?" asked Bruce quietly.

Kathlyn had gone to her room to hide her tears.

"Want you! But no!" The colonel wrung the young man's hand and turned to go back to Kathlyn.

"Wait a moment, Colonel. Supposing I wanted to go, what then? Supposing I should say to you what I dare not yet say to your daughter, that I love her better than anything else in all this wide world; that it will be happiness to follow wherever she goes . . . even unto death?"

The colonel wheeled. "Bruce, do you mean that?"

"With all my heart, sir. But please say nothing to Kathlyn till this affair ends, one way or the other. She might be stirred by a sense of gratitude, and later regret it. When we get out of this—and I rather believe in the prophecy of Ahmed's guru or fakir—then I'll speak. I have always been rather a lonely man. There's been no real good reason. I have always desired to be loved for my own sake, and not for the money I have."

"Money?" repeated the colonel. Never had he in any way associated this healthy young hunter with money. Did he not make a business of trapping and selling wild animals as he himself did? "Money! I did not know that you had any, Bruce."

"I am the son of Roger Bruce."

"What! the man who owned nearly all of Peru and half the railroads in South America?"

"Yes. You see, Colonel, we are something alike. We never ask questions. It would have been far better if we had. Because I did not question Kathlyn when I first met her I feel half to blame for her misfortunes. I should have told her all about Allaha and warned her to keep out of it. I should have advised her to send native investigators, she to remain in Peshawur till she learned the truth. But the name Hare suggested nothing to me, not till after I had left her at Singapore. So I shall go back with you. But please let Kathlyn continue to think of me as a man who earns his own living."

"God bless you, my boy! You have put a new backbone in me. It's hard not to have a white man to talk to, to plan with. Ahmed expects that we shall be ready for the return in the morning. He, however, intends to go back on a racing camel, to go straight to my bungalow, if it isn't destroyed by this time. Perhaps Winnie has not arrived there yet. I trust Ahmed."

"So do I. I have known him for a long time—that is, I thought I did—and during the last few weeks he has been a revelation. Think of his being your head man all these years, and yet steadily working for his Raj, the

British Raj."

"They can keep secrets."

"Well, we have this satisfaction: when Pundita rules it will be under the protecting hand of England. Now let us try to look at the cheerful side of the business. Think of what that girl has gone through with scarcely a scratch! Can't you read something in that? See how strong and self-reliant she has become under such misfortunes as would have driven mad any ordinary woman! Can't you see light in all this? I tell you, there is good and evil working for and against us, and that Ahmed's fakir will in the end prove stronger than your bally old guru. When I am out of the Orient I laugh at such things, but I can't laugh at them somehow when I'm in India."

"Nor I."

That night Kathlyn signified that she wished to go down to the beach beyond the harbor basin. Bruce accompanied her. Often he caught her staring out at the twinkling lights on board the Simla. By and by they could hear the windlass creaking. A volume of black smoke suddenly poured from the boat's slanting funnel. The ship was putting out to sea.

"Why do you risk your life for us?" she asked suddenly.

"Adventure is meat and drink to me, Miss Hare."

The prefix sounded strange and unfamiliar in her ears. Formality. She had been wrong, then; only comradeship and the masculine sense of responsibility. Her heart was like lead.

"It is very kind and brave of you, Mr. Bruce; but I will not have it."

"Have what?" he asked, knowing full well what she meant.

"This going back with us. Why should you risk your life for people who are almost strangers?"

"Strangers?" He laughed softly. "Has it never occurred to you that the people we grow up with are never really our friends; that real friendship comes only with maturity of the mind? Why, the best man friend I have in this world is a young chap I met but three years ago. It is not the knowing of people that makes friendships. It is the sharing of dangers, of bread, in the wilderness; of getting a glimpse of the soul which lies beneath the conventions of the social pact. Would you call me a stranger?"

"Oh, no!" she cried swiftly. "It is merely that I do not want you to risk your life any further for us. Is there no way I can dissuade you?"

"None that I can think of. I am going back with you. That's settled. Now let us talk of something else. Don't you really want me to go?"

"Ah, that isn't fair," looking out to sea again and following the lights aboard the Simla.

It was mighty hard for him not to sweep her into his arms then and there. But he would never be sure of her till she was free of this country, free of the sense of gratitude, free to weigh her sentiments carefully and unbiasedly. He sat down abruptly on the wreck of an ancient hull embedded in the sand. She sank down a little way from him.

He began to tell her some of his past exploits: the Amazon, the Orinoco, the Andes, Tibet and China; of the strange flotsam and jetsam he had met in his travels. But she sensed only the sound of his voice and the desire to reach out her hand and touch his. Friendship! Bread in the wilderness!

*   *   *   *   *   *

Ahmed was lean and deceptive to the eye. Like many Hindus, he appeared anemic; and yet the burdens the man could put on his back and carry almost indefinitely would have killed many a white man who boasted of his strength. On half a loaf of black bread and a soldier's canteen of water he could travel for two days. He could go without sleep for forty-eight hours, and when he slept he could sleep anywhere, on the moment.

Filling his saddle-bags with three days' rations, two canteens of water, he set off on a hagin, or racing camel, for Allaha, three hundred miles inland as the crow flies. It was his intention to ride straight down to the desert and across this to Colonel Hare's camp, if such a thing now existed. A dromedary in good condition can make from sixty to eighty miles a day; and the beast Ahmed had engaged was of Arab blood. In four days he expected to reach the camp. If Winnie had not yet arrived, he would take the road, meet her, warn her of the dangers which she was about to face, and convey her to the sea-port. If it was too late, he would send the camel back with a trusted messenger to the colonel, to advise him.

They watched him depart in a cloud of dust, and then played the most enervating game in existence—that of waiting; for they had decided to wait till they heard from Ahmed before they moved.

Four nights later, when Ahmed arrived at the bungalow, he found conditions as usual. For reasons best known to himself Umballa had not disturbed anything. In fact, he had always had the coming of the younger sister in mind and left the bungalow and camp untouched, so as not to alarm her.

She had not yet arrived. So Ahmed flung himself down upon his cotton rug, telling the keepers not to disturb him; he would be able to wake himself when the time came. But Ahmed had overrated his powers; he was getting along in years; and it was noon of the next day when a hand shook him by the shoulder and he awoke to witness the arrival of Winnie and her woman companion.

For the first time in many years Ahmed cursed his prophet. He that had had time to warn the child, had slept like the sloth of Ceylon!

He went directly to the point. He told her briefly what had happened. He had not the least doubt that Umballa was already aware of her arrival. She must remain hidden in the go-down of the bungalow; her maid also. That night, if Umballa or his men failed to appear, he would lead her off to safety. But there was no hope of stealing away in the daytime. In his heart, however, he entertained no hope; and like the good general he was, he despatched the messenger and camel to the sea. The father and daughter were fated to return.

Ahmed had reckoned shrewdly. Umballa appeared later in the day and demanded the daughter of Colonel Hare. Backed as he was by numerous soldiers, Ahmed resigned himself to the inevitable. They found Winnie and her maid (whom later they sent to the frontier and abandoned) and took them to the palace.

There was no weeping or wailing or struggling. The dark proud face of the young girl gave forth no sign of the terror and utter loneliness of her position. And Umballa realized that it was in the blood of these children to be brave and quiet. There was no mercy in his heart. He was power mad and gold mad, and his enemies lived because he could reach neither of his desires over their dead bodies.

The rigmarole and mummery Winnie went through affected her exactly as it had affected her sister. It was all a hideous nightmare, and at any moment she expected to wake up in her cozy corner at Edendale.

In the bazaars they began to laugh at Umballa and his coronations, or durbars. They began to jest at his futile efforts to crown some one through whom he could put his greedy hand into the treasury. Still, they found plenty of amusement and excitement. And so they filled the square in front of the platform when Umballa put the crown on Winnie's head. How long would this queen last?

And Kathlyn, her father and Bruce were forced to witness the event from behind the cordon of guards, dressed in native costume, their faces stained and their hearts swelling with impotent anger and despair. For it was in such guise they had returned to Allaha.

During a lull in the ceremonies a resonant voice from out the dense throne cried, "Give us a queen of our blood and race, thou black, gutter born dog!"

Ramabai started at the sound of that voice, but caught himself before he looked in the direction from whence it rose. It belonged to one Lal Singh.

Umballa scowled, but gave no other sign that he heard.

But a guard dove into the crowd; uselessly, however.

Kathlyn touched Ramabai's arm.

"Oh, I must speak to her!"

"Be careful, Mem-sahib!" he warned.

But even as she spoke she stepped past him, toward her beloved sister, and offered the flowers she held.

Winnie, not dreaming that this dark veiled creature was her sister, smelled the flowers and beheld a card which had writing on it—English!

"Courage! Father and I have a plan for your escape. Kathlyn."

CHAPTER XVII

LORD OF THE WORLD

Umballa began to go about cheerfully. He no longer doubted his star. Gutter born, was he? A rat from the streets? Very well; there were rats and rats, and some bit so deep that people died of it. He sometimes doubted the advisability of permitting Colonel Hare's head man Ahmed to roam about; the rascal might in the end prove too sharp. Still it was not a bad idea to let Ahmed believe that he walked in security. All Umballa wanted was the colonel, Kathlyn and the young hunter, Bruce. It would be Ahmed, grown careless, who would eventually lead him or his spies to the hiding-place.

That the trio were in the city Umballa did not doubt in the least, nor that they were already scheming to liberate the younger sister. All his enemies where he could put his hand on them!

Cheerful was the word.

The crust of civilization was thin; the true savage was cracking out through it. In the days of the Mutiny Umballa would have been the Nana Sahib's right hand. He would have given the tragedy at Cawnpur an extra touch.

Ten thousand rupees did not go far among soldiers whose arrears called for ten times that sum. So he placed it where it promised to do the most good. It was a capital idea, this of cutting Ramabai's throat with his own money. The lawless element among the troops was his, Umballa's; at least his long enough for the purpose he had in mind.

When the multitude round the platform dissolved and Winnie was led to her chamber in the zenana, Umballa treated himself to a beverage known as the king's peg—a trifle composed of brandy and champagne. That he drank to stupefaction was God's method of protecting that night an innocent child—for Winnie was not much more than that.

Alone, dazed and terrified, she dropped down upon the cushions and cried herself to sleep—exactly as Kathlyn had done. In the morning she awoke to find tea and food. She had heard no one enter or leave. Glancing curiously round her prison of marble and jasper and porphyry, she discovered a slip of white paper protruding through a square in the latticed window which opened out toward the garden of brides.

Hope roused her into activity. She ran to the window and snatched the paper eagerly. It was from Kathlyn, darling Kit. The risk with which it had been placed in the latticed window never occurred to Winnie.

The note informed her that the woman doctor of the zenana had been sufficiently bribed to permit Kathlyn to make up like her and gain admittance to the zenana. Winnie must complain of illness and ask for the doctor, but not before the morning of the following day. So far as she, Kathlyn, could learn, Winnie would be left in peace till the festival of the car of Juggernaut. Ill, she would not be forced to attend the ceremonies, the palace would be practically deserted, and then Kathlyn would appear.

This news plucked up Winnie's spirits considerably. Surely her father and Kit were brave and cunning enough to circumvent Umballa. What a frightful country! What a dreadful people! She was miserable over the tortures her father had suffered, but nevertheless she held him culpable for not telling both her and Kit all and not half a truth. A basket of gems! She and Kit did not wish to be rich, only free and happy. And now her own folly in coming would but add to the miseries of her loved ones.

Ahmed had told her of the two ordeals, the black dungeon, the whipping; he had done so to convince her that she must be eternally on her guard, search carefully into any proposition laid before her, and play for time, time, for every minute she won meant a minute nearer her ultimate freedom. She must promise to marry Umballa, but to set her own date.

Unlike Kathlyn, who had Pundita to untangle the intricacies of the bastard Persian, Winnie had to depend wholly upon sign language; and the inmates of the zenana did not give her the respect and attention they had given to Kathlyn. Kathlyn was a novelty; Winnie was not. Besides, one of them watched Winnie constantly, because the bearded scoundrel had attracted her fancy and because she hoped to enchain his.

So the note from Kathlyn did not pass unnoticed, though Winnie believed that she was without espionage.

Kathlyn, her father, Bruce, Ramabai and Pundita met at the colonel's bungalow, and with Ahmed's help they thrashed out the plan to rescue Winnie. Alone, the little sister would not be able to find her way out of the garden of brides. It was Kathlyn's idea to have Winnie pretend she needed air and sunshine and a walk in the garden after the doctor's visit. The rescue would be attempted from the walls.

Juggernaut, or Jagannath in Hindustani (meaning Lord of the World), was an idol so hideously done in wood that the Prince of Hell would have taken it to be the personification of a damned soul, could he have glimpsed it in the temple at Allaha. The god's face was dark, his lips and mouth were horribly and significantly red; his eyes were polished emeralds, his arms were of gilt, his body was like that of a toad. His temporal reign in Allaha was somewhere near four hundred years, and no doubt his emerald eyes had seen a crimson trail behind his car as many hundred times.

He was married frequently. Some poor, benighted, fanatical woman would pledge herself and would be considered with awe till she died. But in these times no one flung himself under the car; nothing but the incense of crushed flowers now followed his wake. His grin, however, was the same as of old. Wood, paint, gilt and emeralds! Well, we enlightened Europeans sometimes worship these very things, though we indignantly deny it.

Outside the temple stood the car, fantastically carved, dull with rubbed gold leaf. You could see the sockets where horrid knives had once glittered in the sunlight. Xerxes no doubt founded his war chariots upon this idea. The wheels, six in number, two in front and two on each side, were solid, broad and heavy, capable of smoothing out a corrugated winter road. The superstructure was an ornate shrine, which contained the idol on its peregrinations to the river.

About the car were the devotees, some holding the ropes, others watching the entrance to the temple. Presently from the temple came the gurus or priests, bearing the idol. With much reverence they placed the idol within the shrine, the pilgrims took hold firmly of the ropes and the car rattled and thundered on its way to the river.

Of Juggernaut and his car more anon.

The street outside the garden of brides was in reality no thoroughfare, though natives occasionally made use of it as a short cut into town. Therefore no one observed the entrance of an elephant, which stopped close to the wall, seemingly to melt into the drab of it. On his back, however, the howdah was conspicuous. Behind the curtains Kathlyn patiently waited. She was about to turn away in despair when through the wicker gate she saw Winnie, attended by one of the zenana girls, enter the garden. It seemed as if her will reached out to bring Winnie to the wall and to hold the other young woman where she was.

But the two sat in the center of the garden, the thoughts of each far away. The attendant felt no worry in bringing Winnie into the garden. A cry from her lips would bring a dozen guards and eunuchs from the palace. And the white girl could not get out alone. More than this, she gave Winnie liberty in order to trap her if possible.

By and by the native girl pretended to feel drowsy in the heat of the sun, and her head fell forward a trifle. It was then that Winnie heard a low whistle, an old familiar whistle such as she and Kit had used once upon a time in playing "I spy." She sat up rigidly. It was hard work not to cry out. Over the wall the drab trunk of an elephant protruded, and something white fluttered into the garden.

Winnie rose. The head of the native girl came up instinctively; but as Winnie leisurely strolled toward the palace, the head sank again. Winnie turned and wandered along the walls, apparently examining the flowers and vines, but all the while moving nearer and nearer to the bit of white paper which the idle breeze stirred back and forth tentatively. When she reached the spot she stooped and plucked some flowers, gathering up the paper as she did so. And still in the stooping posture, she read the note, crumpled it and stuffed it into a hole in the wall.

Poor child! Every move had been watched as a cobra watches its prey.

She was to pretend illness at once. Plans had been changed. She stood up, swayed slightly and staggered back to the seat. In truth, she was pale enough, and her heart beat so fast that she was horribly dizzy.

"A doctor!" she cried, forgetting that she would not be understood.

The native girl stared at her. She did not understand the words, but the signs were enough. The young white woman looked ill; and Umballa would deal harshly with those who failed to stem the tide of any illness which might befall his captive. There was a commotion behind the fretwork of the palace. Three other girls came out, and Winnie was conducted back to the zenana.

All this Kathlyn observed. She bade the mahout go to the house of the zenana's doctor, where she donned the habiliments familiar to the guards and inmates of the zenana.

Everything went forward without a hitch; so smoothly that had the object of her visit been other than Winnie, Kathlyn must have sensed something unusual. She entered the palace and even led the way to Winnie's chamber—a fact which appeared natural enough to the women about, but which truly alarmed Umballa's spy, who immediately set off in search of the man.

One thing assured her: the hands of the zenana's real physician were broad and muscular, while the hands she saw were slender and beautiful, brown though they were. She had seen those hands before, during the episode of the leopards of the treasury.

It was very hard for Kathlyn to curb the wild desire to crush Winnie in her arms, arms that truly ached for the feel of her. Even as she fought this desire she could not but admire Winnie's superb acting. She and her father had misjudged this butterfly. To have come all this way alone in search of them, unfamiliar with the customs and the language of the people! How she had succeeded in getting here without mishap was in itself remarkable.

She took Winnie's wrist in her hand and pressed it reassuringly, then puttered about in her medical bag. Very softly she whispered:

"I shall remain with you till dusk. Give no sign whatever that you know me, for you will be watched. To-night I will smuggle you out of the palace. Take these, and soon pretend to be quieted."

Winnie swallowed the bits of sugar and lay back. Kathlyn signified that she wished to be alone with her patient. Once alone with Winnie, she cast aside her veil.

"Oh, Kit!"

"Hush, baby! We are going to get you safely away."

"I am afraid."

"So are we all; but we must not let any one see that we are. Father and Ahmed are near by. But oh, why did you attempt to find us?"

"But you cabled me to come, weeks ago!"

"I? Never!" And the mystery was no longer a mystery to Kathlyn. The hand of Umballa lay bare. Could they eventually win out against a man who seemed to miss no point in the game? "You were deceived, Winnie. To think of it! We had escaped, were ready to sail for home, when we learned that you had left for India. It nearly broke our hearts."

"What ever shall we do, Kit?" Winnie flung her arms round her sister and drew her down. "My Kit!"

"We must be brave whatever happens."

"And am I not your sister?" quietly. "Do you believe in me so little? Why shouldn't I be brave? But you've always treated me like a baby; you never tried to prove me."

Kathlyn's arms wound themselves tightly about the slender form. . . . And thus Umballa found them.

"Very touching!" he said, standing with his back to the door. "But nicely trapped!" He laughed as Kathlyn sprang to her feet, as her hand sought the dagger at her side. "Don't draw it," he said. "I might hurt your arm in wrenching it away from you. Poor little fool! Back into the cage, like a homing pigeon! Had I not known you all would return, think you I would have given up the chase so easily? You would not bend, so then you must break. The god Juggernaut yearns for a sacrifice to prove that we still love and worship him. You spurned my love; now you shall know my hate. You shall die, unpleasantly."

Quickly as a cat springs he caught her hands and wrenched them toward him, dragging her toward the door. Winnie sprang up from the cushions, her eyes ablaze with the fighting spirit. Too soon the door closed in her face and she heard the bolt outside go slithering home.

Said Umballa from the corridor: "To you, pretty kitten, I shall come later. I need you for my wife. When I return you will be all alone in the world, truly an orphan. And do not make your eyes red needlessly."

Winnie screamed, and Kathlyn fought with the fury of a netted tigress. For a few minutes Umballa had his hands full, but in the end he conquered.

Outside the garden of brides three men waited in vain for the coming of Kathlyn and her sister.

The god Juggernaut did not repose in his accustomed niche in the temple that night. The car had to be pulled up and down a steep hill, and on the return, owing to the darkness, it was left at the top of the hill, safely propped to prevent its rolling down of its own accord. When the moon rose Juggernaut's eyes gleamed like the striped cat's. Long since he had seen a human sacrifice. Perhaps the old days would return once more. He was weary at heart riding over sickly flowers; he wanted flesh and bones and the music of the death-rattle. His cousins, War and Pestilence, still took their tithes. Why should he be denied?

The whispering became a murmuring, and the murmuring grew into excitable chattering; and by ten o'clock that night all the bazaars knew that the ancient rites of Juggernaut were to be revived that night. The bazaars had never heard of Nero, called Ahenobarbus, and being without companions, they missed the greatness of their august but hampered regent Umballa.

Always the bazaars heard news before any other part of the city. The white Mem-sahib was not dead, but had been recaptured while posing as the zenana physician in an attempt to rescue her sister, the new queen. Oh, the chief city of Allaha was in the matter of choice and unexpected amusements unrivaled in all Asia.

Yes, Umballa was not unlike Nero—to keep the populace amused so they would temporarily forget their burdens.

But why the sudden appearance of soldiers, who stood guard at every exit, compelling the inmates of the bazaars not to leave their houses? Ai, ai! Why this secrecy, since they knew what was going to take place? But the soldiers, ordinarily voluble, maintained grim silence, and even went so far as to extend the bayonet to all those who tried to leave the narrow streets.

"An affair of state!" was all the natives could get in answer to their inquiries. Men came flocking to the roofs. But the moonshine made all things ghostly. The car of the god Juggernaut was visible, but what lay in its path could not be seen.

Umballa was not popular that night. But this was a private affair. Well he knew the ingenuity and resources of his enemies at large. There would be no rescue this night. Kathlyn Mem-sahib should die; this time he determined to put fear into the hearts of the others.

Having drunk his king's peg, he was well fortified against any personal qualms. The passion he had had for Kathlyn was dead, dead as he wanted her to be.

Whom the gods destroy they first make mad; and

Umballa was mad.

The palanquin waited in vain outside the wall of the garden of brides—waited till a ripple of the news eddied about the conveyance in the shape of a greatly agitated Lal Singh.

"He is really going to kill her!" he panted. "He lured her to her sister's side, then captured her. She is to be placed beneath the car of Juggernaut within an hour. It is to be done secretly. The people are guarded and held in the bazaars. Ahmed, with an elephant and armed keepers, will be here shortly. I have warned him. Umballa runs amuck!"

Suddenly they heard voices in the garden, first Umballa's, then Kathlyn's. Sinister portents to the ears of the listeners, father and lover and loyal friends. The former were for breaking into the garden then and there; but a glance through the wicket gate disclosed the fact that Umballa and Kathlyn were surrounded by fifteen or twenty soldiers. And they dared not fire at Umballa for fear of hitting Kathlyn.

The palanquin was lastly carried out of sight.

At the end of the passage or street nearest the town was a gate that was seldom closed. Through this one had to pass to and from the city. Going through this gate, one could make the hill (where the car of Juggernaut stood) within fifteen minutes, while a detour round the walls of the ancient city would consume three-quarters of an hour. Umballa ordered the gates to be closed and stationed a guard there. The gates clanged behind him and Kathlyn. This time he was guarding every entrance. If his enemies were within they would naturally be weak in numbers; outside, they would find it extremely difficult to make an entrance. More than this, he had sent a troop toward the colonel's camp.

The gates had scarcely been closed when Ahmed, his elephant and his armed keepers came into view. The men sent Pundita back to camp, and the actual warfare began. They approached the gate, demanding to be allowed to pass. The soldiers refused. Instantly the keepers flung themselves furiously upon the soldiers. The trooper who held the key threw it over the wall just before he was overpowered. But Ahmed had come prepared. From out the howdah he took a heavy leather pad, which he adjusted over the fore skull of the elephant, and gave a command.

The skull of the elephant is thick. Hunters will tell you that bullets glance off it as water from the back of a duck. Thus, protected by the leather pad, the elephant becomes a formidable battering-ram, backed by tons of weight. Only the solidity of stone may stay him.

Ahmed's elephant shouldered through the gates grandly. For all the resistance they offered that skull they might have been constructed of papier mache.

Through the dust they hurried. Whenever a curious native got in the way the butt of a rifle bestirred him out of it.

Umballa had lashed Kathlyn to a sapling which was laid across the path of the car. The man was mad, stark mad, this night. Even the soldiers and the devotees surrounding the car were terrified. One did not force sacrifices to Juggernaut. One soldier had protested, and he lay at the bottom of the hill, his skull crushed. The others, pulled one way by greed of money and love of life, stirred no hand.

Harold MacGrath

But Kathlyn Mem-sahib did not die under the broad wheels of the car of Juggernaut. So interested in Umballa were his men that they forgot the vigilance required to conduct such a ceremony free of interruption. A crackling of shots, a warning cry to drop their arms, the plunging of an elephant in the path of the car, which was already thundering down the hill, spoiled Umballa's classic.

CHAPTER XVIII

PATIENCE

While Bruce and two of his men carried Kathlyn out of harm's way to the shelter of the underbrush, where he liberated her, Ahmed drove Umballa and his panic-stricken soldiers over the brow of the hill. Umballa could be distinguished by his robes and turban, but in the moonlight Ahmed and his followers were all of a color, like cats in the dark. With mad joy in his heart Ahmed could not resist propelling the furious regent down-hill, using the butt of his rifle and pretending he did not know who it was he was treating with these indignities. And Umballa could not tell who his assailant was because he was given no opportunity to turn.

"Soor!" Ahmed shouted. "Swine! Take that, and that, and that!"

Stumbling on, Umballa cried out in pain; but he did not ask for mercy.

"Soor! Tell your master, Durga Ram, how bites this gun butt as I shall tell mine the pleasure it gives me to administer it. Swine! Ha, you stumble! Up with you!"

Batter and bang! Doubtless Ahmed would have prolonged

Harold MacGrath

this delightful entertainment to the very steps of the palace, but a full troop of soldiers appeared at the foot of the hill, and Ahmed saw that it was now his turn to take to his heels.

"Swine!" with a parting blow which sent Umballa to his knees, "tell your master that if he harms the little Mem-sahib in the palace he shall die! Let him remember the warnings that he has received, and let him not forget what a certain dungeon holds!"

Umballa staggered to his feet, his sight blinded with tears of pain. He was sober enough now, and Ahmed's final words rang in his ears like a cluster of bells. "What a certain dungeon holds!" Stumbling down the hill, urged by Ahmed's blows, only one thought occupied his mind: to wreak his vengeance for these indignities upon an innocent girl. But now a new fear entered his craven soul, craven as all cruel souls are. Some one knew!

He fell into the arms of his troopers and they carried him to a litter, thence to the palace. His back was covered with bruises, and but for the thickness of his cummerbund he must have died under the beating, which had been thorough and masterly. "What a certain dungeon holds!" In his chamber Umballa called for his peg of brandy and champagne, which for some reason did not take hold as usual. For the first time in his life Durga Ram, so-called Umballa, knew what agony was. But did it cause him to think with pity of the agonies he had caused them? Not in the least.

When Ahmed rejoined his people Kathlyn was leaning against her father's shoulder, smiling wanly.

"Where is Umballa?" cried Bruce, seizing Ahmed by the arm.

"On the way to the palace!" Ahmed laughed and told what he had accomplished.

Bruce raised his hands in anger.

"But, Sahib!" began Ahmed, not comprehending.

"And, having him in your hands, you let him go!"

Ahmed stood dumfounded. His jaw sagged, his rifle slipped from his hands and fell with a clank at his feet.

"You are right, Sahib. I am an unthinking fool. May Allah forgive me!"

"We could have held him as hostage, and tomorrow morning we all could have left Allaha free, unhindered! God forgive you, Ahmed, for not thinking!"

"In the heat of battle, Sahib, one does not always think of the morrow." But Ahmed's head fell and his chin touched his breast. That he, Ahmed, of the secret service, should let spite overshadow forethought and to be called to account for it! He was disgraced.

"Never mind, Ahmed," said Kathlyn kindly. "What is done is done. We must find safety. We shall have to hide in the jungle to-night. And there is my sister. You should have thought, Ahmed."

"Umballa will not harm a hair of her head," replied Ahmed, lifting his head.

"Your work has filled his heart with venom," declared Bruce hotly.

"And my words, Sahib, have filled his veins with water,"

Harold MacGrath

replied Ahmed, now smiling.

"What do you mean?" demanded the colonel.

"Ask Ramabai. Perhaps he will tell you."

"That," returned Ramabai, "is of less importance at this moment than the method to be used in liberating the daughter of Colonel Sahib. Listen. The people are angry because they were not permitted to be present at the sacrifice to Juggernaut. To pacify them Umballa will have to invent some amusement in the arena."

"But how will that aid us?" interrupted the colonel.

"Let us say, an exhibition of wild animals, with their trainers."

"Trainers?"

"Yes. You, Colonel Sahib, and you, Kathlyn Mem-sahib, and you, Bruce Sahib, will without difficulty act the parts."

"Good!" said Ahmed bitterly. "The three of them will rush into the royal box, seize Winnie Mem-sahib, and carry her off from under the very noses of Umballa, the council and the soldiers!"

"My friend Ahmed is bitter," replied Ramabai patiently.

"Ai, ai! I had Umballa in my hands and let him go! Pardon me, Ramabai; I am indeed bitter."

"But who will suggest this animal scheme to Umballa?" inquired Bruce.

"I." Ramabai salaamed.

"You will walk into the lion's den?"

"The jackal's," Ramabai corrected.

"God help me! If I only had a few men!" groaned the colonel, raising his hands to heaven.

"You will be throwing away your life uselessly, Ramabai," said Kathlyn.

"No. Umballa and I will understand each other completely."

"Ramabai," put in Ahmed, with his singular smile, "do you want a crown?"

"For myself? No, again. For my wife? That is a different matter."

"And the man in the dungeon?" ironically.

Ramabai suddenly faced the moon and stared long and silently at the brilliant planet. In his mind there was conflict, war between right and ambition. He seemed to have forgot those about him, waiting anxiously for him to speak.

"Ramabai," said Ahmed craftily, "at a word from you a thousand armed men will spring into existence and within twelve hours set Pundita on yonder throne. Why do you hesitate to give the sign?"

Ramabai wheeled quickly.

"Ahmed, silence! I am yet an honorable man. You know

and I know how far I may go. Trifle with me no more."

Ahmed salaamed deeply.

"Think not badly of me, Ramabai; but I am a man of action, and it galls me to wait."

"Are you wholly unselfish?"

It was Ahmed's turn to address mute inquiries to the moon.

"What is all this palaver about?" Bruce came in between the two men impatiently.

"God knows!" murmured the colonel. "One thing I know, if we stand here much longer we'll all spend the rest of the night in prison."

There was wisdom in this. They marched away at once, following the path of the elephant and the loyal keepers. There was no pursuit. Soldiers with purses filled with promises are not overeager to face skilled marksmen. The colonel and his followers, not being aware of this indecision, proposed camping in the first spot which afforded protection from the chill of night, not daring to make for the bungalow, certain that it was being watched. In this they were wise, for a cordon of soldiers (with something besides promises in their purses) surrounded the camp on the chance that its owner might hazard a return.

"Now, Ramabai, what is your plan?" asked the colonel, as he wrapped Kathlyn in the howdah blanket. "We are to pose as animal trainers. Good. What next?"

"A trap and a tunnel."

"Ah!"

"There used to be one. A part of it caved in four or five years ago. It can be reexcavated in a night. The men who do that shall be my own. Your animals will be used. To Kathlyn Mem-sahib your pet leopards will be as play fellows. She has the eye, and the voice, and the touch. She shall be veiled to her eyes, with a bit of ocher on her forehead. Who will recognize her?"

"The sight of you, Ramabai, will cause him to suspect."

"That remains in the air. There must be luck in it."

"If Umballa can be lured to drink his pegs." Then, with an impatient gesture Ahmed added: "Folly! What! Umballa and the council will not recognize the Colonel Sahib's hair, the Mem-sahib's golden head?"

"In the go-down of Lal Singh, the cobbler, there are many things, even wigs and false beards," retorted Ramabai slyly.

Ahmed started, then laughed.

"You are right, Ramabai. So then we have wigs and beards. Go on." He was sitting cross legged and rocking back and forth.

"After the tricks are done Kathlyn Mem-sahib will throw aside her veil and stand revealed, to Umballa, to the council, to the populace."

Bruce jumped to his feet.

"Be patient, Bruce Sahib," reproved Ramabai. "I am not yet done."

Bruce sat down again, and Kathlyn stole a glance at his lean unhappy face. How she longed to touch it, to smooth away the lines of care! The old camaraderie was gone; there seemed to be some invisible barrier between them now.

"She will discover herself, then," proceeded Ramabai. "Umballa will at once start to order her capture, when she shall stay him by crying that she is willing to face the arena lions. Remember, there will be a trap and a tunnel."

"And outside?" said Ahmed, still doubting.

"There will be soldiers, my men. But they will at that moment be elsewhere."

"If you have soldiers, then, why not slip them into the palace and have them take the young Mem-sahib by force?"

"My men are not permitted to enter the palace, Ahmed. Umballa is afraid of them. To go on. Winnie Mem-sahib will stand up and exclaim that she will join her sister, to prove that she is no less brave."

"But the lions!"—from Bruce. From his point of view the plan was as absurd as it was impossible.

Ramabai, however, knew his people and Bruce did not.

"Always remember the trap and the tunnel, Bruce Sahib. At the entrance of the lions the trap will fall. Inside the tunnel will be the Colonel Sahib and Bruce Sahib. Outside will be Ahmed and the brave men he had with him this night. And all the road free to the gates!"

"Ah, for those thousand men!" sighed Ahmed. "I can not

forget them."

"Nor I the dungeon-keep," replied Ramabai. "I must go my own way. Of the right and wrong of it you are not concerned, Ahmed."

"By the Lord!" exclaimed the colonel, getting up. "I begin to understand. He is alive, and they hold him there in a den, vile like mine was. Alive!"

Ramabai nodded, but Ahmed clapped his hands exultantly.

"Umballa did not put him there. It was the politics of the council; and this is the sword which Umballa holds over their heads. And if I summoned my thousand men their zeal for me . . ."

"Pardon, Ramabai!" cried Ahmed contritely. "Pardon!"

"Ah! finally you understand?"

"Yes. You are not only a good man but a great one. If you gave the sign to your men there would be no one in yonder dungeon-keep alive!"

"They know, and I could not stay the tempest once I loosed it. There, that is all. That is the battle I have fought and won."

The colonel reached down and offered his hand.

"Ramabai, you're a man."

"Thanks, Sahib. And I tell you this: I love my people. I was born among them. They are simple and easily led. I wish to see them happy, but I can not step over the dead body of one who was kind to me. And this I add: When you, my friends, are free, I will make him free also. Young men are my followers, and in the blood of the young there is much heat. My plan may appear to you weak and absurd, but I know my people. Besides, it is our only chance."

"Well, Ramabai, we will try your plan, though I do so half heartedly. So many times have we escaped, only to be brought back. I am tired, in the heart, in the mind, in the body. I want to lie down somewhere and sleep for days."

Kathlyn reached out, touched his hand and patted it. She knew. The pain and terror in his heart were not born of his own miseries but of theirs, hers and Winnie's.

"Why doesn't my brain snap?" she queried inwardly. "Why doesn't the thread break? Why can't I cry out and laugh and grow hysterical like other women?"

"I shall take charge of everything," continued Ramabai. "Your tribulations affect my own honor. None of you must be seen, however; not even you, Ahmed. I shall keep you informed. Ahmed will instruct the keepers to obey me. No harm will come to them, since no one can identify them as having been Umballa's assailants. My wife will not be molested in any way for remaining at the bungalow."

Without another word Ramabai curled himself up and went to sleep; and one by one the others followed his example. Bruce was last to close his eyes. He glanced moodily round, noted the guards patrolling the boundaries of their secluded camp, the mahout sleeping in the shadow of the elephant; and then he looked down at Kathlyn. Only a bit of her forehead was exposed. One brown shapely hand clutched the howdah blanket. A patch of moonshine touched her temple. Silently he stooped and laid a kiss upon the hand, then crept over to Ahmed and lay down with his back to the Mohammedan's.

After a while the hand clutching the howdah blanket slid under and finally nestled beneath the owner's chin.

But Winnie could not sleep. Every sound brought her to an upright position; and to-night the palace seemed charged with mysterious noises. The muttering of the cockatoo, the tinkle of the fountain as the water fell into the basin, the scrape and slither of sandals beyond the lattice partitions, the rattle of a gun butt somewhere in the outer corridors—these sounds she heard. Once she thought she heard the sputter of rifle shots afar, but she was not sure.

Kit, beautiful Kit! Oh, they would not, could not let her die! And she had come into this land with her mind aglow with fairy stories!

One of the leopards in the treasury corridors roared, and Winnie crouched into her cushions. What were they going to do to her? For she understood perfectly that she was only a prisoner and that the crown meant nothing at all so far as authority was concerned. She was indeed the veriest puppet. What with Ahmed's disclosures and Kathlyn's advice she knew that she was nothing more than a helpless pawn in this oriental game of chess. At any moment she might be removed from the board.

She became tense again. She heard the slip-slip of sandals In the corridor, a key turn in the lock. The door opened, and in the dim light she saw Umballa.

He stood by the door, silently contemplating her. "What a

certain dungeon holds!" still eddied through the current of his thoughts. Money, money! He needed it; it was the only barrier between him and the end, which at last he began to see. Money, baskets and bags of it, and he dared not go near. May the fires of hell burn eternally in the bones of these greedy soldiers, his only hope!

His body ached; liquid fire seemed to have taken the place of blood in his veins. His back and shoulders were a mass of bruises. Beaten with a gun butt, driven, harried, cursed—he, Durga Ram! A gun butt in the hands of a low caste! He had not only been beaten; he had been dishonored and defiled. His eyes flashed and his fingers closed convulsively, but he was sober. To take yonder white throat in his hands! It was true; he dared not harm a hair of her head!

"Your sister Kathlyn perished under the wheels of the car of Juggernaut."

Winnie did not stir. The aspect of the man fascinated her as the nearness of a cobra would have done. Vipers not only crawl in this terrible land; they walk. One stung with fangs and the other with words.

"She is dead, and to-morrow your father dies."

The disheveled appearance of the man did not in her eyes confirm this. Indeed, the longer she gazed at him the more strongly convinced she became that he was lying. But wisely she maintained her silence.

"Dead," he repeated. "Within a week you shall be my wife. You know. They have told you. I want money, and by all the gods of Hind, yours shall be the hand to give it to me. Marry me, and one week after I will give you means of leaving Allaha. Will you marry me?"

"Yes." The word slipped over Winnie's lips faintly. She recalled Ahmed's advice: to humor the man, to play for time; but she knew that if he touched her she must scream.

"Keep that word. Your father and sister are fools."

Winnie trembled. They were alive. Kit and her father; this man had lied. Alive! Oh, she would not be afraid of any ordeal now. They were alive, and more than that they were free.

"I will keep my word when the time comes," she replied clearly.

"They are calling me Durga Ram the Mad. Beware, then, for madmen do mad things."

The door opened and shut behind him, and she heard the key turn and the outside bolt click into its socket.

They were alive and free, her loved ones! She knelt upon the cushions, her eyes uplifted.

Alone, with a torch in his shaking hand, Umballa went down into the prison, to the row of dungeons. In the door of one was a sliding panel. He pulled this back and peered within. Something lay huddled in a corner. He drew the panel back into its place, climbed the worn steps, extinguished the torch and proceeded to his own home, a gift of his former master, standing just outside the royal confines. Once there, he had slaves anoint his bruised back and shoulders with unguents, ordered his peg, drank it and lay down to sleep.

On the morrow he was somewhat daunted upon meeting Ramabai in the corridor leading to the throne room, where

Winnie and the council were gathered. He started to summon the guards, but the impassive face of his enemy and the menacing hand stayed the call.

"You are a brave man, Ramabai, to enter the lion's den in this fashion. You shall never leave here alive."

"Yes, Durga Ram. I shall depart as I came, a free man."

"You talk like that to me?" furiously.

"Even so. Shall I go out on the balcony and declare that I know what a certain dungeon holds?"

Umballa's fury vanished, and sweat oozed from his palms.

"You?"

"Yes, I know. A truce! The people are muttering and murmuring against you because they were forbidden to attend your especial juggernaut. Best for both of us that they be quieted and amused."

"Ramabai, you shall never wear the crown."

"I do not want it."

"Nor shall your wife."

Ramabai did not speak.

"You shall die first!"

"War or peace?" asked Ramabai.

"War."

"So be it. I shall proceed to strike the first blow."

Ramabai turned and began to walk toward the window opening out upon the balcony; but Umballa bounded after him, realizing that Ramabai would do as he threatened, declare from the balcony what he knew.

"Wait! A truce for forty-eight hours."

"Agreed. I have a proposition to make before you and the council. Let us go in."

Before the council (startled as had Umballa been at Ramabai's appearance) he explained his plans for the pacification and amusement of the people. Umballa tried to find flaws in it; but his brain, befuddled by numerous pegs and disappointments, saw nothing. And when Ramabai produced his troupe of wild animal trainers not even Winnie recognized them. But during the argument between Umballa and the council as to the date of the festivities Kathlyn raised the corner of her veil. It was enough for Winnie. In the last few days she had learned self-control; and there was scarcely a sign that she saw Kit and her father, and they had the courage to come here in their efforts to rescue her!

It was finally arranged to give the exhibition the next day, and messengers were despatched forthwith to notify the city and the bazaars. A dozen times Umballa eyed Ramabai's back, murder in his mind and fear in his heart. Blind fool that he had been not to have seen this man in his true light and killed him! Now, if he hired assassins, he could not trust them; his purse was again empty.

Ramabai must have felt the gaze, for once he turned and caught the eye of Umballa, approached and whispered: "Durga Ram, wherever I go I am followed by watchers

Harold MacGrath

who would die for me. Do not waste your money on hired assassins."

As the so-called animal trainers were departing Kathlyn managed to drop at Winnie's feet a little ball of paper which the young sister maneuvered to secure without being observed. She was advised to have no fear of the lions in the arena, to be ready to join Kathlyn in the arena when she signified the moment. Winnie would have entered a den of tigers had Kathlyn so advised her.

Matters came to pass as Ramabai had planned: the night work in the arena, the clearing of the tunnel, the making of the trap, the perfecting of all the details of escape. Ahmed would be given charge of the exit, Lal Singh of the road, and Ali (Bruce's man) would arrange that outside the city there should be no barriers. All because Ramabai thought more of his conscience than of his ambitions for Pundita.

And when, late in the afternoon, the exhibition was over, Kathlyn stepped upon the trap, threw aside her veil and revealed herself to the spectators. For all her darkened skin they recognized her, and a deep murmur ran round the arena. Kathlyn, knowing how volatile the people were, extended her hands toward the royal box. When the murmurs died away she spoke in Hindustani:

"I will face the arena lions!"

The murmurs rose again, gaining such volume that they became roars, which the disturbed beasts took up and augmented.

Again Kathlyn made a sign for silence, and added: "Provided my sister stands at my side!"

To this Umballa said no. The multitude shouted defiance. In the arena they were masters, even as the populace in the old days of Rome were masters of their emperors.

Winnie, comprehending that this was her cue, stepped forward in the box and signified by gestures that she would join her sister.

The roaring began again, but this time it had the quality of cheers. A real spectacle! To face the savage African lions unarmed! A fine spectacle!

Winnie was lowered from the box, and as her feet touched the ground she ran quickly to Kathlyn's side.

"Winnie, I am standing on a trap. When it sinks be not alarmed."

"My Kit!" cried Winnie, squeezing her adored sister's hand.

The arena was cleared, and the doors to the lions' dens were opened. The great maned African lions stood for a moment blinking in the sunshine. One of them roared out his displeasure, and saw the two women. Then all of them loped toward what they supposed were to be their victims.

That night in the bazaars they said that Umballa was warring in the face of the gods. The erstwhile white queen of the yellow hair was truly a great magician. For did she not cause the earth to open up and swallow her sister and herself?

CHAPTER XIX

MAGIC

Through the tunnel, into the street, into the care of Ahmed and Lal Singh, then hurriedly to the house of Ramabai. The fact that they had to proceed to Ramabai's was a severe blow to Bruce and the colonel. They had expected all to be mounted the instant they came from the tunnel, a swift unobstructed flight to the gate and freedom. But Ahmed could not find his elephants. Too late he learned that the mahouts he had secretly engaged had misunderstood his instructions and had stationed themselves near the main entrance to the arena!

The cursing and railing against fate is a futile thing, never bearing fruit: so Ramabai suggested his house till transportation could be secured. They perfectly understood that they could not remain in the house more than a few hours; for Umballa would surely send his men everywhere, and quite possibly first of all to Ramabai's.

Still, Ramabai did not appear very much alarmed. There were secret stairways in his house that not even Pundita knew; and at a pinch he had a plan by which he could turn away investigation. Only in the direst need, though, did he intend to execute this plan. He wanted his friends out of Allaha without the shedding of any blood.

"Well," said Ahmed, angrily casting aside his disguise; "well, Ramabai, this is the crisis. Will you strike?"

Lal Singh's wrinkled face lighted up with eagerness.

"We are ready, Ramabai," he said.

"We?" Ramabai paused in his pacing to gaze keenly into the eyes of this old conspirator.

"Yes, we. For I, Lal Singh, propose to take my stand at your right hand. I have not been idle. Everywhere your friends are evincing impatience. Ah, I know. You wish for a bloodless rebellion; but that can not be, not among our people. You have said that in their zeal your followers, if they knew, would sweep the poor old king out of your path. Listen. Shall we put him back on the throne, to perform some other mad thing like this gift of his throne to the Colonel Sahib?"

Ramabai, watched intently by the two conspirators for the British Raj and his white friends, paced back and forth, his hands behind his back, his head bent. He was a Christian; he was not only a Christian, he was a Hindu, and the shedding of blood was doubly abhorrent to his mind.

"I am being pulled by two horses," he said.

"Act quickly," advised Ahmed; "one way or the other. Umballa will throw his men round the whole city and there will not be a space large enough for a rat to crawl through. And he will fight like a rat this time; mark me."

Ramabai paused suddenly in front of his wife and smiled down at her.

"Pundita, you are my legal queen. It is for you to say what shall be done. I had in mind a republic."

Lal Singh cackled ironically.

"Do not dream," said Ahmed. "Common sense should tell you that there can be no republic in Allaha. There must be an absolute ruler, nothing less. Your Majesty, speak," he added, salaaming before Pundita.

She looked wildly about the room, vainly striving to read the faces of her white friends; but their expressions were like stone images. No help there, no guidance.

"Is the life of a decrepit old man," asked Lal Singh, "worth the lives of these white people who love and respect you?"

Pundita rose and placed her hands upon her husband's shoulders.

"We owe them our lives. Strike, Ramabai; but only if our need demands it."

"Good!" said Lal Singh. "I'm off for the bazaars for the night. I will buy chupatties and pass them about, as they did in my father's time at Delhi, in the Great Mutiny."

And he vanished.

Have you ever witnessed the swarming of bees? Have you ever heard the hum and buzz of them? So looked and sounded the bazaars that night. At every intersection of streets and passages there were groups, buzzing and gesticulating. In the gutters the cocoanut oil lamps flickered, throwing weird shadows upon the walls; and squatting about these lamps the fruit sellers and candy sellers and cobblers and tailors jabbered and droned. Light women, with their painted faces, went abroad boldly.

And there was but one word on all these tongues: Magic!

Could any human being pass through what this white woman had? No! She was the reincarnation of some forgotten goddess. They knew that, and Umballa would soon bring famine and plague and death among them. Whenever they uttered his name they spat to cleanse their mouths of the defilement.

For the present the soldiers were his; and groups of them swaggered through the bazaars, chanting drunkenly and making speech with the light women and jostling honest men into the gutters.

All these things Lal Singh saw and heard and made note of as he went from house to house among the chosen and told them to hold themselves in readiness, as the hour was near at hand. Followed the clinking of gunlocks and the rattle of cartridges. A thousand fierce youths, ready for anything, death or loot or the beauties of the zenanas. For patriotism in Southern Asia depends largely upon what treasures one may wring from it.

But how would they know the hour for the uprising? A servant would call and ask for chupatties. Good. And the meeting-place? Ramabai's garden. It was well. They would be ready.

Flicker-flicker danced the lights; flicker-flicker went the tongues. And the peaceful oriental stars looked down serenely.

Umballa remained in the palace, burning with the fires of

murder. Messenger after messenger came to report that the fugitives were still at large. Contrary to Ahmed's expectations, Umballa did not believe that his enemies would be foolhardy enough to seek refuge in the house of Ramabai. The four roads leading out of the city were watched, the colonel's bungalow and even the ruins of Bruce's camp. They were still in the city; but where?

A king's peg, and another; and Umballa stormed, his heart filled with Dutch courage.

Ramabai made his preparations in case the hunters entered the house. He opened a secret door which led into a large gallery, dim and dusty but still beautiful. Ancient armor covered the walls; armor of the days when there existed in Delhi a peacock throne; armor inlaid with gold and silver and turquoise, and there were jewel-incrusted swords and daggers, a blazing helmet which one of Pundita's ancestors had worn when the Great Khan came thundering down from China.

"Here," said Ramabai to the colonel, "you will be safe. They might search for days without learning this room existed. There will be no need to remain here now. Time enough when my servant gives warning."

They filed out of the gallery solemnly. Kathlyn went into the garden, followed by Bruce.

"Do you know," said Kathlyn, "the sight of all that armor, old and still magnificent, seemed to awaken the recollection of another age to me?"

He wanted to take her in his arms, but he waited for her to continue the thought.

"I wonder if, in the dim past, I was not an Amazon?"

She stretched out her arms and suddenly he caught them and drew them down.

"I love you, Kathlyn!"

"No, no!" She struggled back from him. "Let us return to father and Winnie," she said.

During this talk in the garden Umballa had not been inactive. He ordered his captain of the guard to proceed at once to the house of Ramabai and learn if they were there, or had been.

The captain salaamed and departed with his men.

As Bruce and Kathlyn reached the door leading into the house they were met by Ramabai, whose face was grave.

"Ah, Mem-sahib, you ought not to have come out here. You might be seen." The servant who had been watching the street burst in with the cry: "Soldiers!"

The colonel, Winnie and Pundita appeared. For a moment they believed that Ramabai was going to guide them to the secret gallery. But suddenly he raised his head and stared boldly at the gate. And by that sign Bruce and the colonel understood: Ramabai had taken up the dice to make his throw. The two men put their hands on their revolvers and waited.

Soon the captain and his men came rushing in, only to stop short at a sign from Ramabai.

"Be with me on the morrow, and I promise out of my own chest will I pay you your arrears and earnest money for the future. On the other hand, what will you gain by taking us prisoners to Umballa?"

"My lord's word is known. I myself will take charge of the affairs at the palace; and Umballa shall go to the burning ghats. I will announce to him that I found you not."

The captain and his men departed, while Ramabai and his friends reentered the house, to find the imperturbable Lal Singh decked out in his lawful finery.

"All is ready," he announced.

"Dawn," replied Ramabai.

"The servant goes forth for the chupatties."

* * * * * *

Dawn. The garden was filling with silent armed men. With Ramabai, in the secret gallery, were the chiefs. Ramabai indicated the blazing swords.

"My friends, choose among these weapons. The gems are nothing, but the steel is tried and true."

Lal Singh selected the simplest, salaamed and slid the scabbard through his cummerbund.

As for Kathlyn, she could not keep her eyes off the beautiful chain cuirass which had once upon a time been worn by one of Pundita's forebears, a warrior queen.

"Beautiful, beautiful!" she exclaimed. "Pundita, may I put it on? And tell me the story of the warrior queen. To be brave like that, to fight side by side with the man she loved!" She put the cuirass on.

The sky was yellow when the little army started off upon

its desperate enterprise. A guard was left behind for the women.

Pundita solemnly gave each of the girls a dagger. War! Rebellion! Great clamor and shouting before the palace stairs!

"Give us Umballa and the council!"

Umballa heard the shouting, and at first did not understand; but soon the truth came to him. The city was in revolt. He summoned what servants he could trust and armed them. And when the captain of the guard entered to seize Umballa he was himself overpowered. The despatch with which this was accomplished stunned the soldiers, who knew not what to do without their leader.

* * * * * *

When Lal Singh staggered into the house of Ramabai holding his side in mortal agony, dying, Kathlyn felt the recurrence of that strange duality which she had first known in the Temple of the Lion.

"We have failed," whispered Lal Singh. "The palace soldiers betrayed us! All are prisoners, shortly to be shot. . . . The secret gallery . . . Food and water there! . . . Fly!" And thus Lal Singh gave up his cobbler's booth.

As in a dream Kathlyn ran from the house into the street.

With the sun breaking in lances of light against the ancient chain armor, her golden hair flying behind her like a cloud, on, on, Kathlyn ran, never stumbling, never faltering, till she came out into the square before the palace. Like an Amazon of old, she called to the scattering revolutionists, called, harangued, smothered them under her scorn and contempt, and finally roused them to frenzy.

In her madness Kathlyn turned the tide; and when her father's arms closed round her she sank insensible upon his breast.

CHAPTER XX

BATTLE, BATTLE, BATTLE

"Kit, Kit!" cried Kathlyn's father when she came to her senses. "My girl, my girl!"

They left the palace immediately.

The overthrow of Umballa seemed to be complete. Everywhere the soldiers surrendered, for it was better to have food in the stomach than lead.

When Kathlyn left the palace a thunder of cheers greeted her. Kathlyn was forced to mount the durbar throne, much as she longed to be off. But Bruce anticipated her thought and despatched one of the revolutionists to the house of Ramabai. Kathlyn held out her hands toward the excited populace, then turned to Ramabai expressively. Ramabai, calm and unruffled as ever, stepped forward and was about to address the people, when the disheveled captain of the guard, whom Umballa had sent to the arena lions, pushed his way to the foot of the platform.

"The arena lions have escaped!"

And there were a dozen lions in all, strong, cruel, and no doubt hungry!

Panic. Men who had been at one another's throat, bravely and hardily, turned and fled. It was a foolish panic, senseless, but, like all panics, uncontrollable. Those on the platform ran down the steps and at once were swallowed up by the pressing trampling crowd.

Bruce and the colonel, believing that Kathlyn was behind them, fought their way to a clearing, determined to secure nets and take the lions alive. When they turned Kathlyn was gone. For a moment the two men stood as if paralyzed. Then Bruce relieved the tension by smiling. He laid his hand on the colonel's shoulder.

"She has lost us; but that will not matter. Ordinarily I should be wild with anxiety; but to-day Kathlyn may go where she will, and nothing but awe and reverence will follow her. Besides, she has her revolver."

At the same time Kathlyn was fighting vigorously to get free of the mob, Winnie was struggling with Pundita, striving to wrench the dagger from the grief-stricken wife's hand.

"No, no, Pundita!"

"Let me go! My lord is dead, and I wish to follow!"

As the latter's eyes opened wildly Winnie heard a pounding at the door. She flung open the door.

"Pundita?" cried the man.

Winnie caught him by the sleeve and dragged him into the chamber.

"Highness," he cried, "he lives!" And he recounted the startling events of the morning.

"They live!" cried Pundita, and covered her face.

To return to Kathlyn: by and by she was able to slip into a doorway, and the bawling rabble passed on down the narrow street. The house was deserted, and the hallway and what had been a booth was filled with rubbish. Kathlyn, as she leaned breathlessly against the door, felt it give. And very glad she was of this knowledge a moment later, when two lions galloped into the street, their manes stiff, their tails arched. Doubtless, they were badly frightened.

Kathlyn reached for the revolver she carried and fired at the animals, not expecting to hit one of them, but hoping that the noise of the firearm would swerve them into the passage across the way. Instead, they came straight to where she stood.

She stepped inside and slammed the door, holding it and feeling about in vain for lock or bolt.

She then espied a ladder which gave to the roof top, and up this she climbed. They could not possibly follow her up the ladder, and as she reached the top and it turned back at her pressure, she knew that for the present she had nothing to fear from the lions.

Then, round the passage she saw a palanquin, carried by slaves. She leaned far over.

"Help!" she cried. "Help!"

The bearers paused abruptly, and the curtain of the palanquin was swept back. The dark sinister visage of Umballa was revealed.

Umballa left the palanquin, opened the door of the house,

espied the rubbish in the hall; was in the act of mounting the first steps when one of the lions roared again. Drunk as he was, filled with a drunkard's courage, Umballa started back. The lions! Out into the street he went. He turned to the bearers and ordered them to fire the inflammables in the hall. But they refused, for they recognized the chain armor. Mad with rage Umballa struck at them, entered the hall again, and threw a lighted match into the rubbish.

CHAPTER XXI

THE WHITE GODDESS

The painted dancing girl in the house where Umballa had taken temporary refuge began to gather her trinkets, her amber and turquoise necklaces, bracelets and anklets. These she placed in a brass enameled box and tucked it under her arm. Next she shook the sodden Umballa by the sleeve.

"Come!" she cried.

"I would sleep," he muttered.

She seized a bowl containing some flowers and cast the contents into his face. "Fire, fire and death!" she shrilled at him.

The douche brought the man out of his stupor.

"Fire?" he repeated.

"Come!"

This time he followed her docilely, wiping his face on his sleeve.

They heard a great shouting in the street, but did not tarry to learn what had caused it.

One of Umballa's bearers, upon realizing what his master had done, had run down the street for aid. He had had two objects in view—to save the white goddess and to buy his freedom.

A few hundred yards away, in another street, the colonel, Bruce and Ahmed were dragging a net for the purpose of laying it for a lion at bay in a blind alley. Into their presence rushed the wild-eyed bearer.

"Save the white goddess!" he cried.

Bruce seized him by the shoulder. "What is that?"

"The white goddess, Sahib! She is on the roof of a burning house. Durga Ram, my master, set fire to it. He is drunk and hiding in a house near by."

"The man is mad," declared the colonel. "Kit would not have lost her way this far. He is lying. He wants money."

Ahmed spoke. The bearer fell upon his knees.

Three shots, at intervals!

The colonel and Bruce stared into each other's eyes.

"God in Heaven!" gasped the colonel; "those are revolver shots!"

"Bring the net!" shouted Ahmed. To the trembling bearer he said: "Lead us; we follow. And if you have spoken the truth you shall not only have your freedom, but rupees for your old age."

A lion's net is a heavy affair, but with the aid of the keepers the men ran as quickly and lightly as if burdenless. Smoke. There was a fire. The hearts of the white men beat painfully. And the same thought occurred to both of them; they should have gone to Ramabai's house first, then turned their attention to the lions. And Umballa was hiding in a house near by!

Well for them that they entered the doomed quarter as they did. Kathlyn saw them, and the muzzle of the revolver which she was pressing to her heart lowered, the weapon itself slipping from her hand to the roof. God was not going to let her die like this.

"Spread out the net!" commanded Bruce. "Kathlyn, can you hear me?" he shouted, cupping his hands before his mouth. Faintly he heard her reply. "When I give the word, jump. Do not be afraid."

Kathlyn stepped upon the parapet. A great volume of smoke obscured her for a moment. Out of the windows the vivid tongues of flame darted, flashing upward. She summoned all her courage and waited for the call of the man she loved. Inside a floor gave way with a crash and the collateral walls of the building swayed ominously. A despairing roar accompanied the thunder of falling beams. The lions had gone to their death.

"Jump!"

Without hesitation Kathlyn flung herself into space. A murmur ran through the crowd which had, for the moment, forgot its own danger in the wonder of this spectacle. The men holding the net threw themselves backward as Kathlyn struck the mesh. Even then her body touched the street cobbles and she was bruised and shaken severely, but, oh, alive, alive! There rose the great shouting which Umballa and the dancing girl had heard.

Shortly after the house collapsed. The fire spread to the houses on each side.

Bruce seized the bearer by the arm. "Now, the house which Umballa entered?"

Eagerly enough the slave directed him. For all the abuse and beatings the slave was to have his hour. But they found the house empty, except for a chattering monkey and a screaming parrakeet, both attached to pedestal perches. Bruce liberated them and returned to the colonel.

"Gone! Well, let him hide in the jungle, a prey to fear and hunger. At least we are rid of him. But I shall die unhappy if in this life we two fail to meet again. Kit!"

"John!" She withdrew from her father's arms and sought those of the man who loved her and whom she loved, as youth will and must. "Let him go. Why should we care? Take me to my sister."

Ahmed smiled as he and his men rolled the net. This was as it should be. For what man was a better mate for his golden-haired Mem-sahib? And then he thought of Lal Singh, and he choked a little. For Lal Singh and he had spent many pleasant hours together. They had worked together in play and in war, shared danger and bread and glory, all of which was written in the books of the British Raj in Calcutta.

It was the will of Allah; there was but one God, and Mahomet was His prophet. Then Ahmed dismissed Lal Singh and the past from his thoughts, after the philosophical manner of the Asiatic, and turned to the more vital affairs under hand.

At Ramabai's house there was a happy reunion; and on her knees Pundita confessed to her lord how near she had been to Christian damnation. She had fallen from grace; she had reverted to the old customs of her race, to whom suicide was no sin, Ramabai took her in his arms and touched the forehead with his lips.

"And now," said the colonel, "the king!"

Ramabai's head sank.

"What is the matter? Is he dead?"

"If I knew that," answered Ramabai, "I would rest content."

"But you searched the royal prison?"

"And found nothing, nothing!"

"What do you believe?"

"I believe that either the council or Umballa has forestalled us. We shall visit the council at once, They are prisoners. If they have had no hand in the disappearance of the king then we are facing a stone wall over which we can not leap. For Umballa has fled, whither no one knows, and with him has gone the secret. Come; we shall go at once to the palace prison."

The council which had ruled so long in Allaha was very humble indeed. They had imprisoned the king because he had given many evidences of mental unbalance. Perhaps unwisely they had proclaimed his death. Durga Ram had discovered what they had done and had held it over their heads like a sword blade. That the king was not in his dungeon, why and wherefor, was beyond their knowledge. They were in the power of Ramabai; let him work his will upon them. They had told the truth. And Ramabai, much as he detested them, believed them. But for the present it was required that they remain incarcerated till the king was found, dead or alive.

In the palace soldiers and servants alike had already forgot Umballa. To them it was as if he had not existed. All in a few hours. There was, however, one man who did not forget. Upon a certain day Umballa had carelessly saved his life, and to his benefactor he was now determined to devote that life. This man was the majordomo, the chief servant in the king's household. It was not that he loved Umballa; rather that he owed Umballa a debt and resolved to pay it.

Two days later, when the fires were extinguished and the populace had settled back into its former habits, this majordomo betook himself to Umballa's house. It was well guarded, and by men who had never been close to Umballa, but had always belonged to the dissatisfied section, the frankly and openly mutinous section. No bribery was possible here; at least, nothing short of a fabulous sum of money would dislodge their loyalty to Ramabai, now the constitutional regent. No one could leave the house or enter it without scrutiny and question.

The servants and the women of the zenana remained undisturbed. Ramabai would have it so. Things had been put in order. There had not been much damage done by the looters on the day of the revolt. They had looked for treasure merely, and only an occasional bit of vandalism had marked their pathway.

On the pain of death no soldier might enter the house.

The majordomo was permitted to enter without question.

He passed the guards humbly. But once inside, beyond observation, he became a different man. For in Umballa's house, as in Ramabai's, there were secret chambers, and to-day the majordomo entered one of them—through a panel concealed behind a hanging Ispahan rug.

On the night after the revolt, Umballa, sober and desperate, had slunk back disguised as a candy seller. The house was not guarded then; so he had no difficulty in gaining admittance. But he had to gain entrance through a window in the zenana. He would not trust either his servants, his slaves, or his chief eunuch. To the women of his own zenana he had always been carelessly kind, and women are least bribable of the two sexes.

Umballa entered at once his secret chamber and food and water were brought, one of the women acting as bearer. On the morning after the guards arrived, and Umballa knew not how long he might have to wait. Through one of the women he sent a verbal message to the majordomo with the result that each day he learned what was taking place in the palace. So they hunted for the king.

He was very well satisfied. He had had his revenge; and more than this, he was confident when the time came he would also gain his liberty. He had a ransom to pay: the king himself!

Now then, Ramabai felt it incumbent on him to hold a banquet in the palace, there to state to his friends, native and white, just what he intended to do. And on the night of this sober occasion he sat in the throne room before a desk littered with documents. As he finished writing a note he summoned the majordomo.

"Have this delivered at once to Hare Sahib, whom you will find at his bungalow outside the city. Tell him also that he must be present to-night, he, his friend and his daughters. It is of vital importance."

Pundita, who was staring out of the window, turned and asked her lord what he was sending the Colonel Sahib that he could not give him at the banquet.

"A surprise, an agreeable surprise."

The majordomo cocked his ears; but Ramabai said nothing more.

At the colonel's bungalow there was rejoicing. Ramabai had written that, since the king could not be found he would head the provisional government as regent, search for and arrest Umballa, and at any time the Colonel Sahib signified would furnish him with a trusty escort to the railway, three days' journey away. He added, however, that he hoped the Colonel Sahib would be good enough to remain till order was established.

The majordomo contrived to tarry long enough to overhear as much of the conversation as needed for he understood English—and then returned to the city to carry the news to Umballa. To him Umballa gave a white powder.

"To-night, you say, Ramabai gives a banquet?"

"Yes, Huzoor."

"Well, put this in his cup and your obligation to me is paid."

The majordomo stared a long time at that little packet of powder. A cold sweat formed upon his brow under his turban.

"Well?" said Umballa ironically.

"Huzoor, it is murder!"

Umballa shrugged and held out his hand for the packet.

The majordomo swallowed a few times, and bowed his head. "It shall be done, Huzoor. My life is yours to do with as you please. I have said it."

"Begone, then, and bring me the news on the morrow that Ramabai is dead. You alone know where the king is. Should they near the hut in which I have hidden him, see that he is killed. He is also useless."

The majordomo departed with heavy heart. Ramabai was an honest man; but Durga Ram had spoken.

At the banquet, with its quail and pheasant, its fruits and flowers, its rare plates and its rarer goblets for the light wines high castes permitted themselves occasionally to drink, Ramabai toyed idly with his goblet and thoughtlessly pushed it toward Kathlyn, who sat at his right.

Imbued with a sense of gratitude for Ramabai's patience and kindness and assistance through all her dreadful ordeals, Kathlyn sprang up suddenly, and without looking reached for what she supposed to be her own goblet, but inadvertently her hand came into contact with Ramabai's. What she had in mind to say was never spoken.

The majordomo stood appalled. This wonderful white woman over whom the gods watched as they watched the winds and the rains, of whom he had not dared speak to Umballa. She? No! He saw that he himself must die. He seized the goblet ere it reached her lips, drank and flung it aside, empty. He was as good as dead, for there were no antidotes for poisons Umballa gave. Those seated about the table were too astonished to stir. The majordomo put his hands to his eyes, reeled, steadied himself, and then Ramabai understood.

"Poison!" he gasped, springing up and catching the majordomo by the shoulders. "Poison, and it was meant for me! Speak!"

"Lord, I will tell all. I am dying!"

It was a strange tale of misplaced loyalty and gratitude, but it was peculiarly oriental. And when they learned that Umballa was hidden in his own house and the king in a hut outside the city, they knew that God was just, whatever His prophet's name might be. Before he died the majordomo explained the method of entering the secret chamber.

The quail and pheasant, the fruits and wine remained untouched. The hall became deserted almost immediately. To the king, first; to the king! Then Umballa should pay his debt.

They found the poor king in the hut, in a pitiable condition. He laughed and babbled and smiled and wept as they led him away. But in the secret chamber which was to have held Umballa there was no living thing.

For Umballa had, at the departure of the majordomo, conceived a plan for rehabilitation so wide in its ramifications, so powerful and whelming, that nothing could stay it; once it was set in motion. The priests, the real rulers of Asia; the wise and patient gurus, who held the most compelling of all scepters, superstition! Double fool that he had been, not to have thought of this before! He knew that they hated Ramabai, who in religion was an outcast and a pariah, who worshiped but a single God whom none had ever seen, of whom no idol had been carved and set up in a temple.

Superstition!

Umballa threw off his robes and donned his candy seller's tatters, left the house without being questioned by the careless guard, and sought the chief temple.

Superstition!

To cow the populace, to bring the troops to the mark, with threats of curses, famine, plague, eternal damnation! Superstition! And this is why Ramabai and his followers found an empty chamber.

CHAPTER XXII

BEHIND THE CURTAINS

In the rear of the temple Umballa sought was a small chamber that was used by the priests, when they desired to rest or converse privately, which was often. The burning temple lamps of brass emphasized the darkness of the room rather than dispelled it. A shadow occasionally flickered through the amber haze—an exploring bat. A dozen or more priests stood in one of the dim corners, from which their own especial idol winked at them with eyes like coals blown upon. The Krishna of the Ruby Eyes, an idol known far and wide but seen by few.

In the temple itself there was a handful of tardy worshipers. The heat of the candles, the smell of the eternal lotus flower and smoking incense sticks made even the huge vault stifling. Many of the idols were bejeweled or patched with beaten gold leaf, and many had been coveted by wandering white men, who, when their endeavor became known, disappeared mysteriously and were never more known in the haunts of men.

A man in tatters appeared suddenly in the great arched doorway. His turban came down almost to his eyes and a neckcloth covered his mouth. All that could be seen of him in the matter of countenance was a pair of brilliant eyes and a predatory nose. He threw a quick piercing glance about, assured himself that such devotees as he saw were harmless, then strode boldly, if hurriedly, toward the rear chamber, which he entered without ado. Instantly the indignant priests rushed toward him to expel him and give him a tongue-lashing for his impudence, when a hand was thrust out, and they beheld upon a finger a great green stone. They stopped as suddenly as though they had met an invisible electric current.

The curtain fell behind the man in tatters, and he remained motionless for a space. A low murmuring among the priests ensued, and presently one of their number—the youngest—passed out and stationed himself before the curtain. Not even a privileged dancing girl might enter now.

The man in tatters stepped forward. He became the center of the group; his gestures were quick, tense, authoritative. At length priest turned to priest, and the wrinkled faces became more wrinkled still: smiles.

"Highness," said the eldest, "we had thought of this, but you did not make us your confidant."

"Till an hour gone it had not occurred to me. Shall Ramabai, then, become your master, to set forth the propaganda of the infidel?"

"No!" The word was not spoken loudly, but sibilantly, with something resembling a hiss. "No!"

"And shall a king who has no mind, no will, no strength, resume his authority? Perhaps to bring more white people into Allaha, perhaps to give Allaha eventually to the British Raj?"

Again the negative.

"But the method?"

Umballa smiled. "What brings the worshiper here with candles and flowers and incense? Is it love or reverence or superstition?"

The bald yellow heads nodded like porcelain mandarins.

"Superstition," went on Umballa, "the sword which bends the knees of the layman, has and always will through the ages!"

In the vault outside a bell tinkled, a gong boomed melodiously.

"When I give the sign," continued the schemer, "declare the curse upon all those who do not bend. A word from your lips, and Ramabai's troops vanish, reform and become yours and mine!"

"While the king lives?" asked the chief priest curiously.

"Ah!" And Umballa smiled again.

"But you, Durga Ram?"

"There is Ramabai, a senile king, and I. Which for your purposes will you choose?"

There was a conference. The priests drifted away from Umballa. He did not stir. His mien was proud and haughty, but for all that his knees shook and his heart thundered. He understood that it was to be all or nothing, no middle course, no half methods. He waited, wetting his cracked and swollen lips. When the priests returned to him, their heads bent before him a little. It represented a salaam, as much as they had ever given to the king himself. A glow ran over Umballa.

"Highness, we agree. There will be terms."

"I will agree to them without question."

Life and power again; real power! These doddering fools should serve him, thinking the while that they served themselves.

"Half the treasury must be paid to the temple."

"Agreed!" Half for the temple and half for himself; and the abolishment of the seven leopards. "With this stipulation: Ramabai is yours, but the white people are to be mine."

The priests signified assent.

And Umballa smiled in secret. Ramabai would be dead on the morrow.

"There remains the king," said the chief priest.

Umballa shrugged.

The chief priest stared soberly at the lamp above his head. The king would be, then, Umballa's affair.

"He is ill?"

"He is moribund . . . Silence!" warned Umballa.

The curtains became violently agitated. They heard the voice of the young priest outside raised in protest, to be answered by the shrill tones of a woman.

"You are mad!"

"And thou art a stupid fool!"

Umballa's hand fell away from his dagger.

"It is a woman," he said. "Admit her."

The curtains were thrust aside, and the painted dancing girl, who had saved Umballa from death or capture in the fire of his own contriving, rushed in. Her black hair was studded with turquoise, a necklace of amber gleamed like gold around her neck, and on her arms and ankles a plentitude of silver bracelets and anklets. With her back to the curtains, the young priest staring curiously over her shoulder, she presented a picturesque tableau.

"Well!" said Umballa, who understood that she was here from no idle whim.

"Highness, you must hide with me this night."

"Indeed?"

"Or die," coolly.

Umballa sprang forward and seized her roughly.

"What has happened?"

"I was in the zenana, Highness, visiting my sister, whom you had transferred from the palace. All at once we heard shouting and trampling of feet, and a moment later your house was overrun with men. They had found the king in the hut and had taken him to the palace. That they did not find you is because you came here."

"Tell me all."

"It seems that the majordomo gave the poison to Ramabai, but the white goddess . . ."

"The white goddess!" cried Umballa, as if stung by a cobra's fang.

"Ay, Highness. She did not die on that roof. Nothing can harm her. It is written."

"And I was never told!"

She lived, lived, and all the terrors he had evoked for her were as naught! Umballa was not above superstition himself for all his European training. Surely this girl of the white people was imbued with something more than mortal. She lived!

"Go on!" he said, his voice subdued as was his soul.

"The white goddess by mistake took Ramabai's goblet and was about to drink when the majordomo seized the goblet and drained the poison himself. He confessed everything, where the king was, where you were. They are again hunting through the city for you. For the present you must hide with me."

"The white woman must die," said Umballa in a voice like one being strangled.

To this the priests agreed without hesitation. This white woman whom the people were calling a goddess was a deadly menace to that scepter of theirs, superstition.

"What has gone is a pact?"

"A pact, Durga Ram," said the chief priest. With Ramabai spreading Christianity, the abhorred creed which gave people liberty of person and thought, the future of his own religion stood in imminent danger. "A pact," he reflected. "To you, Durga Ram, the throne; to us half the treasury and all the ancient rites of our creed restored."

"I have said it."

Umballa followed the dancing girl into the square before the temple. He turned and smiled ironically. The bald fools!

"Lead on, thou flower of the jasmine!" lightly.

And the two of them disappeared into the night.

But the priests smiled, too, for Durga Ram should always be more in their power than they in his.

There was tremendous excitement in the city the next morning. It seemed that the city would never be permitted to resume its old careless indolence. Swift as the wind the news flew that the old king was alive, that he had been held prisoner all these months by Durga Ram and the now deposed council of three. No more the old rut of dulness. Never had they known such fetes. Since the arrival of the white goddess not a day had passed without some thrilling excitement, which had cost them nothing but shouts.

So they deserted the bazaars and markets that morning to witness the most surprising spectacle of all: the king who was dead was not dead, but alive!

He appeared before them in his rags. For Ramabai, no

mean politician, wished to impress upon the volatile populace the villainy of Umballa and the council, to gain wholly, without reservation, the sympathy of the people, the strongest staff a politician may lean upon. Like a brave and honest man he had cast from his thoughts all hope of power. The king might be old, senile, decrepit, but he was none the less the king. If he had moments of blankness of thought, there were other moments when the old man was keen enough; and keen enough he was to realize in these lucid intervals that Ramabai, among all his people, was loyalest.

So, in the throne room, later, he gave the power to Ramabai to act in his stead till he had fully recovered from his terrible hardships. More than this, he declared that Pundita, the wife of Ramabai, should ultimately rule; for of a truth the principality was lawfully hers. He would make his will at once, but in order that this should be legal he would have to destroy the previous will he had given to Colonel Hare, his friend.

"Forgive me, my friend," he said. "I acted unwisely in your case. But I was angry with my people for their cowardice."

"Your Majesty," replied the colonel, "the fault lay primarily with me. I should not have accepted it or returned. I will tell you the truth. It was the filigree basket of gold and precious stones that brought me back."

"So? And all for nothing, since the hiding-place I gave you is not the true one. But of that, more anon. I want this wretch Durga Ram spread out on an ant hill . . ."

And then, without apparent reason, he began to call for Lakshmi, the beautiful Lakshmi, the wife of his youth. He ordered preparations for an elephant fight; rambled, talked as though he were but twenty; his eyes dim, his lips loose and pendulent. And in this condition he might live ten or twenty years. Ramabai was sore at heart.

They had to wait two days till his mind cleared again. His first question upon his return to his mental balance was directed to Kathlyn. Where was the document he had given to his friend Hare? Kathlyn explained that Umballa had taken it from her.

"But, Your Majesty," exclaimed the colonel rather impatiently, "what difference does it make? Your return has nullified that document."

"Not in case of my death. And in Allaha the elder document is always the legal document, unless it is legally destroyed. It is not well to antagonize the priests, who hold us firmly to this law. I might make a will in favor of Pundita, but it would not legally hold in justice if all previous wills were not legally destroyed. You must find this document."

"Did you ever hear of a law to equal that?" asked Bruce of the colonel.

"No, my boy, I never did. It would mean a good deal of red tape for a man who changed his mind frequently. He could not fool his relations; they would know. The laws of the dark peoples have always amazed me, because if you dig deep enough into them you are likely to find common sense at the bottom. We must search Umballa's house thoroughly. I wish to see Ramabai and Pundita in the shadow of their rights. Can't destroy a document offhand and make a new one without legally destroying the first. Well, let us be getting back to the bungalow. We'll talk it over there."

At the bungalow everything was systematically being prepared for the homeward journey. The laughter and chatter of the two girls was music to their father's ears. And sometimes he intercepted secret glances between Bruce and Kathlyn. Youth, youth; youth and love! Well, so it was. He himself had been a youth, had loved and been beloved. But he grew very lonely at the thought of Kathlyn eventually going into another home; and some young chap would soon come and claim Winnie, and he would have no one but Ahmed. If only he had had a boy, to bring his bride to his father's roof!

Pictures were taken down from the walls, the various wild animal heads, and were packed away in strong boxes. And Ahmed went thither and yon, a hundred cares upon his shoulders. He was busy because then he had no time to mourn Lal Singh.

Bruce's camp was, of course, in utter ruin. Not even the cooking utensils remained: and of his men there was left but Ali, whose leg still caused him to limp a little. So Bruce was commanded by no less person than Kathlyn to be her father's guest till they departed for America. Daily Winnie rode Rajah. He was such a funny old pachyderm, a kind of clown among his brethren, but as gentle as a kitten. Running away had not paid. He was like the country boy who had gone to the big city; he never more could be satisfied with the farm.

The baboon hung about the colonel's heels as a dog might have done; while Kathlyn had found a tiger cub for a plaything. So for a while peace reigned at the camp.

They found the much sought document in the secret chamber in Umballa's house (just as he intended they should); and the king had it legally destroyed and wrote a new will, wherein Pundita should have back that which the king's ancestors had taken from her—a throne.

After that there was nothing for Colonel Hare to do but proceed to ship his animals to the railroad, thence to the ports where he could dispose of them. Never should he enter this part of India again. Life was too short.

High and low they hunted Umballa, but without success. He was hidden well. They were, however, assured that he lingered in the city and was sinisterly alive.

Day after day the king grew stronger mentally and physically. Many of the reforms suggested by Ramabai were put into force. Quiet at length really settled down upon the city. They began to believe that Umballa had fled the city, and vigilance correspondingly relaxed.

The king had a private chamber, the window of which overlooked the garden of brides. There, with his sherbets and water pipe he resumed his old habit of inditing verse in pure Persian, for he was a scholar. He never entered the zenana or harem; but occasionally he sent for some of the women to play and dance before him. And the woman who loved Umballa was among these. One day she asked to take a journey into the bazaars to visit her sister. Ordinarily such a request would have been denied. But the king no longer cared what the women did, and the chief eunuch slept afternoons and nights, being only partly alive in the mornings.

An hour later a palanquin was lowered directly beneath the king's window. To his eye it looked exactly like the one which had departed. He went on writing, absorbed. Had he looked closely, had he been the least suspicious . . . !

This palanquin was the gift of Durga Ram, so-called

Umballa. It had been built especially for this long waited for occasion. It was nothing more nor less than a cunning cage in which a tiger was huddled, in a vile temper. The palanquin bearers, friends of the dancing girl, had overpowered the royal bearers and donned their costumes. At this moment one of the bearers (Umballa himself, trusting no one!) crawled stealthily under the palanquin and touched the spring which liberated the tiger and opened the blind. The furious beast sprang to the window. The king was too astonished to move, to appreciate his danger. From yon harmless palanquin this striped fury!

The tiger in his leap struck the lacquered desk, broke it and scattered the papers about the floor.

Ramabai and his officers were just entering the corridor which led to the chamber when the tragedy occurred. They heard the noise, the king's cries. When they reached the door silence greeted them.

The room was wrecked. There was evidence of a short but terrific struggle. The king lay dead upon the floor, the side of his head crushed in. His turban and garments were in tatters. But he had died like a king; for in the corner by the window lay the striped one, a jeweled dagger in his throat.

Ramabai was first to discover the deserted palanquin, and proceeded to investigate. It did not take him more than a minute to understand what had happened. It was not an accident; it was cold-blooded murder, and back of it stood the infernal ingenuity of one man.

Thus fate took Allaha by the hair again and shook her out of the pastoral quiet. What would happen now?

This!

Harold MacGrath

On the morning after the tragic death of the old king, those who went early to worship, to propitiate the gods to deal kindly with them during the day, were astounded to find the doors and gates of all the temples closed! Nor was any priest visible in his usual haunts. The people were stunned. For there could be but one interpretation to this act on the part of the gurus: the gods had denied the people. Why? Wherefore? Twenty-four hours passed without their learning the cause; the priests desired to fill them with terror before they struck.

Then came the distribution of pamphlets wherein it was decreed that the populace, the soldiery, all Allaha in fact, must bow to the will of the gods or go henceforth accursed. The gods demanded the reinstatement as regent of Durga Ram; the deposing of Ramabai, the infidel; the fealty of the troops to Durga Ram. Twenty-four hours were given the people to make their choice.

Before the doors of all the temples the people gathered, wailing and pouring dust upon their heads, from Brahmin to pariah, from high caste matrons to light dancing girls. And when the troops, company by company, began to kneel at the outer rim of these gatherings, Ramabai despatched a note to Colonel Hare, warning him to fly at once. But the messenger tore up the note and flew to his favorite temple. Superstition thus won what honor, truth and generosity could not hold.

Strange, how we Occidentals have stolen out from under the shadow of anathema. Curse us, and we smile and shrug our shoulders; for a curse is but the mouthing of an angry man. But to these brown and yellow and black people, from the steps of Lhassa to the tangled jungles of mid-Africa, the curse of fake gods is effective. They are really a kindly people, generous, and often loyal unto death, simple and patient and hard-working; but let a priest raise his hand in anathema and at once they become mad, cruel and remorseless as the tiger.

Allaha surrendered; and Umballa came forth. All this happened so quickly that not even a rumor of it reached the colonel's bungalow till it was too late. They were to have left on the morrow. The king dead, only a few minor technicalities stood an the way of Ramabai and Pundita.

Bruce and Kathlyn were fencing one with the other, after the manner of lovers, when Winnie, her eyes wide with fright, burst in upon them with the news that Umballa, at the head of many soldiers, was approaching. The lovers rushed to the front of the bungalow in time to witness the colonel trying to prevent the intrusion of a priest.

"Patience, Sahib!" warned the priest.

The colonel, upon seeing Umballa, made an attempt to draw his revolver, but the soldiers prevented him from carrying into execution his wild impulse.

The priest explained what had happened. The Colonel Sahib, his friend Bruce Sahib, and his youngest daughter would be permitted to depart in peace; but Kathlyn Mem-sahib must wed Durga Ram.

When the dazed colonel produced the document which had been legally canceled, Umballa laughed and declared that he himself had forged that particular document, that the true one, which he held, was not legally destroyed.

Burning with the thought of revenge, of reprisal, how could Durga Ram know that he thus dug his own pit? Had he let them go he would have eventually been crowned, as surely as now his path led straight to the treadmill.

Ahmed alone escaped, because Umballa had in his triumph forgot him!

CHAPTER XXIII

REMORSE

There is an old saying in Rajput that woman and the four winds were born at the same time, of the same mother: blew hot, blew cold, balmily, or tempestuously, from all points at once. Perhaps.

In the zenana of the royal palace there was a woman, tall, lithe, with a skin of ivory and roses and eyes as brown as the husk of a water chestnut. On her bare ankles were gem-incrusted anklets, on her arms bracelets of hammered gold, round her neck a rope of pearls and emeralds and rubies and sapphires. And still she was not happy.

From time to time her fingers strained at the roots of her glossy black hair and the whites of her great eyes glistened. She bit her lips to keep back the sobs crowding in her throat. She pressed her hands together so tightly that the little knuckles cracked.

"Ai, ai!" she wailed softly.

She paced the confines of her chamber with slow step, with fast step; or leaned against the wall, her face hidden in her arms; or pressed her hot cheeks against the cool marble of the lattice.

Human nature is made up of contraries. Why, when we have had the courage coolly to plan murder, or to aid or suggest it, why must we be troubled with remorse? More than this, why must we battle against the silly impulse to tell the first we meet what we have done? Remorse: what is it?

Now, this woman of the zenana believed not in the God of your fathers and mine. She was a pagan; her Heaven and hell were ruled by a thousand gods, and her temples were filled with their images. Yet this thing, remorse, was stabbing her with its hot needles, till no torture devised by man could equal it.

She was the poor foolish woman who loved Durga Ram; loved him as these wild Asiatic women love, from murder to the poisoned cup. Loved him, and knew that he loved her not, but used her for his own selfish ends. There you have it. Had he loved her, remorse never would have lifted its head or raised its voice. And again, had not Umballa sought the white woman, this butterfly of the harem might have died of old age without unburdening her soul. Remorse is the result of a crime committed uselessly. Humanity is unchangeable, for all its variety of skins.

And here was this woman, wanting to tell some one!

Umballa had done a peculiar thing: he had not laid hand upon either Ramabai or Pundita. When asked the reason for this generosity toward a man who but recently put a price on his head, Umballa smiled and explained that Ramabai was not only broken politically, but was a religious outcast. It was happiness for such a person to die, so he preferred that Ramabai should live.

Secretly, however, Ramabai's revolutionary friends were

still back of him, though they pretended to bow to the yoke of the priests.

So upon this day matters stood thus: the colonel, Kathlyn, Bruce and Winnie were prisoners again; Ahmed was in hiding, and Ramabai and his wife mocked by those who once had cheered them. The ingratitude of kings is as nothing when compared to the ingratitude of a people.

A most ridiculous country: to crown Kathlyn again (for the third time!) and then to lock her up! Next to superstition as a barrier to progress there stands custom. Everything one did must be done as some one else had done it; the initiative was still chained up in the temples, it belonged to the bald priests only.

But Umballa had made two mistakes: he should have permitted the white people to leave the country and given a silken cord to the chief eunuch, to apply as directed. There are no written laws among the dark peoples that forbid the disposal of that chattel known as a woman of the harem, or zenana. There are certain customs that even the all powerful British Raj must ignore.

The catafalque of the dead king rested upon the royal platform. Two troopers stood below; otherwise the platform was deserted. When Ramabai and Pundita arrived and mounted the platform to pay their last respects to a kindly man, the soldiers saluted gravely, even sorrowfully. Ramabai, for his courage, his honesty and justice, was their man; but they no longer dared serve him, since it would be at the expense of their own lives.

"My Lord!" whispered Pundita, pressing Ramabai's hand. "Courage!" For Pundita understood the man at her side. Had he been honorless, she would this day be wearing a crown.

"Pundita, they hissed us as we passed."

"Not the soldiers, my Lord."

"And this poor man! Pundita, he was murdered, and I am powerless to avenge him. It was Umballa; but what proof have I? None, none! Well, for me there is left but one thing; to leave Allaha for good. We two shall go to some country where honor and kindness are not crimes but virtues."

"My Lord, it is our new religion."

"And shall we hold to it and go, or repudiate it and stay?"

"I am my Lord's chattel; but I would despise him if he took the base course."

"And so should I, flower of my heart!" Ramabai folded his arms and stared down moodily at the man who, had he lived, could have made Pundita his successor. "Pundita, I have not yet dared tell you all; but here, in the presence of death, truth will out. We can not leave. Confiscation of property and death face us at every gate. No! Umballa proposes to crush me gradually and make my life a hell. No man who was my friend now dares receive me in his house. Worship is denied us, unless we worship in secret. There is one pathway open." He paused.

"And what is that, my Lord?"

"To kneel in the temple and renounce our religion. Do we that, and we are free to leave Allaha."

Pundita smiled. "My Lord is not capable of so vile an act."

"No."

And hand in hand they stood before the catafalque forgetting everything but the perfect understanding between them.

"Ai, ai!"

It was but a murmur; and the two turned to witness the approach of the woman of the zenana. She flung herself down before the catafalque, passionately kissing the shroud. She leaned back and beat her breast and wailed. Ramabai was vastly puzzled over this demonstration. That a handsome young woman should wail over the corpse of an old man who had never been anything to her might have an interpretation far removed from sorrow. Always in sympathy, however, with those bowed with grief, Ramabai stooped and attempted to raise her.

She shrank from his touch, looked up and for the first time seemed to be aware of his presence. Like a bubble under water, that which had been striving for utterance came to the surface. She snatched one of Ramabai's hands.

"Ai, ai! I am wretched. Lord, wretched! There is hot lead in my heart and poison in my brain! I will confess, confess!"

Ramabai and Pundita gazed at each other, astonished.

"What is it? What do you wish to confess?" cried Ramabai quickly. "Perhaps . . ."

She clung to his hand. "They will order my death by the silken cord. I am afraid. Krishna fend for me!"

"What do you know?"

"His majesty was murdered!" she whispered.

"I know that," replied Ramabai. "But who murdered him? Who built that cage in the palanquin? Who put the tiger there? Who beat and overpowered the real bearers and confiscated their turbans? Speak, girl; and if you can prove these things, there will be no silken cord."

"But who will believe a poor woman of the zenana?"

"I will."

"But you can not save men from the cord. They have taken away your power."

"And you shall give it back to me!"

"I?"

"Even so. Come with me now, to the temple."

"The temple?"

"Aye; where all the soldiers are, the priests . . . and Durga Ram!"

"Ai, ai! Durga Ram; it was he! And I helped him, thus: I secured permission to go into the bazaars. There an assault took place under the command of Durga Ram, and my bearers were made prisoners. Durga Ram, disguised as a bearer, himself freed the tiger which killed the king. Yes! To the temple! She who confesses in the temple, her person is sacred. It is the law, the law! I had forgot! To the temple, my Lord!"

Before the high tribunal of priests, before the unhappy Kathlyn, before the astonished Umballa, appeared Ramabai and Pundita, between them the young woman of the zenana, now almost dead with terror.

"Hold!" cried Ramabai when the soldiers started toward him to eject him from the temple.

"What!" said Umballa; "will you recant?"

"No, Durga Ram. I stand here before you all, an accuser! I know the law. Will you, wise and venerable priests, you men of Allaha, you soldiers, serve a murderer? Will you," with a wave of his hand toward the priests, "stand sponsor to the man who deliberately planned and executed the miserable death of our king? Shall it fly to Benares, this news that Allaha permits itself to be ruled and bullied by a common murderer; a man without family, a liar and a cheat? Durga Ram, who slew the king; you turned upon the hand that had fed and clothed you and raised you to power. . . . Wait! Let this woman speak!"

A dramatic moment followed; a silence so tense that the fluttering wings of the doves in the high arches could be heard distinctly. Ramabai was a great politician. He had struck not only wisely but swiftly before his public. Had he come before the priests and Umballa alone, he would have died on the spot. But there was no way of covering up this accusation, so bold, direct; it would have to be investigated.

Upon her knees, her arms outstretched toward the scowling priests, the woman of the zenana tremblingly told her tale: how she had saved Umballa during the revolt; how she had secured him shelter with her sister, who was a dancer; how she had visited Umballa in his secret chamber; how he had confided to her his plans;

how she had seen him with her own eyes become one of the fake bearers of the palanquin.

"The woman lies because I spurned her!" roared Umballa.

"Away with her!" cried the chief priest, inwardly cursing Umballa for having permitted this woman to live when she knew so much. "Away with her!"

"The law!" the woman wailed. "The sanctity of the temple is mine!"

"Hold!" said Kathlyn, standing up. In her halting Hindustani she spoke: "I have something to say to you all. This woman tells the truth. Let her go unafraid. You, grave priests, have thrown your lot with Umballa. Listen. Have you not learned by this time that I am not a weak woman, but a strong one? You have harried me and injured me and wronged me and set tortures for me, but here I stand, unharmed. This day I will have my revenge. My servant Ahmed has departed for the walled city of Bala Khan. He will return with Bala Khan and an army such as will flatten the city of Allaha to the ground, and crows and vultures and tigers and jackals shall make these temples their abiding-places, and men will forget Allaha as they now forget the mighty Chitor." She swung round toward the priests. "You have yourselves to thank. At a word from me, Bala Khan enters or stops at the outer walls. I have tried to escape you by what means I had at my command. Now it shall be war! War, famine, plague!"

Her young voice rang out sharp and clear, sending terror to all cowardly hearts, not least among these being those beating in the breasts of the priests.

"Now," speaking to the soldiers, "go liberate my father, my sister and my husband-to-be; and woe to any who disobey me! For while I stand here I shall be a queen indeed! Peace; or war, famine and the plague. Summon the executioner. Arrest Durga Ram. Strip him before my eyes of his every insignia of rank. He is a murderer. He shall go to the tread-mill, there to slave till death. I have said it!"

Far in the rear of the cowed assemblage, near the doors, stood Ahmed, in his old guise of bheestee, or water carrier. When he heard that beloved voice he felt the blood rush into his throat. Aye, they were right. Who but a goddess would have had at such a time an inspiration so great? But it gave him an idea, and he slipped away to complete it. Bala Khan should come in fact.

So he did not see Umballa upon his knees, whining for mercy, making futile promises, begging for liberty. The soldiers spat contemptuously as they seized him and dragged him off.

The priests conferred hastily. Bala Khan was a fierce Mohammedan, a ruthless soldier; his followers were without fear. The men of Allaha might put up a good defense, but in the end they would be whelmed; and the gods of Hind would be cast out to make way for the prophet of Allah. This young woman with the white skin had for the nonce beaten them. Durga Ram had played the fool: between the two women, he had fallen. They had given him power, and he had let it slip through his fingers for the sake of reprisal where it was not needed. Let him go, then, to the treadmill; they were through with him. He had played his game like a tyro. They must placate this young woman whom the people believed was their queen, but who they knew was the plaything of politics and expediencies.

The chief or high priest salaamed, and Kathlyn eyed him

calmly, though her knees threatened to refuse support.

"Majesty, we bow to your will. Allaha can not hope to cope with Bala Khan's fierce hillmen. All we ask is that you abide with us till you have legally selected your successor."

"Who shall be Pundita," said Kathlyn resolutely.

The chief priest salaamed again. The movement cost him nothing. Once Bala Khan was back in his city and this white woman out of the country, he would undertake to deal with Ramabai and Pundita. He doubted Bala Khan would stir from his impregnable city on behalf of Ramabai.

The frail woman who loved Umballa raised her hands in supplication.

Kathlyn understood. She shook her head. Umballa should end his days in the treadmill; he should grind the people's corn. Nothing should stir her from this determination.

"Majesty, and what of me?" cried the unhappy woman, now filled with another kind of remorse.

"You shall return to the zenana for the present."

"Then I am not to die, Majesty?"

"No."

"And Bala Khan?" inquired the priest.

"He shall stand prepared; that is all."

The people, crowding in the temple and in the square

before it, salaamed deeply as Kathlyn left and returned to the palace. She was rather dizzy over the success of her inspiration. A few days might pass without harm; but sooner or later they would discover that she had tricked them; and then, the end. But before that hour arrived they would doubtless find some way of leaving the city secretly.

That it would be many days ere Pundita wore the crown— trust the priests to spread the meshes of red tape!— Kathlyn was reasonably certain.

"My girl," said the colonel, "you are a queen, if ever there was one. And that you should think of such a simple thing when we had all given up! They would not have touched Umballa. Kit, Kit, whatever will you do when you return to the humdrum life at home?"

"Thank God on my knees, dad!" she said fervently. "But we are not safe yet, by any means. We must form our plans quickly. We have perhaps three days' grace. After that, woe to all of us who are found here. Ah, I am tired, tired!"

"Kit," whispered Bruce, "I intend this night to seek Bala Khan!"

"John!"

"Yes. What the deuce is Allaha to me? Ramabai must fight it out alone. But don't worry about me; I can take care of myself."

"But I don't want you to go. I need you."

"It is your life, Kit, I am certain. Everything depends upon their finding out that Bala Khan will strike if you call upon him. At most, all he'll do will be to levy a tribute which Ramabai, once Pundita is on the throne, can very well pay. Those priests are devils incarnate. They will leave no stone unturned to do you injury, after to-day's work. You have humiliated and outplayed them."

"It is best he should go, Kit," her father declared. "We'll not tell Ramabai. He has been a man all the way through; but we mustn't sacrifice our chances for the sake of a bit of sentiment. John must seek Bala Khan's aid."

Kathlyn became resigned to the inevitable.

Umballa. He tried to bribe the soldiers. They laughed and taunted him. He took his rings from his fingers and offered them. The soldiers snatched them out of his palm and thrust him along the path which led to the mill. In Allaha political malefactors and murderers were made to serve the state; not a bad law if it had always been a just one. But many a poor devil had died at the wrist bar for no other reason than that he had offended some high official, disturbed the serenity of some priest.

When the prisoners saw Umballa a shout went up. There were some there who had Umballa to thank for their miseries. They hailed him and jeered him and mocked him.

"Here is the gutter rat!"

"May his feet be tender!"

"Robber of the poor, where is my home, my wife and children?"

"May he rot in the grave with a pig!"

"Hast ever been thirsty, Highness?"

"Drink thy sweat, then!"

"Give the 'heaven born' irons that are rusted!"

The keepers enjoyed this raillery. Umballa was going to afford them much amusement. They forced him to the wrist bar, snapped the irons on his wrist, and shouted to the men to tread. Ah, well they knew the game! They trotted with gusto, forcing Umballa to keep pace with them, a frightful ordeal for a beginner. Presently he slipped and fell, and hung by his wrists while his legs and thighs bumped cruelly. The lash fell upon his shoulders, and he shrieked and grew limp. He had fainted.

* * * * * *

Among the late king's papers they found an envelope addressed to Kathlyn. It was in grandiloquent English. Brevity of speech is unknown to the East Indian. Kathlyn read it with frowning eyes. She gave it to her father to read; and it hurt her to note the way his eyes took fire at the contents of that letter. The filigree basket of gold and gems; the trinkets for which he had risked his own life, Kathlyn's, then Winnie's. In turn Bruce and Ramabai perused the letter; and to Ramabai came the inspiration.

They would seek this treasure, but only he, Ramabai, and Pundita would return. Here lay their way to freedom without calling upon Bala Khan for aid. The matter, however, had to be submitted to the priests, and those wily men in yellow robes agreed. They could very well promise Durga Ram his freedom again, pursue these treasure seekers and destroy them; that would be Durga Ram's ransom.

The return to the palace was joyous this time; but in her heart of hearts Kathlyn was skeptical. Till she trod the deck of a ship homeward bound she would always be doubting.

Bruce did not have to seek Bala Khan. The night of Kathlyn's defiance Ahmed had acquainted them with his errand. He was now on his way to Bala Khan. They need trouble themselves no longer regarding the future.

"All goes well," said Ramabai; "for, to reach the hiding-place, we must pass the city of Balakhan. I know where this cape is. It is not large. It juts off into the sea, the Persian Gulf, perhaps half a dozen miles. At high tide it becomes an island. None lives about except the simple fishermen. Still, the journey is hazardous. The truth is, it is a spot where there is much gun running; in fact, where we found our guns and ammunition. I understand that there are great secret stores of explosives hidden there."

"Any seaport near?" asked the colonel.

"Perhaps seventy miles north is the very town we stopped at a few weeks ago."

The colonel seized Kathlyn in his arms. She played at gaiety for his sake, but her heart was heavy with foreboding.

"And the filigree basket shall be divided between you and Pundita, Kit."

"Give it all to her, father. I have begun to hate what men call precious stones."

"It shall be as you say; but we may all take a handful as a keepsake."

Two days later the expedition was ready to start. They intended to pick up Ahmed on the way. There was nothing but the bungalow itself at the camp.

Umballa was thereupon secretly taken from the treadmill. He was given a camel and told what to do. He flung a curse at the minarets and towers and domes looming mistily in the moonlight. Ransom? He would destroy them; aye, and take the treasure himself, since he knew where it now lay, this information having been obtained for him. He would seek the world, choosing his habitation where he would.

Day after day he followed, tireless, indomitable, as steadfast upon the trail as a jackal after a wounded antelope, never coming within range, skulking about the camp at night, dropping behind in the morning, not above picking up bits of food left by the treasure seekers. Money and revenge; these would have kept him to the chase had he been dying.

As for Bala Khan, he was at once glad and sorry to see his friends. Nothing would have pleased him more than to fall upon Allaha like the thunderbolt he was. But he made Ramabai promise that if ever he had need of him to send. And Ramabai promised, hoping that he could adjust and regulate his affairs without foreign assistance. They went on, this time with Ahmed.

Toward the end of the journey they would be compelled to cross a chasm on a rope and vine bridge. Umballa, knowing this, circled and reached this bridge before they did. He set about weakening the support, so that the weight of passengers could cause the structure to break and fall into the torrent below. He could not otherwise reach the spot where the treasure lay waiting.

The elephants would be forced to ford the rapids below the bridge.

Kathlyn, who had by this time regained much of her old confidence and buoyancy, declared that she must be first to cross the bridge. She gained the middle, when she felt a sickening sag. She turned and shouted to the others to go back. She made a desperate effort to reach the far end, but the bridge gave way, and she was hurled into the swirling rapids. She was stunned for a moment; but the instinct to live was strong. As she swung to and fro, whirled here, flung there, she managed to catch hold of a rock which projected above the flying foam.

A mahout, seeing her danger, urged his elephant toward her and reached her just as she was about to let go.

CHAPTER XXIV

THE INVINCIBLE WILL

"Those ropes were cut," declared Ahmed.

"But who in the world could have cut them?" demanded the colonel.

Ahmed shrugged. "We may have been followed by thieves. They could have got here before us, as we were forced to use the elephant trails. Let us keep our eyes about us, Sahib. When one speaks of gold, the wind carries the word far. And then . . ." He paused, scowling.

"And then what?"

"I do not want the Mem-sahib to hear," Ahmed whispered. "But who shall say that this is not the work of the gurus, who never forget, who never forgive, Sahib."

"But they would not follow!"

"Nay, but their servant would, on the fear of death. I will watch at night hereafter."

Ahmed searched thoroughly about the ledge from which the east side of the bridge had swung, but the barren rocks told him nothing. Armed with his rifle, he plunged boldly back along the elephant trail, but returned without success. Whoever was following them was an adept, as secret as a Thuggee. All this worried Ahmed not a little. He readily understood that the murderous attempt had not been directed against Kathlyn alone, but against all of them. But for her eagerness and subsequent warning some of them would have been dead at this moment.

"Sahib, it would be better to make camp on the other side of the ford. The Mem-sahib is weak from the shock and might collapse if we proceeded."

"I leave everything to you, Ahmed. But is there not some place farther below where the water does not run so fast?"

"Ramabai will know."

But Ramabai knew only the bridge. They would have to investigate and explore the bank. Half an hour's journey— rather a difficult one—brought them to still and shallow water. Here they crossed and made camp beyond in a natural clearing. They erected the small tent for Kathlyn, inside of which she changed her clothes, drank her tea and lay down to sleep.

"What does Ahmed think?" asked Bruce anxiously.

"That we are being followed by some assassins hired by our friends, the priests."

"Colonel, let us make straight for the seaport and let this damnable bushel of trinkets stay where it is," urged Bruce, the lover.

"That is not possible now," replied Ramabai. "We can now reach there only by the seacoast itself, or return to the desert and journey over the old trail. We must go on."

The colonel smoked his pipe moodily. He was pulled between necessity and desire. He had come to Asia for this filigree basket, and he wanted it, with a passion which was almost miserly. At one moment he silently vowed to cast the whole thing into the sea, and at the next his fingers would twitch and he would sigh.

Sometimes it seemed to him that there was some invisible force working in him, drawing and drawing him against the dictates of his heart. He had experienced this feeling back in California, and had fought against it for weeks, without avail. And frequently now, when alone and undisturbed, he could see the old guru, shaking with the venom of his wrath, the blood dripping from his lacerated fingers, which he shook in the colonel's face flecking it with blood. A curse. It was so. He must obey that invincible will; he must go on and on.

His pipe slipped from his fingers and his head fell upon his knees; and thus Kathlyn found him.

"Let him sleep, Mem-sahib," warned Ahmed from across the fire. "He has been fighting the old guru."

"What?" Kathlyn whispered back. "Where?"

Ahmed smiled grimly and pointed toward his forehead.

"Is there really such evil, Ahmed?"

"Evil begets evil, heaven born, just as good begets good. The Colonel Sahib did wrong. And who shall deny some of these gurus a supernatural power? I have seen; I know."

"But once you said that we should eventually escape, all of us."

"And I still say it, Mem-sahib. What is written is written," phlegmatically.

Wearily she turned toward her tent, but paused to touch the head of her sleeping father as she passed. Her occidental mind would not and could not accept as possibilities these mysterious attributes of the oriental mind. That a will could reach out and prearrange a man's misfortunes was to her mind incredible, for there were no precedents. She never had witnessed a genuine case of hypnotism; those examples she had seen were miserable buffooneries, travesties, hoodwinking not even the newsboys in the upper gallery. True, she had sometimes read of such things, but from the same angle with which she had read the Arabian Nights—fairy stories.

Yet, here was her father, thoroughly convinced of the efficacy of the guru's curse; and here was Ahmed, complacently watching the effects, and not doubting in the least that his guru would in the end prove the stronger of the two.

One of the elephants clanked his chains restlessly. He may have heard the prowling of a cat. Far beyond the fire, beyond the sentinel, she thought she saw a naked form flash out and back of a tree. She stared intently at the tree for a time; but as she saw nothing more, she was convinced that her eyes had deceived her. Besides her body seemed dead and her mind too heavy for thought.

Umballa, having satisfied himself that the camp would not break till morning, slunk away into the shadows. He had failed again; but his hate had made him strong. He was naked except for a loin clout. His beard and hair were matted, the latter hanging over his eyes. His body was smeared with ashes. Not even Ahmed would have recognized him a yard off. He had something less than nine hours to reach the cape before they did; and it was necessary that he should have accomplices. The fishermen he knew to be of predatory habits, and the promise of gold would enmesh them.

The half island which constituted the cape had the shape of a miniature volcano. There was verdure at the base of its slope and trees lifted their heads here and there hardily. It was a mile long and half a mile wide; and in the early morning it stood out like a huge sapphire against the rosy sea. Between the land and the promontory there lay a stretch of glistening sand; there was half a mile of it. Over this a flock of gulls were busy, as scavengers always are. At high tide, yonder was an island in truth.

Sometimes a British gunboat would drop down here suddenly; but it always wasted its time. The fishermen knew nothing; nothing in the way of guns and powder ever was found; and yet the British Raj knew that somewhere about lay the things for which it so diligently and vigorously sought.

On the beach fishermen were disembarking. A sloop with a lateen sail lay at anchor in the rude harbor. Some of the fishermen were repairing nets, and some were tinkering about their fishing boats. Beyond the beach nestled a few huts. Toward these other fishermen were making progress.

The chief of the village—the head man—disembarked from this sloop. He was met by his wife and child, and the little one clambered about his legs in ecstasy. Among the huts stood one more imposing than the others, and toward this the chief and his family wended their way. In front of the hut stood an empty bullock cart. Attached to one of the wheels was a frisking kid. The little child paused to play with her pet.

Absorbed in her pastime, she did not observe the approach of a gaunt being with matted hair and beard and ash-besmirched body. Children are gifted with an instinct which leaves us as we grow older; the sensing of evil without seeing or understanding it. The child suddenly gazed up, to meet a pair of eyes black and fierce as a kite's. She rose screaming and fled toward the house.

The holy man shrugged and waited.

When the parents rushed out to learn what had frightened their little one they were solemnly confronted by Umballa.

"I am hungry."

The chief salaamed and ordered his wife to bring the holy man rice and milk.

"Thou art an honest man?" said Umballa.

"It is said," replied the chief gravely.

"Thou art poor?"

"That is with the gods I serve."

"But thou art not without ambition?"

"Who is?" The chief's wonder grew. What meant these peculiar sentences?

"Wouldst put thy hand into gold as far as the wrist and

take what thou couldst hold?"

"Yee, holy one; for I am human. Whither leads these questions? What is it you would of me?"

"There are some who need to be far away to see things. Well, good man, there is a treasure under your feet," falling into the vernacular.

The chief could not resist looking down at the ground, startled.

"Nay," smiled Umballa, "not there. Think; did not something unusual happen here five years ago?"

The chief smoothed the tip of his nose. "My father died and I became head man of the village."

"Would you call that unusual?" ironically.

"No. Ha!" suddenly. "Five years ago; yes, yes, I remember now. Soldiers, who made us lock ourselves in our huts, not to stir forth on the pain of death till ordered. My father alone was permitted outside. He was compelled to row out to the island. There he was blindfolded. Only two men accompanied him. They carried something that was very heavy. My father never knew what the strange shining basket held. Then the soldiers went away and we came out. No one was allowed on the island till my father died."

"Did he tell you what it was he helped bury yonder?"

"No, holy one. He was an honorable man. Whatever the secret was, it passed with him. We were not curious."

"It was the private treasure of the king of Allaha, and the

man was the king himself."

The fisherman salaamed.

"And I am sent, because I am holy, to recover this treasure, which was willed to the temple of Juggernaut."

"And, holy one, I know not where it is hidden!"

"I do. What I want is the use of your sloop and men I can trust. To you, as much gold as your hands can hold."

"I will furnish you with men as honest as myself."

"That will be sufficient; and you shall have your gold."

The word of a holy man is never subjected to scrutiny in India.

Umballa was in good humor. Here he was, several hours ahead of his enemies. He would have the filigree basket dug up and transferred to the sloop before the Colonel Sahib could reach the village. And Umballa would have succeeded but for the fact that the wind fell unaccountably and they lost more than an hour in handling the sloop with oars.

When the sloop left the primitive landing the chief returned to his hut and told his wife what had taken place, like the good husband he was. They would be rich.

Suddenly the child set up a wailing. Through the window she had seen a bold leopard trot over to the bullock cart and carry away the kid. The chief at once summoned his remaining men, and they proceeded to set a trap for the prowler. The cat had already killed one bullock and injured another. They knew that the beast would not return for some hours, having gorged itself upon the kid. But it was well to be prepared.

Toward noon the other treasure seekers drew up within a quarter of a mile behind the village. The men-folk thought it advisable to reconnoiter before entering the village. One never could tell. Winnie declared her intention of snoozing while they waited, and curled up in her rugs. Kathlyn, however, could not resist the longing to look upon the sea again. She could see the lovely blue water through the spaces between the trees. Soon she would be flying over that water, flying for home, home!

She went farther from the camp than she really intended, and came unexpectedly upon the leopard which stood guarding its cubs while they growled and tore at the dead kid. Kathlyn realized that she was unarmed, and that the leopard was between her and the camp. She could see the roofs of the village below her; so toward the huts she ran. The leopard stood still for a while, eying her doubtfully, then made up its mind to give chase. She had tasted blood, but had not eaten.

Meantime the little child had forgot her loss in her interest in the bullock cart with its grotesque lure; and she climbed into the cart just as Kathlyn appeared, followed by the excited leopard. She saw the child and snatched her instinctively from the cart. The leopard leaped into the cart at the rear, while Kathlyn ran toward the chief's hut, into which she staggered without the formality of announcing her advent.

The father of the child had no need to question, though he marveled at the white skin and dress of this visitor, who had doubtless saved his child from death. He flung the door shut and dropped the bar. Next he sought his gun and fired through a crack in the door. He missed; but the noise and smoke frightened the leopard away.

And later, Bruce, wild with the anxiety over the disapp-earance of Kathlyn, came across the chief battling for his life. He had gone forth to hunt the leopard, and the leopard had hunted him. Bruce dared not fire, for fear of killing the man; so without hesitance or fear he caught the leopard by the back of the neck and by a hind leg and swung her into the sea.

The chief was severely mauled, but he was able to get to his feet and walk. The white woman had saved his child and the white man had saved him. He would remember.

Thus the leopard quite innocently served a purpose, for all her deadly intentions; the chief was filled with gratitude.

When the colonel and the others came into view the former seized Kathlyn by the shoulders and shook her hysterically.

"In God's name, Kit, don't you know any better than to wander off alone? Do you want to drive me mad?"

"Why, father, I wasn't afraid!"

"Afraid? Who said anything about your being afraid? Didn't you know that we were being followed? It is Umballa! Ah! that gives you a start!"

"Colonel!" said Bruce gently.

"I know, Bruce, I sound harsh. But you were tearing your hair, too."

"Forgive me," cried Kathlyn, penitent, for she knew she had done wrong. "I did not think. But Umballa?"

"Yes, Umballa. One of the keepers found a knife by that bridge, and Ramabai identified it as belonging to Umballa. Whether he is alone or with many, I do not know; but this I do know: we must under no circumstances become separated again. Now, I'm going to quiz the chief."

But the chief said that no person described had passed or been seen. No one but a holy man had come that morning, and he had gone to the island in the sloop.

"For what?"

The chief smiled, but shook his head.

"Was it not a basket of gold and precious stones?" demanded the colonel.

The chief's eyes widened. There were others who knew, then? Bruce noticed his surprise.

"Colonel, show the good chief the royal seal on your document."

The colonel did so, and the chief salaamed when he saw the royal signature. He was mightily bewildered, and gradually he was made to understand that he had been vilely tricked.

"To the boats!" he shouted, as if suddenly awakening. "We may be too late, Lords! He said he was a holy man, and I believed."

They all ran hastily down to the beach to seize what boats they could. Here they met a heartrending obstacle in the refusal of the owners. The chief, however, signified that it was his will; and, moreover, he commanded that the fishermen should handle the oars. They would be paid. That was different. Why did not the white people say so at once? They would go anywhere for money. Not the most auspicious sign, thought Ramabai. They got into the boats and pushed off.

On the way to the island the colonel consulted the map, or diagram, he held in his hand. It was not possible that Umballa knew the exact spot.

A filigree basket of silver, filled with gold and gems! The man became as eager and excited as a boy. The instinct to hunt for treasure begins just outside the cradle and ends just inside the grave.

To return to Umballa. Upon landing, he asked at once if any knew where the cave was. One man did know the way, but he refused to show it. There were spirits there, ruled by an evil god.

"Take me there, you, and I will enter without harm. Am I not holy?"

That put rather a new face upon the situation. If the holy man was willing to risk an encounter with the god, far be it that they should prevent him. An ordinary seeker would not have found the entrance in a lifetime. Umballa had not known exactly where the cave was, but he knew all that the cave contained. When they came to it Umballa sniffed; the tang of sulphur became evident both in his nose and on his tongue. He understood. It was simply a small spring, a mineral, in which sulphur predominated. He came out with some cupped in his hands. He drank and showed them that it was harmless. Besides, he was a holy man, and his presence made ineffectual all evil spirits which might roam within the cave.

Umballa, impatient as he was, had to depend upon patience. By dint of inquiries he learned that wild Mohammedans had cast the spell upon the cave, set a curse upon its threshold. Umballa tottered and destroyed this by reasoning that the curse of a Mohammedan could not affect a Hindu. Finally, he offered each and all of them a fortune—and won.

Torches were lighted and the cave entered. There were many side passages; and within these the astute Umballa saw the true reason for the curse of the Mohammedans: guns and powder, hundreds and hundreds of pounds of black destruction! A lower gallery—the mouth of which lay under a slab of rock—led to the pit wherein rested the filigree basket. . . . For a time Umballa acted like a madman. He sang, chanted, dug his hands into the gold and stones; choked, sobbed. Here was true kingship; the private treasures of a dozen decades, all his for the taking. He forgot his enemies and their nearness as the fortune revealed itself to him.

As his men at length staggered out of the lower gallery with the basket slung upon an improvised litter he espied his enemies marching up the hill! Back into the cave again. Umballa cursed and bit his nails. He was unarmed, as were his men, and he had not time to search among the smuggled arms to find his need.

"Heaven born," spoke up the man who had known where the cave was, "there is an exit on the other side. We can go through that without yonder people noticing us."

"A fortune for each of you when you put this on the sloop!"

Back through the cave they rushed, torches flaring. Once a bearer stumbled over a powder can, and the torch holder all but sprawled over him. Umballa's hair stood on end. Fear impelled the men toward the exit.

"There is powder enough here to blow up all of Hind! Hasten!"

At the mouth of the exit the men with the torches, finding no further need of them, carelessly flung them aside.

"Fools!" roared Umballa; "you have destroyed us!"

He fled. The bearers followed with the burden. Down the side of the promontory they slid. Under a projecting ledge they paused, sweating with terror. Suddenly the whole island rocked. An explosion followed that was heard half a hundred miles away, where the gunboat of the British Raj patrolled the shores. Rocks, trees, sand filled the air, and small fires broke out here and there. The bulk of the damage, however, was done to the far side of the promontory, not where the frightened Umballa stood. A twisted rifle barrel fell at his feet.

"To the sloop!" he yelled. "It is all over!"

On the far side the other treasure seekers stood huddled together, scarce knowing which way to turn. The miracle of it was that none of them was hurt. Perhaps a quarter of an hour passed before their faculties awoke.

"Look!" cried Kathlyn, pointing seaward.

What she saw was Umballa, setting adrift the boats which had brought them from the mainland.

Came a second explosion, far more furious than the first. In the downward rush Kathlyn stumbled and fell, the debris falling all about her.

CHAPTER XXV

ON THE SLOOP

Blinded by the dust, tripped by the rolling stones, Bruce turned to where he had seen Kathlyn fall. The explosion—the last one—had opened up veins of strange gases, for the whole promontory appeared to be on fire. He bent and caught up in his arms the precious burden, staggered down to the beach, and plunged into the water. A small trickle of blood flowing down her forehead explained everything; a falling stone had struck her.

"Kit, Kit! I hope to God the treasure went up also." He dashed the cold water into her face.

The others were unhurt, though dazed, and for the nonce incapable of coherent thought or action.

"The boats!" Bruce laid Kathlyn down on the sand and signed to Winnie. "Tend to her. I must take a chance at the boats. We could cross the neck of sand at ebb, but Umballa will be far away before that time. Kit, Kit; my poor girl!" He patted her wrists and called to her, and when finally her lips stirred he rose and waded out into the sea, followed by four hardy fishermen. The freshening breeze, being from the southwest, aided the swimmers, for the boats did not drift out to sea, but in a northeasterly direction. The sloop was squaring away for the mainland.

Did Umballa have the treasure? Bruce wondered, as at length his hand reached up and took hold of the gunwale of the boat he had picked out to bring down. Would Umballa have possessed tenacity enough to hang on to it in face of all the devastation? Bruce sighed as he drew himself up and crawled into the boat. He knew that treasure had often made a hero out of a coward; and treasure at that moment meant life and liberty to Umballa. On his return to the island he greeted the colonel somewhat roughly. But for this accursed basket they would have been well out of Asia by this time.

"Umballa has your basket, Colonel. If he hasn't, then say good-by to it, for it can never be dug from under those tons and tons of rock. . . . Here! where are those fishermen going?" he demanded.

The men were in the act of pushing off with the boats, which they had only just brought back.

Ramabai picked up his discarded rifle.

"Stop!"

"They are frightened," explained the chief.

"Well, they can contain their fright till we are in safety," Ramabai declared. "Warn them."

"Hurry, everybody! I feel it in my bones that that black devil has the treasure. Get those men into the boats. Here, pick up those oars. Get in, Kit; you, Winnie; come, everybody!"

Kathlyn gazed sadly at her father. Treasure, treasure; that

first. She was beginning to hate the very sound of the word. The colonel had been nervous, impatient and irritable ever since the document had been discovered. Till recently Kathlyn had always believed her father to be perfect, but now she saw that he was human, he had his flawed spot. Treasure! Before her or Winnie! So be it.

"Colonel," said Bruce, taking a chance throw, "we are less than a hundred miles from the seaport. Suppose we let Umballa clear out and we ourselves head straight up the coast? It is not fair to the women to put them to any further hardship."

"Bruce, I have sworn to God that Umballa shall not have that treasure. Ramabai, do you understand what it will mean to you if he succeeds in reaching Allaha with that treasure, probably millions? He will be able to buy every priest and soldier in Allaha and still have enough left for any extravagance that he may wish to plunge in."

"Sahib," suggested Ramabai, "let us send the women to the seaport in care of Ahmed, while we men seek Umballa."

"Good!" Bruce struck his hands together. "The very thing."

"I refuse to be separated from father," declared Kathlyn. "If he is determined to pursue Umballa back to Allaha, I must accompany him."

"And I!" added Winnie.

"Nothing more to be said," and Bruce signed to the boatmen to start. "If only this breeze had not come up! We could have caught him before he made shore."

Umballa paced the deck of the sloop, thinking and planning. He saw his enemies leaving in the rescued boats. Had he delayed them long enough? As matters stood, he could not carry away the treasure. He must have help, an armed force of men he could trust. On the mainland were Ahmed and the loyal keepers; behind were three men who wanted his life as he wanted theirs. The only hope he had lay in the cupidity of the men on the sloop. If they could be made to stand by him, there was a fair chance. Once he was of a mind to heave the basket over the rail and trust to luck in finding it again. But the thought tore at his heart. He simply could not do it.

Perhaps he could start a revolt, or win over the chief of the village. He had known honest men to fall at the sight of much gold, to fight for it, to commit any crime for it—and, if need be, to die for it. But the chief was with his enemies. Finally he came to the conclusion that the only thing to be done was to carry the treasure directly to the chief's hut and there await him. He would bribe the men with him sufficiently to close their mouths. If Ahmed was on the shore, the game was up. But he swept the mainland with his gaze and discovered no sign of him.

As a matter of fact, Ahmed had arranged his elephants so that they could start at once up the coast to the seaport. He was waiting on the native highway for the return of his master, quite confident that he would bring the bothersome trinkets with him. He knew nothing of Umballa's exploit. The appalling thunder of the explosions worried him. He would wait for just so long; then he would go and see.

Every village chief has his successor in hope. This individual was one of those who had helped Umballa to carry the treasure from the cave; in fact, the man who had guided him to the cave itself. He spoke to Umballa. He said that he understood the holy one's plight; for to these yet simple minded village folk Umballa was still the holy one. Their religion was the same.

"Holy one," he said, "we can best your enemies who follow."

"How?" eagerly.

"Yonder is the chief's bullock cart. I myself will find the bullocks!"

"What then?"

"We shall be on the way south before the others land."

"An extra handful of gold for you! Get the oars out! Let us hurry!"

"More, holy one; these men will obey me."

"They shall be well paid."

Umballa had reached the point where he could not plan without treachery. He proposed to carry the basket into the jungle somewhere, bury it and make way with every man who knew the secret; then, at the proper time, he would return for it with a brave caravan, his own men or those whose loyalty he could repurchase.

The landing was made, the basket conveyed to the bullock cart, which was emptied of its bait and leopard trap; the bullocks were brought out and harnessed—all this activity before the fishing boats had covered half the distance.

"I see light," murmured Umballa.

He tried to act coolly, but when he spoke his voice cracked and the blood in his throat nigh suffocated him.

"Sand, holy one!"

"Well, what of sand?"

"You can dig and cover up things in sand and no one can possibly tell. The sand tells nothing."

They drove the bullocks forward mercilessly till they came to what Umballa considered a suitable spot. A pit was dug, but not before Umballa had taken from the basket enough gold to set the men wild. They were his. He smiled inwardly to think how easily they could have had all of it! They were still honest.

The sand was smoothed down over the basket. It would not have been possible for the human eye to discover the spot within a perfect range. Umballa drove down a broken stick directly over where the basket lay. He had beaten them; they would find nothing. Now to rid himself of these simple fools who trusted him.

The man who longed to become the chief's successor was then played upon by Umballa; to set the two factions at each other's throats; a perfect elimination. Umballa advised him to rouse his friends, declare that the white people had taken the gold away from the holy man, to whom it belonged as agent.

Thus, in this peaceful fishermen's village began the old game of gold and politics, for the two are inseparable. Umballa, in hiding, watched the contest gleefully. He witnessed the rival approach his chief, saw the angry gestures exchanged, and knew that dissension had begun. The men of the village clustered about.

"Where have you hidden it?" demanded the chief. "It belongs to the Sahib."

"Hidden what?"

"The treasure you and the false holy one took from the forbidden cave!"

"False holy one?"

"Ay, wretch! He is Durga Ram, the man who murdered the king of Allaha."

The mutineer laughed and waved his hand toward the smoking ruins of the promontory.

"Look for it there," he said, "under mountains of rock and dirt and sand. Look for it there! And who is this white man who says the holy one is false?"

"I say it, you scoundrel!" cried the colonel, advancing; but Bruce restrained him, seeing that the situation had taken an unpleasant and sinister trend.

"Patience, Colonel; just a little diplomacy," he urged.

"But the man lies!"

"That may be, but just at present there seem to be more men standing back of him than back of our chief here. We have no way of getting a warning to Ahmed. Wait!"

"Jackal," spoke the chief wrathfully, "thou liest!"

"Ah! thou hast grown too fat with rule."

"Ay!" cried the men back of the mutinous one.

"Sahib," said the chief, without losing any of his natural dignity, "the man has betrayed me. I see the lust of gold in their eyes. Evil presage. But you have saved the life of my child and mine, and I will throw my strength with you."

"Father, can't you see?" asked Kathlyn.

"See what?"

"The inevitable. It was in my heart all the way here that we should meet with disaster. There is yet time to leave here peacefully."

But her pleading fell upon the ears of a man who was treasure mad. He would not listen to reason. Ahmed could have told Kathlyn that the old guru stood back of her father, pushing, pushing.

"He is mad," whispered Bruce, "but we can not leave him."

"What would I do without you, John!"

From down the beach the chief's little girl came toddling to the group of excited men. She was clutching something in her hand. Her father took her by the arm and pulled her back of him. Kathlyn put her hand upon the child's head, protectingly. The child gazed up shyly, opened her little hand . . . and disclosed a yellow sovereign!

The argument between the chief and his mutinous followers went on.

"John," said Kathlyn, "you speak the dialect. I can understand only a word here and there. But listen. Tell the chief that all we desire is to be permitted to depart in peace later," she added significantly.

"What's up?"

"The child has a coin—a British sovereign—in her hand. She knows where Umballa has secreted the treasure. Since father can not be budged from his purpose, let us try deceit. You speak to the chief while I explain to father."

To the chief Bruce said: "The treasure is evidently lost. So, after a short rest, we shall return to our caravan and depart. We do not wish to be the cause of trouble between you and your people."

"But, Sahib, they have the gold!"

"The false holy one doubtless gave them that before the explosion." Bruce laid hold of his arm in a friendly fashion apparently, but in reality as a warning. "All we want is a slight rest in your house. After that we shall proceed upon our journey."

The mutineers could offer no reasonable objections to this and signified that it was all one to them so long as the white people departed. They had caused enough damage by their appearance and it might be that it was through their agency that the promontory was all but destroyed. The fish would be driven away for weeks. And what would the fierce gun-runners say when they found out that their stores had gone up in flame and smoke? Ai, ai! What would they do but beat them and torture them for permitting any one to enter the cave?

"When these men come," answered the chief, with a dry smile, "I will deal with them. None of us has entered the cave. They know me for a man of truth. Perhaps you are right," he added to the mutineer. "There could not have been a treasure there and escape the sharp eyes of those Arabs. Go back to your homes. These white people shall be my guests till they have rested and are ready to depart."

Reluctantly the men dispersed, and from his hiding-place Umballa saw another of his schemes fall into pieces. There would be no fight, at least for the present. The men, indeed, had hoped to come to actual warfare, but they could not force war on their chief without some good cause. After all, the sooner the white people were out of the way the better for all concerned.

Did the leader of this open mutiny have ulterior designs upon the treasure, upon the life of Umballa? Perhaps. At any rate, events so shaped themselves as to nullify whatever plans he had formed in his gold-dazzled brain.

The colonel was tractable and fell in with Kathlyn's idea. It would have been nothing short of foolhardiness openly to have antagonized the rebellious men.

"You have a plan, Kit, but what is it?"

"I dare not tell you here. You are too excited. But I believe I can lead you to where Umballa has buried the basket. I feel that Umballa is watching every move we make. And I dare say he hoped—and even instigated— this mutiny to end in disaster for us. He is alone. So much we can rely upon. But if we try to meet him openly we shall lose. Patience for a little while. There, they are leaving us. They are grumbling, but I do not believe that means anything serious."

"Now, then, white people," said the chief, "come to my house. You are welcome there, now and always. You have this day saved my life and that of my child. I am grateful."

Inside the hut Kathlyn drew the child toward her and

gently pressed open the tightly clutched fingers. She plucked the sovereign from the little pink palm and held it up. The child's father seized it, wonderingly.

"Gold! They lied to me! I knew it."

"Yes," said Bruce. "They did find the treasure. They brought it here and buried it quickly. And we believe your little girl knows where. Question her."

It was not an easy matter. The child was naturally shy, and the presence of all these white skinned people struck her usually babbling tongue with a species of paralysis. But her father was patient, and word by word the secret was dragged out of her. She told of the stolen bullock cart, of the digging in the sand, of the holy one.

In some manner they must lure Umballa from his retreat. It was finally agreed upon that they all return to the camp and steal back at once in a roundabout way. They would come sufficiently armed. Later, the chief could pretend to be walking with his child.

So while Umballa stole forth from his hiding-place, reasonably certain that his enemies had gone, got together his mutineers and made arrangements with them to help him carry away the treasure that night, the rightful owners were directed to the broken stick in the damp sand.

That night, when Umballa and his men arrived, a hole in the sand greeted them. It was shaped like a mouth, opened in laughter.

CHAPTER XXVI

THE THIRD BAR

It was Ahmed's suggestion that they in turn should bury the filigree basket. He reasoned that if they attempted to proceed with it they would be followed and sooner or later set upon by Umballa and the men he had won away from the village chief. The poor fishermen were gold mad and at present not accountable for what they did or planned to do. He advanced that Umballa would have no difficulty in rousing them to the pitch of murder. Umballa would have at his beck and call no less than twenty men, armed and ruthless. Some seventy miles beyond was British territory and wherever there was British territory there were British soldiers. With them they would return, leaving the women in safety behind.

"The commissioner there will object," said the colonel.

"No, Sahib," replied Ahmed. "The Mem-sahib has every right in the world to this treasure. You possess the documents to prove it, and nothing more would be necessary to the commissioner."

"But, Ahmed," interposed Bruce, "we are none of us British subjects."

"What difference will that make, Sahib?"

"Quite enough. England is not in the habit of protecting anybody but her own subjects. We should probably be held up till everything was verified at Allaha; and the priests there would not hesitate to charge us with forgery and heaven knows what else. Let us bury the basket, by all means, return for it and carry it away piecemeal. To carry it away as it is, in bulk, would be courting suicide."

Ahmed scratched his chin. Trust a white man for logic.

"And, besides," went on Bruce, "the news would go all over the Orient and the thugs would come like flies scenting honey. No; this must be kept secret if we care to get away with it. It can not be worth less than a million. And I've known white men who would cut our throats for a handful of rupees."

For the first time since the expedition started out the colonel became normal, a man of action, cool in the head, and foresighted.

"Ahmed, spread out the men around the camp," he ordered briskly. "Instruct them to shoot over the head of any one who approaches; this the first time. The second time, to kill. Bruce has the right idea; so let us get busy. Over there, where that boulder is. The ground will be damp and soft under it, and when we roll it back there will be no sign of its having been disturbed. I used to cache ammunition that way. Give me that spade."

It was good to Kathlyn's ears to hear her father talk like this.

At a depth of three feet the basket was lowered, covered and the boulder rolled into place. After that the colonel stooped and combed the turf where the boulder had temporarily rested. He showed his woodcraft there. It would take a keener eye than Umballa possessed to note any disturbance. The safety of the treasure ultimately, however, depended upon the loyalty of the keepers under Ahmed. They had been with the colonel for years; yet . . . The colonel shrugged. He had to trust them; that was all there was to the matter.

A sentinel came rushing up—one of the keepers.

"Something is stampeding the elephants!" he cried.

Ahmed and the men with him rushed off. In Ahmed's opinion, considering what lay before them, elephants were more important than colored stones and yellow metal. Without the elephants they would indeed find themselves in sore straits.

"Let us move away from here," advised Bruce, picking up the implements and shouldering them. He walked several yards away, tossed shovel and pick into the bushes, tore at the turf and stamped on it, giving it every appearance of having been disturbed. The colonel nodded approvingly. It was a good point and he had overlooked it.

They returned hastily to camp, which was about two hundred yards beyond the boulder. Kathlyn entered her tent to change her clothes, ragged, soiled and burned. The odor of wet burned cloth is never agreeable. And she needed dry shoes, even if there was but an hour or two before bedtime.

Only one elephant had succeeded in bolting. In some manner he had loosed his peg; but what had started him on the run they never learned. The other elephants were swaying uneasily; but their pegs were deep and their chains stout. Ahmed and the keepers went after the truant on foot.

The noise of the chase died away. Bruce was lighting his pipe. The colonel was examining by the firelight a few emeralds which he had taken from the basket. Ramabai was pleasantly gazing at his wife. Kathlyn and Winnie were emerging from the tent, when a yell greeted their astonished ears. The camp was surrounded. From one side came Umballa, from the other came the mutineers. Kathlyn and Winnie flew to their father's side. In between came Umballa, with Bruce and Ramabai and Pundita effectually separated. Umballa and his men closed in upon the colonel and his daughters. Treasure and revenge!

Bruce made a furious effort to join Kathlyn, but the numbers against him were too many. It was all done so suddenly and effectually, and all due to their own carelessness.

"Kit," said her father, "our only chance is to refuse to discover to Umballa where we have hidden the basket. Winnie, if you open your lips it will be death—yours, Kit's, mine. To have been careless like this! Oh, Kit, on my honor, if Umballa would undertake to convoy us to the seaport I'd gladly give him all the treasure and all the money I have of my own. But we know him too well. He will torture us all."

"I have gone through much; I can go through more," calmly replied Kathlyn. "But I shall never wear a precious stone again, if I live. I abhor them!"

"I am my father's daughter," said Winnie.

"Put the howdahs on the two elephants," Umballa ordered.

The men obeyed clumsily, being fishermen by occupation and mahouts by compulsion.

Kathlyn tried in vain to see where they were taking Bruce and the others. Some day, if she lived, she was going to devote a whole day to weeping, for she never had time to in this land. The thought caused her to smile, despite her despair.

When the elephants were properly saddled with the howdahs Umballa gave his attention to the prisoners. He hailed them jovially. They were old friends. What could he do for them?

"Conduct us to the seaport," said the colonel, "and on my word of honor I will tell you where we have hidden the treasure."

"Ho!" jeered Umballa, arms akimbo, "I'd be a fool to put my head into such a trap. I love you too well. Yet I am not wholly without heart. Tell me where it lies and I will let you go."

"Cut our throats at once, you beast, for none of us will tell you under any conditions save those I have named. Men," the colonel continued, "this man is an ingrate, a thief and a murderer. He has promised you much gold for your part in this. But in the end he will cheat you and destroy you."

Umballa laughed. "They have already had their earnest. Soon they will have more. But talk with them—plead, urge, promise. No more questions? Well, then, listen. Reveal to me the treasure and you may go free. If you refuse I shall take you back to Allaha—not publicly, but secretly—there to inflict what punishments I see fit."

"I have nothing more to say," replied the colonel.

"No? And thou, white goddess?"

Kathlyn stared over his head, her face expressionless. It stirred him more than outspoken contempt would have done.

"And you, pretty one?" Umballa eyed Winnie speculatively.

Winnie drew closer to her sister, that was all.

"So be it. Allaha it shall be, without a meddling Ramabai; back to the gurus who love you so!" He dropped his banter. "You call me a murderer. I admit it. I have killed the man who was always throwing his benefits into my face, who brought me up not as a companion but as a plaything. He is dead. I slew him. After the first, what are two or three more crimes of this order?" He snapped his fingers. "I want that treasure, and you will tell me where it is before I am done with you. You will tell me on your knees, gladly, gladly! Now, men! There is a long journey before us."

The colonel, Kathlyn and Winnie were forced into one howdah, while Umballa mounted the other. As for the quasi-mahouts, they were not particularly happy behind the ears of the elephants, who, with that keen appreciation of their herd, understood instinctively that they had to do with novices. But for the promise of gold that dangled before their eyes, threats of violent death could not have forced them upon the elephants.

They started east, and the jungle closed in behind them.

As for Umballa, he cared not what became of the other prisoners.

They were being held captive in one of the village huts. The chief had pleaded in vain. He was dishonored, for they had made him break his word to the white people. So be it. Sooner or later the glitter of gold would leave their eyes and they would come to him and beg for pardon.

Moonlight. The village slept. Two fishermen sat before the hut confining the prisoners, on guard. An elephant squealed in the distance. Out of the shadow a sleek leopard, then another. The guards jumped to their feet and scrambled away for dear life to the nearest hut, crying the alarm. Bruce opened the door, which had no lock, and peered forth. It was natural that the leopards should give their immediate attention to the two men in flight. Bruce, realizing what had happened, called softly to Ramabai and Pundita; and the three of them stole out into the night, toward the camp. Bruce did not expect to find any one there. What he wanted was to arm himself and to examine the boulder.

Meantime, Ahmed returned with the truant elephant to find nothing but disorder and evidence of a struggle. A tent was overturned, the long grass trampled, and the colonel's sola-topee hat lay crumpled near Kathlyn's tent.

"Ai, ai!" he wailed. But, being a philosopher, his wailing was of short duration. He ran to the boulder and examined it carefully. It had not been touched. That was well. At least that meant that his Sahib and Mem-sahib lived. Treasure! He spat out a curse . . . and threw his rifle to his shoulder. But his rage turned to joy as he discovered who the arrivals were.

"Bruce Sahib!"

"Yes, Ahmed. Umballa got the best of us. We were tricked by the truant elephant. He has taken Kathlyn back toward Allaha."

"And so shall we return!"

Ahmed called his weary men. His idea was to fill the elephant saddle-bags with gold and stones, leave it in trust with Bala Khan, who should in truth this time take his tulwar down from the wall. He divided his men, one company to guard and the other to labor. It took half an hour to push back the boulder and dig up the basket. After this was done Bruce and Ramabai and Ahmed the indefatigable carried the gold and precious stones to the especially made saddle-bags. All told, it took fully an hour to complete the work.

With water and food, and well armed, they began the journey back to Allaha, a formidable cortege and in no tender mood. They proceeded in forced marches, snatching what sleep they could during the preparation of the meals.

Many a time the impulse came to Bruce to pluck the shining metal and sparkling stones from the saddle-bags and toss them out into the jungle, to be lost till the crack of doom. There were also moments when he felt nothing but hatred toward the father of the girl he loved. For these trinkets Kathlyn had gone through tortures as frightful almost as those in the days of the Inquisition. Upon one thing he and Ahmed had agreed, despite Ramabai's wild protest; they would leave the treasure with Bala Khan and follow his army to the walls of Allaha. If harm befell any of their loved ones not one stone should remain upon another. And Bruce declared that he would seek Umballa to the ends of the earth for the infinite pleasure of taking his black throat in his two hands and squeezing the life out of it.

Eventually and without mishap they came to the walled city of the desert, Bala Khan's stronghold. Bala Khan of necessity was always ready, always prepared. Before night of the day of their arrival an army was gathered within the city.

Ramabai sat in his howdah, sad and dispirited.

"Bala Khan, we have been friends, and my father was your good friend."

"It is true."

"Will you do a favor for the son?"

"Yes. If the Colonel Sahib and his daughter live, ask what you will."

Ramabai bowed.

"I will set my camp five miles beyond your walls and wait. When I see the Mem-sahib I will salaam, turn right about face, and go home. Now, to you, Bruce Sahib: Leave not your treasure within my walls when I shall be absent, for I can not guarantee protection. Leave it where it is and bring it with you. Save myself, no one of my men knows what your saddle-bags contain. Let us proceed upon our junket—or our war!"

* * * * * *

Umballa reached the ancient gate of Allaha at the same time Bruce stopped before the walls of Bala Khan's city. He determined to wring the secret from either the colonel or his daughter, return for the treasure and depart for Egypt down the Persian Gulf.

He made a wide detour and came out at the rear of his house. No one was in sight. He dismounted and entered, found three or four of his whilom slaves, who, when he revealed his identity, felt the old terror and fear of the man. His prisoners were brought in. A slave took the elephants to the stables. He wanted to run away and declare Umballa's presence, but fear was too strong.

Ironically Umballa bade the fishermen to enter to eat and drink what they liked. Later he found them in a drunken stupor in the kitchen. That was where they belonged.

He ordered his prisoners to be brought into the Court of Death and left there.

"You see?" said Umballa. "Now, where have you hidden the treasure?"

Kathlyn walked over to one of the cages and peered into it. A sleek tiger trotted up to the bar; and purred and invited her to scratch his head.

"I am not answered," said Umballa.

A click resounded from the four sides, and a bar disappeared from each of the cages.

"That will be all for the present," said Umballa. "Food and water you will not require. To-morrow morning another bar will be removed."

And he left them.

Early the next morning the town began to seethe in the squares. Bala Khan's army lay encamped outside the city!

When Bruce, Ramabai, Pundita and Ahmed halted their

elephants before the temple they were greeted by the now terrified priests who begged to be informed what Bala Khan proposed to do.

"Deliver to us the Mem-sahib."

The priests swore by all their gods that they knew nothing of her.

"Let us enter the temple," said Ramabai. "Ahmed, bring the treasure and leave it in the care of the priests." A few moments later Ramabai addressed the assemblage. "Bala Khan is hostile, but only for the sake of his friends. He lays down this law, however—obey it or disobey it. The Colonel Sahib and his daughters are to go free, to do what they please with the treasure. Pundita, according to the will of the late king, shall be crowned."

The high priest held up his hand for silence. "We obey, on one condition—that the new queen shall in no manner interfere with her old religion nor attempt to force her new religion into the temple."

To this Pundita agreed.

"Ramabai, soldiers! To the house of Umballa! We shall find him there," cried Ahmed.

Umballa squatted upon his cushions on the terrace. The second bar had been removed. The beasts were pressing their wet nozzles to the openings and growling deep challenges.

"Once more, and for the last time, will you reveal the hiding-place of the treasure?"

Not a word from the prisoners.

"The third bar!"

But it did not stir.

"The third bar; remove it!"

The slave who had charge of the mechanism which operated the bars refused to act.

The events which followed were of breathless rapidity. Ramabai and Umballa met upon the parapet in a struggle which promised death or the treadmill to the weaker. At the same time Bruce opened the door to the Court of Death as the final bar dropped in the cage. At the sight of him the colonel and his daughters rushed to the door. Roughly he hurled them outside, slamming the iron door, upon which the infuriated tigers flung themselves.

* * * * * *

The young newspaper man to whom Winnie was engaged and the grizzled Ahmed sat on the steps of the bungalow in California one pleasant afternoon. The pipe was cold in the hand of the reporter and Ahmed's cigar was dead, which always happens when one recounts an exciting tale and another listens. Among the flower beds beyond two young women wandered, followed by a young man in pongee, a Panama set carelessly upon his handsome head, his face brown, his build slender but round and muscular.

"And that, Sahib, is the story," sighed Ahmed.

"And Kathlyn gave the treasures to the poor of Allaha? That was fine."

"You have said."

"They should have hanged this Umballa."

"No, Sahib. Death is grateful. It is not a punishment; it is peace. But Durga Ram, called Umballa, will spend the remainder of his days in the treadmill, which is a concrete hell, not abstract."

"Do you think England will ever step in?"

"Perhaps. But so long as Pundita rules justly, so long as her consort abets her, England will not move. Perhaps, if one of them dies. . . . There! the maids are calling you. And I will go and brew the Colonel Sahib's tea."

Choose from Thousands of 1stWorldLibrary Classics By

A. M. Barnard
Ada Leverson
Adolphus William Ward
Aesop
Agatha Christie
Alexander Aaronsohn
Alexander Kielland
Alexandre Dumas
Alfred Gatty
Alfred Ollivant
Alice Duer Miller
Alice Turner Curtis
Alice Dunbar
Allen Chapman
Alleyne Ireland
Ambrose Bierce
Amelia E. Barr
Amory H. Bradford
Andrew Lang
Andrew McFarland Davis
Andy Adams
Angela Brazil
Anna Alice Chapin
Anna Sewell
Annie Besant
Annie Hamilton Donnell
Annie Payson Call
Annie Roe Carr
Annonaymous
Anton Chekhov
Archibald Lee Fletcher
Arnold Bennett
Arthur C. Benson
Arthur Conan Doyle
Arthur M. Winfield
Arthur Ransome
Arthur Schnitzler
Arthur Train
Atticus
B.H. Baden-Powell
B. M. Bower
B. C. Chatterjee
Baroness Emmuska Orczy
Baroness Orczy
Basil King
Bayard Taylor
Ben Macomber
Bertha Muzzy Bower
Bjornstjerne Bjornson

Booth Tarkington
Boyd Cable
Bram Stoker
C. Collodi
C. E. Orr
C. M. Ingleby
Carolyn Wells
Catherine Parr Traill
Charles A. Eastman
Charles Amory Beach
Charles Dickens
Charles Dudley Warner
Charles Farrar Browne
Charles Ives
Charles Kingsley
Charles Klein
Charles Hanson Towne
Charles Lathrop Pack
Charles Romyn Dake
Charles Whibley
Charles Willing Beale
Charlotte M. Braeme
Charlotte M. Yonge
Charlotte Perkins Stetson
Clair W. Hayes
Clarence Day Jr.
Clarence E. Mulford
Clemence Housman
Confucius
Coningsby Dawson
Cornelis DeWitt Wilcox
Cyril Burleigh
D. H. Lawrence
Daniel Defoe
David Garnett
Dinah Craik
Don Carlos Janes
Donald Keyhoe
Dorothy Kilner
Dougan Clark
Douglas Fairbanks
E. Nesbit
E. P. Roe
E. Phillips Oppenheim
E. S. Brooks
Earl Barnes
Edgar Rice Burroughs
Edith Van Dyne
Edith Wharton

Edward Everett Hale
Edward J. O'Biren
Edward S. Ellis
Edwin L. Arnold
Eleanor Atkins
Eleanor Hallowell Abbott
Eliot Gregory
Elizabeth Gaskell
Elizabeth McCracken
Elizabeth Von Arnim
Ellem Key
Emerson Hough
Emilie F. Carlen
Emily Bronte
Emily Dickinson
Enid Bagnold
Enilor Macartney Lane
Erasmus W. Jones
Ernie Howard Pie
Ethel May Dell
Ethel Turner
Ethel Watts Mumford
Eugene Sue
Eugenie Foa
Eugene Wood
Eustace Hale Ball
Evelyn Everett-green
Everard Cotes
F. H. Cheley
F. J. Cross
F. Marion Crawford
Fannie E. Newberry
Federick Austin Ogg
Ferdinand Ossendowski
Fergus Hume
Florence A. Kilpatrick
Fremont B. Deering
Francis Bacon
Francis Darwin
Frances Hodgson Burnett
Frances Parkinson Keyes
Frank Gee Patchin
Frank Harris
Frank Jewett Mather
Frank L. Packard
Frank V. Webster
Frederic Stewart Isham
Frederick Trevor Hill
Frederick Winslow Taylor

Friedrich Kerst
Friedrich Nietzsche
Fyodor Dostoyevsky
G.A. Henty
G.K. Chesterton
Gabrielle E. Jackson
Garrett P. Serviss
Gaston Leroux
George A. Warren
George Ade
Geroge Bernard Shaw
George Cary Eggleston
George Durston
George Ebers
George Eliot
George Gissing
George MacDonald
George Meredith
George Orwell
George Sylvester Viereck
George Tucker
George W. Cable
George Wharton James
Gertrude Atherton
Gordon Casserly
Grace E. King
Grace Gallatin
Grace Greenwood
Grant Allen
Guillermo A. Sherwell
Gulielma Zollinger
Gustav Flaubert
H. A. Cody
H. B. Irving
H.C. Bailey
H. G. Wells
H. H. Munro
H. Irving Hancock
H. R. Naylor
H. Rider Haggard
H. W. C. Davis
Haldeman Julius
Hall Caine
Hamilton Wright Mabie
Hans Christian Andersen
Harold Avery
Harold McGrath
Harriet Beecher Stowe
Harry Castlemon
Harry Coghill
Harry Houidini

Hayden Carruth
Helent Hunt Jackson
Helen Nicolay
Hendrik Conscience
Hendy David Thoreau
Henri Barbusse
Henrik Ibsen
Henry Adams
Henry Ford
Henry Frost
Henry James
Henry Jones Ford
Henry Seton Merriman
Henry W Longfellow
Herbert A. Giles
Herbert Carter
Herbert N. Casson
Herman Hesse
Hildegard G. Frey
Homer
Honore De Balzac
Horace B. Day
Horace Walpole
Horatio Alger Jr.
Howard Pyle
Howard R. Garis
Hugh Lofting
Hugh Walpole
Humphry Ward
Ian Maclaren
Inez Haynes Gillmore
Irving Bacheller
Isabel Cecilia Williams
Isabel Hornibrook
Israel Abrahams
Ivan Turgenev
J.G.Austin
J. Henri Fabre
J. M. Barrie
J. M. Walsh
J. Macdonald Oxley
J. R. Miller
J. S. Fletcher
J. S. Knowles
J. Storer Clouston
J. W. Duffield
Jack London
Jacob Abbott
James Allen
James Andrews
James Baldwin

James Branch Cabell
James DeMille
James Joyce
James Lane Allen
James Lane Allen
James Oliver Curwood
James Oppenheim
James Otis
James R. Driscoll
Jane Abbott
Jane Austen
Jane L. Stewart
Janet Aldridge
Jens Peter Jacobsen
Jerome K. Jerome
Jessie Graham Flower
John Buchan
John Burroughs
John Cournos
John F. Kennedy
John Gay
John Glasworthy
John Habberton
John Joy Bell
John Kendrick Bangs
John Milton
John Philip Sousa
John Taintor Foote
Jonas Lauritz Idemil Lie
Jonathan Swift
Joseph A. Altsheler
Joseph Carey
Joseph Conrad
Joseph E. Badger Jr
Joseph Hergesheimer
Joseph Jacobs
Jules Vernes
Julian Hawthrone
Julie A Lippmann
Justin Huntly McCarthy
Kakuzo Okakura
Karle Wilson Baker
Kate Chopin
Kenneth Grahame
Kenneth McGaffey
Kate Langley Bosher
Kate Langley Bosher
Katherine Cecil Thurston
Katherine Stokes
L. A. Abbot
L. T. Meade

L. Frank Baum
Latta Griswold
Laura Dent Crane
Laura Lee Hope
Laurence Housman
Lawrence Beasley
Leo Tolstoy
Leonid Andreyev
Lewis Carroll
Lewis Sperry Chafer
Lilian Bell
Lloyd Osbourne
Louis Hughes
Louis Joseph Vance
Louis Tracy
Louisa May Alcott
Lucy Fitch Perkins
Lucy Maud Montgomery
Luther Benson
Lydia Miller Middleton
Lyndon Orr
M. Corvus
M. H. Adams
Margaret E. Sangster
Margret Howth
Margaret Vandercook
Margaret W. Hungerford
Margret Penrose
Maria Edgeworth
Maria Thompson Daviess
Mariano Azuela
Marion Polk Angellotti
Mark Overton
Mark Twain
Mary Austin
Mary Catherine Crowley
Mary Cole
Mary Hastings Bradley
Mary Roberts Rinehart
Mary Rowlandson
M. Wollstonecraft Shelley
Maud Lindsay
Max Beerbohm
Myra Kelly
Nathaniel Hawthrone
Nicolo Machiavelli
O. F. Walton
Oscar Wilde

Owen Johnson
P.G. Wodehouse
Paul and Mabel Thorne
Paul G. Tomlinson
Paul Severing
Percy Brebner
Percy Keese Fitzhugh
Peter B. Kyne
Plato
Quincy Allen
R. Derby Holmes
R. L. Stevenson
R. S. Ball
Rabindranath Tagore
Rahul Alvares
Ralph Bonehill
Ralph Henry Barbour
Ralph Victor
Ralph Waldo Emmerson
Rene Descartes
Ray Cummings
Rex Beach
Rex E. Beach
Richard Harding Davis
Richard Jefferies
Richard Le Gallienne
Robert Barr
Robert Frost
Robert Gordon Anderson
Robert L. Drake
Robert Lansing
Robert Lynd
Robert Michael Ballantyne
Robert W. Chambers
Rosa Nouchette Carey
Rudyard Kipling
Saint Augustine
Samuel B. Allison
Samuel Hopkins Adams
Sarah Bernhardt
Sarah C. Hallowell
Selma Lagerlof
Sherwood Anderson
Sigmund Freud
Standish O'Grady
Stanley Weyman
Stella Benson
Stella M. Francis

Stephen Crane
Stewart Edward White
Stijn Streuvels
Swami Abhedananda
Swami Parmananda
T. S. Ackland
T. S. Arthur
The Princess Der Ling
Thomas A. Janvier
Thomas A Kempis
Thomas Anderton
Thomas Bailey Aldrich
Thomas Bulfinch
Thomas De Quincey
Thomas Dixon
Thomas H. Huxley
Thomas Hardy
Thomas More
Thornton W. Burgess
U. S. Grant
Upton Sinclair
Valentine Williams
Various Authors
Vaughan Kester
Victor Appleton
Victor G. Durham
Victoria Cross
Virginia Woolf
Wadsworth Camp
Walter Camp
Walter Scott
Washington Irving
Wilbur Lawton
Wilkie Collins
Willa Cather
Willard F. Baker
William Dean Howells
William le Queux
W. Makepeace Thackeray
William W. Walter
William Shakespeare
Winston Churchill
Yei Theodora Ozaki
Yogi Ramacharaka
Young E. Allison
Zane Grey

www.ingramcontent.com/pod-product-compliance
Lightning Source LLC
Chambersburg PA
CBHW020257030726
47499CB00001B/230